Journey To Fate

Journey To Fate

A Novel

Scott Ottesen

iUniverse, Inc.
New York Lincoln Shanghai

Journey To Fate

iUniverse books may be ordered through booksellers or by contacting:

iUniverse
2021 Pine Lake Road, Suite 100
Lincoln, NE 68512
www.iuniverse.com
1-800-Authors (1-800-288-4677)

ISBN-13: 978-0-595-40405-6 (pbk)
ISBN-13: 978-0-595-84780-8 (ebk)
ISBN-10: 0-595-40405-7 (pbk)
ISBN-10: 0-595-84780-3 (ebk)

Printed in the United States of America

In memory of my brother Chris.

CHAPTER 1

▼

Emotions were rampant in Brad Preston on this frigid February evening. He unconsciously had a strangle hold on the steering wheel, as he navigated the all wheel drive Audi through the slick winding roads on his drive home from work. His mind was swirling in thought from the three different scenarios he had to choose from concerning his future, two of which would create a big change for him and his family. His stomach turned sour recognizing it was now time to make a decision on his career and the possibility of having to move his family to another state.

The stress of having to make a decision soon was exacerbated by the fact that he would be confronting Greg and Kristy tonight at one of his best friend's birthday party. Greg was one reason he wasn't playing major league baseball at this time, and Kristy was his old high school girlfriend. Brad placed his left hand firmly on his abdomen and pressed hard to try to ease the knot in his stomach.

Brad couldn't believe his emotions were running wild tonight causing him unusual stress. He had almost always had control of himself for most of his life, but the decisions that were on the table for him at this time would impact his family's life, especially if he decided on getting back into baseball and moving to California. He loved his job in Indianapolis as well as living in his hometown, but the thought of getting back into baseball was intriguing, even if it meant moving to the West coast.

The car shifted slightly on a slippery curve, but automatically made the proper adjustments to keep it from sliding off the road, startling Brad back to the task at hand of driving home on this dreary winter evening. Brad was glad he bought the four wheel drive Audi over the BMW 535, because he thought the Audi's quattro system handled the winter roads much better. He needed the four wheel drive to negotiate the few curves that bordered some treacherous ravines on this section of road he traveled everyday. One particular curve had a section of the guardrail missing, which could be hazardous for someone if they slide off the road. He wondered why the highway department had not replaced it yet.

Brad reached for the volume knob of the radio without taking his eyes off the road. He thought an updated weather report was in order since he and Anne would be going out this evening. The meteorologist was in the middle of his report stating the temperature would fall to twenty-five degrees tonight, with snow accumulations of up to four inches by tomorrow.

"God, I should take the job in North Carolina or California rather than put up with this long winter crap in Indiana. What keeps me here, other than my parents living here and my job?" he said out loud to himself. He then remembered that his parents had decided to move to Florida in the near future, nullifying one positive aspect of staying in Indiana.

He gave a quick faint smile as he decided on eliminating one option from the three. He would definitely take the North Carolina or California job and leave this cold nasty weather. He knew Anne would be happy if they moved back to her hometown of Charlotte, North Carolina and Brianna was too young to care either way.

A good feeling came to Brad as he thought of Brianna, his adorable two and a half year old girl. Brad loved Brianna with all his heart. He loved to be with her in his spare time, which had been getting sparse lately with his demanding job. Anne wasn't very pleased with his additional time spent at work either, which added some stress to their relationship.

Maybe I should just take the position in North Carolina, he thought. It would get us out of this weather and make Anne happy. But he knew he had to fulfill the California position sooner or later. He had a contract from a few years earlier that he would have to honor.

"I don't know what to do," he said to himself as he pulled into the driveway, waiting for the garage door to open. A snowflake softly floated through the cold night air twisting and turning due to the north wind blowing. He watched the flake falling to earth until it landed softly on the windshield of the Audi as the garage door opened. He drove the car into their garage being careful not to hit Brianna's new bicycle that sparkled in the bright headlights of the road salt covered car.

Brianna loved her new two wheeler with training wheels. It was her favorite Christmas present from Santa. She couldn't wait to ride it when the weather warmed up and the streets melted of the dirty snow.

As he pulled the keys out of the ignition, his thoughts switched to the party he must attend, and he once again shuddered at the thought of seeing Kristy and Greg there. He knew they would attend since Kristy was Carol's best friend, and she wouldn't miss Carol's birthday. He disliked Greg, or maybe loathed was the correct term to use for his feelings toward him. The motion of the door opening from inside the house broke up Brad's unpleasant thoughts.

"Daddy, your home," cried out Brianna.

Brad jumped out of the car and hurried to Brianna. He pulled her close to him. "I missed you honey. How was your day?"

"Mommy and I made chocolate chip cookies for us. I want to take some to grandma and grandpa's house tonight," Brianna said, not letting go of Brad as they held hands walking towards Anne.

"Hi," Brad said as he walked up to Anne and gave her a kiss. "I understand the two of you made your special cookies today." He sniffed the air to gather in the special, sweet delectable scent of the cookies. "Umm, the fresh aroma of warm cookies is still in the air."

"Yes, that was the excitement of our day," Anne said in a disgruntled tone. "Brad, this long winter is killing me. I wish we could move to warmer weather. Wouldn't you like to be able to walk outside and feel a nice warm breeze in your face? Or do you like to freeze your you know what off up here?" she asked in her sexy southern accent.

"I was thinking about that on my drive home. I guess I need to meet with Bill about the position in Charlotte."

Anne smiled at Brad lovingly and gave him a long hug. "Were you really?"

"Yes, I was thinking about the Charlotte and the California job. We have to make a decision real soon you know," he said with an unsure look on his face.

"I know. I just like having you around and it hasn't been enough lately. Charlotte would be my choice you know." She knew a baseball career would take Brad away from them more than she liked, and she hated the thought of having to live that life.

"Yes, I'm well aware that you'd prefer to move back to Charlotte, and we'll work on spending more time together." He gave her a passionate kiss and smiled. "You know that baseball would keep me in top shape and not allow me to get fat."

"I don't worry about that with you. You're way too vain to let that happen to yourself," Anne replied. She couldn't help but feel pleasure from the chance of going home again to the Charlotte area. A glow came over her beautiful fine-featured face, with perfect cheekbones and refined chin. Her shoulder length blond hair glistened from the light in the kitchen. Her big round brown eyes were infectious, and tonight she tried to use them to sway him more on moving to North Carolina.

Anne's looks were stunning. She is the woman you would expect to see standing at the Miss America beauty contest as they announced "Miss North Carolina." She was five feet eight inches tall, possessing the perfect body. From her slender neck, to her proportionate breasts, down through her slender waist, she was a head turner. If you were able to get past that, she had the perfect bottom, attached to long sleek legs that tapered down to her perfectly pedicured size eight feet. She would be the definition of a southern beauty, if there was one in the dictionary.

Anne had lacked self confidence until she met Brad. She had always been a beautiful girl that hid from her natural born gift of good looks. She came from a wealthy family, causing other kids her age not to know where to put her in the social structure. Her classmates held her in contempt for her natural beauty and proclaimed her to be conceited by confusing her shyness for what they perceived as too much vanity.

Brad brought out her confidence when they started dating and allowed her to be her special self. Anne was sweet and very smart, two strong assets that drew her to him. He just wasn't overly impressed with looks alone, although it was one factor that brought them together. He wanted a complete woman with sincere intentions.

Brad felt the warmth of Anne's flirting as it brought on a charge of energy racing through his body. Anne could be the most beautiful person in the world, both physically and personally, and it had been a while since she displayed her true inner beauty, and Brad was taken by it.

They stared at each other until Brianna spoke up, "Don't forget I'm here."

Brad and Anne broke out in laughter simultaneously as they both embraced Brianna with a huge three person hug. "We won't forget you honey," Anne said to her as she ran her fingers through Brianna's fine blond hair.

Brad thought about how lucky Brianna was because she was a miniature Anne in looks. There was a splash of Brad here and there, but she was definitely a clone of Anne. He gave a quick look at his watch. "Hey, we better get moving here if we're going to get you to your grandparents in time for dinner. They're having your favorite tonight."

"We're having grandma's yummy chicken with mashed potatoes?" Brianna asked in her cute toddler voice that sounded like a commercial that would pull at anybody's heartstrings to buy their fried chicken.

"Yes, and chocolate cake with chocolate icing, just the way you like it." Brad was still smiling from Brianna's playfulness. God, I adore this little girl of mine. I don't know how I could ever live without her, he thought to himself.

They broke from their hug, and Brad grabbed a fresh baked cookie as he headed to the closet to hang his coat. He took a big bite out of the cookie and moaned with delight from the wonderful flavor. "I'm going to change real quick," he said as he raced to their bedroom.

"Don't get crumbs all over the house, I just vacuumed today," Anne warned as she followed him to the bedroom. Brad already had his shirt off by the time Anne reached the bedroom. She flopped down on their king size bed that was decorated with what seem like a hundred pillows. Anne wrapped her arms around the biggest, fluffiest pillow and watched intently as Brad stripped down.

Brad was an unusually handsome man. He was six feet three inches tall with broad shoulders. His body was cut like a finely tuned athlete, almost equaling the athleticism he possessed. Brad's hair was sandy brown in color, sporting a stylish cut. But it was Brad's eyes that could stop anybody in their tracks. They were large blue eyes with eyelashes long enough to be accused of using false ones. The physical appearance of his eyes was just the start though because he communicated through them channeling his thoughts and desires to his recipient in an unmistakable way. There was a softness that radiated through his eyes, along with a command that he was in control of any situation.

Anne was already getting warm from watching him. She admired his muscular chest with just the right amount of chest hair. His arms were long, highlighted by well developed biceps and triceps, giving her a feeling of security when they surrounded her body. She loved his large, but tender hands. Anne's favorite part was his firm, well shaped butt that connected to powerful long legs. She knew he was built to be the perfect athlete. "Why don't we drop off Brianna and come back home to make love all night?"

Brad turned to look at her and felt the stirring of arousal light up his body as he watched her hugging the pillow that he wished was him instead. Just as he was getting ready to reply, Brianna walked in.

"Are you guys hiding from me?" she asked with a giggle.

"No, your dad's just getting ready for the evening, and I thought I'd visit with him," said Anne as she sat up in bed. "Go finish your movie while we get ready please."

"I want to visit with daddy too," Brianna said, pouting.

Brad walked up to Brianna and kneeled down to her giving her a hug and kiss. "You can visit with me all you want. I thought you wanted to finish your Winnie the Pooh movie."

"It's over now," Brianna said as she returned Brad's kiss. "I love you daddy very, very much. And you too mommy."

"We love you too honey very, very much," Brad said in the same toddler talk. He then turned towards Anne. "You know, that sounds good, but it's Carol's birthday party, and she's one of my best friends. Carol would never forgive me if we stood her up."

"I know," Anne replied in a disappointing tone. "I just thought it'd be nice, and we need the time together with just the two of us."

"I won't argue with that," Brad said as he pulled his favorite wool sweater over his head. He straightened the collar on his shirt and checked his hair in the mirror to make sure it was still in place. "I'm ready when you are."

"I have Brianna's night bag packed already and Carol's present is wrapped." Anne sprayed her neck with Escada perfume. She knew Brad loved the smell of Escada on her, and tonight she wanted to be at her best.

Brad walked up to Anne and pulled her tight against his body so he could feel her warmth. He felt the blood flow through his body at an accelerated rate, and he tenderly pressed his lips against hers to help satisfy the hunger he felt for her.

Anne returned the kiss with more aggression. They broke apart knowing they had to leave, and with Brianna still home with them, they knew it would not be possible to finish what they were getting started.

"My oh my Mr. Preston, you sure do know how to seduce us southern ladies," she said in an accent that reminded Brad of Scarlet O'Hara

"Us northern men know how to treat you southern ladies," Brad said with a grin on his face that lit up the whole room. Brad realized something special was happening between them once more, which felt good. He was determined to not let this feeling go, so he promised himself it would be a short evening at Carol's and then get home for a night of romance.

"Are you thinking what I'm thinking?" Anne asked, with a devilish smile.

He patted her on the butt to urge her to get going. "Yes ma'am, I do believe so."

"Let's go Brianna," Brad said. "And don't forget the cookies for grandma and grandpa."

"I won't," Brianna said as her little legs moved in a double pace towards the door. "I can't wait to see them."

They put on their winter coats, and Brad carried Brianna out to the car while Anne handled the other items.

Something definitely had changed between Brad and Anne this evening. The flame of the strong love between them was lit again as they both felt the strong feelings for each other that had brought them together.

CHAPTER 2

▼

Earlier in time

Miles and Margaret Preston lived in a lovely two story traditional brick home located in an upscale subdivision in suburban Indianapolis. The driveway was always lined with red and white impatiens in the summertime, outlining the blend of evergreens and other varieties of plants Mrs. Preston had planted over the years.

Miles Preston was a handsome man with a powerful presence. He was quite the athlete in his time and was still in good physical condition. Golf had become his game, and he carried a five handicap at Brandywine Country Club. His successful career in investment banking allowed him a good lifestyle. He was well educated and had a strong sense of what the market was going to do. He played the stock market well when it was going through the roof with the tech stocks leading the charge. He bought them cautiously knowing there was no real value in them due to the lack of assets. He then sold off the tech stocks with perfect timing, while directing his clients to do the same, earning him much respect from his clients and colleagues because shortly thereafter the tech stocks collapsed.

He and his wife Margaret had three children. Margaret was very attractive and could still turn men's heads. She was a proud woman that came from the Boston area. She carried herself in a way that warranted instant respect making people feel like they were around someone important. Margaret had a kindness that was second to none, but she would be the first to let you know if you wronged somebody. She taught English in high school, and her students loved her because she brought so much enthusiasm to the classroom. Her passion for literature and the correct use of the English language rubbed off on her students so much that her students averaged a B in her class, and it wasn't because of charity.

Margaret gave birth to three children. All three Preston children grew up to be a perfect mix of their parents. David, the oldest son, lived in Florida and achieved success following his father as an investment banker.

Rebecca was the middle child and the only daughter. She was well on her way in to be a sensational real estate agent in Boca Raton, taking advantage of the high demand of the rich lifestyle in that area.

Bradford was their youngest and going to college at Duke University. Ever since Brad was a child, he had always dreamed of playing profession baseball or football. He excelled in every sport he participated in from a young age. Brad was all state in basketball and football in high school, and rated as one of the ten best high school baseball players in the country. He made the honor roll carrying a 3.9 grade point average.

The only time he disappointed his parents was when he decided to go to Duke University and not Notre Dame where his father had graduated. Brad had almost committed to play football at Notre Dame, but became very interested in baseball after spending time with the Notre Dame Baseball Coach. The Irish Coach was a very classy individual that had the interest of his players first. Brad had spent hours talking with the Notre Dame Coach, which led to his decision to play baseball rather than football in college. Brad felt terrible when he finally decided on Duke because of the respect he held for the Irish Coach.

Brad recognized that Duke Baseball was not near the program as Notre Dame's, but the warm weather swayed him to Duke, along with his preference to Dukes medical school. It was a great letdown for Notre Dame and his father, but it was a decision Brad felt he should make for his future.

The decision to play baseball instead of football was just as hard on Brad, but he believed he would have a longer playing life on the diamond rather than the gridiron. He studied the longevity of professional football players and their pay, and compared it to the life and income of profession baseball players, and decided on the later. Besides, he had interviewed several ex-professional football players that explained to him they had trouble getting out of bed every morning from the abuse their bodies took playing the game, and Brad didn't want to live his life that way after he retired from sports.

Brad's parents weren't the only ones disappointed in his decision to attend Duke. His long time girlfriend Kristy was heartbroken when she found out he was going out of state to college. Brad and Kristy had been dating since seventh grade. They had broken up a few times during high school, but only for a short time. Everybody assumed they would marry and raise a family. She had enrolled at Indiana University to pursue her interest in music. Kristy's thought process on her decision to attend IU also centered on Brad's plan to attend Notre Dame. Bloomington was only a five hour drive to South Bend and would make it possible to see Brad now and then.

Brad first met Kristy in the seventh grade. Kristy had long blond hair and stunning blue eyes. He wanted to be with her the instant he saw her. It was the same feeling for Kristy as she fell in love at first sight with Brad. They experienced the middle school puppy love that grew into a full fledged love in high school. They made a beautiful couple and were envied by most of their fellow students. They would flow together as they held hands walking down the halls between classes.

Kristy turned out to be a very attractive woman. She had a great figure to go with her pretty face, but her personality made her a beauty queen. She was liked by everyone because she was always smiling. She lifted the spirits of those around her since her good moods were contagious. Her personality impressed Brad the most as well as her deep love for him that she openly expressed to him. Kristy's good looks were just a bonus. Overall, Brad appreciated all of her qualities, and he loved her for them.

The closeness they shared made Brad's sudden changes of colleges hard on Kristy. She suspected that their time together would be very limited. It hurt her in a way she had never felt before. Her initial reaction was to break up with Brad, but after a few weeks of reflection she decided that she did not want to live her life without him. Kristy apologized for her hasty and immature handling of the situation, admitting to Brad that she could not live without him. Brad let her know he felt the same way, so they prepared themselves to be able to cope with a long tem relationship.

When school started, the two of them talked daily on the phone and they wrote each other constantly, either by mail or e-mail. During the holidays they spent almost the entire time with each other, but as time went on, the long distance between each other gradually starting tearing away at their relationship. They had started another level of life, but not together. College brought on new challenges and was quite different than high school. They recognized the problem, and vowed to stay together, and work through the struggle, and lonely times.

With the start of their junior year of college a new problem came about. Greg Somanski transferred to Indiana University. Greg was a childhood friend to Brad early on, but their friendship turned to hatred on Greg's part because he was so competitive with Brad in everything, especially sports. Brad was by far a better athlete, and Greg couldn't handle that fact. At the beginning of their friendship, Greg's over aggressive competitiveness was just innocent behavior on his part. At least that is the way Brad perceived it. But as time went by, Greg showed contempt towards Brad he could not hide. Greg resented Brad being picked first when they choose teams to play neighborhood games. To make matters worse, Brad was always the pitcher when they played baseball or the quarterback when it was football season. The problem was the fact that everyone knew Brad was better than Greg at everything, including school and women, except for Greg.

By the start of high school, it was axiomatic to everybody including Brad that Greg's fanatical obsession of competing against Brad was at an unhealthy level. Brad endured the rivalry as well as anyone could, but it was very trying on him. He didn't have much choice though, because Greg was a good athlete, and he started in the same sports as Brad.

Greg was a decent looking young man with short brown hair that would curl wildly if he let it grow longer. He had deep brown eyes that were sinister looking when angered. Greg was well built with a muscular physique, making him look like a jock. He had a rounded face that could make you feel good when he smiled. He became the class clown to overcome his inadequacies, and everybody liked him. Overall, he was a good person with a big problem, his self-imposed rivalry with Brad. When high school ended, everyone went their separate way, making it best time of Greg's life. He no longer had to face daily life with Brad. Greg knew his feelings against Brad were shallow, but he could not shake them off. It grew into an obsession that was instilled deep into Greg's subconscious. He had become mentally deranged.

Greg went to a junior college in Illinois for his first two years of college. He was able to maintain a good grade average and did well in the school's baseball program allowing Indiana University to offer him a scholarship to play baseball there. Upon his arrival at IU, he instantly went after Kristy. He had always liked her, and there couldn't be a much better way to show up Brad than take his high school girl friend away from him.

Kristy made it a point that she was not interested in Greg and made it clear to him that she loved Brad.

Greg was persistent though. He worked Kristy hard by making up stories about Brad that she started to believe. Greg was very attentive to Kristy's needs and put on a good show to her to try and get her to fall for him.

Kristy began to have doubts about Brad due to Greg's lies, magnified by her growing loneliness. She allowed all of the negatives to overwhelm her elevating the friction to worsen between her and Brad.

Brad didn't help himself in his relationship with Kristy either. He was studying hard on his major, which took much more time than the general studies classes the previous two years. He also had become a big time pitcher in college. He was ranked number one and receiving a great deal of attention from the major league scouts. All of this took its toll on Brad and Kristy's relationship. They talked less than before, and suspicions grew on Kristy's part even more than before with the aid of Greg insinuating there might be another woman.

The situation came to a head during Christmas vacation. Brad was able to come home for a few days and decided to visit Kristy at her parent's house. Greg had known that Brad would be dropping by her house today, so he dropped in uninvited just minutes before Brad arrived. Greg had timed things well. He had Kristy under the mistletoe, in what Kristy thought was an innocent peck when Brad entered the house. Their relationship ended on the spot after Brad stormed out and never allowed Kristy to explain. It was the best Christmas present Greg could have ever dreamed of. He beat Brad at something, and it felt great. It was the first time Greg felt a euphoric charge through his entire body from beating Brad at something.

Brad was very upset by whole episode, because he seriously thought Kristy was cheating on him with Greg. After all, they had grown apart since the start of this school year, and he didn't recognize how absorbed he had become in his studies and baseball. Brad hadn't realized Kristy felt abandoned by him.

It turned out to be a blessing for Brad in some ways. He turned his full attention to school and baseball, and totally focused on both. Spring baseball started, and he was dominating as a pitcher. He had an astounding 1.08 earned run average. The coach hated the fact that Brad couldn't play every day because his batting average was .386.

Brad was excelling in school maintaining a 3.9 grade average. Everything was going Brad's way. He was the force behind Duke being in the midst of winning their conference title in baseball and possibly qualifying for the college world series.

Unknowing to Brad, things were about to change in his life. It was the third day of May, on a bright sunny day in North Carolina. The temperature was eighty-two degrees, and it was very humid. Indiana University was on the field warming up for the game against Duke. Normally, Duke wouldn't play Indiana during the regular season this late in the year, but this was a make up game from earlier in the season. This made it possible for the day to come when Brad and Greg would be on the same field together again. This time they were on opposite teams. Brad was scheduled to start for Duke, but Greg was a relief pitcher for IU, so it would not be a pitching dual between the two.

Greg strutted up to Brad and shook Brad's hand like they were best friends. Brad saw the arrogance in Greg's swagger and the hate in Greg's beady eyes, and it turned his stomach.

"Good to see you again." Brad had to force the words from his mouth.

"Yeah, it's good to see you too. Let's see if you're as good as everybody says you are. Oh, Kristy said to say hi," Greg added, throwing a jab at Brad.

Brad felt like Greg kicked him in the groin. His body tensed up and his stomach ached, making him feel nauseous. Brad shook off the feeling as best he could. He stared straight at Greg, with fire in his eyes. "Give her my best."

Greg knew he hit a nerve with Brad, giving him a feeling of power he had felt once before. It was a great feeling to have Brad sweating. What a high he was getting from it.

The game started, and Brad was focused like never before. Indiana couldn't touch his pitches with their bats the first three innings, as Brad struck out the first nine batters. The score was six to nothing after the first six innings, and IU didn't have a hit. It was a performance of a lifetime for Brad. He could put the ball anywhere he wanted. His curve had a snap in it like never before. His fastball was around ninety-four mph and would tail up slightly moving in on the right hand batters. Brad stuck out the side again in the top of the seventh.

Duke had taken total control of the game and they were scoring wildly in the bottom half of the seventh. There were no outs, and Duke had run the score up to nine to nothing. Normally, Brad would be pulled at this time, but he was throwing a perfect game, and the coach wanted to give him the chance to complete the game. Brad was on deck to hit when the pitcher hit the batter at the plate with a wild pitch.

Indiana's coach went out to the mound and signaled for Greg Somanski to come into the game. The IU coach had no idea of the relationship between Greg and Brad, so he thought nothing of pitching this particular relief pitcher against Brad. Greg threw his warm up pitches, all the while giving Brad a look. Greg had seen the article in Sports Illustrated with Brad on the front cover, so he knew Brad was still going to be a tough out, plus he remembered Brad always had his number.

Brad was intrigued by this situation. He was always able to hit Greg, but it had been three years since he had faced him. Brad watched Greg closely, noticing he had really bulked since high school. So Brad went to the plate not knowing what to expect. He just hoped he would get a curve ball.

Greg's first pitch to Brad was wild causing the catcher to work hard to keep the ball from going to the backstop.

Brad dug in, stroking the bat across the plate in a slow motion waiting for Greg's next pitch.

Greg checked the runners, kicked his left leg high in the air while cocking his right arm back and released the ball. He threw a curve ball in hope to regain his composure. Brad saw it coming, and took a mighty swing at it. The ball exploded off the bat making a cracking noise heard several blocks away. The ball sailed out of the stadium just to the left side of the left field foul ball pole.

Brad was disappointed the ball was out of play, knowing he hit the ball with the sweet part of the bat. He trotted back to home plate and dug back in waiting for the next pitch.

Greg threw the new ball hard into his glove as his hatred for Brad shot through his entire body. He wasn't going to allow Brad to make him look bad. Greg's eyes narrowed as he stared at his self proclaimed enemy. His hate fueled his body with more energy. He went through a quick windup and threw the ball with all of his might aiming it at Brad's head.

It was a fastball that seemed to jump out of Greg's hand from Brad's perspective, and it was heading right for his head. Brad had no choice at this time but to jerk his body back as fast as he could, so he wouldn't take the full brunt of the ball hitting him. He rapidly threw his right shoulder back in order to get his body moving away from the pitch and then twisted his upper body quickly. At that time, he heard a snap in his right shoulder just before the ball hit him on his upper left arm that he had used to cover his face with.

Everybody in the stadium gasped at the same time. Brad's coach ran out to the plate to check on him, while the umpire threw his arm in the air and ejected Greg from the game. It was obvious to everyone that Greg intended to hit Brad.

Brad held his left arm and thought he was well enough to continue to play. The pain from the ball hitting his left arm made Brad forget the snap he felt in his right shoulder. The coach conferred with Brad, asking him if he was ok. Brad forced a smile and said he was fine, before he trotted to first base while receiving applause of appreciation from the stands.

Duke scored three more runs, including Brad scoring on a close play at home, before the inning ended. The eighth inning started with Brad on the mound. He felt a tightness and slight pain in his right shoulder, but he was pumped up from last inning and wanted to continue pitching. On Brad's second pitch of the inning his shoulder exploded in pain. You could hear his shoulder pop from the dugout.

Brad was bent over in pain as the entire team stood lifeless in disbelief.

Coach Culley ran to the mound while his stomach soured from seeing his star player injured. "Brad, are you ok?" Coach asked, searching Brad's eyes for an answer.

"Just pull the knife out of my shoulder, and I'll be fine," Brad said as he winced in pain.

"Don't move your shoulder until Doc takes a look," Coach Culley replied as he studied the situation.

At that time, Doc made it to the pitcher's mound to join the rest of the team. Doc bent over Brad to see what the problem was. "Tell me where it hurts the most son?"

Brad pointed to his right shoulder blade with his left hand. "Right there."

Doc felt the area where Brad pointed to, but couldn't feel anything wrong. "Let's get him to the hospital for an x-ray and MRI. I can't tell by feeling what's wrong."

Brad slowly got to his feet with the assistance of two of his teammates. He felt like he was going to throw up as he stood upright. He carefully made his way to the dugout and thanked Dennis and Brian for their help.

CHAPTER 3

▼

Duke baseball coach, Pat Culley, waited impatiently beside Brad as they sat waiting for the use of the MRI diagnostic machine. Coach Culley had rushed to the hospital immediately after the game ended. Duke had beaten Indiana, seventeen to nothing, securing Brad's win and shutout, but it was a mute point at this time. Brad's injury was the focal point of their conversation at this time.

"The x-ray didn't reveal any problems, so your rotator cup is ok," Coach said as he patted Brad on his right hand.

"The pain is behind my shoulder blade and burns like hell. I felt a snap back there when I tried to get out of the way of the bean ball. I didn't think much of it at the time. I was irritated at Greg for being vindictive enough towards my success that he would actually throw at me. I realized as I grew older, he was jealous of me. I just didn't know how jealous."

"Maybe the ball just got away from him Brad. His first pitch was way outside."

"It's possible, but I really doubt it. He's partly responsible for my break up with Kristy." Brad still felt the hurt from his loss of Kristy.

"Look, let's just concentrate on what the problem is and get you healed up properly. You have a great career ahead of you in the majors. I have never coached or seen a player perform like you. And most of your toughness is mental. Focus on the mental toughness right now. Put that positive force to good use." Pat gave Brad a smile of encouragement.

"You're right, I need to be positive. I can overcome anything." Brad saw a movement down the hall and was glad to see the doctor approaching them.

"Gentlemen, please follow me if you will," Doctor Athinson said, pausing a brief moment to allow Pat and Brad to get to their feet.

"What's the verdict Tom?" Pat asked the doctor. Pat knew Dr. Tom Athinson very well and didn't think anything about calling him Tom.

"I want to show you what we found before I say anymore," Dr. Athinson replied in a professional manner.

The coach's body shook slightly from fear. "That doesn't sound good to me Tom."

The three men entered the doctor's office and each one of them sat down. Dr. Athinson pulled a chart with the results of the MRI. He tilted his head down slightly and directed his attention towards Brad. "Look son, you really damaged your Teres Majer. It's the muscle that ties into the side of your shoulder blade. I've never seen such a muscle tear like this from throwing a ball. This is such an unusual muscle to damage from throwing."

"Well I felt a snap in that area while I was at the plate trying to keep from getting beaned in the head by a wild pitch. How bad is it?" Brad asked in a whisper.

The doctor turned the computer monitor towards them and typed Brad's name into the keyboard. An image came up on the screen as Dr. Athinson pointed to an area on the monitor. "See that right there? That's the problem area. It appears to me this muscle is badly torn. It'll take surgery to see how severe the actual damage is, but it's not good anyway you look at it. I'm sorry to be the bearer of bad news Pat," the doctor said as he turned towards the coach. "He's definitely out for the rest of this year and probably longer."

The news hit Brad like a ton of bricks. He felt numb all over and tried to ask the doctor a question, but was unable to talk.

There was dead silence in the room until Pat spoke. "Is it repairable?"

"I'm sure it's repairable, but to what extent I can't say at this time. I feel surgery is the best and only solution, and at that time I can give you a better prognosis. Right now it's somewhat of a guessing game. I know you both have many concerns and more questions to ask, but let's schedule surgery first, and then repair the damage, and work on rehab from there," Dr. Athinson said, trying to hide his true concern. He had seen Brad play many times and was impressed by the talent he displayed. "We should call your parents Brad and let them know what happened. I'm sure that they'll want to be here for the surgery."

"Thanks, Dr. Athinson," Brad said, finally able to talk again. "How soon do you want to perform the surgery?"

"I think the sooner the better. Tomorrow is not too soon. I'll make the arrangements with the hospital and my team to do you tomorrow. Is that alright with you?"

"Sure, let's get it done." Brad knew full well that he had no other choice at this time.

Pat's heart sunk feeling like it was now in his stomach from seeing Brad go through this. Pat loved Brad as a son. He couldn't have wished for a better person to be around. He knew his team would not be as successful if Brad had not been on the team, but that was his last concern at this time. This was a great kid with all the right stuff. Brad's work habits were far superior to anyone he had coached before, and the leadership he exhibited was equal to his as a coach. The thing Pat liked about Brad the most was his personality. Brad would light up an entire room when he entered. Why did this have to happen to him? Did that Greg kid try to hit him on purpose? It started to bother the coach, thinking about these unanswered questions.

Brad's parents took the news hard. They recognized how hard Brad had worked to get his game to this level. They also knew Brad had planned to play profession baseball or football since high school. They took the next available flight to North Carolina, and arrived at the Duke Medical Center in Durham at 9:45 p.m. that same day.

The Prestons took the elevator to the floor were Brad's room was and didn't have any trouble finding it because it was surrounded by his teammates.

"I guess they don't have limits on the number of visitors here," Miles stated jokingly as he and Margaret walked in the room filled with Brad and his teammates.

"We should leave guys," Dennis said. Dennis was the catcher for the team and was now the best choice for team leader, with Brad out for the season.

"You boys don't have to leave because we're here," Miles exclaimed.

"No, it's time for us to get back to our rooms," stated Brian, the team's starting shortstop.

"We'll see you later Brad," they all said at the same time as they left the room.

Dennis and Brian stepped back into the room as the other teammates left. "Hell of a game out there today," they both said.

"It was an honor to be catching for you today," Dennis added.

"We're all pulling for the surgery to go well. Take care man. Good night Mr. and Mrs. Preston," they both said in unison, before they departed again.

"Nice young men," Miles said.

"Yeah, they're both great. Dennis really made me a better pitcher by the way he could manage a game," Brad replied. "And Brian has saved me many times by making spectacular plays at shortstop.

"You look good son. How are you feeling?" Mr. Preston asked as he looked Brad over, searching for the truth of Brad's mental state as well as his physical health.

"As well as can be expected. Thanks for coming down here. I know it's a lot of trouble," Brad said, trying to hold back tears.

Mrs. Preston gave Brad a hug. "Don't be ridiculous Brad. We wouldn't let you go through this by yourself. You should know better than that." She sensed that Brad was upset, and it was making her more emotional. She held back the tears that were waiting to flood her eyes.

"I guess it doesn't take but an instant to change your life," Brad said.

"I know things look bad now son, but it'll work out. You have a lot of other qualities other than baseball. Besides, it's too soon to let go of your dream of playing in the majors," Miles said. He knew how Brad had planned his life out so carefully by choosing the right classes to back up the possibility that he may not make it in baseball. He was proud of the way his son was leading his life. Very mature for twenty-one years of age, his father thought to himself.

The three of them chatted for a few minutes as Brad filled them in on what happened at the game.

Coach Culley had made his way to Brad's room and gave a quick knock, before opening the door slowly giving them time to finish their thoughts.

"Come on in Coach. You remember my parents Miles and Margaret?"

"Good evening Mr. and Mrs. Preston," Pat said, extending his hand towards Miles. "It's good to see you again. I just wish it was under better circumstances."

Pat and Miles shock hands while Miles stated, "It's good to see you again. I can't tell you how much Brad talks about you. We appreciate the way you've taken care of him…" Miles turned towards Brad and nodded his head at him. "We know these things happen sometimes."

"You're right, accidents do happen, but they shouldn't happen on my watch. I feel responsible for this. I should've taken him out of the game when he was hit by that pitch."

"Hey, we can look back and say that we should have done this or we should have done that, but it won't do any good. What has happened is done. I don't blame you or this school. I believe I would have kept Brad in the game under the circumstances. It's not often you see a perfect game performed," Miles replied honestly. "What's next for Brad?"

"Surgery first thing in the morning, then we get the status report from the doctor on how extensive the damage was in his shoulder, and what he did to repair it. From there, we formulate a rehabilitation process to get Brad back in shape. He's young and should heal quickly. The key is Brad. He's the one that'll make the mental and physical effort to get back to where he was before this happened," Coach Culley explained

"Thank you Mr. Culley," Margaret said, chiming in on the conversation. "I appreciate your candor. What do you believe the damage is at this time?"

"Well, I can only go by what the doctor said earlier, but it doesn't look real good. He believes that there is a severe muscle tear and maybe more damage elsewhere. At this time, we need to allow this surgery to take place and then see what the complete damage is. I'm sure that Dr Athinson will fill you in tomorrow morning before he performs surgery. I've known Tom for years, and he's the best," Coach Culley stated with confidence.

"Coach is right Mom and Dad. Why don't you two go check into your hotel room so we can all get some rest? Tomorrow will be a tough day for all of us. Coach, can you direct my parents to their hotel?"

"Sure Brad."

They all said their goodbyes and left Brad alone in his room. Brad gave a sigh of relief glad to have a few minutes to himself. So much had changed for him today, and he wanted some time to reflect on it. He went over the game, especially his at bat against Greg. He wondered if Greg intentionally hit him. After going over the at bat several times in his mind, he came to the conclusion that Greg definitely did try to hit him and did so with intentions to do harm to him.

Brad's thoughts turned to Greg's involvement of his breakup with Kristy. As he remembered that awful day in Kristy's house, his blood turned hot and he felt a hatred envelope him towards Greg. He knew he still had feelings for her. Thoughts of Kristy filled his mind as he fell asleep.

Miles and Margaret Preston arrived at the hospital at six in the morning. They knew that Brad's future in sports hinged on the success of today's surgery. Miles was prepared for Brad to be in a somber mood, with some degree of doubt, so he entered the stark hospital room with a big smile. "Well, did you sleep any last night or did you stay awake in anticipation for today?"

"I actually slept fine. They had to wake me," Brad said, returning the smile. "I know that Dr. Athinson will perform the surgery to the best of his ability, and he's one of the best doctors in the country. It will be up to me to take care of the rest. I know that baseball might not be in my future, but I can handle it if that is how it turns out. You two raised me right."

His mom gave him a big hug as she kissed Brad on the cheek. "You have turned into a wise man at such an early age. We know this is hard on you, but we feel confident there will be more difficult times in your life. There always are hard times, and this is just a challenge to help you get through them down the road."

"Are you worried about the procedure in any way?" Mr. Preston asked, concerned.

"Not really. I'm young and very healthy, so going under doesn't bother me. I've studied the body enough to know the difficulty of getting the muscle attached to the shoulder properly. And I know that it will take some time to build that portion of my shoulder back to normal, but I'll do it." Brad felt confident he would overcome this set back.

"We know it also Brad. You're one of the strongest individuals I've ever known. It doesn't surprise me much since you're my son," Miles said, laughing.

"Boy, are you a happy crowd today," Dr. Athinson said as he entered the room. "This must be the wrong room. I was scheduled to perform major surgery on someone in this room today." He walked up to the Prestons to introduce himself.

After shaking the elderly Preston's hands, the doctor explained the surgery in detail. He acknowledged the fact that the shoulder may never be the same and there would be extensive rehab for Brad to get it back within eighty percent of normal. After that process, it would be more difficult to get the strength back to one hundred percent. With that said, the nurses came in and helped Brad on the gurney to take him to surgery.

Before leaving, Brad's parents told him that everything would be all right and they would see him in recovery room.

CHAPTER 4

▼

Dr. Athinson met Mr. and Mrs. Preston in a post surgical room to fill them in on the surgery. He explained to them that there was extensive damage beyond what the MRI revealed. He told them that his team did a remarkable job of repairing the damage and reconnecting the torn section of the Teres Major muscle. It would be an extensive rehabilitation for Brad, and it would be a long time before he could pitch again, if ever. The good news was Brad made it through with no problems, and he would not be crippled in that area of his back. The doctor then asked them if they had any questions, then said he would see them a little later when he checked on Brad later this afternoon.

The Prestons thanked the doctor for the good news and for his concern for their son, and then waited to be called into Brad's intensive care room.

While the doctor and his parents where talking, Brad was having a strange dream. It was like the "Wizard of Oz" movie. His world was spinning around so fast, and he could see his life go by. He wanted to see the future, but couldn't. He arrived in a strange land wanting to know if he was going to be able to perform as a pitcher in the majors, but nobody could answer him. They said follow the road to recovery. It was painted red, not the yellow brick road like the movie. He followed the road and experienced a great deal of pain because the road was full of abusive work he had to perform to build his shoulder back to normal.

There were people telling him he would never be able to pick up a fork to eat with his right arm again. Trainers were pushing him so hard he passed out, but he continued down the long red road, crawling at times because he was so spent from working out.

All at once, the road magically turned to a yellow road paved with bricks. There was Yankee Stadium right in front of him with his name on the marquis naming him as the starting pitcher. He walked faster towards the stadium and then started running. Fans were applauding as he approached. It had worked. All of the pain and suffering he went through was for the good. Then suddenly, a puff of smoke appeared, and Greg Somanski stood in front of him laughing. He held a baseball and unleashed it towards Brad so fast that he couldn't get out of the way. Brad's reflexes moved his body too fast causing a snap in his shoulder.

Brad woke up with sweat running down his face. He felt a damp cloth wipe his face delicately. His eyes opened, and there was the most beautiful girl in the world standing over him. She had the most stunning look he had ever seen. Her eyes threw darts of pleasure through his entire body while her smile warmed him within. He tried to smile back, but all he could say was, "Are you a good witch or bad witch?"

She broke out laughing and spoke in the sexiest southern accent, "Well now, I can honestly say that I've never been asked that question before. You must've had a terrible dream. Your body was jerking all over this bed. This is recovery time, so you have to be still for awhile." She smiled at him thinking what a handsome man he was. No, not handsome, he was beautiful. His eyes could steal your heart in a second.

"Am I awake or is this still a dream?" Brad asked, still groggy.

"You're waking up. I heard your surgery went well," she said as she started to take his blood pressure.

"I'm sorry. I didn't mean to call you a witch. I was having the strangest dream or nightmare. I'm not sure which."

"Yes, you were having a nightmare I believe. You must've watched the Wizard of Oz one to many times when you were a child. Are you ok?" the nurse asked with sincere concern.

Brad focused on the question and went through a test of his body to see if everything worked. He noticed pressure in his right shoulder, which would inflict a lot pain when the drugs wore off. "Everything seems ok."

"Good. Your vitals are just fine. I'm Anne. I'll be with you the rest of the day. Well, at least until four o'clock," she said, still smiling

"How'd I get so lucky as to get such a beautiful nurse? Did Coach work this out?"

"No, you're not that special. It's just my shift, so lay there and be good for me." She turned around and started out the door.

"Hey, where're you going?" Brad asked. He was having difficulty keeping his eyes focused because his head was still unclear from the drugs. Everything looked blurry, as if he was looking through someone's eye glasses that were for severe near-sightedness.

"I have other things to do. You aren't my only patient," she said, not telling the whole truth. She was really on her way to get his parents, so they could visit with him. She walked out the door waving her hand over her face in a fanning motion while she looked at the girl behind the desk.

"What's the matter Anne? Is he too hot for you?" the red headed nurse asked, laughing. She got a kick out of seeing Anne flustered by a man because it had never happened.

"Have you seen him? My God, he's gorgeous. And those eyes," Anne stated, feeling a stirring in her body.

"No I haven't had a chance to get a look at him, but I definitely will now that I've seen your reaction. My word girl, I've never seen you like this before. You know, he was some star baseball player. I hear that every major league team was looking at him," the red head stated.

Anne gave the girl a quick nod. "I'm going to get his parents. Please keep your ears open for any problems." She walked fast, anxious to see what his parents were like. Why was she acting this way, she asked herself? She wasn't fond of jocks, but he was different.

Brad's parents were just down the hall in a small waiting room. Anne walked in and asked, "Are you the parents of Brad Preston?"

Miles and Margaret both stood up at the same time and answered in unison, "Yes we are."

Anne introduced herself and asked them to follow her to Brad's room. She told them that Brad had just awakened and was still a little doped up, but he could talk.

The three of them entered Brad's room. Miles walked up to the bed looking at Brad carefully. "Well you made it just fine. The doctor said that you should heal well."

"How are you Brad?" Mrs. Preston asked, relieved to see him. She was a strong person, but found it hard seeing her son this way.

"As well as can be expected I guess. I still feel groggy. Heck, I asked this pretty woman here if she was a witch," Brad said, embarrassed.

They all laughed together, and Anne's face turned red. "I believe he was having a very weird dream or nightmare. I just happened to be around when he opened his eyes, and he naturally took me for an ugly old witch," Anne playfully explained with an exaggerated southern accent.

"Do you two know each other?" Brad's mother asked.

"No, we just met today," Brad answered.

"I've been going to school at Duke for three years taking medical classes and training here at the hospital for the past two years. They put me in post-op intensive care a few months ago. I just happened to be scheduled to work this area today. It's strange that we've never crossed paths on campus," Anne replied.

Anne was a very sophisticated woman as well as attractive. The Prestons could see she came from a good family. Margaret was doing an appraisal of her and rated Anne with high marks. She appreciated the natural beauty Anne possessed and the manner that she carried herself. Anne didn't seem to let her beauty run her life, but she did everything right to present her stunning looks and perfect body.

Margaret wondered if Brad noticed the same things. She assumed Kristy was still on his mind at times, but Brad didn't talk about that relationship at all, so she wasn't sure what he felt for Kristy at this time. This young woman standing in front of Mrs. Preston was more beautiful in looks, but it would take someone special to be more beautiful in personality than Kristy. Nevertheless, Margaret liked Anne and hoped Brad would show some interest in her.

The door swung open, and in walked Dr. Athinson and Coach Culley. "Well Brad it's good to see you awake. Are you still groggy?" asked the doctor.

"I'm getting most of my senses back. The drugs must be wearing off. I can tell because the pain is really increasing. But I'd rather have pain than be numb in the mind. I can't stand not having my mental capacities," Brad stated as he fought off the feeling of hot needles sticking in his back muscle.

"I have filled in your parents and Pat on the outcome of the procedure. We did a very good job on repairing the damage. It couldn't have gone any better from that standpoint. The problem we couldn't control was the severity of the damage you did to the muscles, ligaments, and joint. It was extensive. You'll be all right, but your pitching days are over for a long time, maybe forever. Now the rest of the process is up to you. It will take a lot of hard work and agony on your part to strengthen your shoulder area to get it to eighty percent. I know that isn't what you wanted to hear, but those are the facts. I'm sorry I can't give you better news on that front," Dr. Athinson stated empathetically.

Everyone turned to Brad to see his reaction. It was hard to read how Brad took the news. He just laid there without changing his facial expression. Finally, he let out a long breath shaking his head side to side while biting his lower lip ever so gently. He forced a smile. "It's a good thing I planned for this type of stumbling block by studying hard and taking classes that will do me good in real life. Looks like I'm going to have to fall back on them now. Sorry Coach, I hate to let you and the team down in a year that we could have gone a long way in the College World Series."

"Brad, you didn't let anybody down. I can't tell you just how much good you've brought to this team. Just help me keep these guys up in spirits by coming to practices and staying positive," Coach Culley asked.

"That would be great. At least I can still be a part of the team through the end of this season," Brad stated, already missing playing the game.

The Prestons and Anne had to choke back tears. They all knew Brad was disappointed, yet he was handling the situation like a man far beyond his years. Anne realized he was a much different person than anybody she had ever been around. He was not a jock like she expected, but instead a classy gentleman that she hoped to see more of after he left the hospital.

Dr. Athinson told Brad he would like for him to stay in the hospital for two more days, and if possible, then be released Sunday morning. He exited the room leaving the other five behind.

Anne checked Brad's vitals again and left the room allowing the three remaining visitors to talk with her new patient.

The three Prestons and Coach Culley discussed the situation at length. Coach explained to them that Brad would not lose his scholarship, which was the least of their worries since Miles was very capable of paying for the remainder of Brad's education. Coach Culley then excused himself, having to get to the practice field with the rest of the players. He turned to Brad. "Don't worry about the team. Just take care of yourself. Everything will work out for the best."

The rest of the day went by slowly. Anne would check on Brad often while the Preston family talked about the injury and what the future would hold.

Kristy McDonnell had heard about Brad's injury and was very upset from the news. The rumor was, Greg intentionally tried to hit Brad with a pitch, and from that caused Brad to throw his shoulder out. It was early Friday morning, and she had just started her nine-hour drive to Durham, North Carolina to visit Brad. Maybe she would discover the truth about Greg's accusations of Brad's infidelity. No matter what she would find out, she was excited to see him again. Her heart still belonged to Brad, even though she had been dating Greg off and on.

The drive was long, but beautiful. The mountains were somewhat of a challenge to drive through, but the scenery was great. She found the culture very different in the south compared to central Indiana, and thought it was a nice slower pace. She wondered if Brad enjoyed living down here.

Kristy started thinking about her past with Brad and began asking herself questions. What would she do if Brad had found someone else? Would she be able to handle it if he had? "This is the worst thing about a long drive," she said out loud to herself. Too much idle time while you're driving leads you to think too much. You just can't keep your brain from looking ahead, she thought. At least it made the travel time go fast since she was already on the outskirts of Durham. She calculated that she would be at the hospital in about twenty-five minutes, allowing time for traffic. That would put her there about five-thirty.

Mr. and Mrs. Preston spent the entire day at the hospital again. They felt better about Brad's misfortune believing he had accepted his fate very maturely. They were so proud of their youngest child by the way he planned ahead for such an event knowing very few men his age would have done the same.

It was getting close to five thirty, and they were hungry. They ate little lunch because they didn't care too much for the hospital food. They decided to go to a nice restaurant for dinner and offered to bring Brad a filet mignon back to the hospital for him to eat, and he seemed enthused about the offer.

As they left, they passed Anne in the hallway. It had been her day off, and she was dressed in a pair of jeans cut to show off her perfect body. She wore a pale blue, rounded neck pull over top, with short sleeves, making her more stunning than yesterday. They stopped for a quick chat as Anne explained she had come to get her paycheck and decided to see how Brad was doing.

Margaret told Miles that she suspected something was in the air between the two. They both smiled at the prospect of that happening because they liked Anne and believed she would be good for him at this time. She would be a nice distraction from the daily grind facing Brad they both agreed.

Anne gave a soft knock on Brad's door and opened it slightly, whispering, "Is it ok if I come in?"

Brad recognized her voice and asked her to enter. He had to catch his breath from seeing her beauty as she walked up to him. "You look different without your hospital clothes."

She smiled affectionately. "I do live another life away from here."

Kristy had estimated her time of arrival to the hospital fifteen minutes too early. It was 5:45 p.m. when she asked the front desk the room number for Brad Preston. The receptionist looked it up and sent her to the fourth floor, room 415.

She exited the elevator and looked for the nurse's station. She was nervous about seeing Brad again. She knew he was not expecting her, and wondered what his reaction would be to her visit. She approached the desk and asked the attending nurse for room 415.

The nurse told her it was located three doors down on the right, stating that he was awake, so it was ok to see him. The nurse didn't tell her another woman was in the room with him as she didn't think much of it since it was Anne.

Kristy's pace quickened as she approached the door to 415.

Brad had complained to Anne that his IV needle was bothering him. She bent down and gently grabbed his hand to look at it. Brad was looking at her in a very caring way, not noticing the door to his room open slightly.

Kristy glanced in the room and witnessed Brad and a stunning blond woman together holding hands, in what she perceived as a romantic exchange between the two. She quietly closed the door and rested her head against the door frame as tears rolled down her cheeks. This couldn't be happening, she thought. Greg was right. Brad must have been cheating on her. And how could she compete with such a beautiful woman, she thought to herself?

Kristy almost ran back to the elevator as she left the hospital, believing Brad had found someone else. How could she be so naïve as to drive a full day down here to see him?

The end to their relationship was official. They both blamed the other for its failure. To make matters worse, they still felt a love for one another that neither would admit.

CHAPTER 5

▼

Brad was released from the hospital and went back to his hard work at school. The only difference now was Brad couldn't participate in practices or games. He was now a cheerleader for his teammates, although they didn't look at Brad that way in any respect. They looked up to him in a way that Brad couldn't grasp. They thought the world of him and privately dedicated the rest of the season to Brad.

Coach Culley's stomach was in knots seeing Brad sit on the sidelines. He knew Brad was having a difficult time being a spectator. Brad was far too competitive to sit idle and watch. Coach tried to keep Brad involved as much as possible, but it just wasn't the same. He was amazed at how well Brad was able to hide his emotions from the team, and he knew his team was playing well above their ability because of Brad.

"Hell, I don't need to be out here," the Coach said to himself. "I could let Brad take charge of this team and they would probably win every game." He shook his head and smiled to himself, knowing the truth of about Brad's leadership abilities.

Brad and Anne hadn't seen each other since his release from the hospital. Anne thought about him more than he thought about her. She was determined to make it a point to see him again. She asked several friends on campus if they knew Brad Preston and finally came across someone that shared a class with him. She thought carefully on how to manufacture an innocent meeting between the two of them.

Anne decided to be honest with him, so she waited outside the door of his advanced trigonometry class as it ended. She wasn't to be let down as he walked out of the classroom with the other students.

Brad noticed her standing by the door when he exited the room. He walked towards her still stricken by her beauty. He realized at that point that he had missed her the past few weeks, and gave her a shy smile and a look that made his eyes much more dangerous.

She almost melted at the sight of him. She thought he was more than handsome and his personality was at an even keel with his looks. He looked different than in the hospital bed. This man was in charge of life and the people around him, and he didn't even care about that fact, or he didn't realize it. She couldn't tell one way or the other. It wasn't important though because he was perfect in her mind. She remembered the reaction she received when she asked other classmates about him.

The students she had talked to had all heard great things about him, even if they didn't know him.

She stood there with weak knees as he approached her. All she was able to get out of her mouth was a simple, "Hi," in an almost inaudible tone.

Brad felt her feelings for him and was pleased as well as honored. He had heard nothing but good things about her. He had done some investigation work on his own towards her also. "Good morning," he replied. "What brings you here? We've been on campus together for three years, and this is the first time we've run into each other." He smiled even bigger.

"I planned on being here. I wanted to see how you were doing." She looked him over admiring his perfect body that was highlighted by a tight fitting shirt and tailored trousers. "Actually, I wanted to see you again," she said, revealing herself to him in a way that she had never done before with anyone.

"Well, I'm glad you did. I missed you too." He caught himself and rephrased his words by adding, "You did so much for me in the hospital." He could see the disappointment in her face from his last statement. Why was he so defensive about going into a possible relationship, he thought to himself? She seemed to be a wonderful person.

"Is that the only reason you're glad to see me, because I was there for you at the hospital?" she replied as the color left her face.

His face turned red, and a guilty smile took over his face. "I'm sorry. I've been so caught up in school work and baseball these past few years that I forgot how to act around a woman. Please forgive me?"

"You're forgiven," she said, looping her arm in and around his muscled arm, being alert enough to latch on to his left arm. "How's your shoulder?"

He gave his right arm a quick glance. "The pain is minimal now, but I still can't do much with my right arm."

Anne led him down the hall. "I'll walk you to your next class."

"Actually, that was my last final exam for this semester. Where should we go to celebrate?" he asked, holding on to her even tighter.

Anne thought for a minute and suggested that they go to an espresso café a short distance away. They walked as the warm sun showered them with brilliant rays of light, adding to the heat they were creating between themselves. They took turns talking about themselves and their pasts, to allow each to learn as much about their life as possible in such a short amount of time. They were both relieved that there was not a significant other in either one of their lives, and marveled that it took three years for them to run into each other. The next few hours went by quickly, before Brad announced he had to get to the practice field.

"I thought baseball was over for you for awhile," Anne stated, not wanting their time to end now.

"I work out a little and help out Coach Culley with the pitchers. I think the team likes me to be there for them. Why don't you come and watch?"

"I don't want to be in the way. Besides, I've never been that much of a sports fan," she stated, embarrassed by her lack of knowledge of the game.

Brad persisted by asking her what else she had to do. He assumed her finals were over as well. "Come on," he said, grabbing her hand. "Just this one time, and if you don't like it I won't ask again."

"I'll give it a try." She smiled affectionately while her face glowed; enjoying the way people looked at the two of them.

Anne sat attentively on the bleachers watching Brad interact with the other players. She began to understand just how important Brad was to the team. She witnessed how he took control of any situation without trying. Even the coach looked up to Brad. Anne began to enjoy baseball, and she now regretted the fact she never did see Brad play. From everything she heard and from what she witnessed today, Anne could only conclude that he was a special player. She knew he was a unique person that would go far in life.

Anne had been lost in her thoughts and was startled when Coach Culley sat down beside her.

"He's a good young man with exceptional qualities, isn't he?" Coach asked.

"I'm beginning to realize that more and more," she said, stunned by the fact that Duke's head baseball coach was sitting next to her.

Coach Culley leaned back to get a better look at her. "You're the young lady from the hospital, aren't you?"

"Why yes I am," Anne answered shyly. "I'm Anne Weatherby, and I go to school here as well as work at the hospital. It's nice to talk to you since Brad has given you such high praises."

The coach stared at her without realizing it, admiring her beauty and the proper manners she possessed. "Be good to him please. I've grown to love that kid, and I want the very best for him. And I do believe you could be the very best for him, so don't take me wrong. It's just that he has a long road ahead of him to get his shoulder healed properly, and there will be some trying times."

They both sat in silence starring at the practice field before the coach smiled at her while getting to his feet. "It's a pleasure to meet you Anne."

Anne had a lot to absorb from the events of the day. She learned so much more about Brad and it was all too good to be true. She never saw one negative aspect about him. What was she heading for she, thought to herself? Was this man too big for her? She had never in her life asked that question to herself. She felt her stomach turn from fear. A fear acknowledging the fact that she could get hurt from this relationship. "Relationship," she said out load to herself. "Heck, we're not that far along yet."

Anne sat there until practice ended, not sure of what to do next. She wasn't sure she was willing to set herself up for a major heartbreak, but she didn't want to walk away from someone so special. She knew in her heart and in her mind that she would never meet such a man again. He was a once in a lifetime catch.

"Did you see a ghost?" Brad asked her as he walked up to her. "You look a little pale. Are you alright?"

She fumbled with her purse with her shaky hands. "I think so."

"What's wrong Anne?"

"I guess I've been doing too much thinking. I haven't been with a guy for some time now. Then I finally meet someone, and I find out he's larger than life. I'm somewhat overwhelmed by that thought right now," Anne stated, while staring at his handsome face.

"Anne, I'm not larger than life. I really don't understand why you think that. Look at you. You have class and you're intelligent, plus you're beautiful. Heck, I feel overwhelmed being with you."

Her fingers stopped playing with the purse as a smile replaced the frown on her face allowing her big brown eyes to light up the world as they made the light of the sun seem dim. She stood up and looked him in the eyes trying to read anything that might be contrary to what he spoke, but there was nothing to say different. She touched his left hand and brought it up to her lips giving it the slightest kiss. "What do you say we get cleaned up and have a nice dinner together?"

"That sounds good to me. Maybe we should keep this on neutral ground for awhile. What did you have in mind?"

Anne thought for a minute and then suggested Antonio's, a quaint Italian restaurant, located on the edge of town. She offered to pick Brad up at his dorm, and he agreed.

Brad and Anne had a nice dinner that evening, keeping everything at a slight distance. They both had built a wall around themselves hindering a positive, loving relationship. But that was what they wanted at this time because Anne did not want to be hurt, and Brad was protecting himself from what had happened between him and Kristy. He was still hurt by his breakup with Kristy and still had some feelings for her, but they were slowly fading away because of Anne.

They departed that evening admitting openly that they wanted to see each other again, but revealing a tight schedule the next couple of weeks. Anne's work schedule was heavy, and Brad had to travel with the team for the conference tournament in a few days, which would lead Duke to the College World Series if they won it

Brad and Anne talked a few times on the phone during this brief time away from each other, both realizing the more contact they had with each other, the stronger their feelings grew for one another.

Brad returned from the tournament on the Friday morning before Memorial Day weekend. Duke lost in the semi finals of the conference tournament, ending their season.

Anne had been pondering the question of asking Brad to her parent's house for the weekend. She really wanted him to stay with them, but she wasn't sure how he would react to the question. She finally determined that he couldn't say yes or no, if she didn't ask him.

Brad met Anne in the hospital cafeteria as planned. His feelings for her were ignited again as soon as he saw her. He couldn't remember having these strange sensations with another woman before.

Anne's feelings were the same for Brad. Every time she was near him, her heart raced and she felt weak in the knees. She had to take a deep breath to regain her composure.

They sat down to eat, before she felt confident enough to ask Brad if he would join her this weekend at her parent's home to celebrate Memorial Day. Anne explained that there was plenty of room, and she really wanted to be with him.

After a brief dialog about the proposed weekend, Brad agreed to the idea. It really intrigued him because he wanted to be with Anne and see the parents of this unique woman. He could only imagine that her family would be a pleasure to be around.

CHAPTER 6

▼

Anne arrived on time to pick up Brad for their holiday weekend. It was such an odd situation for both of them, and they were both a little nervous after acknowledging this was an unusual way to start a relationship. Brad hoped it wouldn't be awkward for the Weatherbys since Anne's parents had no knowledge that she was even dating anyone.

Anne's parents were surprised by her announcement of bringing a boy home for the weekend, but they were looking forward to meet the young man that stole their daughter's heart.

As they drove to Charlotte, Anne talked about her family to fill Brad in on what to expect. She went on to explain that her father was Norris Weatherby, a successful attorney in Charlotte. He specialized in business law, especially working out details on international trade matters. He was a graduate of Duke and number one in his class at law school.

Grace Anne Pinker was Anne's mother's maiden name. She came from old money as her ancestors survived the Civil War, or as the Southerner's called it "The War of Northern Aggression." Her family had owned a large cotton plantation and then started a highly successful textile business.

"Mother is very proper and definitely a southern bell. Don't worry though; they'll both be very impressed with you. We will have a great time this weekend," she said, giving him a smile and patting his hand in encouragement.

Brad sat in the passenger seat of the Camry, picturing in his head her family. "I'm not worried. In fact I'm looking forward to this. It will be good to see what made you the way you are."

"Oh, I forgot to tell you about my younger brother Nathan. He's a cute kid, fourteen years old, and he loves sports. Especially baseball."

"You have a brother that loves baseball, and you haven't mentioned him to me yet? Are you ashamed of him?" Brad asked, kidding.

"No, I think the world of him. I didn't know where you and I would end up, so I didn't bring him up. I didn't want you to focus on him since he was a sports fanatic, and leave poor old me out in the cold," she said playfully, in her exaggerated southern charm accent.

Brad laughed and shook his head. "You're the most beautiful woman I've met. A fourteen year old boy won't stand in your way."

Anne sped down the highway as the landscaped changed to friendly looking housing subdivisions outlining the highway. The closer they got to Charlotte, the denser the housing became. With the hilly terrain, they could see the mixture of middle income subdivisions, blending in with high end developments, giving Charlotte the look of a city on the go.

Anne turned off of the expressway and drove a mile of winding, hilly roads, before turning into a very upscale development. The houses were on small acreage lots, and all of the homes were luxurious and large. She slowed down as they approached a long driveway that led to a plantation style house, outlined with immaculate landscaping. There was a circle drive with a water fountain in the middle that led to the front of the house. The annuals were planted and already displaying their vibrant colors.

Brad was very impressed, and complimented Anne on having such a nice home. They both got out of the car at the same time and went to the trunk.

Anne's mother was peeking out the window to get a glimpse of this special guest. She didn't get a good look at Brad right away since he had his back to her. She watched Anne handing him one piece of luggage, before gathering the additional suitcase and cosmetic bag herself, and then hauling the load to the house. Grace was aghast that the young man was not carrying the luggage. She was taken back though when she got a full view of Brad. He had a stunning look and a powerful physique. "God I hope he isn't a stupid jock with good looks," she said to herself.

Norris opened the door and stepped out on the piazza to welcome Anne and her friend home.

Grace walked towards the front door, and yelled out, "Nathan, please give your sister a hand with the luggage."

Brad heard her and felt embarrassed that he was unable to take care of that small task. His right side wasn't able to handle the job at this time.

Anne's father greeted her with a big hug, and then extended his hand to Brad and introduced himself to the young man.

Brad set down the bag he was carrying and extended his left hand. "It's great to meet you Mr. Weatherby. I am Brad Preston. I apologize that I can't shake with my right hand, but I just recently had surgery on my right shoulder, and I'm still incapacitated on that side."

"Brad Preston?" Nathan asked, excited. "Are you the Brad Preston that's the famous pitcher for Duke?"

"Well I was a pitcher until recently. You must be Nathan. Anne spoke highly of you. And you must be Mrs. Weatherby," Brad said as she approached him. "It's a pleasure to meet you ma'am. Excuse me for extending my left hand, but my right arm is not up to par at this time. I met Anne in the hospital after my surgery."

"Well, it's a pleasure to meet you," Grace replied, a little embarrassed by her quick judgment of him as a loser. But she didn't feel bad about her concern because she only wanted the best for her daughter. "Where are you from Brad? I can tell that you aren't from the south. You don't have the accent."

"I'm from the Indianapolis area," Brad replied, hoping that would not be a problem.

They all entered the foyer of the small mansion. Brad stopped, and took a long look at the inviting entry way. He loved the Italian marble that covered the large foyer and the winding stairwell that led to the second floor. The tall ceilings were finished off at the wall intersection with a massive crown molding, highlighted with a rope design. To the left there were ornate columns that led to a formal dining room. The parlor was on the right, and furnished in what appeared to be early eighteenth century furniture. Brad recognized the quality of the house and the furnishings, and complimented the Weatherbys for their outstanding taste.

Grace was taken back from seeing a twenty-one year old having the ability to recognize and appreciate the old southern furnishings from her family as well as the hand picked antiques she labored to find to fit into her decorating style. Maybe he is someone to consider for Anne, she thought. "Why thank you Brad. Dinner will be served at 7:00, so why don't the two of you go unpack your belongings and then join us in the parlor for a cocktail."

"Yes ma'am." Anne laughed, knowing how pushy her mother could be at time. "What are we having?"

"Southern ham with the usual side dishes. Is that ok with the two of you?"

"That'll be fine." Anne turned to Brad. "Mom serves the best ham."

Nathan grabbed the bags and followed his sister and Brad upstairs. He couldn't believe the star of Duke's baseball team was going to be in his house for the weekend.

After Nathan dropped off the luggage, Anne showed Brad his room. She informed him that they should probably change into more formal clothing for the evening.

Brad acknowledged her by pulling a nice pair of trousers and a dress shirt from the suitcase, raising them up to his body for her approval. "I assumed I'd need these this weekend. By the way, you have a really nice home. Did you grow up here?"

"Basically, I did. I was seven when we moved in." She walked up to him and gave him a quick peck on the cheek. "Thank you for coming with me this weekend. I think they like you."

"I'm sure it's too early for them to make that appraisal," Brad replied, recognizing Anne's desire to put him at ease.

"Don't be so sure. Dad is a lawyer, and mom is a busy body. They have good instincts about people. Now hurry up and change, so we can spend time together. I really enjoy you being with me this way. It feels good." Anne couldn't hold off her feelings for Brad, and gave him a lovingly smile.

"Yes it does. What are you going to wear?"

"I plan on wearing a simple cotton dress that will compliment your choice of clothing for the evening." She walked out of the room and then peeked her head back into the room. "See you downstairs."

Brad changed into a pair of black slacks, accompanied by a silk blend black button down shirt with small splashes of gold accents. He finished his GQ look with stylish Italian black tasseled loafers, and then waited for Anne to exit her room. "You look beautiful. But you always do," he said, grabbing her hand and leading her to the parlor.

"Ah, what a handsome couple we have here," Mrs. Weatherby stated as the young couple entered the room. "You two really make a good pair. Brad, I assume your parents met Anne in the hospital. What do your parents think of you and Anne?"

"You're correct. They did meet her in the hospital when Anne was my nurse. They mentioned to me that she was a great girl and suggested I ask her out. I guess that would give her positive marks as well as endorsing the two of us," he replied as he recalled their comments.

"You never told me they said that to you." Anne gave Brad a scolding look, followed by a quick smile.

Brad laughed and put his hands up in defense. "I don't want to tell you everything. I don't know you well enough for that." He took a quick step back to avoid a possible slap. "You know I'm just kidding. We didn't talk about that subject so I never brought it up."

Anne went up to him and looked into his eyes smiling. "I do plan on getting to know you very well, and this weekend is a start." She grabbed his arm, and laid her head on his shoulder softly.

Mr. and Mrs. Weatherby were surprised to see Anne show this much affection towards anyone. She had been standoffish with her past boyfriends, but she had never brought home the likes of Brad before. They both recognized he was intelligent and had the looks of a movie star, highlighted by the fact that he was a very humble person.

"What would you two like to drink?" Norris asked. "We have almost everything, so don't be shy."

"A glass of red wine would be fine," Brad answered.

"I'll take the same," Anne said. "Do we have Merlot?"

"Of course," Miles replied. "Is that alright with you Brad?"

"Yes sir, that'll be just fine."

Norris opened a fresh bottle of Merlot while Brad asked Mrs. Weatherby and Nathan if he could get them something to drink.

"I'll get a coke for myself, thank you," Nathan replied. "Mom will have a vodka and tonic, with a lime."

Brad prepared the vodka and tonic for Grace carefully measuring the shot of vodka, so he wouldn't overpower the drink.

"Why thank you Brad. You're such a gentleman. I can see why Anne wanted to bring you home," Mrs. Weatherby said, taking the drink from Brad.

Grace Weatherby was a pretty woman that didn't show her age. Her hair wasn't as blond as Anne's, but more of a sandy color instead. She had brown eyes, much like Anne's, but hers could make you feel welcome if she wanted, or let you know you crossed the line. She was definitely in control of herself and the people around her. Her manners and posture portrayed her upbringing in a strict high society environment. She had the look of success, and carried herself like a royal figure. She didn't act pretentious, just well bred.

Mr. Weatherby handed Brad and Anne their glasses, and then picked up a glass of wine for himself. "Here's to family and our special guest."

They all clicked their glasses together and took a sip of their drink.

"Brad, would you tell me how you injured yourself?" Nathan asked.

"Sure, but there isn't too much to tell you about the incident. It started when a wild pitch was racing towards my head. It was a fastball that didn't give me much time to get out of the way. I jerked back hard and fast, to try to keep from getting hit by the pitch. That was a waste because the ball still hit me, although it hit my arm and not my head. I felt something snap in my shoulder when I jerked back, but I didn't think much of it because the ball hurt me, and I was concentrating on that pain alone. I was too pumped up with anger and excitement, so I didn't say anything to the coach since I had a perfect game going at the time, and I wanted to finish. The second pitch I threw the next inning was my last pitch. I tore my shoulder muscles so bad that they had to do surgery to repair the damage. The only good thing about this is getting to meet Anne, and of course the rest all of you." Brad answered, red faced from the anger he held concerning Greg's willful act to hurt him.

Anne could see the emotion that had built up in Brad, so she put her arm around his back and pulled him closer to her. She knew Brad missed the game, and she could only imagine how he felt talking about the incident.

"I heard the guy that hit you did it on purpose. The two of you were rivals in high school, and he was jealous of your success," Nathan broke in to get the scoop.

"I can't say for sure he tried to hit me on purpose or not. He used to be a friend when I was younger, but he seemed to always try to out do me. I'd have to guess he did throw the ball at me though, because I believe he resents me that much," Brad said pointedly.

"I can tell you from experience Brad that there are people in this world willing to do almost anything to get ahead or get their vengeance on someone," Grace firmly said. "You seem to be a good person. Just be careful in life not to allow anyone to use you or take advantage of you. There will be many more people like this boy that will resent your abilities and your successes in life."

Brad looked into Grace's eyes and gave her a slight nod, acknowledging her words.

"Well Brad," Norris broke in. "What do you have planned as your next step? I'm sure that you have thought about that since your surgery."

"I've been studying human anatomy in school, along with an assortment of medical classes as a plan B. I always knew that something like this could happen, and I needed something for my life after sports. My father taught me to have a secondary plan. Thank God I listened to him. To answer your question, it's premature to cut off my baseball career, but it doesn't look near as promising as a month ago. I'm sure I can get into a business profession where I can make good money though. I'll just see what's available when I graduate."

"You know Brad; I have a good friend that is the president of a prosthetic and orthopedic company here in Charlotte. I know they're expanding and looking for good talent. With your education background, that might be a good field to consider. I hear there's big money in that industry," Norris stated.

"I appreciate the lead. That would fit well with the classes that I've taken. What is the name of your friend?"

"He's Bill Matthews. If you're interested, I can arrange for you to meet with him. In fact he might be at the country club tomorrow night," Miles replied, glancing over at Grace for confirmation of that statement.

"They're supposed to be there tomorrow," Mrs. Weatherby acknowledged.

"Let me give it some serious thought. I really don't want to be a doctor, and this fits in with some of my interests," Brad said appreciatively.

Grace grabbed Anne's hand. "I hate to break this up, but I need Anne to help me in the kitchen. I let Audrey go home this evening, so we could all be together privately, leaving the two us to put dinner on the table."

Anne and her mother went into the kitchen leaving the men to be by themselves. But Mrs. Weatherby really wanted to be with Anne for a few minutes to chat about Brad. As soon as they were out of hearing distance from the men, she asked Anne, "How long have you known him?"

Anne smiled proudly. "Not quite a month. I met him in the hospital just like Brad said."

"I like him. You must be serious about him to have him stay for the weekend."

"We have both been so consumed with school and our other work that we haven't had much time together. Each day we are together builds more of a bond between us, although we haven't been that romantic yet. Barely a kiss, but I think things are changing between us for the better." Anne stood in the kitchen fumbling with the dinnerware.

"I can tell you're falling for him or maybe have already fallen for him. It's such a rare sight to see you taken by a man the way you are with Brad, but I enjoy seeing it. It's early for my observation, however, I believe he's a good man for you, and I hope things work out. You two make a beautiful couple and seem to have similar backgrounds." Grace went to the pantry with a little extra bounce to her step, to pull out the fresh bread Audrey had baked earlier. She was smiling when she set the bread on a platter. "What are his parents like?"

"You'll like them. They're super nice people and a lot like you and dad. It's like Brad stated, we met while I was his nurse, and there wasn't anything between us at the time, so I didn't get to know them that well. Brad and I are just getting to know each other more and more each day. We're both going at a slow pace because we're cautious about getting hurt."

"Well, you two take the time to build a love from the heart and not with sex," Grace said with a warning glare.

"Mom, we haven't even come close to sex. Like I said, we've barely kissed. I almost wish he would try to get me to bed. At least then, I'd know he was attracted to me in some way. I think he cares for me in a loving way, but he's so polite that he hasn't shown any aggressiveness towards me. Tonight he has shown more feelings for me than he ever has before. Help me out her Mom, what should I do?"

"I believe I've seen signals from him tonight indicating stronger feelings for you than just a friend. You can see it in his eyes. You need to be more aggressive with him by showing him your true feelings, or better yet, tell him how you feel. I know that may difficult for you since it isn't your nature to be the pursuer, but he seems to be worth it. Besides honey, you've fallen in love with him. I can tell." Grace smiled at her daughter, knowing the turmoil she was feeling.

"Thanks Mom for helping me. This is a first for me. And you're right. I'm falling in love with him, or I've already fallen in love and just haven't had the guts to admit it to myself." Anne had tears welling up in her eyes. "My God, what has happened to me? I'm an emotional wreck." She picked up a napkin and wiped the tears from her eyes.

"That's love Anne, and you have a few choices to make. Pursue him, wait for him to pursue you, or take a let's see what happens approach. I suggest you take my previous advice and pursue him. I don't know him that well yet, but my instincts say he's a special person." Mrs. Weatherby glanced in the oven window to check on the ham.

"He's special Mom. The once in a lifetime man. Maybe he's too special."

"Nobody is too special for you. You're just as special as he. Now let's get dinner on the table, so they won't think we've been in here all this time talking about Brad." Grace opened the oven door and savored the sweet aroma of the ham that filled the room.

Dinner went well with small talk about Brad and Anne's schedule with school and work.

After thoroughly enjoying the southern cooking, Brad requested seconds and complimented Mrs. Weatherby for the outstanding dinner. He then took care of the seconds with no problem by cleaning his plate once again.

They all retired to the family room after the men actually helped clean up the dinner table, and had light conversation before retiring for the night.

The next morning arrived with a beautiful sunrise, featuring shades of orange and pink that painted the eastern sky. Brad woke up early, impressed to find Anne in the kitchen making coffee. "Good morning" Brad said cheerfully. "I'm surprised to find you up so early."

"I'm an early riser. Do you want some coffee?"

"Yes, I will thank you. Just make it black." Brad walked up to Anne and gave her a hug from behind.

Anne finished pouring the coffee and leaned her body into his warm body. Her body trembled when their two bodies meshed together. She enjoyed being around Brad more than anyone before, so she took advantage of being wrapped up in his long arms. She gently caressed his arms. "This is a nice way to start the day."

"I agree." Brad drew a long breath of air through his noise capturing her scent. The flavor of her skin smelled wonderful, and he didn't want to let go of her so he held her tighter. He realized for the first time since his break up with Kristy that he could fall for someone else. The thought confused him and brought fearful thoughts of getting hurt again. He slowly let go of her, recognizing the strong feelings for each other went both ways. "What's on our agenda today?"

"We're doing nothing today. We both need some rest and relaxation, so I think we will hang around the pool to relax and maybe doze off now and then on the loungers. We'll need the sleep because mom and dad want us to go to the country club tonight for a dinner party, if that's all right with you? I think they want to show us off as a happy young couple," she said, making a funny look.

"I like how you think concerning today's activities, or lack of activity. And come to think of it, I haven't been to a dinner party for some time and it sounds fun. My parents would take us to a party at the country club at times when we were younger. I imagine your parents belong to a nice country club."

"Only the best for them." Anne took his hand and led him to the back patio, so they could enjoy the sunrise together.

They sat together for an hour sipping coffee, talking seldom, while staring at the horizon and at each other.

Mr. and Mrs. Weatherby had awakened and were now sitting in the kitchen watching Anne and Brad on the patio.

"I believe Anne is in love honey. What do you think?" Norris asked.

"I have no doubts that she's fallen for him. What do you think of Brad?"

"From what I have seen so far, I really like him. He's very smart, good looking, and has a good head on his shoulders. It might be premature for me to say, but I hope they make it together for a long time."

"Norris, are you saying you want them to get married?"

"I didn't say that, but at this time it wouldn't bother me. There's something about him that just impresses me." Norris took a drink of his orange juice.

"I hope they agree to come to the country club tonight. I want to show them off," Grace said mischievously.

Anne's parents walked out to the patio to join the young couple. "What time did you two get up this morning?" Mrs. Weatherby asked.

"A little over an hour ago," Anne answered.

"Do you two want to do anything special today?" Anne's mother asked.

"We just want to relax around the pool today. And by the way, we're planning on going with you tonight for dinner at the country club."

"I'm glad to hear that," Grace said, turning to Norris with a huge smile.

The rest of the day was spent basking in the hot sun while periodically cooling off in the pool. Brad had been overwhelmed with desire when he first saw Anne in her bikini. Her looks were stunning, magnified by the swimsuit she was wearing that was light brown in color, with swirls of yellow, accenting her tanned body and blond hair. He just couldn't believe her stunning beauty and how voluptuous her body was. Brad had a tingling feeling all day.

They lay by the pool in their loungers that were butted up tight to allow their bodies to touch. They couldn't sleep much because the electrical flow between the two set off a sexual excitement in each of them adding to their other feelings they had for each other.

The afternoon was passing ever so quickly as they both ached for each other, which was something Anne had never experienced before. She reluctantly got up from the lounger feeling dizzy from excitement that ran threw her entire body. "I hate to get up Brad, but I need to shower and do my hair for this evening."

"I know it's getting that time" he replied, watching her closely. "I'll need to do the same." He carefully lifted himself from the lounger. "I assume you asked me to bring a sports coat so I could wear it tonight?"

"Yes, that was my intention. I wasn't sure if we would be going tonight, but I thought we should be prepared." Anne gave a devilish smile.

Brad grinned, seeing her personality evolve. "I think we'll have a good time tonight. I'm anxious to see the clubhouse as well as the lay out of the golf course."

"It's too bad you can't go out and play a round with dad, but with your shoulder that's not possible this time." She walked up to him and whispered in his ear, "I may be selfish, but I'm glad you can't play golf now. I really enjoyed being with you." She gave his ear a mild bite and then gave him a long kiss.

Brad closed his eyes momentarily. "I can play golf some other time. I enjoyed today, and we needed it."

Anne went up to shower, and Brad jumped in the pool to cool off in a couple of ways.

The Hidden Hills Country Club stood up to its claim to fame as the elite club of Charlotte. The golf course was immaculate, with neatly groomed narrow fairways, well trimmed shrubbery, and greens that looked like carpet. There were plenty of shapely sand traps that would test your skills if your ball entered them. Brad could see it was indeed a professional course both in quality and competitiveness. As they drove up to the elaborate clubhouse, he recognized this was the place to belong if you were successful. The surroundings made other clubs he had visited look second class.

"Very nice," Brad said to the Weatherbys.

"Thank you Brad," Norris replied. "I hope you enjoy this evening. The food has a five star rating, and there's supposed to be a good band here tonight, so I hope you enjoy dancing." Norris buttoned his jacket and gave a proud look at the surroundings.

"It's been awhile since I've danced, but I'm sure we'll enjoy the music."

The valet parked their car, and they entered the main building. The atmosphere of the club house radiated opulence the moment you stepped in the door. The feeling of success and upper class was overpowering. Brad enjoyed this style of living. He had grown up with similar surroundings, but not as classy Hidden Hills, with the tall ceilings splattered with massive crystal chandeliers that sparkled like diamonds as the light reflected from them onto multi colored walls. The woodwork was remarkable and plentiful, and the rich tones of the woods gave this large imposing structure a feeling of luxury and warmth. It was built in the early 1920's, and demonstrated the superior skills of the local crafts men at that time.

Tonight was an annual event that brought most members to the club in celebration of the start of summer. They were dressed in a variety of formal wear, but most men wore the standard country club sport jacket. The women were dressed in the latest styles from the top name designers and accented their eveningwear with the finest jewelry money could buy. Brad felt good in this atmosphere and remembered why he wanted to succeed in life. He made a mental note to work extra hard to get his shoulder and arm back to full strength, so he could make enough money to participate in this type of atmosphere.

Anne touched him softly and whispered, "It's a remarkable place, isn't it?"

"It's grandiose," Brad replied. He looked around the club knowing he wasn't the type of person that wanted to belong to a place like Hidden Hills to show off his success, if and when he achieved that status in life. Brad just liked being around people that were successful and proud of their achievements in life. He respected the people that took chances in life and worked hard to get here.

Several couples approached their foursome, wanting to greet the Weatherbys and satisfy their curiosity on who the young man was accompanying Anne. One of the couples was Bill Matthews and his wife Ruth. Bill appeared to be in his early fifties from what Brad could tell, and he was a good looking man that kept himself in good shape.

"Good evening Norris and Grace," Bill said, shaking Norris's hand and then giving Grace a kiss on the cheek. "My God Anne, you've become more beautiful. I didn't think that could happen since your beauty has always out shined any other woman I've seen, except for my wife and Grace of course," he said with a laugh. "Your gentleman friend here looks familiar," Bill added, turning to Brad.

"Good evening sir." Brad extended his hand towards Bill being careful not to allow a hard handshake. "I'm…"

"Brad Preston," Bill broke in immediately as he recalled the mature, well-mannered voice from a television interview Brad had once given. He instantly recognized the surprised look on Brad's face. "I wouldn't have expected to see you here tonight. I'm sorry to have cut you off, but I've seen you play ball several times. You were very impressive. In fact, the best I've ever seen at the college level. I'm sorry to hear about your injury though. Are you going to be able to play again?"

"That's yet to be determined, but I'll give it everything I have to make it happen." Brad had a surprised look on his face from the knowledge Bill had of him.

"I'm sure you will," Bill said with confidence. He then turned towards Anne. "How did you come to hook up with this remarkable young man?"

"We met in the hospital. I was assigned to his room after he came out of surgery," Anne explained and then turned to Brad with a bashful smile.

"Well, I hope this works out for you two. It is a good fit," Bill said, admiring the couple.

Anne looked at Brad with a burning love she had never experienced before. "Yes, it is a good fit, and he's a great person that I enjoy being with. We just haven't had a chance to spend enough time together until this weekend."

"Oh my, Grace," Mrs. Matthews said. "They make a beautiful couple. Why didn't you say anything to me?"

Grace smiled proudly. "This was kind of sprung on us at the last minute Ruth."

Bill fished in his wallet and pulled out a business card. "I don't want to bother you tonight Brad, but I'd like to get together with you sometime. My company has been working on a computer program that could mold a perfect throwing motion customized to the individual's body. It's an interesting concept that could be a benefit to you. And if things don't work out with your baseball career, we could talk about you working for me. I can always use a person like you."

"That sounds intriguing Mr. Matthews. How long have they been working on this program?"

"It's in the beginning stages. It could be a few years before it will materialize, but you could be the one to help them along. Here is my card. Call me when you have time to talk."

Brad took the card and read it to himself, and then looked up to Bill. "Thank you sir. I will call you soon."

Brad knew he would meet many people tonight that he would have trouble remembering their names, but he wouldn't forget Bill Matthew's name.

Brad turned his attention to Anne. He couldn't help but notice how everybody stared at her because her beauty was so striking. He started to see an inward beauty in her that made him realize he was falling in love with her. He pulled Anne close to his body and gave her a quick kiss on the lips to let her know he cared for her.

Anne was surprised by his sudden display of affection. He had not been aggressive towards her to this point. She looked deep into his blue eyes, realizing he had feelings for her. Anne's heart beat faster while she found it difficult to breathe. She wanted to grab him and kiss him forever, and she would have if they hadn't been at the country club surrounded by her parent's best friends. Instead, she held his hand tight. It was amazing how her life had changed since meeting Brad. He brought a renewed look at life, and she now looked forward to her post school days.

The traditional dinner for the Memorial weekend was an elaborate barbeque that consisted of charcoal grilled filet mignon, fresh fish, grilled lobster, and barbeque baby back ribs with all of the southern side dishes. It was a tremendous feast, and most everybody there ate too much. The food had been prepared to perfection, and Brad couldn't place having as good a meal as he had this evening.

Club members mingled as dinner ended, allowing Brad and Anne a chance to talk. They both reflected on the weekend and how they enjoyed this particular evening. Anne questioned Brad on his future plans for the first time. He explained to her that his future was uncertain at this time as far as his career was concerned. He told her he had always wanted to play a professional sport if possible when he was a young child, and that was still his dream at this time, but things had changed in several ways since his injury. He was prepared to go into the business world to make his living as long as it allowed him to live a nice lifestyle.

"What is the dream of your future?" she asked him.

"I was raised in a well to do family. Not as elaborate as your family, but my parents have done well for themselves. I'd say they're very similar to your parents. Dad worked hard and smart, allowing them to be financially independent. My mother came from an upper class Boston family that dates back to royalty. I guess my answer to your question is; I want to have the financial freedom to live my life as our parents have. I haven't thought that much about a family, but I'd like to marry and raise a couple of children."

"That is good to hear. I'd like the same things in life. I just want to share it with the right man." Anne's brown eyes transmitted the excitement in her.

"That is what will make life special. You have to spend it with the right person. My parents truly love each other, but there have been times in their life that they have been tested."

"Same with my parents and every married couple out there. I guess that's why I've never dated anybody seriously. I've never felt comfortable until I met you. You took me by surprise."

Before Brad could respond, the band started playing, making it difficult to talk. They were going to take the conversation outside, but they were both carried onto the dance floor by her parents and their friends. It seemed they all wanted the two of them to make it as a couple. Brad and Anne took the hint, and played along by joining everyone on the dance floor. Besides, it was a good song, and the band was very good.

After a few dances, Brad and Anne started back to their table. They had almost reached their seats when a slow song started playing. It was a perfect song for the two of them, and Brad took Anne back to the dance floor, pulling her close to him and displaying his ability as a good dancer. They both held on tight and found the right rhythm as they swayed together like they had done it hundreds of times before.

This had been the first time Brad had slow danced with anyone since Kristy. It was a bit awkward at first, but it soon felt very natural to him. They seemed to be as well in tune with each other as he and Kristy, and this was their first dance. He realized how much he missed being with a woman and concluded that Anne was special, making him determined to make this work.

As the song ended, Anne's parents expressed their feelings on how good it was to see them dancing so splendidly together and told them they made cute couple. Norris and Grace truly liked Brad and thought he would make a great addition to their family, so they had a notion that parental encouragement wouldn't hurt one bit.

The young couple didn't mind the positive feed back. They both felt it was important for their parents to like their choice of a mate.

The rest of the night flew by as they all danced, talked, and had a great time together.

Brad and Anne sat on the couch in the family room as her parents bid them a good night. Brad thanked the Weatherbys for a great evening before Miles grabbed Grace's hand and led her upstairs leaving their daughter alone with Brad.

Anne turned towards Brad and took his hand between her hands. There were many thoughts going on in both of their heads.

Anne played with Brad's hand while staring blankly. She looked up at Brad. "I've fallen in love with you. You're the first person that has brought these feelings out in me, and I'm not sure how to handle it."

"I'm falling in love with you too," Brad stated, and then pulled her close to him and gave her a long loving kiss with much passion and eagerness.

Blood pumped through Anne's body sending tingling sensations throughout her. "I wasn't sure how you felt, but that kiss said a lot. It seemed like I wasn't that important to you. I'm ignorant about your past and wasn't sure if there was someone else back home, or maybe you just didn't have feelings for me." Tears rolled down her cheeks.

Brad tenderly wiped the tears from her face and held her close. He carefully put his fingers through her long blond hair stroking it gently. They both backed away slowly, so they could look each other in the eye, both knowing the eyes were the gateway to the soul. What they saw was a deep love and affection for each other.

"Look," Brad said. "There are many things we both want and need to know about each other. Time will reveal many things we will love and dislike about each other, although I feel confident there is nothing bad enough to discover to make us depart. I apologize for allowing you to have to second guess my feelings. I wasn't prepared to find someone like you."

"You don't have to apologize for that. I've held back my true feelings until this weekend. I was afraid, and I'm still somewhat afraid. I don't want to be hurt, and I don't know how to love someone. It just hasn't happened to me before."

"Anne, it's natural for you to be afraid. I am too. I've been hurt before, and you're the first woman that has made me think about anything other than school or baseball."

"So there had been another woman. I was pretty sure of it though. What happened to the two of you anyway?" Anne asked, hoping his feelings for her had passed.

"I'm a little embarrassed to talk about it, but you deserve to know." Brad thought carefully on what to say, trying to word everything properly so he wouldn't push Anne away. He wasn't sure he wanted her to know how deep his love had been for Kristy.

There was a brief silence between the two as each prepared for a history lesson on one another.

Brad started to talk first, giving Anne a complete run down on his relationship with Kristy. He explained the break up between them as best he could since he really wasn't sure of all the facts. He just knew Greg had been involved with Kristy, and that was enough. He told her he had been too caught up in his life at school and baseball since the breakup, admitting that he had probably been hiding from the hurt he had felt when he and Kristy broke up.

"Did you ever talk to her after you two broke up?" Anne asked.

"We never did converse with each other again. It just ended. Things happen in life for a reason. I've had some tough breaks this past year, but they have led me on a path to you. And for that I'm thankful."

"Are you sure about that?"

"I know I love you." He gently ran his finger tips down the side of her face. "I also know I probably wouldn't have met you if I had not been injured, resulting in surgery and having you as my nurse. As far as Kristy goes, we were very young when we started dating and had never dated anybody else. My past with her has helped me grow as a man and a person. Now tell me about you. Why have you never dated anybody? You have to be the most beautiful person I have seen." Brad felt he was honest with her, so he sat back to admire her beauty

"I've never met a boy that made me feel like I wanted to be with him. I never felt those tingling feelings all over…until I met you. You're a first for me, and you excite me when I see you, and I'm sad when I'm not with you. I almost wish you didn't think I was the most beautiful person you have met. I grew up with good looks and was treated differently. Most boys were afraid to ask me out because they thought I'd turn them down. Please don't take me wrong, and think I'm conceited. I feel I'm attractive, but there is more to me that nobody tried to find. At least until I met you."

"I can tell you I had some reservations about you at first because I didn't want to go out with a person that was too caught up with her good looks. But you're nothing like." Brad paused a moment to catch his breath and allow his heart to slow down. "The more I've gotten to see the real you, the more I fell for you. I still believe you have more in you to give someone."

"I think you're right Brad. Please give me some time to learn to love someone and really let out my inner self. You won't be disappointed. I have a lot to give." Anne touched his face ever so gently.

"Yes you do. I can see it, and I want to experience the whole you. I like the way you carry yourself, and I like your intelligence. But I want to know you and become familiar with your complete inner beauty that you're hiding. If you let that out all of the way, I could never turn away from you." He kissed her softly.

"There is something you should know that I'm proud of, but somewhat embarrassed to admit in today's world. I have never had sex before," she said sheepishly.

"You're still a virgin?"

Anne laughed. "That's what a virgin is honey."

They both laughed together before they wrapped one another up in their arms and made out for the next ten minutes.

"I don't want to lose my virginity the first night I admit to you I'm still pure," she said jokingly.

"Don't worry; I wasn't planning on taking advantage of you tonight. I was going to wait until tomorrow."

"Oh, that's the way it works. No wonder I never dated," Anne said, trumping his tease.

"Seriously Anne, we have a lot of time before we do anything. I don't want to put that pressure on you at this time."

"Do I turn you on?"

"I can honestly say that you turn me on very much and refraining from having sex with you is a challenge," Brad replied, feeling the heat build up in his groin.

Anne smiled satisfied with his answer. "I don't plan on being a virgin for the rest of my life you know. I never met the right person until now." She kissed him softly knowing that he would be the one.

They both ended up falling asleep on the couch cuddled up next to each other.

CHAPTER 7

▼

Senior year of college

The summer flew by in a flash as Anne and Brad continued to date each other, but finding it hard to move their relationship to the next level due to their busy schedules. This led to some insecurity on both of them because they felt more time should have been spent together. The fear that one was losing desire for the other was creeping in their minds, so they dug in deeper to their school work and other duties to keep their emotions under check.

Anne had been working at the hospital full time while taking medical classes, while Brad had started his rehabilitation on his shoulder and was taking a full load of classes in preparation of a different career other than baseball. It was not a good recipe for a growing relationship, but their love for each other was there, which would have been good if they had time to express it towards each other. Neither one of the two realized the full extent of the love that each held for the other.

Some unexpected news happened this past summer. Brad was picked in the second round of the baseball draft by the Los Angeles Dodgers, which was one of the last teams he wanted to play for. It wasn't the Dodger organization, but it was Los Angeles that bothered him. He wasn't thrilled with the lifestyle there. Brad was surprised by the high draft pick though, since it was uncertain whether or not he would be able to pitch again at the high level he achieved this past year.

The start of their senior year classes brought new life to their relationship. Anne cut her hours at the hospital, allowing her some additional time to spend with Brad. They even had two classes together that allocated more time together.

With the arrival of fall, Brad's romantic side came out. The flavors of the changing season brought out more of his true feelings for Anne. Brad always enjoyed fall because it brought memories of his past. He remembered his high school days of walking hand and hand with Kristy, bringing a longing for that feeling again. He smiled knowing he had found it again with Anne.

Brad was trying to enjoy this special time of year because he needed something to keep him up in spirits with his shoulder rehab dragging along at a snail's pace. He was frustrated with the fact that he was unable to control his body the way he wanted to. He did appreciate the way Anne helped him through this ordeal. She was a wise woman and explained to him it was going to take a lot of time. She expressed her concern to him that pushing himself too much would only delay his progress.

Anne had become his soul mate, and he was determined to let her know how deep his love was for her. They spent more time together now than ever before. Anne felt his love more than ever bringing about a glow from her that Brad could see and feel. They were becoming one, and Brad thought of marriage on occasions. He just wasn't sure if the time was right. He thought he might be pushing it along too fast.

Anne's anxiety towards their relationship had diminished, allowing her inward self to become totally exposed. She had never allowed it to happen before, and it felt good to finally unleash her true personality. Her inner beauty compared equally with her outer beauty, and Brad was now overcome by her completeness.

They still had not made love together, but both knew that would not last long. Their love was too intense now, and neither one could hold out much longer.

With October now half over, Brad and Anne were still working hard at school, along with their other duties. They had both studied hard for a major exam, and today was the test day. The sidewalks were damp from an early morning rain as the two walked to their class together. They never heard the squishing sound their shoes made from the moisture beneath their soles because they were so caught up with each other.

While the humid air brought out the smell of the changing season, the site of the leaves in the beginning stage of turning the magnificent colors was equal in embellishing the campus and bringing forth the feeling that fall had indeed arrived. The love stricken couple didn't take the special ambiance for granted, but instead allowed the change of season to enhance the romance between them.

Brad asked Anne questions he thought might be on the exam while Anne answered each question with no problems, clutching Brad's hand and enjoying the flavor of the new season.

She stopped for no reason and pulled Brad towards her. "I love you." She smiled, before giving him a long kiss.

"I love you too," he replied, holding her close. He gazed into her sparkling eyes knowing her love for him was deep. The electricity between them was stronger than ever, and Brad just wanted to make love to her right there. He led her to class dreaming of her naked in his arms.

The exam was as intense as they expected; leaving them both mentally drained when they left class.

"Why don't we meet at the Italian Village tonight for pizza and a few beers?" Brad asked.

"That sounds good to me. We haven't let loose for a long time, and we deserve it, not to mention the fact that we need it. We've been working too hard."

After a long kiss they departed for their next class while looking forward to the evening and a well deserved restful weekend.

Italian Village was a quaint restaurant within walking distance of the college. It was well known for great pizza, Italian beef sandwiches, and basic pasta dishes. It was a red brick building on the outside that was not fancy looking, but inviting. The interior was dimly lit and decorated with grapevines, wine bottles, and red and white table cloths. It was romantic in its own special way.

Having just left the hospital, Anne entered the restaurant by herself. She had changed into a pair of jeans that accented her well shaped bottom and slender legs. She wore a dark yellow sweater that highlighted her blond hair. Anne looked fantastic and wasn't aware of all the stares she was getting from everyone. She was only interested in seeing Brad.

Brad saw her first and stood up from the booth he was sitting in to rush over and meet her. He gave her a quick kiss and led her back to their table. They were both tired from the non-stop life they each lived daily. Brad's days consisted of a full load of classes, at least two hours of working out, and studying until late at night.

Anne's schedule was much the same as Brad's, with the exception of her work at the hospital instead of a physical work out. This harsh routine had taken its toll on both of them, and they needed some time together to recharge their relationship as well as their bodies.

Anne noticed a pitcher of beer on the table with one empty glass and another glass half full. "Starting without me tonight?" she asked with a sexy smile on her face.

"I'm sorry." Brad poured a beer for Anne and topped his glass off. "We normally don't do the typical college things like drink, blow off school, and enjoy our young years away from home, so I thought I'd indulge tonight."

"You sound like you resent the fact you've worked so hard here at school and missed out on the social side of things."

He sipped his beer. "I resent it somewhat. I've worked my ass off making straight A's and working out hard to play baseball, and I don't know if I'll be able to pitch again."

"You have worked hard because that is who you are. You wouldn't be satisfied with yourself if you were the average student." She knew he was having a difficult time with the slow progress of his shoulder healing, as he had only regained fifty percent of his strength at this point.

"I know I'm feeling sorry for myself with the injury, but I do resent not being able to have the time with you that I really need and want. I love you so much and would like to be with you all of the time." His eyes threw darts of true love at her.

Anne set her elbows on the table and leaned forward to hear his loving words better while she kicked her shoe off and rubbed his leg with her foot. She loved Brad more than life itself, but was not able to really show it because of the lack of time they had together. She felt in her heart they were meant for each other, and Brad was finally verifying the fact he felt the same way. "I love you so much Brad. I apologize I don't show you how much sometimes. It's hard to express my true love for you when we have so much on our plate. But I've put myself our there for you to have, and now I see you've accepted my offer."

Brad was overwhelmed with Anne's love and beauty at this point. There was nobody on earth that could compete with her when she let her true self come out of its shell. The glow she projected tugged at every emotion he had. He just wanted to take her there and make her a part of him so they could become just one. His actions being limited, Brad took both of her hands and gazed into her love glazed eyes not knowing what to say or do.

After a minute or so, Brad blurted out, "I have been thinking a lot lately about us getting married…"

"Oh my God, Brad. Are you serious? How many beers have you had?"

"That isn't exactly the response I wanted to hear," he said as his face lost color.

"Oh Brad, I'm sorry. I didn't mean it that way. I knew you cared for me, but I had no idea you felt that way about me. I'd marry you tomorrow, I love you so much." Her face was overcome by an uncontrollable smile.

Brad's color went from pale white to beet red. "That's good to hear. You almost gave me a heart attack," Brad said, holding his heart.

"Well join the club then because you almost gave me one too. I just didn't know you felt that much love for me to even have the thought cross your mind," she answered with so much life in her voice.

"It crosses my mind, just like you're on my mind all of the time. It's you that gets me through the pain of working out. That's why I said earlier that I somewhat resent the fact I've spent so much time on school and baseball, and not enough time on my personal life. Our life," he added, correcting himself.

Anne was taken back by his words. "Our life," was something that at one time she had only dreamed of hearing from Brad. She never expected to be swept off her feet as she had been with Brad. Yes, she knew one day she would meet someone she would want to spend her life with, but she never expected it would come so fast and so hard.

Anne had always had the fairy tale wedding in mind with a big wedding party, glamorous reception, and the whole works. But she felt different about a big wedding if she married Brad because it wasn't necessary for her to be happy. She was being selfish in her thinking by not wanting to share the special day of her wedding with her friends. Maybe some of it had to do with the fact that she really didn't have many acquaintances in her life that were true friends. So many things were bouncing back and forth in her brain.

"What's wrong Anne? You look sad."

"I saw my life go by and realized I've been a turtle all of these years. I've hidden in my shell and missed out on so much. Thank you for allowing me to see life as it should be." Happy tears ran down her face.

"We are so much alike. I've been so absorbed in sports and having to be perfect in everything I do. There is nothing wrong with that."

"I know, but at least you had a special relationship in your life before me. You know, this love thing is hard. It brings out every emotion that is hiding in your body. I never realized how emotional I could be. It's nice in one respect, but hard in others." She shook her head side to side vigorously.

Brad squeezed her hand while smiling at her. "It's what life is all about you know. They can't teach it or prepare you for it. It just happens, and I don't believe many people have experienced it the way we have with each other. We must spend more time together, which is one reason I wanted to have this evening together. I enjoy you so much." He leaned across the table and gave her a long kiss.

The kiss was interrupted as their waitress addressed their table, by her asking if they were ready to order.

Brad's face turned red, and he sat straight up to answer. "We'll take a large pizza with everything except onion and anchovies please."

"Would you like anything else to drink?" the waitress asked kindly.

"Bring us another pitcher of beer please," Anne replied. "And a couple glasses of water also."

"Thank you," the waitress said with a smile. She took the menus and went to retrieve their drink order.

"So, where were we?" Anne asked as her big brown eyes danced with excitement.

Brad gave an anxious laugh. "I believe somewhere between marriage and just getting to know each other."

They stared at each other in silence until they were brought back to earth when the waitress set the pitcher of beer and their waters on the table.

"Thank you," Brad said to the waitress. He poured Anne another beer and refilled his glass before returning his attention back to Anne. "What do you want out of life?"

Anne sat up straight and gave a quizzical look. She dug deep into her inner soul to answer him and then drew a deep breath. "I've always wanted the dream life of most women and men, I presume. I'd like a successful job in the medical field, but I'm not sure I want a doctor's life. Maybe a high ranking assistant or nurse would be satisfying. A perfect marriage with two children and a nice house with an upscale lifestyle would put the finishing touches on my dream life. It's funny though, because at one time I thought this was just a pipe dream. But that changed after I had spent time with you. I do believe that if we were to marry, it'd be a perfect life for me."

"If we do get married down the road, I'll make that come true. The timing just has to be right you know."

"Yes, I know that, and I appreciate the fact you recognize it also," Anne said, feeling secure in their mature approach.

They turned their conversation towards school, Anne's work at the hospital, and how their parents would react towards a possible marriage between them. They skirted the issue of Brad's uncertain future in baseball, knowing Brad was still struggling through his rehab with his shoulder.

Anne wasn't sure how she felt about the possibility of being a baseball wife. She wasn't sure she wanted to share the man she loved and adored with the rest of the world. It wasn't in a bad way; she just wanted him home with her every night. She needed him.

The pizza arrived as steam rose from the thick melted cheese. They both dug into the pizza, not realizing how hungry they were. The pizza was half gone before they said anything, causing them to laugh at each other while acknowledging to one another that they had been pigging out. However, it didn't bother them because they reached for another piece.

"I forgot how good food tasted," Anne said while finishing another piece. "With the fast pace life we're living, I don't take time for these small luxuries of sitting down and eating."

"I know. This sounded good to me today, which is why I suggested we come here tonight. Plus, food tastes better when you eat it with the one you love," he added, before wiping a small amount of pizza sauce from his mouth.

"Absolutely correct Mr. Preston," she said, laughing. Life was great for her at this moment in time, and she never wanted it to end.

The waitress politely interrupted them when she asked if everything was alright.

The love stricken couple told their kind waitress the pizza was great and to bring another pitcher of beer.

After eating all the pizza they could handle, they turned their conversation to where they would like to settle down when they married.

Brad took a long swig of his beer, and then stated he liked the southern lifestyle and better weather of North Carolina. He enjoyed the mountains that were close by and the charm of Charlotte. He thought Indianapolis was nice, but it had more of a rural feel to it

He brought up the possibility of a baseball future, stating he would prefer to play for Chicago or St. Louis because they were his favorite boyhood teams. He recognized he would more than likely be playing for the Dodger organization since they drafted him. He just prayed he could handle California.

Anne was so simple in her ways expressing her desire to stay around Charlotte. She loved it there and really wasn't that interested in having to experience the rest of the country.

Brad just shook his head in amazement by her down home thinking. Brad would have expected someone like her to want a ritzy lifestyle, by traveling around the world to see all of the sights and mingle with the upper class. It just made her that much more irresistible.

Brad took her hand in his. "Why haven't you found someone before me?"

"Why do you ask me that question now?"

"I'm just dumbfounded that some other guy hasn't figured you out to be a beautiful intelligent, modest, down to earth girl that is perfect."

Her face turned red. "Thanks." Anne shrugged her shoulders, and wrapped her napkin around her index finger, and then looked Brad squarely into his eyes. "Probably because I've never allowed anyone to see the real me. As I told you before, everybody thought I was pretty, but conceited, therefore causing them to shy away from me. And I probably over reacted by staying to myself due to the hurt they inflicted on me from their harsh words, consequently fulfilling their image of me as self indulged."

Brad finished the last of his beer and set his glass on the table. "I'm just proud to be the lucky guy to unlock your soul. I just can't imagine how I've been able to do that while I've been so busy with my other activities, not to mention my self centered pity of my baseball career. I'm sorry I haven't been the person you really deserve."

"You're way too hard on yourself Brad. Haven't you taken time to look in a mirror and see the great looks you possess? And don't you realize you're a very giving person? Yes, you do sulk a little now and then about your uncertain future in baseball. But you do it with some class." She gave him a big smile.

Tears came to Brad's eyes. "Whoa, I must've had one too many beers. I'm getting soft with my emotions." He slapped his face softly trying to erase the alcohol-induced effect he had on his brain.

"That's just the way you are Brad. You're so humble that you don't even know how much people adore you. I could see the respect your teammates had for you by the way they looked up to you when they came to the hospital to visit with you. And your coach had tears in his eyes at times when he witnessed your struggle with your injury. That told me a lot about you."

They stared at each other for a long time. The waitress broke their spell when she dropped the bill off at the table.

Brad looked at the check, left a nice tip, and went up to pay for their dinner.

They walked hand in hand to Anne's place in a very good mood, both feeling a strong bond between them.

CHAPTER 8

▼

Anne's apartment was modest and very neat. It was accented with fashionable furnishings to remove the sterile feelings of the quarters. She shared her apartment with her friend, April, that she had met in college. April was from Wilmington, and had gone home for the weekend, allowing Anne the chance to relax with Brad with nobody else around.

Anne was now on her home turf, which felt good to her. As the door closed, she pinned Brad to the wall and gave him a long kiss while rubbing her body against his. The electricity was high voltage between them like multiple strikes of lighting during a thunderstorm on a muggy evening.

Anne then pulled Brad to the couch and sat him down as she put her knees on each side of his legs, straddling him as she sat on his lap. She leaned her head towards him and then abruptly pulled it back, flinging her blond hair back out of her perfect face. She then brought her head towards his and gave a mischievous smile.

Brad was shocked by her aggressiveness, but was enjoying the mood. "What is on that brilliant mind of yours?"

"Nothing in particular," she answered as she applied a long loving kiss to Brad.

"Well, I like your nothing in particular style," he replied as he felt sharp spasms in his body.

Just as quickly as she sat him down on the couch, she jumped up from his lap and headed to the kitchen.

Brad was disappointed by her sudden departure. His body was on fire from her aggressiveness and he wanted more. Much more.

"How about a glass of wine Honey?" she asked. "I have some good red wine I think you'll enjoy."

"Probably not as much as I enjoyed you just now. But, I will have a glass."

Anne reentered the room and handed Brad his wine. She resumed her previous position of sitting on his lap. "There, is that better?" she asked as she wiggled her butt against his lap.

"I don't think it could be any better." He thought to himself that it could be better if he was lying next to her naked body.

Anne read his mind. "I bet it does get better than this." Then in her sexy southern accent she added, "But this little ole southern girl wouldn't know about those things."

Brad pulled her close and caressed her body with his big, but gentle hands. "I bet this little ole southern girl has an idea of how it gets better than this though. She sure knows how to turn on this northern gentleman."

"You know...April is gone for the weekend...and I want you to spend the weekend here with me...And that includes spending the night also," Anne stated, even shocking herself by what she said.

"Oh, you're playing the old game of the girl getting the guy drunk and then taking advantage of him. I see how you are," Brad replied, laughing.

"Is that how it goes? No wonder I'm still a virgin. I thought it was the other way around."

They both broke out in laughter, halting their sensual caresses while staring at each other with anticipation of what was going to happen next.

Brad's desire took over as his passion fueled his hands to aggressively caress Anne's body, touching her in places he had never touched her before. He kissed her harder and pulled her even closer to his body. He wanted to take her there on the couch.

Anne returned his fury by rubbing her body hard against his, all the while sucking on his lips as she inserted her tongue deep into Brad's mouth. All at once she pulled away and took one last drink of her wine. She threw her head back to get the hair out of her face and stood up grabbing Brad's hand, leading him to the bedroom.

"I'm going to change into something more comfortable," Anne stated as she walked towards the closet. "There's an extra toothbrush in the bathroom in the top drawer if you want to brush your teeth before bed."

She changed into a long tee shirt and met Brad with a kiss as he exited the bathroom.

"You taste nice and fresh now. Give me a minute and I will too," she said, before she headed into the bathroom. Anne looked into the mirror as she brushed her teeth and silently talked to herself about what she was doing. She acknowledged she was a little drunk, but that was not the reason she wanted to go to bed with him at this time.

"I love him so much," she told her image in the mirror, reinforcing her decision. "Besides, I am an adult," she added, while turning out the light and rushing to the bedroom where Brad was waiting for her.

"You might want to get a little bit more comfortable than that," she said amused, seeing that Brad was still fully dressed.

"I wasn't sure what to do." He watched Anne pull back the bed covers.

Anne snuggled into the cool sheets as Brad removed his clothing, except for his briefs.

"Hurry up and keep me warm," she said.

Brad cuddled up against her, excited by the mere fact that his bare legs were touching her bare legs. He told himself to be careful and not do anything to upset Anne. He thought he would let her set the pace. It was going to be difficult to lay there next to her and not enjoy the full bloom of her delicious body if she was not ready to make love. This was a harder test than the exam they had earlier today in school.

Anne's breathing accelerated as her heart beat faster from the sensation of Brad's almost naked body next to her. She explored his physique with her smooth hands and felt stirrings inside her body that she never knew existed. Her lips were swelling from the long hard kisses while an intense heat was intensifying in her genitals.

Then suddenly, she pulled away from Brad at his disappointment, only to remove her final piece of clothing, the long tee shirt, and then went straight back to her lover. She slowly worked his underwear off his body and almost exploded as their completely naked bodies rubbed against each other. How could she have missed this wonderful feeling all of her life, she thought to herself.

Brad was having the same reaction. Anne's body felt perfect to him, and he was having a hard time holding himself back. He ran his hands up her leg and over her tender bare bottom, feeling a rush of excitement causing him to do it over and over again.

Anne was more aggressive now rubbing her naked body hard against him. They rolled slightly as he ended up on top of her. Anne's eyes were almost glazed from being so excited. She kept rocking against him while she spread her legs drawing him closer to her.

Brad wasn't sure what to do next, and he was at the point beyond his control.

They both stopped thinking about anything and allowed their bodies to take over. Both couldn't get enough of one another. They were made for each other, and soon their bodies became one as Brad entered her in a slow loving way. They found a perfect rhythm and slowly increased their pace to a full frenzy that took their passion to an exploding point as their bodies discharged spasms of joy.

There was no regret from either one as the entire night was spent with small sleep sessions and more lovemaking. They finally got up the following morning at eleven o'clock and were sharing a pot of coffee together when the phone rang.

"I wonder who that could be?" Anne asked, reaching for the phone with a small groan from being sore from their nighttime activities.

She answered the phone and then handed the phone to Brad. Anne covered the mouthpiece of the phone and whispered, "It's Bill Matthews for you."

Brad took the phone from Anne's tender hand and responded to the call, "Hello, this is Brad Preston."

"Brad, this is Bill Matthews. I called Anne to get your phone number and was fortunate to catch you there. I'm sorry to bother you and interfere with your time with Anne, but I wanted to get with you on a few things. Would you mind coming to my office in Charlotte and spend some time with me on a few things? I believe I have some interesting ideas you'll find intriguing."

"I'm sure that Anne and I can drive to Charlotte some weekend to visit her parents," Brad replied as he looked towards Anne for approval.

Anne shook her head yes and smiled. She had been intending to visit her parents in the near future anyway.

"Great Brad, how about this next weekend? I could pick you up at the Weatherby's and fill you in with some of the details on the way to my office." Bill jotted the date down on his daily planner.

Brad asked Anne if next weekend would work, and she told him to schedule the appointment. They would call Bill if there was a problem that would cause them to cancel.

"Anne seems to think that'll be ok Mr. Matthews."

"Great, and call me Bill please. Just to fill you in with some teasers about what I have in mind, I want to talk to you about your future. Whether it's in baseball or another profession, I would like to be involved," Bill said with enthusiasm.

"That does sound intriguing. I look forward to meeting with you next week. I'll call you later this week to confirm our meeting with a more exact time. Is that alright with you?"

"Yes Brad, that'll be fine. I have spoken with Anne's father about my idea, so he won't be surprised when you two call them," Bill stated, slapping his desk in success.

"Alright then Mr. Matthews, I mean Bill. Next weekend it'll be. Now I have a whole week to try and figure out what you have in mind," Brad said, taking the bait.

"Don't worry about anything bad. What I want to talk to you about is nothing but good. I'll see you next week. Please give Anne my best," Bill said, before he hung up the phone.

"What was that about?" Anne asked Brad.

"I'm not sure. He wants to talk to me about my future. He sounds like he'd like to be involved in it in some way or another. I know he has connections in the big leagues, but what other profession would he want to help me out in?"

"He's in the prosthetics and orthopedic business. With your education in anatomy and the medical field, along with your business classes, I'd guess he'd like for you to work with him. You'd be an asset to his company."

"Well it's sure worth the time to talk to him. It'd be nice to plan on an alternative profession since I have no idea what my arm will ever do for me in the majors. It would be an interesting profession working with prosthetics. It definitely would go along with what I've studied. I just thought I'd use it more in the sports world."

"Don't be so quick to rule out sports Brad. You still have plenty of time to get back to form. But if you don't, you should feel good about using your education in a field in which you studied. This whole thing with Bill works out good you know. You can work on your future, and I can see my parents again. I was trying to plan a trip to see them soon, so this will work out fine, especially with you coming with me. They really like you."

"I look forward to visiting them again also," Brad replied as he emptied his coffee cup in the sink. "It's a good thing our parents approve of our relationship. My mom's always asking about you."

"She does? How come you never mentioned that to me?"

"I don't want you to feel too confident about us you know," he said as he ducked back, anticipating a quick slap on the arm.

Anne went ahead and smacked him, just because he expected it. "I'll never feel too confident about us. I do feel better now than before though. And last night was great by the way," she said, admitting to herself that her sore body was a small price to pay for the extreme pleasure she experienced.

Brad gave a shy smile as his cheeks turned pink. "Yes, it was great. You're great, and I love how you feel next to me. I hope I didn't push myself on you."

"I was a very willing participant, and we have the rest of the weekend to work on it more. But we do have to get our assignments done. Are you going to work out today?"

"I think I'll pass on working out today. I'd rather spend today with you." He kissed her hard.

Anne was impressed. Brad had never given up any time in the past for anyone when it came to his rehab. She hoped it was because of her and not the fact that he was losing faith in himself. She knew he had been working out so hard on rebuilding his shoulder and arm strength, and she thought he was making good progress.

They spent the rest of the weekend together discovering each other more, while doing minimal work in finishing their class assignments. Their relationship was at an all time high, and they knew that they were made for each other, so they committed themselves to make time for each other.

CHAPTER 9

▼

Bill Mathews was right on time Saturday morning to pick up Brad. In fact, he was early enough to share a cup of coffee with Brad and the Weatherbys. Bill gave the family a quick run down of what he had in mind for Brad, leaving them all excited from what they heard.

Bill then began to explain in full detail his plans to Brad when they were alone in the car. Bill explained his connections to some major league teams. He was close to the Dodger organization, and acknowledged to Brad that he was a major force in the Dodgers drafting him so high with the unanswered question hanging out there of whether or not he would ever be good enough to play in the big leagues.

Bill went on to explain further, a new computer program his company had been working on for some time. It was a program based on a theory that proper body movement could be orchestrated to each person's body profile and build. This was important for designing prosthesis for each individual to maximize the use of their artificial limb.

"You mentioned that to me before. How does it fit in for me?" Brad asked.

"I've watched you pitch in person, and I've seen film of you pitching, and noticed that your delivery is a hybrid between throwing a football and pitching a baseball. Everyone has their own unique style Brad. That's why some players last a long time in the majors and some throw their arm out prematurely. Your throwing motion put an added strain on your shoulder muscles. With continued consecutive motion of your throwing style, you'd probably have experienced problems in your shoulder at some time. The quick jerking motion you made to prevent from being hit by that pitch just accelerated the problem. So to answer your question, I believe we can computer format a pitching motion that will work with your body's make up. We can take pressure off of your shoulder as well as the rotator cup to give you longevity. I also believe we can increase your pitching velocity. You threw hard and fast before, but I think we can increase your speed even more."

Brad's head was spinning from excitement. He had been getting discouraged lately, but this was getting him pumped up again. "What documentation do you have from previous studies and tests of this program?"

"That is the problem," Bill sighed. "The theory is there, and a computer program based on that theory is progressing, although it isn't tested yet. But Brad, I know this will work. I want you to be the first to work on this theory. I want you to succeed as a major league pitcher. You have the right stuff. It's all there in front of you. You just have to painfully work for it."

"So what you're saying, is you want me to change my whole delivery?" Brad asked confused.

"Yes, you'd have to change your pitching mechanics completely. But you'll have to sooner or later. I know Brad because I threw my arm out prematurely, and I know I can help you."

Brad was silent for a minute. He could see how passionate Bill was about this idea, and it really did make sense. He just wasn't fond of the idea of changing his pitching style. Brad then thought of a famous golfer who was already at the top of his game and everyone else's game, and he took almost a year off to reinvent his swing. That golfer then dominated the sport, forcing the others to elevate their game if they were going to compete with him.

Bill saw the frown on Brad's face. "Well, what do you think?"

"It makes a lot of sense. I really didn't realize I had mixed my quarterbacking throwing motion into my pitching motion. There doesn't seem to be a downside to this as long as I don't screw myself up altogether," Brad said with chuckle.

"You won't hurt yourself with a new throwing motion. I guarantee it Brad. We've already witnessed what your old motion did to you. That was a very rare injury to a pitcher. I can only think of two other pitchers with the same injury as yours. It'll also be great research for those less fortunate than you. The individuals that have lost a limb could benefit the most. This will open the door for new technology and ways to make prostheses more like a natural part of their body."

"You mentioned my future on the phone. I'm sure you had an alternate plan for me if I failed to make it to the big leagues. What is it?"

"If you fail at baseball, I want you working for me. You have great management skills as well as the proper education to be a big player in our company.

We're preparing to open a new facility in the Indianapolis area. Would you be interested in managing the Indy office if your other plans don't work out? I would pay you very well because I believe in you." Bill searched Brad's expression for an initial response.

Brad squirmed in his seat, and his heart beat accelerated. He knew he would have to make a decision sooner or later concerning his future. For most of his life he had dreamed of playing some professional sport, but things had changed. He was facing reality, and it was confusing. Brad finally replied, "I really appreciate your confidence in me. I want to work hard on this computer program and change my pitching style. You're right about both aspects. If I don't succeed in baseball, the computer program would be significant in improving prosthetics. I'll keep your job offer at the top of my list. It sounds very interesting, and it could allow us to improve other people's lives."

Bill slapped the steering wheel with his hand in celebration of Brad's commitment to his idea. He wanted Brad to make it in the major league, but the thought of Brad working for him was exciting. "I appreciate your decision Brad. I have everything set up at the office, so we can get right on it."

Brad smiled. "So you were confident I'd agree?"

"I know you're an intelligent man and passionate about the sport, so I felt good about the chance of you agreeing with me. You'll be a rich man one way or another."

"I always knew I'd succeed in life. I just wasn't sure how. But for me it isn't all about the money. I want the wealth for the independence from worrying about the lack of money. And I do like the better lifestyle."

"There's nothing wrong with that Brad. I always felt if you worked hard for it and took a few chances in life, you deserved the awards," Bill said, applauding Brad's goals.

They looked at each other approvingly and shook hands as they pulled into Bill's company parking lot. They worked hard all day on the project, causing them to fall behind schedule on getting home at the promised time, but they both held a tremendous amount of passion for the project causing them to forge ahead.

Upon their arrival to the Weatherby's home, Bill apologized to Anne and her family for keeping Brad all day.

Norris asked Bill to stay for a drink, and Bill accepted. He and Norris were best friends, and he wanted a chance to explain all of the details of his proposal to the rest of them.

It took two drinks for Bill and Brad to tell them about the computer program and how it would apply to Brad. It appeared the idea had merit from the initial testing, and Brad admitted it could create a better pitching motion for him. They just had to develop a better way to monitor motion in the body and tie it in on how it affected muscles and ligaments. Brad had brought up an excellent idea to accomplish that feat, and Bill was going to the research department with the idea for them to expand on.

Anne hugged Brad lovingly, proud of his desire to participate in such an important project. She had worked with amputees at the hospital, and she was excited about the promise this program had.

As he had to rush off for a dinner appointment he had to attend, Bill gave everyone a good bye.

Norris walked him to his car. "You seem to be real high on Brad. We've only been around him for a weekend a few months ago, and we were impressed, but some people can put on a front."

Bill instantly raised both of his hands. "Norris, don't even think that way about him. He is the real thing! You and Grace might prepare yourselves for him to be your son in law in the near future. From what he said to me, he and Anne have become really close, and he has fallen head over heals with her."

"Don't take me wrong Bill. I never thought Brad was being counterfeit with us. I just wanted your input because you have watched him over the past three years at Duke, plus you spent an entire day with him. We like him a lot and appreciate the way he has brought Anne back to life socially."

"Good. You have nothing to worry about with him. I've also noticed the difference in Anne, and it's for the better. She deserves a special person like Brad because she's also very special. You all have a good weekend now. I need to get going before I get in trouble with my wife."

The rest of the weekend went by too fast. Brad and the Weatherbys built a strong foundation for a possible long term relationship.

Brad and Anne went back to Durham with a stronger bond between them and more self assurance about their future. Life was definitely as good as it gets for the young couple.

CHAPTER 10

▼

Brad spent the next week working out harder than ever. He spent several hours with Bill and a programmer at the Duke Medical Center working out details on the computer reading his body movements, so they could coordinate the body make up of an individual with proper muscle usage to insure the ideal limb movement.

School was also demanding on Brad, and when he entered Anne's apartment on Friday night he was exhausted. He wasn't prepared to face a panicky Anne that was crying uncontrollably.

Brad ran up to Anne and held her close, then asked her what was wrong.

"Oh Brad, I'm so sorry," she cried, pulling away from him.

Brad was trembling. "Sorry about what? What happened? Are you ok?"

"I don't know," she whispered.

"Anne, please slow down and stop crying. We can work out any problem. Just pull yourself together and talk to me. I love you, and I can help," he said in a very soothing tone.

Anne sniffed her nose while bringing a Kleenex to her eyes and then patted her nose with a dry area of the tissue. She shook her head several times in small rapid jerks trying to pull her self together, and then she focused her eyes directly on Brad's eyes. She wanted to read his reaction to what she had to say. Her mouth opened slowly, and at first nothing came out. Finally very sheepishly she said, "I think I'm pregnant." She stood back to see his true feelings about what she had just told him.

As if someone had shocked him with a live wire, Brad's body stiffened. He could see she was terrified over the situation because she just stood there without any emotion while staring at him. The silence seemed like hours between them, but it was only about ten seconds. Brad walked up to Anne and pulled her close to him again. He slowly put his hands on her tear-ridden face and carefully wiped the moisture from her eyes.

Anne put her arms around his body and pulled so hard that even Brad was impressed by her strength.

Brad then led her to the couch and sat them down facing each other while holding both of her hands. "Ok, let's start over," he said slowly in a very loving tone. "It's only been a couple of weeks since we had sex. How could you know so soon?"

"I've been like clock work every month since my first period when I was thirteen. I should've started yesterday," she said between sniffs.

Brad's body relaxed, and he gave a big smile. "Anne, it's only one day. Maybe you're just over reacting since it was the first time you had sex."

Anne cried even harder before regaining her composure. "I know it sounds ridiculous for me to think I'm pregnant from being just one day late, but that's how I feel. It might be because I miscalculated the timing for me the night we made love. I don't know honey. What if I am pregnant, what do we do then?"

Brad took the question seriously, by providing her with an answer straight from his heart and inner being. "We get married and raise our child together. It isn't that difficult of a decision for me. What about you?"

"I didn't want to get married this way. I do love you though…more than anything. What will our parents think? They won't be very pleased about this."

Brad stood up and went to get a beer. He brought back two cold ones and started to hand one to Anne, and then he pulled it back. "You can't have one if you're in a motherly way."

"Well at least it's good to see you in a good mood about this. I didn't know what to expect from you, although I suspected you'd handle the situation similar to the way you have. That's a big reason I'd marry you under these circumstances," Anne said as she leaned up against him and took the beer. "I could use one right now."

Anne popped the cap off without any problem and took a long drink.

"Gees, I guess you could've used that beer. Before you drink the rest of the six-pack, let's work this out in an intelligent way. We have to separate the emotion we're experiencing right now and work out a solid plan. But before we put aside the emotion, I want a nice kiss from you, and I want to tell you how much I love you," he said pulling her close to him, before giving her a long loving kiss that brought back the feelings that put them in this situation.

"Let's just get married now," she said as she returned his kiss with one even better.

"That might be the solution to everything between us."

"What do you mean?" she asked as her chin dropped, dragging her mouth wide open.

He stared at Anne without blinking. "First, let's establish that we want to marry each other even if you're not pregnant. I can honestly say I want to marry you no matter what."

Anne's mouth opened even wider, as did her eyes. She felt a wave of excitement run through her entire body as her tension diminished even more. It made her heart accelerate and her head spin for a brief moment. Gathering herself she replied, "I wanted to marry you the first weekend we spent together at my parents, and I want to more than ever now. I love you with all of my heart and soul."

The two embraced each other for a long time while throwing in several hard kisses.

Brad broke the moment with more logic. "Alright, it's established that we love each other and marriage is something we both want to happen between us. I agree with you that our parents will be disappointed and maybe embarrassed if we get married because you're pregnant. So your comment about getting married now might be the answer."

Anne stood motionless not knowing what to say.

Brad's right eyebrow rose in a sexy arc from his concentration on fixing this problem. "And, if you aren't pregnant, we still get what we wanted, which is each other forever."

Tears came to Anne's eyes again.

Brad was concerned as he saw a tear trickle down her tanned cheeks, so he gently wiped it away.

Anne gave a faint smile. "I'm fine honey. I'm just so happy you feel the way you do. So what's your, I mean our plan?"

"We plan an immediate wedding with just us and our parents. Maybe our brothers and sister too. We do it within the week, hopefully at your church with your Pastor," he said as he paced back and forth contemplating the idea.

"How do we explain this sudden decision to our parents Mr. Genius?"

Brad stopped pacing and turned to Anne. "We don't. We just tell them the truth."

"What, that I might be pregnant, and we just want to get ahead of the game by marrying now?" Anne replied with a "get real" stare.

"No not that real reason. The real reason that we want to live together now, and we'll only do it as man and wife. That's the way we are you know."

"You are good! But my parents will want a big wedding with all of the traditional wedding things. You should know that from being around my mom."

"Here's how we do it. I'll call my family now and have them down this coming weekend to meet your parents. It's homecoming next weekend anyway, and they were talking about coming here for the occasion. You call your Pastor and talk him into marrying us next Saturday in a private secret ceremony with just you and me, along with our families. He might argue the point with you, but I'm Catholic, so that should help. They will not know until that moment what we are up to. Yes, they will be upset a little at first, but I truly believe our parents will rejoice in our union. My parents adore you, and I think your parents like me. How does that sound?" Brad asked as he took a deep breath.

Anne was quiet for a minute really mulling the idea over. The frown on her face slowly turned into a smile. "That's probably the best scenario we could plan. You're right, they'll be somewhat disgruntled at first, but they want us happy. I know my parents love you and secretly pray you'll marry me and make me happy. Of course they'll want to plan a wedding reception for their friends you know."

"I have an idea. How much do you trust Bill Matthews?"

"He's my dad's best friend, and he's a close family friend to me. Why do you ask?"

"Can we get Bill to pull off a reception on Saturday evening without spilling the beans to your dad?"

"Good idea. I like how you think. Yes, we can trust Bill because he thinks the world of you, and he wouldn't want to betray your trust," Anne said with more excitement in her voice. "This just might work. What if I'm not pregnant?"

"Our decision is made no matter what happens on that front." Brad took her hand as his sparkling eyes penetrated her wide brown eyes. "Anne will you marry me?"

"Yes, I'll marry you," she replied, giving him a powerful hug and then finishing it off with a long sensual kiss.

"I apologize for not having a ring to offer you at this moment, but we can handle that part tomorrow. We have a lot of work to do tonight. What about Alice?"

"She'll be fine about moving out. She's hinted to me that she wants to move in with Chris, her boyfriend."

"So you're in agreement then? No matter what, we get married next weekend?"

"Yes Brad, we get married next weekend. Now let's get to work, so we can play around later."

"You sure do know how to motivate a guy," he replied, feeling aroused.

"Brad, one very important question. How do we pay for everything? When we marry, I don't expect for our families to take care of us."

"Good point, but I do have some money of my own. Plus I have an idea that should allow us to get a substantial amount of money fairly quick," he said, raising both eyebrows.

"Why don't you fill me in first? I'd like to know what you have in mind because it effects both of us now and our baby," she said, patting her slim belly.

Brad laughed hard for a moment. "I can't believe we're going through all of this because you're one day late. Sorry, I didn't mean it that way."

"I know what you mean, so don't worry. It's sort of funny though. I don't even mind if I am pregnant. You have fulfilled my dreams. I never did want to just work all my life, even though that is what I expected."

Brad shook his head in agreement. "When I was in the car with Bill last Saturday we talked about several things. He mentioned to me that he had a big connection with the Dodgers. He was a key in my high draft pick since there's doubt I'll be able to pitch again. Bill believes in me and his idea, and he hinted to me that he could strike a deal with the Dodger organization for me to sign a contract. If that won't pan out, I believe Bill would sign a contract with me for my commitment to work for him. He told me it didn't matter if I played baseball or worked with him, I would be wealthy. So if I work things out right, we can finish school this year without hardship, and I will have a good job to start our post college days together."

"I can honestly tell you I'm not fond of the idea of you playing baseball. I guess I'm selfish since I want to be with you all of the time. Baseball does require a lot of travel. But, because of my unending love for you, I will support your decision if that is what you want to do as long as it isn't in the minor leagues."

"That's fair. I wouldn't want to just max out playing in the minor leagues either. But I'd have to start in the minors you know?" Brad was excited just talking about his chance of playing baseball again.

"Yes, I do know something about the game. I secretly researched it after I met you," Anne said with a guilty smile. "Hand me the phone please. I need to start our wedding plans, so I better talk to Father Mahoney first. He'll give me a hard time, but I think he'll relent and marry us next weekend."

"Anne, would you be disappointed if it turns out you're not pregnant and miss out on a big wedding? That seems to be most women's big dream."

"We're getting married because we love each other and want to spend the rest of lives together. That means this is between you and me, along with our families. A big wedding is just a show that I don't want to put on for other people. Does that answer your question good enough to put that thought out of your mind for the rest of your life?"

"I will never bring it up again. You just need to sell your mother the same way you sold me. Where's your cell phone? I need to call Bill Matthews," Brad said as he looked around her well kept apartment looking for the phone.

Brad stopped for a moment as the thought just came to his mind that this was soon to be his home also. He never thought much about it, but he had always noticed how spotless her place was. He felt excited knowing that Anne was going to be his wife. He was lucky he had met her. It seemed funny to him how things happen when you face adversity in life. One bad thing happens, and a good thing comes from it. That made him think about the strong possibility that he would become a father, and it took him back a bit as he asked himself, "Am I ready to be a parent? Will I be a good one?"

So many things were happening to him right now. He did believe in fate and would take each adverse situation at hand and work through it.

Anne startled Brad when she handed him the phone. He jerked awkwardly as he took it from her.

"Second thoughts there honey?"

"No, not at all. I was just digesting all of the changes that have taken place in my life since I met you. They're all for the good though, so don't worry. I was just hit in the face with the reality that I might become a father soon. That was something I was not prepared for, but will look forward to. I just hope I'll be a good dad."

"You'll be a great father, so don't worry about it." She put her arm around him and laughed. "Now get on the phone before you are a father!"

"It's good to see you in a better mood about this. You were crying your eyes out earlier."

Anne walked up to him and stared into his eyes seriously. Certain that she had his attention she said, "You did a wonderful job getting me over that part, so I'm now beyond it."

Brad's eyes were laughing, but he wouldn't let his face participate in it as he tried to not show Anne that she won one. "It looks like life is going to be very interesting with you as my wife. I can't wait."

They embraced each other furiously and kissed one another hard, before they both reluctantly broke away from each other and dialed their phones.

After an hour of nonstop conversation with Father Mahoney and Bill Matthews, Anne and Brad sat down exhausted.

"That was tough," Anne said, shaking her head.

"Yeah, me too. How'd your talk go?" Brad asked as he opened another beer.

Anne grabbed the beer and took a drink before she answered. "Well, the outcome was a little different than we planned, but he agreed to marry us next Saturday. What about your conversation with Bill?"

"It went well. He just had one suggestion…"

"That we should not surprise our parents!"

"Ding, ding, ding, you're the big winner. I can see their point though," Brad said as he stretched his long legs out. "Bill was actually very excited about the news and told me to tell you congratulations. He said the same thing you said about your mother. She would've wanted a big wedding. But he thought she would be ok with our plans. Just prepare for a nice reception down the road. He said your mom would want to show us off to all of her friends. She's proud of us and has talked to Ruth at lengths about us, wishing that we would marry. So just call your parents and give them the news." Brad handed the phone to Anne and sat back in the couch.

"You call your parents first," she said, handing the phone back and then grabbing the beer from him. This time she took a good long drink. "I might need that in a few minutes you know."

"You'll be fine," he said as he laid her down on the couch and pressed himself against her.

"That comes later. We still have some work to do. Let's just call our parents at the same time."

"What do we do if our parents can't make it?"

"They will cancel any plans they may have for this. I know them too well," she said with confidence.

Brad was done with his call in thirty minutes, but he noticed that Anne was still on the phone to her parents. He took that time to call his brother and sister to invite them for the weekend. After another fifteen minutes, he was finished with his family calls, so he slowly walked towards Anne to see her conversation was going well. He sighed with relief when he heard laughter in Anne's beautiful voice.

Feeling confident that things were going well, he put both arms around Anne. The smell of her fresh clean body brought pleasure to him. He loved the way she smelled and felt more excited about getting married.

Anne gave him a slight bump with her butt in a joking way to help ease his tension. "Oh Mom, Brad just walked in from talking to his family. You can talk to him now."

Anne had a huge grin on her face, and she had to force the phone in his hand before he would take it. "It's ok," she mouthed without saying the words.

"Hello Mrs. Weatherby." Brad stammered for a second while pacing back and forth. "I guess Anne told you of our impetuous, but well thought out plans."

"You don't have to sell me on the idea Brad. And please call me Grace, or mom, but not Mrs. Weatherby. These wedding plans are on short notice, although I can sincerely say that you have our blessing. I would have liked to have had a large wedding as you two guessed, but this is great news…" Grace breathed hard and tried to fight off tears. "Those are happy tears, by the way. I'll see you two tomorrow, so let me talk to Anne. And Brad, Norris and I both adore you. We're happy to welcome you into our family."

"Thank you Grace. I look forward to have you and Norris as my in laws. I really enjoy you both, and I have a great deal of respect for you and Norris," Brad stated from his heart.

Brad handed Anne the phone and then wandered to the kitchen window that captured glimpses of the campus. Tears came to his eyes, releasing the emotion that had built up in him the past three hours. The plan worked. Everything was set for the two of them to be married. That was the most important thing in his life right now. His baseball days had taken a back seat to Anne.

CHAPTER 11

▼

Friday was already upon them as Brad and Anne's rushed wedding was practically set, with the irreplaceable assistance of Mrs. Weatherby.

Brad stood patiently as he waited for his parents to arrive from their flight from Indianapolis. He was glad his brother and sister decided on a later flight and then rent a car to drive, allowing him more time to prepare for his wedding. Brad was anxious to see his parents again since he hadn't seen them in almost two months. He took a short stroll to look at the monitor of arrivals. Flight 5567 from Indianapolis, on time, the screen revealed. Brad glanced at his watch to verify how accurate the information was and laughed to himself because the flight was already eight minutes late. "I guess they're pretty flexible here about what on time means," he whispered to himself.

The airport wasn't very busy yet for a Friday. He guessed it would be packed when David and Rebecca arrived later in the evening, as they would be mingling with the business travelers coming home for the weekend. He spotted an area with a good view of the runway and then slowly walked up to it to catch a glimpse of the incoming planes. He was particularly looking for a United Airlines jetliner approaching the gate.

He stared out the window, thinking about marrying this wonderful, beautiful woman that was extremely intelligent and possibly pregnant. She still had not started her period and truly believed without a doubt that she was indeed with child. How could he question her instinct? He pictured a cute, healthy baby in his arms, and his hair stood up on his body. He was amazed by the fact that he was excited about being a father. He had never thought about it with baseball being his prime goal in life.

He was startled by the announcement of flight 5567 arriving at gate 23. He missed seeing the plane land from being deep in thought. Brad positioned himself, so he could see his parents as they entered the building. Fortunately they were one of the first ones off the plane.

Brad greeted each of his parents with a big hug, followed by a quick kiss.

Mrs. Preston broke from her hug with Brad and looked him over from head to toe. "I can't believe you're getting married. I thought it would be many years down the road." She kept from adding, "Since your breakup with Kristy."

"I really didn't expect it either Mom. It just happened very fast. Anne is such a special person."

"I agree," Miles said as he entered the conversation. "Congratulations Son. We don't know her that well, but from the little time we spent with Anne, we like her. Is everything ok with you?"

"Couldn't be better Dad. I want to talk with you about a few things sometime this weekend. I have some important things going on that I want your advice on," Brad stated, preparing his father for decisions he had made for his future with Anne.

"Sure, I'd love to give you some advice for a change, especially some consul that you actually asked me for. That is a change for parents," Mr. Preston said with a laugh.

The three of them worked their way to baggage claim while filling each other in with news of what was new in their life. But mostly the talk was about Brad and Anne. They retrieved the enormous amount of baggage from the squeaky carousel in good time.

Brad turned to his mother in disbelief. "Did you bring enough clothes?"

"We didn't know what the weather would bring, so we brought warm weather clothes and fall wear just in case," Margaret said in defense of her over packing.

Miles looked at Brad in disgust and shrugged his shoulders. They loaded everything and headed for the car. "How far do the Weatherby's live from here Brad?"

"I'd guess about fifteen to twenty minutes, depending on traffic," Brad answered, straining from pushing the luggage.

"That gives you some time to fill me in on what you wanted to talk to me about son," Miles said with a command to Brad. "I assume it has to do with your future in baseball or another profession."

"You're correct as usual Dad. I may have an opportunity to sign a contract of some kind with the Dodgers…"

"Oh yeah, how is that?" his dad broke in.

"Anne's father's best friend, Bill Matthews, played professional ball. He has a good contact with the Dodger organization. He told me he pushed them hard to draft me this summer, which explains why I went so high in the draft with an injury hindering my career. He didn't fill me in with too many details, but I expect some good news from him any time. He's a real nice guy. In addition, he owns a prosthetic and orthopedics company and wants me to work with him if baseball doesn't work out right away," Brad said nervously, being cautious not hurt his fathers feelings.

Miles had listened to Brad's possible career choices and concentrated heavily on what was on the table for his son. He stared ahead for a few seconds, digesting what he just heard. "I'll tell you what Brad, that sounds like a couple of great opportunities for you. When you get more details, let's get together and make sure you do this right," Mr. Preston stated, giving Brad a pat on the shoulder. "How is that shoulder anyway?"

"It isn't where I hoped it would be at this time. They tell me it'll take a long time to heal. You two will meet Mr. Matthews this weekend. He and his wife will be at the wedding tomorrow, and I think you'll like him and trust his intentions."

Brad found the car without any problem and loaded the luggage into the trunk with his father's assistance.

"How many people will be at the ceremony tomorrow?" Margaret asked after buckling her seat belt.

"Not very many Mom. We were originally going to have just you, dad, and Anne's parents. But then we thought her brother should come, as well as David and Rebecca, but we expanded the list a little more. I really want to thank you two for understanding our feelings about this, especially on short notice. We were going to surprise everybody at the last minute, but Father Mahoney talked us out of it. He made us realize right a way that would be too stressful for everyone involved."

"Yes," his mother said sternly. "That would have been awkward for all of us. And you don't have to thank us for coming. We wouldn't miss this special event you know."

"That's right Brad," his dad chided in. "It's not what we expected, but we are happy for you. As long as you're happy and you think you're doing the right thing."

"I couldn't be more sure," Brad answered proudly. "You'll love Anne. She's a very special person. Very bright and classy. I couldn't do any better."

The drive went well, and they turned into the Weatherby's driveway.

"Well it looks like she comes from a good family," Margaret stated, getting excited to get to know Anne better and to meet her parents. She noticed an attractive; no beautiful would be a more appropriate description of the young woman walking out of the impressive house. She forgot how pretty Anne was. Actually Anne was more stunning dressed in fashionable clothing, rather than hospital scrubs. Margaret noticed Miles eyebrows raise in pleasure as he watched her approach.

He quickly turned to Brad saying, "She certainly is an attractive girl Brad."

Anne opened the back door of the car to allow Mrs. Preston to exit. As Margaret slid out of the back seat and got to her feet, Anne hugged her. "Thanks for making the trip down here. I hope your flight went well."

Brad's mom gave Anne a quick kiss on the cheek. "We wouldn't miss this for the world. And yes, our flight was just fine."

Miles immediately gave Anne a big hug. "Do you remember me? Miles Preston."

Anne hugged him hard and gave Mr. Preston a kiss. "Of course I remember you. How could I forget either one of you? You were so kind to me in the hospital."

"Come on you three. Let's get their wardrobe out of the trunk and get everybody settled in. There's much to do yet today," Brad said as he opened the trunk, staring at the abundance of luggage.

"Oh my," Anne said with a laugh. "You two travel just like my parents. I know we'll all get along just fine."

At that same time, Norris and Grace Weatherby walked out to greet them. There was a friendly exchange of introductions and small talk before they took the Preston's belongs into the house. Miles and Margaret were taken to their room, so they could settle in and get comfortable.

"You get unpacked and refreshed, and we'll meet you in the parlor for a drink where we can talk further. Please take your time, and I'll see you downstairs," Norris told them in his southern style, gentlemanly manner.

The Prestons took only fifteen minutes to organize their things and then joined Brad and the Weatherbys in the parlor.

Norris took their drink order and prepared their favorite in a prompt professional way, displaying his love to entertain. "Here you go," Norris said as he handed his future in laws their drink. "If I need to adjust them, please let me know."

Miles sipped his absolute martini that was prepared with a splash of vermouth and two large green olives on a cocktail spear. "It's just right, thank you. It hits the spot after the trip here."

Grace stepped forward and addressed the Prestons. "Now that we're all together, I'd like to get your ideas and input of what you'd like in the ceremony tomorrow. It's very short notice for all of this, and I want you both to feel like you had a hand in the wedding plans. I'm open to any ideas, and I won't be hurt if you disagree with anything we may have to change. After all, we planned for this in less than a week," Grace explained, while giving Anne a look to let her know she would have liked more time to plan.

"Well, we really don't have any particular tradition to follow. Our families are both Catholic, and the wedding is in the Catholic Church…I feel very confident that everything will be just perfect. I do want to thank you for putting this together so fast. I'm not sure why these two did this last minute," Margaret said, shaking her finger at Brad and Anne. She then gave a happy smile.

Anne stepped forward pulling Brad with her. "We've decided that we want both sets of parents standing at the altar with us. I'll still have my father walk me up the aisle, but he'll remain there with us along with you all. I know that isn't tradition, but that's our way of letting you all know how much you mean to us."

The parents just stood there stunned by the news while looking back and forth at each other.

Norris broke the silence as he raised his glass for a toast. "Here is to all of us. Great parents…with great kids."

"I second that." Miles clicked his glass against Norris's and then did the same with the others.

The tension of meeting prospective in laws had faded. They all realized this was a marriage that was meant to be. Everyone in the room had a strong feeling that the two families would get along just fine. They were both well off in a monetary way, shared the same values, and had raised their children with love and attention, while directing them to be the best that they could be.

After finishing their drinks, they drove to the church for a quick run through and to make sure that things were in place for the big day tomorrow.

They then met up with the rest of the family at a fine Italian restaurant for a nice dinner to top off the evening.

CHAPTER 12

▼

The church was decorated exquisitely with dozens of flower arrangements neatly spaced throughout the church. Each arrangement was made of three red roses, accompanied by white carnations, with baby's breath mixed in for a perfect effect. The exception to this design consisted of two dozen long stem red roses integrated with fern leaves, flanking each side of the pulpit.

Brad entered the sanctuary and marveled at the beauty and craftsmanship of the church. It was built in the early 1900's, and represented the superior quality that was practiced at that time. Hand carved appliqués were applied to the rich woods, putting the finishing touches to the interior of the great structure. The multi colored stained glass windows flooded the room with a prism of color and light. Jesus hung on the cross just behind the pulpit to remind everybody of his great sacrifice. It presented an aura of tranquility with a divine presence.

There were three rolls of pews separated by a wide red carpet that led to the altar. Family and special guests filled the first three rows of the pews.

Brad was happy to see Coach Culley present, sitting next to the Matthews. There were a few people that Brad did not recognize, but he figured he would meet them after the ceremony.

Brad walked up slowly to the vessel of holy water, and gently dipped the tip of his first two fingers in the sacred water, and then did the sign of the cross as he bent his head down towards the pulpit. He then prayed quietly, "Dear God, please bless our families on this special day and bless this reunion in your name. I ask you to shine your light on us all. Please help make this marriage strong. We trust your decision on Anne's possible pregnancy. Thank you for everything." He did the sign of the cross in unison with, "In the name of the father, son, and holy spirit, amen."

Brad searched the church from where he was standing to see if Anne and the rest of the wedding party were preparing to enter the sanctuary, but did not see any sign of them. Just as he was about to walk back towards the door, his brother David peeped into the room and gave Brad a "thumbs up."

Brad's attention then turned to Father Mahoney as the priest approached the altar prepared to perform his duties in God's way.

Being motioned by the robed holy man, Brad started his walk towards the altar to start his new life. His stomach rolled slightly from his anxiety. He wasn't nervous about getting married, he just wanted to do it right. Making his way down the aisle, he smiled after noticing how the flowers were arranged. He determined that Anne had made a symbolic gesture with the three red roses surrounded by all of the carnations with a mix of baby's breath. "Not bad. The two of us and the baby surrounded by family. She's very clever," he said to himself.

He made it up to the altar and stood to Father Mahoney's left. Brad acknowledged the priest respectfully and turned around to face the guests, his family, his soon to be wife, and his future in laws.

The procession started with David Preston escorting his mother holding on to his arm. Miles and Rebecca Preston were next in line, following just twenty-five feet behind. The four of them were smiling with pride as they approached.

Brad shook David's hand as he dropped their mother off at Brad's side. They both kissed their mother, and then David took a seat with the other guests.

Miles and Rebecca made their way up to the altar as Brad hugged his dad and gave Rebecca a quick hug and kiss, and then Mr. Preston followed suit doing the same to his daughter, before she took her seat along side David.

Nathan Weatherby escorted his mother down the aisle. He gave her a kiss after he dropped her off on the right side of the priest and then eagerly accepted Brad's handshake. He then held his head high while he strutted to join the others in their special seats.

The organ player then started the traditional song everyone identifies as, "Here Comes the Bride." The entire party of guests and family stood up as Norris proudly walked Anne down the aisle.

Brad had goose bumps overtake his entire body from seeing this amazing woman walking towards him. Words could not describe how beautiful she was.

Anne's blond hair was pulled back, so it wouldn't interfere with the veil. Her face had the right amount of makeup, accentuating her cheekbones and allowing her large brown eyes to captivate everyone around her.

The wedding gown had been modified to fit this wedding theme. It had been Margaret's gown when she married Norris, and it originally had been designed for a more elaborate wedding. Anne had the long train removed and a layer of lace taken off the bottom. The upper portion was fitted to accent her breasts and was made of an off white satin with a hint of lace around the bosom. The lower section of the dress was the same satin underlay with a rich looking lace that fell to the floor. The combination looked like a custom fitted gown that was perfect for Anne and the type of wedding they choose. Margaret did a grand job getting the seamstress to do such a good job at short notice.

Anne was glowing as she floated down the aisle towards the man she loved. She could hear a few gasps from family and guests, making her smile even more rampant. Anne proudly displayed a bouquet of three roses combined with carnations and baby's breath as she held the arrangement carefully in her hands. Only Brad realized her true symbolic meaning of the arrangement.

Norris escorted Anne to Brad's side with pride and ease. It was surprising to Mr. Weatherby that it felt so natural to offer his only daughter to Brad, whom he had not known that well. It was a sign to him that Brad was the right person for his lovely daughter; perhaps the only man for his daughter that would instill the confidence in Norris to make her happy.

Mr. Weatherby took both of Anne's hands in his and whispered he loved her as tears filled his eyes. Norris gave Anne a quick kiss, followed by a firm hand shake with Brad, and then he took his place next to his wife as he put his arm around her and kissed her on the cheek.

Tears filled most everybody's eyes from the emotional display of Norris' love for his daughter.

It was now time for the ceremony to start as the priest cleared his voice and started to proceed. "Dearly beloved, we are gathered here to unite Bradford Preston and Anne Weatherby in holy matrimony."

As Brad faced Anne, he could see her glow while he gleamed with joy from the fact that they were becoming one. Brad thought Anne looked so beautiful standing just inches away from him. He was having trouble holding back from grabbing her and pulling her close to him, so he could give her an unending kiss. He took both of her soft hands in his and stared into her deep brown eyes that cried out, "I love you so much!"

Anne looked into his eyes having the same thoughts, wishing the ceremony would end soon, so she could kiss his sexy lips. She couldn't believe how much her sex drive had changed since her first time of making love.

They were both so mesmerized with each other that they almost missed their small speaking part of the ceremony.

Miles handed Brad the beautiful wedding ring made of fourteen carat gold, with a one carat diamond, surrounded by another carat of smaller diamonds. It was a ring that Anne had seen last summer when she was dreaming of becoming Brad's wife while she was out window shopping. She saw the ring in the window and went in the jewelry store to try it on. Anne fell in love with it, and by fate it was still at the store waiting for them to buy it.

Brad slid the ring on her hand while repeating his vows to Anne, as she received the token of their pledge to be man and wife for life, with tears falling like a steady April rain shower.

Anne then repeated the same vow and put Brad's wedding band on his ring finger sealing the vow of being his wife for life.

Father Mahoney ended the ceremony by declaring the two of them husband and wife.

Brad and Anne kissed each other hard for a longer than usual kiss for a Catholic wedding.

The guests didn't seem to mind as they applauded and laughed at the young married couple.

Brad and Anne's journey had officially started.

After the traditional wedding line and the throwing of the rice, the family members and special guests gathered at the Hidden Hills Country Club for a small, but elaborate reception.

Brad was especially interested in talking to one guest that he did not know before the wedding. His name was Keith Olsen, and he worked in the front office of the Dodger organization. Brad's curiosity was in full drive after finding out who Keith was. It seemed odd to Brad that someone from the Dodgers would be at his wedding, especially since his wedding was small and intended for a few close friends and basic family members.

The reception was a huge success. The food was ordered from the menu to satisfy everyone's taste buds, which also allowed the food to be served hot and fresh. There was a beautiful three tier cake that was more than delicious. The white cream icing melted in their mouths, and the white cake was so moist and light that it had many people wanting a second piece, especially the bride and groom. Of course they wasted one piece feeding each other per wedding tradition. The champagne was none other than Dom Perignom, which made all of the toasts to the new couple extra special.

Due to such short notice, a live band was not available; however a top DJ brought a great musical show to them. It was a grand time, allowing Brad and Anne to celebrate their wedding with much joy along with all of the special guests that admired the young couple.

Brad had wanted to talk with Keith Olson more than he had a chance to at the reception, but time wouldn't allow it. Brad did find out why Keith was there. It turned out that Bill and Keith played baseball together in the majors. Bill tried to set Keith up with his sister, but it just so happened she was into the arts more than sports, and she married Keith's brother instead, who had just starting out in the film making business. Bill and Keith stayed close all of these years, helped by the fact that they were somewhat related.

Keith did tell Brad that he wanted to meet with him tomorrow along with Bill, Mr. Weatherby, and Brad's father and left it at that. Keith didn't want to bring business to this special occasion.

Brad found Keith quite interesting and a pleasure to be around with Keith's easy going personality. Keith was a good looking man just shy of being six feet tall. His red hair was combed back, allowing his kind, blue eyes to dazzle you. He had a friendly smile that set you at ease the moment you were around him, escalating Brad's desire to talk with him more.

The festive evening came to a close as the newlyweds departed to spend their honeymoon night in the most luxurious hotel Charlotte offered, thanks to the Weatherbys. A stretched limousine with a perfectly chilled bottle of champagne awaited them as the newlyweds gave everybody their thanks and said their good byes. As they settled into the plush seat of their ride, they each breathed a sigh of relief, followed by a passionate kiss.

"What a great day!" Brad said, undoing his tie and unbuttoning his top shirt button.

"It couldn't be better," Anne replied, exhausted. "I can't believe how well it went with such short notice."

"Your mom did a fantastic job."

"That's her forte you know. She loves these types of parties. I don't think she's as disappointed having a small ceremony after such a successful wedding. I don't know how it could have been better, do you?" She gave him a long kiss.

Brad pulled her close as his blood flowed quicker. "It seems to me that an explanation point will soon be applied to this special day."

Brad prepared two flutes of champagne and handed one to Anne. "Here's to the rest of our life together." And with the dinging sound that only the best crystal makes from the click of their flutes, they toasted their marriage.

The final seal of their wedding was yet to be made. A night filled with endless lovemaking would put the final stamp on their day.

The newlywed couple arrived at the Weatherby's house at 1:30 p.m. the following day. There was a glow from both of them that revealed how much they were in love with each other.

Grace had a special lunch prepared for everyone to end the weekend. The Matthews were present, as well as Keith Olson, and Brad's immediate family. A meeting was scheduled with Keith and Bill concerning Brad's future after the lunch.

Brad's curiosity was killing him on what was gong to be proposed to him.

The Prestons thought Grace did herself proud by serving a superb lunch. They were genuinely impressed with the southern hospitality she displayed; adding more assurance Brad had married the right girl. In fact, they made a special toast to all demonstrating their true feelings of the marriage.

It was time for David and Rebecca Preston to leave to catch their flight back to Florida. Brad told them he was happy to see them again and thanked his brother and sister for coming. After a few tears and several hugs, his siblings drove the rental car back to the airport for their flight home.

It was now time for business as Brad and Anne were ushered to her father's home office. Norris's study was magnificent in order and detail, blending in perfectly with the southern plantation style home. Detailed moldings, adding to the richness of the wood enhanced the walnut walls. The bookcases behind the early 1800 hundreds antique desk were filled with books on law and several personal favorites of Mr. Weatherby.

When Brad entered the room, he was inundated with the feeling he was in a world of high finance or preparing for a very important legal case. It was a large room that easily handled the small crowd of Brad, Anne, Miles, Norris, Bill, and Keith. Neatly organized on the antique desk, were several documents that Keith and Bill had prepared. Brad sat nervously with Anne at his side, flanked by their fathers.

"Let's get this started," Bill said as he picked up a document. "I want you all to know that Brad is not obligated to agree to, or sign these contracts today. However, I believe that they're very fair to all parties. With Norris's knowledge of business contracts, and Miles expertise in finance, I can't think of any better representation on Brad's behalf, as well as Anne's."

Keith Olson stepped forward and straightened his shirt collar. "I represent the Los Angeles Dodgers management and have full authority to execute these documents on their behalf. I'll say that Bill has driven a hard bargain on this agreement, and I feel that our organization is taking a risk. But from everything we have seen of Brad, and the hard sell that Bill applied to us, we have agreed on these terms."

"Let's see the details. We can determine the fairness on the evidence," Norris broke in, displaying his abilities as a savvy contract attorney.

"This is a three party contract," Bill said as he started to explain the deal. "My company is the third party in this agreement. It's a win, win situation for Brad."

"This is going to be very interesting," Norris said as his curiosity rose to an elevated level.

Anne was the only one to observe Brad squirming in his chair. She took her hand and put it on his arm and gently rubbed it trying to soothe his nerves.

It helped as he relaxed somewhat, giving her a smile of thanks.

"Let me explain my thinking about this situation," Bill said as he wanted to take control. "Brad was no doubt the number one college player in the States this year before he injured his shoulder. There's no guarantee he'll ever be able to play at that level again. I feel strongly that he will and maybe better than before. Brad and I have been working on a program that will orchestrate his throwing motion with his body and muscle make up. If this theory works, it will benefit many people. We can work with pitchers to make them better, and we can work this into the prosthetic field to make the computerized replacement limbs better than ever."

"Brad filled me in on your idea Friday after he picked us up from the airport. It's a very interesting theory," Miles said. "I think I see where you're coming from. Please continue with your presentation."

"I have a contract for Brad that works two ways," Keith broke in impatiently. "We are willing to pay Brad a $500,000.00 signing bonus to either play for the Dodgers in the future, or coach for us for a minimum of three years. As I said earlier, it's a gamble, but we believe Brad is worth it. He'll be an asset as a player or a coach."

Brad and Anne looked at each other trying to conceal their smile. Anne grabbed Brad's hand and held it tight. "That's a lot of money Mr. Olson," she said. "What's the catch?"

"There's no catch," Keith said in a matter of fact tone. "We want him in our organization and not with another team. Brad has great leadership qualities that we can use. I talked to Coach Culley, and he verified Bill's assessment of Brad."

"There might be a slight catch," Bill chided in. "I have a contract for Brad to sign to make this whole plan work. Brad will agree to be employed with my company for at least one year to work on our project. This will give us time to work on this program and apply it towards Brad's rehabilitation and pitching motion. He needs to have a different throwing motion, so he won't put so much pressure on his damaged shoulder. And while he's working for me, he'll be working out to strengthen his arm and shoulder per the data from the computer program."

Norris gave a brief laugh and then turned to Bill. "So you'll have a contract with the Dodgers also? I should've known you had a motive in this deal to work so hard on closing it."

"Now Norris, Brad is the winner in this matter," Bill said defensively.

"I was just kidding you Bill. I believe that we all appreciate the effort you made in putting this together, right Miles?"

"Sounds like a great deal to me," Miles said, astonished from the monetary figure and the back up plan for his son. "What are you planning to pay Brad for his service to your company Bill?"

"I will pay him a fair weekly salary while he's still in school and then an executive salary after graduation. He will be compensated well, I guarantee it," Bill replied.

"What is well?" Norris asked.

"It'll depend on Brad's progress with his rehab and working on his new throwing motion. This could take a few years to make him the player that he wants to be. The Dodger organization doesn't want him to pitch if he isn't one hundred percent. So to answer your question, I might need to send Brad to Indiana to help open our new facility there if he hasn't progressed enough physically to play ball. That would be a two hundred K plus per year job. I can't see a risk on his behalf."

"I'd like to get this contract signed before I leave. No pressure though," Keith said with a big smile as he handed Brad the contract.

Norris stood up, and walked up to his desk, and grabbed two contracts. He took one contract for himself and handed the other to Miles with a wink.

Miles took the contract with a sense of pride. He was grateful for the Weatherbys and glad for Brad's decision to marry Anne.

An hour later, the contracts were signed and a large check was handed to the newly married couple. Everyone was a winner in this deal. Brad would make sure of that.

CHAPTER 13

▼

Fall turned into winter as the once color filled trees shed their leaves, giving the appearance that they had died. The air was cold, which was normal for mid January in North Carolina, but it was a cloudless day with the sun bringing life to the winter day.

Today was Anne's first visit to the doctor since her suspicion of being pregnant. She dressed in a baggy sweater and loose fitting jeans. She had only put on a few additional pounds, so nobody would even guess she might be pregnant. She thought that by waiting long enough to verify the new life in her, would put doubt in her mind that she might not have been pregnant when she wed. It wasn't for her alone, but for others, like both sets of parents.

Anne had been eating more than usual since Brad had moved in after their wedding, so that might explain the few extra pounds she had added to her cute body. She still had not had a period since the first time they made love, giving her good reason to believe she was indeed pregnant. She just wasn't real sure when she conceived. Today should answer that question. It was three months to the day since that marvelous weekend of lovemaking that relieved her of her virginity.

Anne had not told Brad about her appointment today. He had been urging her to go doctor to see if she was indeed pregnant to erase their uncertainty.

Anne opened the door to the hospital like she had done hundreds of times before. Her shift didn't start for two hours allowing her plenty of time to spend with her doctor. She went to a different floor today and checked in at the front desk. She didn't know anyone working the desk today, which gave her some relief.

"Don't worry about it. You're married now, and it doesn't matter if you turn up pregnant," she said to herself. Anne walked over to a magazine rack and picked up "First Baby," a book she assumed was about going through your first pregnancy.

She had read enough of the book to validate her suspicion that it was about going through your first pregnancy from the first trimester to the actual birth itself. She was really getting into the book when the nurse called her name. Hearing the words Anne Preston brought a big smile to her face because she loved being married to Brad. If only they had more time together without homework or business papers to review.

"Right this way Mrs. Preston," the nurse said as her arm motioned her to a small room. They both entered the sterile feeling room that had a cold environment.

Anne shuddered when she saw the stainless steel table with the stirrups, hating the thought of lying there with her legs spread for the whole world to see.

The nurse watched Anne closely sensing her nervousness. "Why don't you just sit down and relax for a minute while I take your vitals."

Anne sat down and gave the nurse a friendly smile. "Thank you. I guess I'm pretty nervous. This is the first time I've been for a pregnancy test."

By the time the nurse took her blood pressure and temperature, Anne had settled down somewhat. It was all too familiar with her, but she was always on the other side of doctor patient relationship.

"Everything looks great here," the nurse said as she wrote down a few things on Anne's chart. The nurse rose to her feet asking Anne to undress and put on the gown that she handed her, and then told Anne the doctor would be in shortly.

Thankfully it was only a few minutes when there was a knock on the door.

"Is it alright to come in now?"

"Yes, I'm in the gown now," Anne answered, pulling at her gown to cover herself. Anne was thankful that her doctor was a female. "Good to see you Dr. Phillips. I guess it's my turn to be on the receiving end at the hospital."

"Your not the first nurse here to see me," the doctor answered with a calming smile. "Now what are we here for today?"

Anne's fingers were busy gnawing at the light weight hospital gown. "I need to have a pregnancy test. It's been close to three months since my last period, and I've never been late before."

Dr. Phillips sat down at the small desk as she put her reading glasses on and proceeded to read Anne's chart. She tilted her head down to see Anne over the frame of her glasses. "I don't see anywhere on your chart where you were on birth control. Were you trying to get pregnant?"

Anne blushed as her cheeks turned were bright red. She folded and unfolded her hands. "I wasn't trying to get pregnant," she said meekly. "We just married, and it was the first time I ever had sex, and I thought it was safe."

"Anne, how long have you been a nurse here?" the doctor scolded her. "Well, do you want to be pregnant?"

"I really hadn't planned on it. But we just married, and things happened so fast."

"It's alright now, just relax. I just want to know what your plans are if you turn out to be pregnant. Since you're married, it makes sense to have a baby. It just makes it more cumbersome to start a marriage with a child. How does your husband feel about the possibility of becoming a father?"

"He's like me. It hadn't crossed his mind to have a baby at this time, but he is excited about the possibility of us having one."

"That's a good start," the doctor replied as she stood up. "Before we get a nursery going it might be a good idea to verify the fact you are indeed pregnant. Don't you agree?"

Anne laughed. "Yes, that's what I learned in school."

"Let's do a quick blood test just to make it more accurate. I'll send Linda in to pull blood, and I'll return in a minute to give you a check up. Have you taken a test at home?"

"No, I thought it'd be better to do it here. It's not out of my way to come here," Anne answered, not wanting the doctor to know the real reason she had not done a home pregnancy test.

Dr. Phillips gave a brief laugh as she left the room.

Anne stood up and paced the room looking at all of the medicines and medical equipment she worked with daily. What seemed weird to her, was the fact she wanted to be pregnant. The three months of preparation had made her think so much about all of the positive aspects of having a baby that now she wanted it to be true. She kept thinking just how beautiful this child would be.

A quick knock at the door brought her back to the present as an elderly nurse came in to pull her blood. The nurse was an expert and pulled the blood sample without any trouble. It didn't even hurt. Nurse Linda stood up and grabbed the handle to the door. "That should do it honey. The doctor will be right back."

Within a few minutes Dr. Phillips reentered the exam room where Anne was waiting. "We will get the test back shortly. In the meantime, I want to give you a complete examination if you don't mind?"

"That's fine with me. It's been a while," Anne replied as she got to her feet and went to the examination table.

The exam went well, verifying Anne's good health and not revealing any problems. After a short question and answer session, they were interrupted by the phone ringing. Dr. Phillips answered the phone and wrote down some notes on Anne's chart.

Anne's stomach was turning at this time as the anxiety of knowing for sure if she was pregnant or not had peaked. She was sure the call was from the lab with her results. Her fingernails dug into the cushion of her chair as she prepared herself for the news. She hoped it was positive. That is, she hoped the test was positive. She wanted Brad's baby.

Dr. Phillips finished writing and turned her attention to Anne. "Well Mrs. Preston, the test shows that you're pregnant."

Anne's entire body filled with excitement, and her mind was full of wonderful thoughts as she digested the news. "Oh good!"

"Well good then. I wasn't sure how you'd feel about the news."

"I know it isn't the best way to start off a marriage, but it will add something more special to an already great relationship. We'll both be out of school by the time the baby is born."

"Well it sounds to me like the two of you are blessed then. I want to see you again in a month to make sure that things are progressing well. That'll finish your first trimester. You know that you should not smoke or drink alcohol, and please stay away from the x-ray area," Dr. Phillips said in a motherly tone.

"I don't smoke, and I won't drink, and I normally don't do anything with x-rays here anyway. Should I quit working here since there are sick people that I'll be in contact with?"

"You have to be more careful on being around certain people that are contagious. Your wing is more of a surgical recovery area that normally does not have that highly contagious patient there. But be cognizant of every patient in your area from now on. You never know," the doctor said with a concerned smile. Dr. Phillips gently grabbed Anne's hand and patted it. "You're a very smart girl. Just watch what you do and rely on your medical skills on doing the right thing. I'll see you in a month."

The remainder of Anne's day at the hospital seemed to last forever. Her four hours of work seemed like twelve. She couldn't wait to get home and tell Brad the news. Her stomach was rolling from being nervous about his reaction. She thought to herself that it was easier for Brad to be bold about the prospect of being a father, but it could be quite different when the news was definite. She also feared both sets of parents would not accept the news of a baby in a good way.

Anne put together a plan for the evening while she worked. Since it was Friday, Brad would expect the two of them to go have pizza at Italian Village, but today would be different.

When work finally ended, she called ahead for a carry out, and stopped by the store to get a special card and some beer for Brad, and then picked up the pizza.

She arrived home relieved to see that Brad was not there yet. It gave her time to prepare everything. She wrote a special note in his card, set the table, and created the right ambience for the mood with candles and dim lighting. She iced down a beer for Brad, so it would be the right temperature for him. After placing the pizza in the warm oven and chilling the rest of the beer in the refrigerator, Anne walked to the window to see if Brad was close to home. She clapped her hands together and rubbed them against her jeans. They were clammy. "Relax!" she yelled out.

Anne started pacing nervously and then went back to the window to see if Brad was coming. Her heart almost leaped out of her body at the sight of him strolling up the sidewalk towards their apartment. His hair was still damp from his shower.

Brad was ambushed with a loving hug and numerous kisses as he walked into his home.

"Missed me that much did you?" he asked lovingly. He hugged her back hard and looked into her eyes. There was a glow there that had been missing lately. He felt guilty they couldn't do more things together outside of schoolwork and their own jobs.

"I always miss you."

"Give me a second to put my things away, and we can continue this." He started sniffing the air in search of the special aroma he picked up on and turned to her upon recognizing the smell of his favorite pizza. "What's up honey? We normally go to IV's on Friday nights."

"I thought we needed a special night at home for a change. We both have tomorrow off you know," she said, feeling guilty about fibbing.

Brad finished putting his things away before he returned to his beautiful wife who was waiting for him with a fresh cold beer and a card. "What's this?"

"I just want to tell you how much I love you," she replied as her eyes sparkled with joy.

"You're doing a fine job of that." He kissed her hard and took a drink of his favorite brew, before opening his card.

Anne stood rigid preparing herself for his reaction. Her insides were in knots and she was having problems breathing.

Brad read the front of the card and then opened it to read what was on the inside. His entire body locked up as he saw the picture of a baby. He went on to read the handwritten message from Anne, stating that they would be sharing their life with their baby. Tears of joy rolled down his cheeks.

"I hope those are happy tears," Anne said anxiously.

"They are honey. So you finally went to the doctor?"

"Yes I did, and everything is great. The test was positive, and I'm healthy."

Brad laid down the card and his beer, and went up to Anne giving her the most loving hug possible. "Do you want a boy or girl?"

"I hadn't thought about it that much yet. I don't care as long as it's healthy. It'd be nice to have a boy that's just like you," she stated as she had a vision of a cute baby boy in her arms.

"I was thinking it would be great to have a girl just like you. Something that beautiful and precious would be a nice addition to this world. Well, I guess we need to add a nursery to this little place. Well, maybe not here though. When's your due date?"

"I'd say somewhere around mid July. Maybe a few weeks later than that. It really depends on when I conceived.

"We graduate in May of next year, so that gives us time to move to a permanent house. I just wonder where we'll be then," Brad said, knowing that he needed to make a decision on the Indianapolis location that Bill wanted him to head up. Time was running out, and now with a baby on the way it added to the urgency for them to decide.

"Yes, we need to make that decision soon." Anne wasn't keen on the idea of moving away. She loved North Carolina, and hated to leave it as well as her family. Anne's stomach did a flip-flop from the thought of her family and the fact that she had to tell them she was pregnant. She prayed they wouldn't assume that she was with child before she wed Brad. Anne slowly walked over to the end table to gather the phone.

"Are you sure you want to call them now?" Brad asked as he grabbed her from behind and pulled her close to him.

"I need to get it over with. Besides, there's good news in this situation. I'm truly excited knowing that I have your baby inside me. I know that sounds weird, but that's how I feel. I just pray that our parents will accept the news as well as we have." She put her hands together and looked up to heaven.

"I'm excited as well. Sometimes you have to believe there's a plan for you beyond your control by the big guy up above. I'll never question his decision in this matter."

"Good, because he trumps your plans anyway. Well, here goes the call to mom and dad," she said as she dialed their number.

Brad stood by Anne's side to make sure the call was going well. He could hear that Grace was sincerely excited by the news. She never questioned Anne about when it happened.

Anne continued to talk to both of her parents while Brad walked over to pick up the card that gave him the big news. He read it several times and then walked over to the living room window. Staring out into the darkness of the evening, he thought of everything that had happened to him over the past year. He knew if he had been told a year ago that at this time in his life he would be married with his wife pregnant and out of baseball, he would have told that person they were nuts. He thought about how funny life is, but that's what makes it so exciting. He turned around to see if Anne was still on the phone.

Anne noticed Brad glancing at her and ended the phone call with her parents, so she could deliver to him their reaction. "They were ecstatic after their initial shock," she said, smiling from ear to ear. "Mom wants to take me shopping soon. You know how she is. We have to get the right maternity clothing and some things for the upcoming baby. God I'm glad that's over. Thank you Brad."

"Thank you for what?"

"Thank you for handling this whole situation in such a positive way. And thank you for having the fore thought of getting married so quick and actually doing it. You're something special, and I'll always remember this for the rest of my life. God I love you!" She rushed over to him to hold him.

"I love you too. It's not like I did you a favor you know. You're a gift to me that I'll always cherish. I can't wait to hold our child in my arms," Brad finished as tears rolled down his face.

Anne's eyes filled with tears also from seeing Brad cry. "I can't wait either," was all she could get out of her mouth.

Brad then called his family with the news, which was received with the same excitement and shock as the Weatherby's.

With the weight of the world off their shoulders, Anne retrieved the pizza from the oven, and they sat down to eat and relax for the rest of the evening.

CHAPTER 14

▼

Brad and Anne finished unpacking the last box, ending the long move from Durham to Indianapolis. June was just a week away, but the temperature felt like summer was already in full bloom. With the help of Brad's parents, the young couple had found a great house perfect for them and their upcoming baby. They closed on the purchase of their new homestead just days after their graduation.

Anne was relieved to get the move out of the way and have the burden of school work finally end. She hated to leave her home state of North Carolina, although the new house helped diminish those feelings. She found Indianapolis to be similar in size to Charlotte, but lacking the southern charm her home town possessed. Anne was happy with her life. She prayed that she would now have more time with Brad because the past eight months had been extremely hectic for both of them.

Brad had been overloaded more than Anne as he had a tough medical class to take that Bill insisted on him enrolling in to help out in his new job. Brad had also been working hard to strengthen his shoulder, which didn't leave much time for the two of them.

Anne's pregnancy could not have gone any better. She was healthy, and so was the unborn baby who was putting extreme pressure on her mid section at this time. But it was all worth it to her because she loved Brad more than ever. Maybe too much she thought at times. She loved the little one in her belly also and couldn't wait to hold the tiny body in her arms and see its cute face.

Brad was more than happy to end his college days. With his sport days gone, college didn't have the special appeal to him that it once had. He was really enjoying his work with prosthetics. He had some major input on some improvements to the product they developed, which led to greater profits for Bill's company. Brad's shoulder was about ninety percent healed at this time, but he refrained from throwing. He wanted to develop the program to customize his form with his body and muscular make up. He knew that he could make the program work.

Brad decided to take the Indianapolis job offer because he felt he owed it to Bill for all he had done for the two of them. Plus, he liked the challenge it offered. The only drawback was he would not have as much time to work on his computer program that would allow him to reinvent his pitching motion. But baseball was not as important as it once was in his life. His marriage to Anne and their child on the way took over his focus. He hoped he now would have time to show Anne that she and the baby were the most important things in his life. Their new life in the Indianapolis area would be the start of their new life together. They not only graduated from college, they graduated into adult/parent hood.

The first seven weeks of their life in Indiana flew by. Brad's work was demanding, causing him to work additional hours. Anne worked hard on getting the house arranged to her liking and preparing the nursery. She wanted the house and nursery to be perfect, which fit her personality.

They had refused to find out the sex of the baby because the mystery of not knowing whether it was a boy or girl was a nice touch. They decided to name the baby Brian if it was a boy or Brianna if it was a girl. Their thinking was the names would be a symbolic combination of the two of them into one child.

Anne woke up with back cramps, and it appeared that the day had finally come to find out what the name of their newborn child would be. Anne's labor pains came on quick and hard. Luckily it was Sunday morning and Brad was home with her. She couldn't imagine how she would have handled the situation if he hadn't been there with her.

Brad gathered the pre-packed suitcase, and loaded it in the car, and then retrieved Anne for their drive to the hospital. He called the hospital from the house, but didn't have time to call their parents, so he waited until they got in the car and called the prospective grandparents from his cell phone.

His mom and dad told Brad they would meet them at the hospital while the Weatherby's informed him they would arrange a flight to Indianapolis right away.

Brad couldn't believe how fast everything was happening. It seemed to him that Anne was about ready to give birth in the car. His panic subsided when he pulled into the parking lot of the hospital. He turned to look at Anne and was shocked by the redness in her face and sweat pouring from her body. He decided that the emergency room entrance would be their best choice.

Getting help from the emergency nurses, they hurried Anne to a birthing room. Fate was with them today as her doctor was present making her morning rounds. The preliminary examination indicated she was already at seven centimeters, which was a surprise to her doctor.

Anne was working hard, but was able to blurt out to Brad, "It has to be a boy. It's just like you, in a big hurry."

Brad was having trouble keeping his emotions in check. The excitement, along with the anxiety of the situation made him want to cry. "We will know shortly," he replied to her.

Twenty minutes later the doctor came back to her room dressed in scrubs prepared to deliver the special gift to both of them. Dr. Miller re-examined Anne and was surprised to find her at almost ten centimeters. "You work fast Mrs. Preston. I'm going to give you a local down here to help with the pain. It might not work in time since you're progressing so fast."

With the particularly hard contractions, Anne was working harder now, which amazed Brad that she was going to deliver without any painkillers.

"It's coming," Dr. Miller shouted calmly. "Ok Anne, give us a big push now."

Anne took her command serious from the doctor by pushing hard and moving the baby down the birth canal.

"I have the head now honey, so give me one more hard push," Dr. Miller ordered after putting her hands under the small wet head of the baby.

In an instant, the baby was born with arms flailing and legs kicking. Brad got a glimpse of his child and started crying from the joy of the arrival of their baby and the knowledge that everything went well.

"Looks like we have a very healthy girl here. Would the father like to cut the cord?" the doctor asked, turning her direction towards Brad.

"Sure," Brad replied. He took the stainless steel scissors from the doctor and attempted to cut the cord. He failed the first time stunned by how tough the cord was. He put the scissors in position and worked it in a saw like action, and this time executed his deed. He noticed that some blood had spurted on his clothing, but it didn't bother him because it was the blood of his daughter, and she was alive and well.

The doctor laid the newborn child on her mother's stomach to allow Anne to see her miracle. Tears tricked down Anne's face, but not enough to hide the love that glowed from her for her baby girl.

"Oh my God!" Anne exclaimed. "She is beautiful! Is everything there?"

"Everything's there, just the way it's supposed to be. She appears to be quite healthy, but we'll do the standard tests to confirm," the doctor replied. "Now let's get the after birth out of the way."

A nurse took the baby to start the clean up process and perform all of the tests while the doctor finished up with Anne.

Brad walked over to watch the nurse while glancing at Anne to make sure everything was going well there. He felt a twinge as they pulled blood from his daughter, causing her to cry out in pain. Poor little thing, he thought.

The nurse cleaned up Brianna and dressed her before she handed Brad his daughter.

The moment Brad held Brianna in his arms, was the moment that his life changed forever. She was the most precious thing he had ever seen. There was an instant bond between the two as she seemed to cuddle up against Brad looking quite content in her father's arms. It was a moment that only happened a few times in anyone's life, and it was overwhelming to Brad. Tears once again flowed from his eyes from the emotional experience.

"Hey you," Anne yelled softly. "Why don't you bring me our little girl?"

"I'm sorry honey. I didn't forget you. I was waiting for the doctor to finish up with you, and I got caught up with the routines they put her through. She's lucky that she isn't a boy, if you know what I mean. That has to hurt," Brad said as he twisted his hips and gave a look of pain.

Anne laughed easily trying not to put any more pressure on her midsection. She took her precious child from Brad and pulled her close to her while staring at the beauty of her newborn baby. "Hello Brianna," she whispered softly. "I'm your mother, and that man that just held you is your father," she said, pointing to Brad with her finger.

She slowly rocked Brianna in her arms and looked up at Brad. "We did good honey."

"Yes we did," Brad said proudly. "It's a whole different life for us now."

"I know," Anne said as she took the baby's hand and wrapped it around her finger. "I can't believe how much I love her already."

"She's so small and precious. I just want to be there to protect her all of the time. I never want anything to happen to her."

"I feel confident that you'll always be there to make sure that nothing bad ever happens to her."

Brad gave her a smile. "I won't let anything happen to either one of you. I love you both, and I'd give my life for you two. By the way, how are you feeling? I can't believe you went through that without any painkillers. You're stronger than I am."

"I'm great. Just a little exhausted right now, but holding her and seeing her has me going strong. You know it hurt like hell, but it was worth it. I'd do it again." Anne stated, staring up at Brad.

"Let's get this one up in age some first," Brad scolded lightly, only to be interrupted by his parents entering the room.

The new grandparents gasped at the first sight of the newborn baby from the pure innocence of the child and knowing that this was their granddaughter. She was a perfect little baby that was almost a mirror of her mother with a splash of her father.

CHAPTER 15

▼

Present day

The fifteen minute drive to Brad's parent's house went by quick, with good conversation and scores of laughs. It had been some time since Brad and Anne had actually taken time to have some playful talk and physical contact, other than having sex every once in a while. The flame was burning hot again between them. Not that there was a loss of love between them, but they had centered so much of their life on Brianna, and Brad had buried himself in his work. It felt good to both of them to once again experience each other the way it should be.

Anne had become a little insecure with less attention from her husband, causing her to hide her true feelings for him. But tonight the spark was ignited, and they both felt it.

Before Brad retrieved his daughter from the jeep, he trotted around the vehicle to open Anne's door and then gave her a hard kiss.

"God I missed that part of you," Anne said, pulling him close to her, returning his kiss. "Let's not lose it again please. I love you so much."

"I promise."

"It's getting cold in here," the little voice in the car seat yelled out. "I want to see grandma."

"Ok honey," Brad said as he attempted to unlatch the child restraints on her seat. He fumbled with the center strap and successfully unsnapped the latch, and then pulled her from the seat and gave her a kiss. "You're getting big."

"Come on Daddy, let's hurry up. I'm hungry," Brianna said, squirming in his arms.

Margaret Preston opened the front door of the house to greet the three special guests. She instantly took Brianna from Brad's arms. "How is my precious Granddaughter tonight?"

"Good Grandma, and I'm hungry for chicken," the toddler said, licking her lips.

"Well you're just in luck. It's about time to eat. What's this?" Margaret asked, seeing the package of treats. "Are these cookies for us?"

"Yep, mommy and I made em today. Daddy said they were delicious," Brianna said with a giggle.

"I bet they are. How are you two doing tonight?" Mrs. Preston added, turning her attention to Brad and Anne. "Are you feeling alright?"

"We're just fine Mom," Brad said.

"It's good to see you," Anne chided in as she gave her mother in law a hug. "How've you been? Is this cold weather getting to you yet?"

"Miles and I were just saying today that it will be nice to leave this nasty weather. But we will miss you three," Mrs. Preston stated with some regret about moving.

Brad pulled Anne close to his side lovingly. "Well, we just might be moving south also. I plan on talking to Bill about the top management job in Charlotte."

"Well that would be good for you guys. Plus it would be closer to us. What made you decide to go for that position?" Margaret asked.

"I haven't decided one hundred percent, but it's a good opportunity for me, plus we're ready to get back down there. Hi Dad," Brad said as his father entered the room.

"What's this I hear about you moving?" Miles asked.

"Well, since the two of you are moving south, and I have the Indy office on course, I think it's time to talk to Bill about his desire for me to practically take over his business," Brad replied, still knowing he had to consider his contract with the Dodgers.

"That's great Son. I'm proud of you on the way you've handled your job. I could have used someone like you in our office when I was working."

"You did have someone like me Dad. It was you," Brad said, laughing. He then pulled Anne towards him and gave her a big hug followed by a kiss on the cheek.

Miles and Margaret were happy to see the closeness between Brad and Anne. They knew from the start there were many challenges a young couple faced from getting married so young, and then to have a baby right away only added to the stress. But it was clear to the proud parents that their son and daughter in law had triumphed over the obstacles in their path.

"I hate to run, but we're going to be late," Brad said as he gave Brianna a kiss good bye.

Anne gave Brianna a hug and a kiss, then sternly said, "Be good for grandma and grandpa, and we'll see you tomorrow." She turned to Margaret and asked, "What time do you want us to pick her up tomorrow?"

"Let's not worry about that now. You two have fun and enjoy yourselves. You need to do that sometimes," Margaret said, shaking her index finger at them.

"You're right. We do need to spend more time together, and tonight we'll have fun," Anne replied with a look of mischief.

Brad and Anne drove off to the party filled with a high level of sexual desire for each other. Brad put his hand on her knee rubbing it slowly. "It's good to see the woman I married back to her old self again."

"It's good to see my husband back to his old self also," Anne replied as she grabbed his thigh and slid her hand upward. "Oops, look's like someone else is glad to see me."

Brad squirmed in his seat and then ran his hand up her thigh. "Well yes I am. We have a party to go to you know?"

Anne gave him a devilish smile. "I know we have to go to Carol's birthday party, but it wouldn't hurt to turn into the golf side of the parking lot at the country club. It should be empty now."

Brad couldn't resist the invitation, so he pulled into the parking lot of the golf course seeing that Anne was correct in her assumption that it would be empty. He found a dark area and parked the Jeep Grand Cherokee. He was surprised to see his wife with her pants off already. "Whoa, you really are serious tonight."

"This is just the appetizer for later. Now make love to me, and show me how much you really love me."

"I do love you very much. I just wish I'd have shown you how much the past two years," he said as he worked hard to pull his trousers off. It was a difficult task with his tall body in a confined area, but he succeeded in his task.

Anne made her way over to her husband and sat on his lap. "You don't need to apologize now. We've both learned our lesson. Now let's quit talking and start rocking," she commanded as she worked her way on him.

They finished their quick session with perfect timing, giving them temporary relief from some of the sexual buildup they brought about earlier. Anne hated to dismount from Brad, but did so after holding him and kissing his delicious lips.

They both struggled getting dressed, but finally got presentable for their dinner party with Carol and the others.

Brad looked at his watch and cringed. "We're going to be a little late. I hope Carol isn't mad."

"She'll be just fine. Besides, we aren't that late. I know how close you two are, but she'll be happy to see you, even if you're late. It's been awhile you know," Anne replied while she straightened her sweater.

"It's been too long. I guess I've been working too hard and missing out on the people that are the most important to me."

"You haven't really missed out on Brianna and me. You've been a great father. You just haven't had a full tank left for me. But I should've been there for you more. I just felt a little insecure about you and me."

"It won't happen again. You two are my life. If I get the big job in Charlotte, I'll not let it run my life or our life. Let's just keep these feelings we shared tonight going strong for the rest of our lives."

"It's a deal. Now get moving. I want to wish Carol a happy birthday."

Brad sped out of the parking lot and headed for the party.

They made it to Carol's house in good time, making their tardiness minimal. Brad knocked on the door and then put his arm around Anne.

Carol answered the door, and Brad immediately said, "Sorry that we're a little late, but something came up at the last minute that put us behind. Happy birthday," he added as he pinched Anne on the butt.

Anne could hardly contain herself from busting out in laughter, so she hugged Carol. "Happy birthday Carol," she said giggling.

"Thanks," Carol replied as she gave them both a curious look. "Come on in and get out of the cold air. We were just having a drink since dinner isn't quite ready. You shouldn't have gotten me a present."

Brad was in a slap happy mood and laughing uncontrollably. "Oh it's not for you. It's for John." He then gave Carol a firm hug.

"Maybe you should just drink a coke Brad," Carol said, kidding.

"Believe it or not, we haven't had anything to drink tonight. Where's John?" Brad asked as he helped Anne with her coat.

Carol pointed towards the family room. "He's in there with the others. You look good tonight Anne," she said, fishing for the reason they were so giddy.

"Thanks Carol. It's been too long since we've gotten out of the house to do something, so I thought I'd take advantage and dress up a little."

John ran into Brad in the kitchen while retrieving drinks. They shook hands and made small talk. John had gone to high school with Brad, and they played football together. He was a fullback and linebacker, and he played with a lot of heart. John saved Brad from getting sacked many times and was one of Brad's favorite receivers. They brought up a few of their favorite football stories as they prepared drinks for the others.

"I'll take these two," John said.

The drinks were for Greg and Kristy, and he knew there were some ill feelings between the three. He just hoped that Greg would behave himself.

Carol and Anne joined them in the kitchen before they all headed off to join the others.

Kristy and Greg, Heather and her husband Rob, and a couple that Brad didn't know were all sitting in the family room having polite conversation with one another. Carol introduced the unknown couple as her new neighbors, Craig and Julie Hamilton.

There was an instant air of coolness from Greg when Brad and Anne entered the room. It was elevated when he saw how happy Brad and Anne were together.

The Prestons were so much in touch with each other that they weren't cognizant of Greg's attitude, even though they said hello to Kristy and him.

Greg sat back and sucked his drink down as he watched how smooth Brad was on getting to know the Hamilton's. He grabbed Kristy's drink and took a big gulp of it before he headed to the kitchen for another.

John decided that it would a good idea to have a quick talk with Greg. He didn't want his wife's birthday party to be ruined by an immature idiot. "Hey buddy, why don't you slow down a bit? We have all night to drink," he said to Greg in a soothing tone.

"What are you talking about?" Greg replied with a grunt.

"Come on Greg, it's Carol's birthday. You don't have to get upset because Brad's here. He's never done anything to you."

"Brad doesn't bother me," Greg said, lying. "I was just thirsty. I had a hard day at work. Besides Brad and I go way back."

As he retreated back to the family room, John left Greg somewhat satisfied that Greg would behave himself. The talk did help a little, or so it seemed, as Greg hid his true feelings from the others. Only Kristy knew that he was putting on a show on concealing his hostility for Brad.

Kristy was unusually quiet tonight as she stared at Brad and Anne. She witnessed how happy they were together and the way they were touching each other. It pulled at her heart to see it because she still loved Brad. Kristy turned her attention totally towards Anne. She never realized just how beautiful Anne was. It was the first time that she had seen Anne so full of energy and personality, and it made her realize that she could never be capable of turning heads the way that Anne could.

Kristy admired Anne's perfect body, thinking no one would have guessed she had delivered a baby a few years earlier. She watched Anne's actions and listened to her talk with her cute southern accent, learning more about Anne than ever before. Kristy was jealous, but not envious. She grew to respect Anne and knew she was no match for Brad's wife. She smiled to herself, thinking that Brad got what he deserved, a beautiful, intelligent, and lively woman.

"Hey I'm still here. Don't forget me just because he's here," Greg said after he poked Kristy. He had been watching Kristy's full attention towards the Prestons, and he didn't like it.

Kristy turned to Greg with a look of disgust and got up to talk to Carol. There wasn't anyone paying any attention to Greg, and that wasn't the way he liked things.

Greg was very insecure about himself. His muscled body had turned a little flabby over the years from not working out, and his hair was just starting to thin. He was a car salesman with a laborer's mindset. He didn't have the charisma that Brad possessed, and tried to make up for it by being funny. What made matters worse, was the fact that everything was so natural for Brad, while they weren't for Greg. Life was so unfair Greg thought. "But I'll change that someday," he said to himself, seething with jealousy. Greg stood up to follow the men out of the room. He went in the kitchen first to refresh his drink though.

That left the five women in the room together. Heather and Julie started asking Anne questions, so they could get to know her better.

Kristy's ears perked when Julie asked Anne how she met Brad.

Anne faced Julie, but moved her eyes to catch a glimpse of Kristy. She noticed Kristy leaning forward and hesitated to answer, but then thought it was best to be honest and tell them all how she met Brad. "We both went to college at Duke University, where I'd been taking nursing classes. I was employed by the Duke Medical Center in the spring of my junior year. Brad had to have surgery on his shoulder, and I just happened to be his nurse. That was the first time we had seen each other in our three years at Duke," she said purposely, to let Kristy know she was not the cause of their breakup.

Kristy's body stiffened while uncontrollable tears spilled from her eyes. Her mind was racing, thinking of all the lies that Greg had told her. She had to know more, but not in front of the others.

Carol sensed her best girlfriend's dilemma and asked the other two girls to help her get the food on the table, leaving Kristy and Anne together alone for the first time.

Meanwhile, Greg realized his wife and Anne were not with the other women, so he found a place to hide to enable him to spy on the two of them. It was too odd for them to be alone.

"Well Kristy, here we are face to face with nobody around," Anne started out, knowing there might be a confrontation.

Kristy wiped the tears from her eyes and looked over at Anne. "You met Brad in the hospital after his surgery?"

"Yes, that is correct," Anne replied a little uneasy.

"I'm sorry to ask you these questions, but it's important to me," Kristy said, embarrassed.

"Look Kristy, I'm not your enemy. Brad told me about you. I'm sure he left out a lot of details, but he filled me in pretty good." Anne got up and walked over to Kristy and sat next to her.

Kristy tilted her head towards Anne studying her even closer. "Was he seeing someone else when he met you?"

"No he wasn't," Anne said as her words sent a sharp pain into Kristy's gut. "I was the only woman after you. Brad felt betrayed and was afraid to see anyone after you two broke up. He just dove into baseball and school that much more. He told me that he was a little timid about starting another relationship." Anne said with a serious expression.

Kristy had more tears in her eyes and she grabbed Anne's hand. "I hope I haven't been a bitch to you. I always thought you were the one that broke us up." Kristy was now beside herself. She realized that she married a man that lied to her over and over, and now showed signs of being abusive to her.

Greg was seething now, seeing his wife upset because of Brad. He knew that she still had feelings for him. He was fighting the rage that had consumed him, but it was too late. This put him over the edge. He was now consumed with revenge since his life was less than mediocre. "Settle down man, there'll be a time to take care of this," he said to himself.

"We better go help the others with dinner," Anne said. "Unless you have other questions for me?"

"No more questions right now," Kristy replied, getting up. "Thanks Anne for being up front with me. I know that it can't be easy on you."

"It's fine," Anne said as she led Kristy into the kitchen.

Dinner was going smoothly with everyone enjoying Carol's homemade lasagna.

Julie broke the silence by asking Brad, "So, you met Anne in the hospital?"

Brad swallowed his food hard, causing him to almost choke. He made a fist with his hand and put it over his mouth to cough slightly. "Yes, I met here after my surgery," he finally replied, after gathering himself. He thought it might be best to add some humor to break any tension in the room. "I'm surprised that she would want to date me after hearing my first words to her."

"And what were the words?" Julie asked curiously. She really liked Anne and was hoping to build a friendship with her.

Brad sipped his wine. "I asked her if she was a good witch or a bad witch."

Everybody but Greg broke out in laughter.

Craig broke in the conversation by asking, "Were you on drugs man?"

Brad laughed hard. "Why yes I was."

Greg couldn't stand the attention that Brad was getting. Plus, he was about totally drunk by now. He decided to throw a jab and a right hook to Brad verbally. "So Brad, how do you feel about being a big shot with a large corporation and not being able to play ball anymore?"

Brad pondered the question, trying to decide if he should do a rope a dope or throw an upper cut to Greg.

He didn't decide by himself, because Anne threw the jab to set up the upper cut by saying, "Well, he's not out of baseball for good. He has a contract with the Dodgers."

Brad was stunned by her aggressiveness and finished the knock out by landing an upper cut to Greg's jaw by saying, "I enjoy my work, but it hasn't kept me out of baseball. We are working on a program that will provide me and other pitchers a customized throwing motion that will put less strain on the critical areas of one's body from throwing hard. I'm one hundred percent healed from the incident that put me out of commission, but I have refused to pitch until I prototype my form. And if I can't pitch again, I have a contract to coach with the Dodgers."

Greg would have been declared knocked out in the boxing ring. The news he heard from Brad came unexpected, and he couldn't respond. He knew that everyone was looking at him like he was a jerk.

John thought quickly by gathering the presents for Carol to open.

That eased the tension at the table for everyone except Greg. He was ready to spit bullets by now, but thought it best to just shut up. He would take care of this matter on his own terms.

Carol opened her presents and was especially pleased with her gift from the Prestons. She had mentioned one time that she wanted a particular set of Waterford wine glasses, but didn't want to spend the money on them. Brad remembered her desire for the glasses and purchased a set of four for his true friend.

Greg's anger elevated to another level from seeing Brad give such a nice present to Carol, whereas the present he and Kristy gave was pale in comparison.

The rest of the evening progressed much better because Greg grabbed Kristy after the cake was served and demanded she take him home.

It was a relief for everyone, except for Kristy. She knew that she was going to get it later from Greg, and it wasn't going to be pretty.

Brad and Anne stayed a little while longer, and then excused themselves to leave. They had made plans earlier, and they were going to stick to them.

"Well, that was quite an evening." Brad stated as they drove away. "I'm sorry to put you through all of that."

"You can't feel like it was your doing tonight. Greg has some serious problems. I feel sorry for Kristy. She's really a nice person. I see now what you saw in her," Anne replied sincerely, while taking Brad's hand in hers.

"But didn't you feel uncomfortable all night?" Brad asked, amazed by her response.

"Only at first, but I relaxed after I talked with Kristy."

"You talked to Kristy?" Brad asked, taken off guard.

"Yes, we had a small talk. Kristy found out some news tonight that shocked her." Anne wasn't sure how much she wanted to say to Brad, but she decided to tell him the whole story. She no longer felt insecure, so she explained everything and made mention that she did not trust Greg. There was evil in him, and she suspected he abused Kristy.

Brad absorbed everything and acknowledged Greg's problem. "It's a good thing that we'll be moving away from here."

"Yes, the timing is right for us to make the move," she said as she pulled his hand to her lips and kissed it softly, sending a sensual sensation through his body.

They spent the entire night making passionate love, with brief sessions of talking about their future. Sleep was not a priority because they were too wound up sexually and full of an array of mixed emotions from the prospect of moving.

Change was always difficult for the two of them.

CHAPTER 16

▼

The wheels were in motion for the young Preston family to move away from the Indianapolis area. Brad made the call to Bill to let him know he was interested in the big job in Charlotte.

Bill was ecstatic with the news, but reminded Brad of his contract with the Dodgers. They decided they would discuss all of the pending issues on Thursday morning.

It was decided that Brad would fly down to Charlotte on Wednesday night by himself since nothing was set in stone about moving to North Carolina. Brad and Anne thought it would be best if he flew down by himself to discuss with Bill the North Carolina job offer and the Dodger's contract, before going further with their plans. If things worked out, Anne would fly down with Brianna on the weekend to look for housing with Brad. That would allow for Anne to take care of some business here at home.

The excitement filled the air throughout their house. They both felt confident that Bill would give Brad the job since Brad had done such a great job getting the Indianapolis location going. The Indy office shouldn't suffer much of a loss because Brad had groomed a young lady to take over his position, and he had no reservations concerning her ability to manage the Indy office.

Brad had worked hard on Wednesday preparing a proposal for a production change on a new prosthetic device. He helped Leslie with all of the details, so she could handle the presentation without any problem. It was an idea he created from his work on maximizing the usage of an artificial limb. He just needed the stamp of approval from the product development supervisor to make sure that they could produce the device and confirm it would work. If his idea proved right, it would give their company an edge over the rest of the competition.

Brad hated to miss out on the proposal, but Leslie would be the champion of the project if he moved to Charlotte, so it was best for her to be involved with the presentation.

Brad packed his briefcase with some paperwork that Bill needed to review, and left for home. He would have a quick dinner with Anne and Brianna and then go to the airport. Everything was planned and on schedule.

Brianna was especially glad to see her father home this evening. She knew he was going to be away for a few days, but wasn't quite sure what that meant. She just knew that he couldn't tuck her in tonight, and she didn't like that. So Brianna hung on to her dad until they left for the airport.

Brad double checked his bags and popped open his briefcase to verify that his airline tickets were there. He let out a moan when he noticed that he mistakenly put the presentation for tomorrow in his briefcase. "Ah gees," he complained.

"What's wrong?" Anne asked concerned.

"Leslie has to give this presentation tomorrow, and I have all of the paperwork with me."

"Can't you just fax it?" Anne stated, trying to come up with a simple solution.

"I could, but there are some x-rays that are part of the proposal, and they won't fax."

She walked up behind Brad and gave him a hug. "What time's the meeting? I can take them to office for you. Don't worry about it."

"If you don't mind honey that would be great. The meeting is first thing in the morning," Brad said, feeling guilty about having Anne take her time to take care of his problem.

"That's ok. Brianna and I can get going a little early tomorrow. Besides, I won't be able to sleep that well with you gone and with everything else going on in our lives right now.

Brad turned around and pulled Anne close to give her a good kiss. "I'm going to miss you two you know."

"And we'll miss you too," Anne replied, holding him tight.

"Yeah daddy, I'm gonna miss you. You won't be here to tuck me in," Brianna said with a cute pucker on her lips.

The three of them did their family hug and then put on their coats to depart for the airport.

Brad put Brianna's car seat in his car since it was a better ride than their SUV.

Anne dropped Brad off at the terminal and then drove Brianna and herself home. She had some things to finish around the house, so it would look pristine when the real estate agent came to do a market analysis on it. She prayed that everything would go their way, so they could move back south. She missed North Carolina.

Morning came too fast, causing Anne to rush around the house getting the two of them ready, so they could deliver the proposal to Brad's work. It had started snowing again, although it wasn't too bad yet. They were calling for three to six inches today.

"Another reason to leave Indiana," she said to herself. Anne decided to take the Audi since it had Brianna's car seat in it. Besides she thought, it handled as well as the jeep in the snow.

Greg Somanski had been busy planning a way to get revenge on Brad ever since he woke up on Saturday morning following Carol's birthday party with a self inflicted hang over. Greg's rage had turned psychotic from the events of the party, and he was now scheming to take Brad out for good. He had left the house early on Monday morning and drove to Brad's subdivision. He tailed Brad to work to get an accurate route of his commute and to get a time line set. Greg then drove the same path back towards his rival's house making mental notes to himself before he drove to work, all the while thinking of ways to execute a plan to kill Brad.

On Tuesday morning Greg positioned his car on a hill that overlooked the road that Brad routinely traveled on his drive to work. He was positioned at the center of the sharp curve where a section of guardrail was missing, leading down to a very deep ravine. Greg considered using his rifle to shoot Brad, but thought better of the idea since it could trace the murder to him. He decided that Brad's death should appear to be an accident instead.

Looking the area over, he determined he could force Brad's car off the road at such an angle as to cause the vehicle to pass through the opening where the missing guardrail was. The driver of the car would surely be killed because the tree-ridden ravine was so deep, it would cause the vehicle to ricochet from tree to tree and more than likely continuously roll down the remainder of the steep incline. Greg was surprised that the County Highway Department hadn't replaced the missing section of guardrail, but he was glad they hadn't as of yet. This was definitely a plan worth looking in to.

The following day Greg did the same thing. He watched Brad drive through the curve at almost the same identical time as the two previous days. He had a good view of the road from both directions to help insure that he could execute the plan without another car driving by to witness the killing. Everything looked good. He even had a vehicle he could use without anyone's knowledge that didn't belong to him. It was a pickup truck he sold to an individual that had a snow plow installed on the front. Greg knew the owner was out of town because the guy had offered Greg the right to hunt on his property. The owner told Greg he would be out of the state for a month, but feel free to hunt anytime he wanted to.

The plan was almost set. Greg just wanted to confirm that the truck was parked where he could get it and also make sure that the owner was indeed out of town. Greg's ears perked when he heard the weather forecast for Thursday. There was a snow watch with a chance of three to six inches. Things were working out just the way he wanted. Thursday would hopefully be Brad Preston's last day on earth. Adrenaline rushed through Greg's body as he was pumped by the idea. It even aroused him sexually. Life was great again.

The snow had started to come down hard now as Anne carefully navigated the Audi through the winding hilly roads on her way to Brad's office. The visibility was getting bad, and the wind had picked up substantially creating small snow-drifts. She considered turning around, but decided it wasn't that bad yet. Besides, she didn't want to let Brad down after promising him she would deliver the pro-posal to his office.

Further up the road a few miles, sat a pickup truck with a snow plow attached to the front. The truck was parked in a well hidden area on the side of a hill that overlooked the road below. In fact, with the snow coming down, it was almost impossible to see the piece of Detroit steel. A man sat behind the steering wheel with a sock hat covering his face and his hands covered with gloves. He was hop-ing to pull off a perfect crime.

Checking his watch, he cursed out loud, "Come on you son of a bitch. You're always like clockwork. Don't let me down today." He adjusted the heat and squinted to the right to see if an Audi was coming his way. "Damn," he blurted as his patience dwindled, making him grow angry.

Anne handled the sharp curve expertly as she now had a short distance of straight highway before a dangerous curve. "I'll just slow down and creep around the next curve," she said to herself, knowing how dangerous it would be today.

The driver of the truck spotted a car coming his way. It had to be Brad he thought. He doubled checked the road from both directions and could only see one vehicle, and it was his target. His heart started beating fast and he became aroused again. "Tonight, I'll screw Kristy just to show both of them that I am the man," he said with a devilish grin on his face.

Brad had been meeting with Bill for fifteen minutes. They took a small break to allow Bill to relieve himself of the coffee he had drank. Brad had been in Bill's office many times before and was still impressed with it. There were framed magazine articles on the wall proclaiming Bill Matthews as a pioneer on high tech prosthetic devices. Displayed proudly was an original Monet painting highlighted by two spotlights. The desk was handmade and built with premium cherry wood, giving it a rich look that any top executive would be proud to own. Everything was in perfect order on the desk. There were two framed pictures that sat proudly on the corner of his workstation that featured his family.

One particular wall was lined with pictures highlighting Bill's baseball career. Brad walked over to the photograph with Bill and President Reagan that was signed by the president to Bill. The office portrayed the success story of Bill Matthews, and Bill was proud of it.

Brad hoped that he could have just half of the success as this man who had become his second father.

"Hey, I have some more coffee here, would you like some more?" Bill asked as he reentered the room. Bill could see Brad's admiration of his life's tokens of success. "I've had quite a good life. I feel blessed to be where I am today. However, it wasn't handed to me. I had some failures in the past also. It's like they say Brad; it's not how far you fall, but how high you bounce back. That's what makes one successful."

"Are you trying to tell me something?"

"Yes I am Son." Bill called him that sometimes because Brad felt like a son to him. "It's been almost four years since you've pitched. I watched you out there toeing the rubber, and you're the best talent I've ever seen at that level. Hell, maybe even better than the next level. The worse thing is, we may never know. Doesn't that bother you?"

Brad walked up behind the fine leather chair that he had been sitting in earlier. He gently rubbed the fine leather with his hands while intentionally not looking at Bill. He reflected back on his baseball days, realizing he really missed the game. Not just the game, but the competition. The thrill of overpowering the batters that faced him. He looked Bill straight in the eyes. "Yes it bothers me. But I still have time. I'm only twenty four years old."

"Brad that's not young in today's professional sports arena, especially since you're a year or two away from being able to compete at that level if you started today. There are many young players out there ready to go. Hell, you haven't even pitched since your injury," Bill added, irritated.

"Do you want me to forget my work here and start playing baseball again? I don't understand. I came here to work under you, so I can learn enough to take over and let you retire someday."

"Brad, I could retire today and leave this company in your hands, and feel confident that you'd run it as well as I could. Maybe even better…because I believe in you son. This company will be here many years from now, but your baseball career won't be. They don't have a senior league you know," Bill said with a laugh. "Have some of this gourmet coffee before it gets cold."

Anne approached the dangerous curve in the road. She slowed down to a crawl to negotiate the curve and maximize her visibility. The wind was driving the snow fiercely by now making it hard to see.

The snow was also hampering the driver of the truck, but he was so focused it didn't bother him enough to keep him from executing his plan. He had such a high from the thrill of the impending kill that he couldn't wait to create the impact that would force the car down the ravine and take out the driver that he loathed. It was now time to complete his dangerous plan.

The truck moved slowly to the edge of the road. The driver lowered the blade slowly to gather snow that should prevent any paint from the car to rub off on the hard steel, therefore leaving no evidence.

Anne was about ten feet from the opening from the missing guardrail when she noticed a movement to her left. She was shocked to see a truck coming from nowhere heading for her car. There was nothing she could do.

The blade of the truck struck the front of the Audi propelling the car straight through the opening. The truck stopped and then sped off, while the car headed down the steep ravine.

The car picked up speed and struck a tree causing the vehicle to turn around and go backwards. A small child was screaming for her mother, but to no avail. The initial impact of the tree had hit the driver door squarely, knocking the driver unconscious. The car ricocheted off of several trees like a steel ball in a pinball machine. It then rolled over several times and finally rested at the bottom of the ravine. The car was mangled, and the occupants were severely injured, leaving one dead.

Bill sipped his coffee, savoring the flavor of the rich blend. He sat down on his plush leather executive chair and leaned back. He could see that Brad was deep in thought, so Bill remained quiet as he watched his young protégé contemplating the words he threw at him. Bill smiled to himself realizing he threw a curve ball right by Brad. He had thought about this conversation for a year now, knowing that it had to be said. It was a hard thing to do because he didn't want to lose Brad as an employee. Bill knew that Brad was a once in a lifetime gift and he produced for the company exceptionally.

Brad made Bill more money than the quarter of million dollars he guaranteed the Dodgers if their signing of Brad didn't pan out. Nobody knew that Bill had backed the contract with the cash guarantee, and he meant to have it that way for life. But the money was not the reason he was pushing Brad to make up his mind on a baseball career. Brad deserved the shot in the big leagues, and he had the talent and other tools to be a star. Actually, it would be a huge advantage to Bill's company to pay the two hundred and fifty thousand to the Dodgers and keep Brad in his company.

Bill was startled from his thought as Brad starting speaking, "You know Bill, I have a clean bill of health now. The doctors say my shoulder has healed one hundred percent. In fact they marveled at the progress. They said my slow and deliberate exercise program allowed everything to heal and strengthen properly. They talked about writing a piece on it in the medical journal."

"That's great news Brad," Bill fired back. "Now you have no excuses. The rest is up to you. What's keeping you from going forward with a baseball career?"

Brad's cheeks blushed as he fumbled for the right explanation. He decided to just tell his true feelings about the matter. "It comes down to two things. I love Anne and Brianna dearly, and I hate to be away from them. Anne isn't to keen about me being away from home so much either."

"That's a good reason. Your family is the most important thing. Your wife is something special, and I want you to know that I've appreciated the way you've loved her and taken care of her. She's like family to me you know," Bill said sincerely.

"Thanks. It's amazing how much they've changed my life. I just can't imagine life without them. But it also comes down to what you said to me when you presented your idea to me about the program to mold my motion. I acknowledge that my form was not the best for me, so I viewed film over and over of my pitching motion and took notes on what to change. But it still comes down to the fact that we don't have this program perfected. We have to develop a way to capture my motion and send that data to the computer to make sure each pitch is the exact same motion as the designed motion. I don't want to start to pitch again until I have the perfect pitching motion. I'll then need to practice that motion over and over again to create the muscle memory to make it consistent every time I throw. When that happens, I'll try to pitch again."

"We have the capability to do that now," Bill stated impatiently.

"Not really Bill. It just doesn't work the way we originally thought it would. I've been working on a new pitching motion, and something is missing. We have to find a way to record the body motion more precisely."

"Once that happens we will be true pioneers and more wealthy than ever. But the most important thing is taking this information to make our prostheses better than ever. There will be many deserving people that will benefit," Bill added, trying to hide his excitement towards Brad going forward with his new pitching style.

"You're right. And that's another reason it's hard for me to decide to play ball again. There's a lot of satisfaction in this line of work."

Bill stared at his desk gathering his thoughts and then looked Brad squarely in the eye. "Alright then, let's do this. I want you down here working with me. We can work together, so you can learn everything you need to know to take this business over when I decide to retire. Now I'll tell you, I don't plan on retiring any time soon. I also enjoy this line of work..."

Brad tried to butt in, but Bill held his hand up and continued, "I want you to spend most of your time getting this program perfected. I'll also bring in the pitching coach of the Dodgers to work with you personally for a few days. It's important to get his input. And I want you to work with Coach Culley at Duke and his pitching staff. You're going to find out if you still have the ability to play professional baseball. Now you may comment if you like."

Bill took a drink of his coffee when the phone rang again. Bill looked at it in disgust as he only wanted emergency phone calls. Bill pushed the button to activate the speaker phone and firmly said, "I thought I told you not to interrupt me."

"I'm sorry Mr. Matthews, but it's Leslie from our Indianapolis office. She needs to talk to Brad, and she said it was important," Bill's personal assistant answered.

"Put her through then."

Brad walked closer to the phone. "What is it Leslie?"

"I don't have the file on our proposal for the meeting this morning," Leslie stated with a panic in her voice.

"I mistakenly took it home last night. Anne was going to deliver it to you first thing this morning," he said while glancing at his watch. "She should have been there by now."

"Well, the weather's bad here" Leslie said. "Maybe she's held up by the snow."

"Let me call her at home to make sure she's on the way. Hold on a sec, and I'll see." Brad put Leslie on hold and dialed his home.

"Hi, this is the Preston residence. We are unable to come to the phone right now. Please leave a message and we will call you as soon as possible," and the phone beeped signaling to leave the message.

"Anne this is Brad. Please call me at the Charlotte office. Love you." He then pushed the button to reconnect Leslie. "Leslie, Anne must be on her way. If you don't mind please have her call me when she arrives."

"Sure thing Brad. Sorry to interrupt your meeting," Leslie replied before she hung up the phone."

"What was that all about?" Bill asked.

The snow was still coming down In Indianapolis. The wind was blowing hard covering any tracks with snow that either vehicle made in the accident that took place earlier. The Audi still rested at the bottom of the ravine with both passengers still in it.

The driver of the truck was safe at work still pumped up after pulling off his crime. Nobody suspected that he had done anything wrong. He was a good salesman when he wanted to be.

Thirty minutes after the accident occurred, another vehicle slid off the road close to the open guardrail. The elderly man pulled his collar up over his neck to block off the harsh wind, and proceeded to check out his situation. He walked to the back of his car and then to the front. It didn't look good. He then walked to the passenger side and did a double take when he looked down the ravine where he thought he saw a car.

He abandoned the inspection of his car and walked over to an area to get a better look at the object in the ravine. Sure enough it was a car, although it didn't resemble one now. The ravine was too steep for his old body to negotiate, so he hurried back to his car to grab his cell phone to call for help on his behalf and the wrecked car. He prayed that there wasn't anyone still inside the car.

"I guess I didn't realize how strong your feelings were concerning my baseball career," Brad said. "Your idea sounds good to me. It would be nice to throw a fast ball again. Do you think I have a chance in the big leagues Bill?"

"You have everything it takes and more. There are good players in the majors that don't have half the talent that you do. Plus, you have more desire and heart than the superstars. Yes, you have what it takes. You just have to start the process.

And I'll help you start that process. Deal?" Bill asked as he extended his hand to Brad.

Brad shook Bill's hand vigorously. "Deal."

"Good, now let's get started," Bill began as he sat down to write some notes. "This is a unique situation we have here. This is a promotion to you and a possible end of your working here for many years. I want the best for you Brad. That's what's important to me."

"Thanks Bill. I really appreciate your concern and prompting. Well, how do we work this out?" Brad asked with growing enthusiasm.

"That's the easy part. I'll pay you to get this computerized program functioning the proper way, plus I'll train you to run this company. From there, we should be able to determine if you'll pitch again, or just coach for a few years and then return to our company."

The phone rang again in Bill's office. "Yes Linda. What is it this time?"

Linda hesitated for a second before answering. "It's Brad's mother on the phone, and she's really upset."

Bill kept the speakerphone on, so he could be involved with any problem.

Brad almost went limp. Why would his mother call him in Charlotte? It must be dad he thought. "What's wrong Mom?"

"Oh Brad" his mother said as she began to cry. "You have to get back here now."

"Is there something wrong with dad?"

"No Brad. It's Anne and Brianna." Mrs. Preston stopped for a few seconds, trying to regain her composure and stop crying. "They were in a bad accident."

"Are they alright mom?" Brad asked, coming to a full panic.

"It's serious Brad. I don't know much. The sheriff's office called just a minute ago to inform us. They told us to get to the hospital as soon as possible. That's all they'd tell us. It doesn't sound good Brad," she added and then cried harder.

Brad sat down, so he wouldn't collapse to the ground. His head was spinning and his stomach felt like it was ready to explode. He couldn't keep up with all of the possibilities of what happened to his wife and daughter. How bad could it be, he wondered? "What hospital did they take them to Mom?"

"Riley's."

Bill interjected, "Look Mrs. Preston, I'll put Brad on a corporate jet immediately and have a limo waiting for him at the airport. You and Miles get to the hospital and take care of Anne and Brianna in the meantime."

"Ok. We'll see Brad at the hospital. The weather's still bad here, so don't force a flight if there's any chance of danger," Margaret added.

"We'll take all precautions to get him there safe and sound. Don't you worry about that," Bill said trying to comfort her.

The phone disconnected, and Brad was crying. He was numb and needed to know what was going on.

Bill's entire body stiffened from realizing that Norris and Grace needed to know there was a terrible accident. How could things change so fast? He looked over at Brad and saw the young man being torn apart. "Brad, we don't know the facts yet. Let's get you on the road to the airport and try to get more information. Where are Norris and Grace now?"

"I know you're right, and I apologize for losing it, but I can't bare the thought of Anne and Brianna injured and laying in the hospital. I think that Anne's parents just got back from vacation. I'll give them a call," Brad said as he gathered himself. "They'll probably want to fly up there with me."

"That'd be great if we can get them to the airport in time to fly with you, but time is passing by quickly, and you need to be with your wife and daughter," Bill said as he tried to come up with some good solutions to this dilemma.

Brad had already dialed his in law's home, but there was no answer. He left a message on their answering machine to call Bill Matthews and then hung up. "They're out of the house right now. I told them…"

"I'll handle it Brad. Take a cab to the airport, and call me when you get there. I'll let you know where to go at that time, and I'll inform you if the Weatherbys will be flying with you. Look Brad, this will work out fine. We can't think the worst right now. Think positive. Now get out of here and call me from the hospital please. And please tell Anne and Brianna I said to get better soon."

Brad walked up to Bill and gave him a quick hug. "Thanks for being so good to me Bill. You're like a father to me you know."

Bill fought back tears as Brad left the room. He had work to do trying to locate Norris and Grace and trying to get some information on what happened in Indianapolis earlier today. He flopped down in his plush chair and leaned back while rubbing his temples. He then sat up straight and reached for his phone, and went to work trying to locate his best friend.

CHAPTER 17

▼

The flight felt like a transcontinental flight that lasted half a day as Brad impatiently sat in the private jet. The only good news was the weather had improved around the Indianapolis area allowing them to land there. It was still snowing, but the fluffy white flakes had subsided a little. The gusting wind was now the worst force working against them making the last part of Brad's flight bumpy, although he didn't pay much attention to the movement of the jet. He was too caught up in thought of what he would find when he arrived at the hospital.

Brad believed it to be rather unusual that nobody could or would let him know the condition of his wife and daughter. "What does that mean?" he kept asking himself. He drew the conclusion that it meant one of two things. Either they were both in serious condition, or they only had minor injuries.

Bill was on a mission trying to track down the Weatherbys. He finally reached Miles Preston at the hospital. The news Miles delivered sent a dagger to Bill's heart. He couldn't believe the accident was that serious. He now had to decide how to handle Norris and Grace if they happened to call him back. He had left messages everywhere for them.

Bill walked over to a hidden cabinet behind his desk and pulled out a bottle of vodka. He hardly ever drank at the office and only kept the hidden bar for occasions when he wanted to have a celebratory drink with a client. But now this was his drink of choice. The coffee had only exacerbated his stress.

Brad found the limo waiting for him as Bill said it would be. He made a mental note to do something special for Bill when this was over. Brad thought the limo driver must have been instructed to get his passenger to the hospital in record time as he sped off and never slowed down. There was a phone next to Brad and a piece of paper with the phone number to the hospital. "God, Bill thinks of everything," Brad said quietly. He stared at the phone, and his heart started racing. He wanted to know what was going on, and he didn't want to know.

He dialed the number and put the communication device to the side of his head while closing his eyes and praying for good news. It took almost five minutes before he could get to someone that would even talk to him. They wouldn't say anything at this time, except that both patients had been brought to this hospital.

The hospital tracked his father down and put him on the phone to Brad. His heart sank from the tone of his father's voice as soon as the first words came out. He knew it was a serious matter.

The only information that Miles offered his son, was the fact that Brianna had just come out of surgery. He told his son that he would meet him at the main entrance doors of the hospital.

The information was not good enough for Brad. He pressed his father for more information. "Come on Dad, what is the status of Anne? Is she alright?"

There was an uncomfortable silence at the other end of the phone. Miles started out somewhat stuttering his words, "It's a grave situation son…" He hesitated for a few seconds and then went on, "She didn't make it Son."

Brad went into panic mode. "What do you mean? Is she dead?"

There was silence on the phone as Miles pulled himself together. He knew he needed to be strong to help his son through this tragic ordeal. It was the most difficult thing he had ever done in his life. Having to identify Anne's body crushed him. At least he was able to take that burden off his son.

"Dad, please answer me. Is Anne dead?" Brad asked, losing his composure altogether now.

"She was dead at the scene," Miles blurted out, heartbroken.

Brad squeezed the phone tight as he felt his entire world fall apart. He bent over as he gagged from the vile that his stomach forced up to his mouth. This couldn't be happening. His father kept asking him if he was still there and if he was alright, but Brad couldn't hear the questions. He was in an emotional shock that nobody should ever have to experience.

Finally the limo driver brought him back to the present as he shook Brad. "Sir, we're here at the hospital."

The physical contact by the driver and the bitterly cold air helped Brad back to his senses.

Miles rushed out to greet his son knowing quite well that he was so badly shaken that he wouldn't remember their meeting place. His heart sunk from seeing the white pale look on Brad's face. He wrapped his arms around Brad embracing him with all of his might. "I'm so sorry Son," is all he could say before he led him into the hospital.

The hot air of the hospital fell on Brad and started to suffocate him. He bent over and put his hands on his knees. It was more than Miles could take. He selfishly wished Margaret was there to help, but she was waiting to be allowed to go in the recovery room to see their precious granddaughter.

A hospital attendant went over to Brad and Miles, and asked if everything was all right.

An angry voice asked, "Where's my wife?"

"Excuse me sir?" the attendant asked.

"I'm Miles Preston, and this is my son Brad," Miles spoke quietly, but with authority. "His wife and daughter were admitted here earlier this morning from a car accident."

The attendant knew right away who Miles was referencing. News traveled fast when there was a death. "Come with me," the attendant said, leading the two Preston men to the morgue.

"Are you sure you want to see Anne now?" Miles asked, not sure if that was the best idea at this time.

"Yes, I want to see my wife." He needed the verification that she was indeed dead. His brain couldn't accept the fact that she was not alive.

Brad was glad it wasn't as hot in the lower section of the hospital where his wife was temporarily laid to rest. It was an eerie feeling being in the lower level away from all of the hubbub of the hospital. He hesitated as he approached a body that was lying on a stainless steel table.

His father took him by the arm. "You don't have to do this right now."

"Yes I do Dad. She was my life, and I need to see her even if she's dead," Brad stated adamantly.

The sight of his badly bruised wife was more than he could take. He broke down crying as he took her limp cold hand in his. He knew the life was out of her, just as it had left him. He couldn't believe that this could be his beautiful wife. He stroked her blond hair and said a prayer stating she was now with God in a better place. He stood over her body holding her hand wanting to bring her back.

Finally Miles said, "Brad, we need to get to Brianna now. She needs you."

Brad kissed Anne softly on her lips to say goodbye. Unexpectedly, there was a peculiar warmth that came from her mouth and traveled through his body that left as fast as it had come. The only thought that came to his mind, was that Anne's soul had left her lifeless body and used Brad as a conduit to heaven. She waited to say goodbye to him the only way she could. The entire episode left goose bumps on Brad's whole body.

Brad stood motionless thinking that now it was up to him to take care of their daughter. The thought of his daughter brought some hope to Brad. How could he raise her by himself? Anne had been such a good mother that there was no way he could replace her.

Once again Miles urged Brad to go see Brianna.

They both left the morgue and the feeling of death it represented, without Brad saying a word of what had just happened.

Margaret ran up to meet her son as he walked out of the elevator. "Brad, are you ok?"

Brad gave his mother a firm hug. "No Mom, I'm not. How's Brianna?"

"I don't know yet. They haven't let me in there," she replied with an annoyed look on her face from the lack of communication the hospital had displayed to this point.

Just as the three of them walked up to the waiting area, a doctor exited the room that Brianna was in. He saw the Prestons and assumed they were related to his patient from the look on their faces. Just to make sure, he walked up to them and asked if they were the family of Brianna Preston.

"I'm her father," Brad spoke up.

"And we are the grandparents," Miles said.

"I'm Dr. Kline," he said as professionally as possible under the circumstances. It was hard on him to see a small child in near death condition. This was the most difficult part of his job. "Come with me please." The doctor led them to a private room. "Please sit down," Dr. Kline said pointing to the vacant chairs. "We have done everything we can."

The three Prestons froze and held their breath. That was not the way they wanted this meeting to start.

After seeing the initial reaction from the father and the grandparents, Dr. Kline continued, "It's all up to her now. She doesn't want to let go. She had severe internal injuries, including a punctured lung when they brought her in this morning. If they'd have found her earlier, it might not have been as bad as it turned out."

Brad knew from all of his medical classes that a punctured lung was danger-ous. It would allow the chest cavity to fill up with air and create severe pressure on all of the organs. It could even move the heart out of place. "May I see my daughter now?"

The doctor sensed they recognized the critical condition of the child and replied, "Yes, please follow me." He felt relieved that he didn't have to say any more at this time. He just hoped the little girl was still alive.

The doctor asked the grandparents to wait outside as he led Brad into the room. Brad was shocked at the sight of all of the tubes and wires connected to Brianna's body. He rushed up to her bed and gently took her little hand in his. His attention was so centered on his daughter that he missed the nurse shaking her head sideways at the doctor. "Brianna, it's your dad. It's ok, I'm here now."

Tears filled the eyes of Dr. Kline and the nurse. They knew it was only a mat-ter of time before the beautiful girl would pass away. It was a miracle she was still alive. They were startled and found some hope when the little girl seemed to react to her father. They stepped forward to get a better view.

Brad felt Brianna give just the slightest of a squeeze to his large hand. It might have been his imagination, but there seemed to be a faint smile from her small lips.

Brianna knew her father was there. She had been waiting for him to come and see her.

Brad turned to the doctor smiling with encouragement. "Did you see that?"

"Yes I did," the doctor answered in amazement. Maybe miracles do happen, he thought to himself.

"I love you honey," Brad continued, trying to comfort his precious daughter.

Those were the words that Brianna wanted to hear. Those three special words her father said, plus the fact he was there with her, is what she held on for. She could now let the inevitable happen. She gave one more brief faint smile to her father and then took her mothers hand and left the world where she felt so much pain, and went to a place with no pain.

Buzzers filled the room as the doctor approached the dead body. There was nothing they could do. Her insides were too damaged. Dr. Kline shocked Brianna's heart with the paddles for Brad's sake only, but it did not bring the small body back to life.

Brad was crying and pleading with the doctor to do more.

"There's nothing more we can do. She had too much damage to her vital organs, and I don't want to put her through more since it would be to no avail," the doctor answered.

Dr. Kline then walked over to Brad and put his hand on Brad's shoulder. In a soothing tone the doctor said, "It was a miracle that she had stayed alive as long as she had. Feel blessed Mr. Preston. Your daughter waited for you to come see her, so she could say goodbye to you. I have never seen anything like it before. It's a miracle."

It was an emotional scene as Brad, Dr. Kline, and nurse just stood there and cried.

The grandparents walked in the room after hearing the buzzers and some of the conversation that followed. Their hearts sunk as they realized they lost Brianna.

Margaret pushed her head into Mile's chest and cried out, "No, this can't be happening. Our baby is gone too."

The distraught grandparents walked up to the body of their granddaughter and looked over her body with tears spilling from their eyes. They each took their turn to say goodbye.

They then hugged Brad as the doctor and nurse stood there with tears spilling from their eyes.

It was an unusual scene in a hospital to see the staff showing so much emotion, but they had just witnessed an amazing thing. They would tell the others in the hospital what had happened in this room today.

Brad turned around to face his daughter. He laid his upper body on her and held her, not wanting to let her go. It was so surreal losing his family all at once. He prayed to God to take her and reunite her with her mother. He then felt a warm feeling enter his body and then leaving almost simultaneously. It was identical to the sensation he felt with Anne before he left her. He sensed it was Anne taking Brianna home by using him as a passageway and letting him know she had her now. He then kissed Brianna on her little lips and got up to leave.

Dr. Kline had been explaining to Brad's parents about the miracle he had witnessed. The doctor had genuinely been touched by the entire episode.

Brad, Miles, and Margaret gave one final look at Brianna and then vacated the room.

Dr. Kline then gave the Prestons a quick run down on what would happen next with Anne and Brianna, and informed them to get in touch with a funeral director to take care of the bodies.

Those words hit the three of them hard as it reinforced the fact that Anne and Brianna were indeed dead.

CHAPTER 18

▼

Brad's life was in turmoil from the deaths of his family, but he had a mountain of work to do with funeral arrangements, the sale of his house, and moving on to Charlotte that would take his mind off the tragedy. Brad's first deed was to call Bill Matthews to fill him in on what had happened with Anne and Brianna.

Bill took the news exceptionally hard and actually broke down a couple of times during their conversation. Bill informed Brad that he still had not heard from Anne's parents, which concerned them both.

Brad discussed with Bill the funeral arrangements he had in mind for Anne and Brianna. He told Bill he decided to have them both buried down in Charlotte. He knew that Anne loved it down there, therefore making it the right decision, especially for her parent's sake. The other plus side of the burials in North Carolina was the fact that Brad was still planning on moving to Charlotte, therefore enabling him to visit the gravesites regularly.

Bill let Brad know that the Weatherbys would be very pleased with his decision.

There was no mention of work at this time because that was the furthest thing on both of their minds. Bill let Brad know that he was there to help in any way. They discussed a strategy on the best way to give the tragic news to Anne's parents and decided that it would be best if Brad told them, but if they called Bill beforehand he would have to let them know.

Meanwhile, Miles had contacted Phil Mullens, a close friend, who was also a funeral director. He explained the tragic accident to Phil and let him know that Brad was probably going to have the burial in Charlotte, but he would greatly appreciate it if Phil would handle everything here.

Phil let Miles know that he would certainly take care of things for Brad, and he would do so in a way as if they were his own children.

Miles appreciated the gesture and then answered a few questions before they ended their conversation.

Miles hung up the phone and rubbed his eyes. He couldn't believe what had happened today. The whole ordeal took everything out of him.

Margaret read his mind and walked up to her husband to hold him tight.

They both started crying again. Not just for the loss of Anne and Brianna, but also for their concern for Brad. How would he be able to go on with life? They knew how dedicated he was to both of them.

Brad approached his parents after his phone call with Bill, and saw them crying together. He walked up to them to make sure they were alright.

They were honest and said no, and then asked if he was going to be able to handle the situation.

"I don't know," Brad said honestly. "I hurt too bad to know anything at all right now. I died today also."

The older Prestons felt like they had been run over by a truck from hearing Brad's response. They were worried sick about Brad.

There was a brief silence that was shattered by the phone ringing, startling all three of them. Miles looked at the caller ID and handed the phone to Brad. It was the Weatherbys.

Brad's body tensed when he saw who it was. It took all he had to say hello.

"Brad, this is Norris. I received your message. What's going on there?" he asked with grave concern.

Brad's stomach turned a somersault after realizing the Weatherbys didn't know about the tragic deaths earlier today. He stumbled with his words, but somehow got them out, "There's been a terrible accident…"

"Is Anne ok?"

Brad broke down as he told Norris that Anne and Brianna had been killed. There was silence on the other end of the phone. "Norris, are you there?"

"I'm still here Brad," he was able to say before his body convulsed and he cried uncontrollably.

Grace witnessed Norris's crying and became panicked as she picked up the phone. "Brad what's wrong?"

Brad didn't have to answer as Norris said, "They're dead Grace. Our girls are dead."

"Oh my God Brad. What happened?" she asked, too shocked to have her emotions take over.

"All I know is they were in a terrible accident. Anne died on impact, and Brianna died as I held her hand in the hospital. It's awful Grace," Brad said as he started crying again.

The news finally hit Grace, and she passed out and fell to the floor. All Brad could hear was Norris trying to wake her up.

Finally Norris got back on the phone and said, "I'll have to call you right back. Grace has passed out, and I need to call an ambulance."

Brad stood there with a dead phone in his hand. He couldn't believe things could have gotten any worse than earlier, but this added to it. He called Bill and explained the situation, and asked if he would check in on the Weatherbys.

Bill assured Brad he would make sure Anne's parents were all right and call him with any news.

Things settled down after that. Norris called Brad back to let him know that Grace was ok now, but heartbroken. After hearing Brad's desire to have Anne and Brianna laid to rest in Charlotte, the Weatherby's thanked Brad for his decision. Waves of emotions came and went with further discussion on burial arrangements. They decided to lay them to rest next to Grace's mom and dad.

Brad was relieved to have gotten everything handled with Norris and Grace, therefore taking him into another mind set. He had to vacate all of his emotions, so he could tolerate what had happened. He turned on his business mind by focusing on legal matters, funeral arrangements, and helping others handle the tragedy. Some would call it shock, but Brad preferred to think of it as survival.

Kristy witnessed Greg in an unusually good mood this particular evening. She also noticed he had a strange look about him. He looked demonic. Kristy stopped what she was doing enabling her to watch Greg more closely. He turned on the early evening news, which was out of the ordinary for him, and sat down to watch the local news while leaning forward as if he was waiting for a particular story.

Kristy jumped when he yelled out, "Hey, bring me a beer."

She darted back to the kitchen and pulled a beer out of the fridge. She wanted to take the glass bottle and smash over his head, but she knew better. He had been showing more signs of abuse lately, but so far he had only slapped her across the face several times. His verbal abuse was much worse than it had ever been before though. She thought about the talk with Anne at Carol's party, which only brought on more contempt towards him. How could she have been such a fool?

"Hey woman, I said bring me a beer. What the hell's wrong with you?" Greg screamed out in an angered voice from the living room.

Kristy hurried into the living room and almost dropped the beer when she heard the report of the tragic accident today that killed Anne Preston and her two-year-old daughter, Brianna.

"God damn it," Greg yelled out in disappointment.

Kristy could tell his disappointment wasn't because of the death of Brad's wife and child. She sensed he was waiting to hear of someone else being killed. She handed him the beer and walked away. She wanted to call Carol, but Greg would be mad at her, so she decided to wait until he wasn't around. Tears filled her eyes. She knew that Brad would be devastated, and she also felt bad because she had started to like Anne. To make matters worse was the fact that their daughter had also been killed. It was too much for Kristy to handle as she broke down weeping.

She didn't notice Greg standing there witnessing her crying. He made her jump when he asked her in a smart ass tone, "What's the matter Kristy? Are you crying for your old boyfriend? I thought you might be glad that his wife was now dead. It might give you reason to have hope on getting him back. But it won't happen babe. I will kill you if you ever try to leave me. Don't ever forget that. You know, it's just too bad that it wasn't Brad in the car."

Kristy turned towards him with a go to hell look, but kept her mouth shut. She wasn't in the mood to be hit right now. "I'm sure that he would prefer to be dead right now. I can't imagine how anyone could cope with the loss of their spouse and only child in one day."

Greg smiled in victory. He hadn't thought about it that way. Knowing how Brad was, his loss today would kill him more than if he actually had died, and he would have to live with it for the rest of his life. Greg took a long drink from his beer and returned to his good mood. He suddenly became aroused again.

Miles reluctantly backed out of the driveway of Brad's house after dropping his son off for the night. He didn't think Brad should be alone tonight, especially in the house he had shared with his wife and daughter. It would do nothing but bring back all of the memories he had of Anne and Brianna. Nevertheless, Brad insisted on staying there tonight. Miles directed him to call them or come stay with them at any time if he couldn't handle being there alone.

Miles worried about his son, even though Brad promised he would be fine and would call if there was a problem. Miles knew that Brad was hiding from facing his true feelings in respect to his traumatic loss. He drove away and then glanced back at the house praying for everything to be all right tonight.

It was the third most difficult thing that Brad had ever done. Entering his house alone, and feeling Anne's presence there, as well as Brianna's, brought him back to reality. He wasn't prepared for the impact. All of his senses were heightened right now. He could smell the scent of Anne's perfume, and he could feel Brianna hugging his leg waiting for him to pick her up and return her hug. All of the personal belongings that each had possessed were there in plain sight. It was almost more than he could handle. He rushed over to the patio door in the breakfast nook and opened it quickly. The rush of cold air hit him hard and eased his urge of getting sick.

Then he started the why game. Why was it them instead of him that drove to his work? Why did he ask her to take the documents on a day that he knew had a chance of snow? Why didn't he take Anne and Brianna with him? He knew he had the job.

"Stop it," he yelled to himself. "It's too late to change anything right now. You need to pull yourself together or just end it."

End it, he thought to himself. That would end his agony for good, and he could spend his eternal years with them. Just then a cold blast of air hit his face. The snow swirled in the backyard creating images of ghostly figures.

He closed the door quickly and went to the couch to sit down. There were many strange things happening today that were not normal. He perceived them as signs from his wife and daughter. Gathering his thoughts again, he put suicide out of his mind for good. His family had been through enough hell. All he would accomplish by killing himself would only add more misery and heartache to everyone.

Brad felt something soft under his hand, so he grabbed the item and pulled it up. Tears fell again as he held Brianna's blanket in his hand. He pulled it to his face to breathe in the fresh smell it projected. He breathed in the full scent of the soft possession; the same way a gourmet cook would savor the aroma of the cuisine to allow the full fragrance to fill his nose. The full flavor of his daughter enveloped his senses bringing pleasure to him. He made a mental note to take the blanket and never wash it.

Brad then realized he could never stay in this house and tonight would be his last night here. He stood up and searched for personal items of Anne's. After an hour he did the same with Brianna's personal belongings. He accomplished his feat by filling a suitcase with items that he would keep forever.

Grace had suggested a couple of outfits that would be proper for Anne and Brianna to be buried in, so Brad fulfilled that task.

It was almost ten o'clock when he heard the phone ring. Checking the caller ID, he noticed it was Carol or John calling. He had been expecting them to call, so he decided to answer it knowing he was going to talk to them about today's injustice sooner or later. Now was the best time he thought. Besides, he needed to speak with a good friend after his loss today.

"I thought you would call."

"I have tried calling several times tonight," Carol replied.

Brad checked his caller ID and was amazed at the number of calls he received tonight that he didn't know about. He was so focused on other things he didn't hear the phone ring.

"I'm sorry Carol. I didn't realize the phone had rung tonight until just now."

"Oh Brad, we're so sorry about Anne and Brianna. Is there anything we can do to help?" Carol asked sincerely, trying to hide the fact she had been crying all night.

"I don't know. There isn't anything anybody can do right now. Nobody can bring them back to me."

"I just can't believe it," Carol said, fighting back tears again. "It was just last weekend that we were all together. And I've never seen the two of you so happy together. My God Brad, how are you able to get through this?"

"Right now it's minute by minute. But I have to be strong because Anne would have wanted it that way. Besides, there are too many people that are hurting just as bad as I am. If they see me struggle, it will only add to their suffering."

"Are you alright?"

"As well as anyone can be under the circumstances," Brad answered in a monotone. "I feel sorry for Anne's parents though. Her mother fainted when she heard the news. Mom and dad are taking it real hard also. They were so close to Brianna, and they really loved Anne."

"Brad, please call us if you need anything. We'd be more than happy to help out after the service."

"Thanks, but I've decided to have the services and burial in Charlotte. I didn't say anything to you the other night, but we were considering moving there soon. That's where I was today. It should have been me in that car Carol."

"You can't talk that way Brad. Things happen for a reason. I don't know if I'll ever understand this one, but the good lord wanted those two up there with him. You have to believe that," Carol replied, trying to soothe Brad's loss.

"After what has happened to me today, I do somewhat believe that," Brad said, remembering the strange sensations he experienced earlier.

"I won't keep you on the phone any longer, but I want to see you tomorrow. Is that ok with you?"

"Yes, that's fine. Just come to my parent's house. I can't stay here. It's too hard on me," Brad said as he looked around the lonely home.

"Ok then. I'll see you tomorrow."

Greg had been harassing Kristy all night. He would make remarks like, "poor Brad" or "one day you'll both be together, but it won't be on earth." It gave Greg a sense of power, which was an aphrodisiac to him. This was his way of foreplay for himself. He was building up for later tonight when he would take his wife the way he wanted to.

Kristy had completed her normal late evening routines and quietly snuck away from Greg as she attempted to do almost every night.

This time Greg was prepared for it. In fact he was more than ready as he had been aroused more than ever after accepting the idea that Brad was miserable and dead in another way. In Greg's sick mind this gave him an extreme power base over his rival because he is the one that caused Brad's loss.

Kristy was in the bathroom preparing for bed. She was standing by the sink bending slightly forward wearing only her panties and a bra. Her stance enhanced her perfect butt, elevating Greg's desire to another level.

He watched intently waiting for the perfect time to take his rebellious wife. It was time to teach her a lesson while fulfilling his pleasure.

Greg stepped back from the door and undressed. He admired his fullness as he patiently waited for Kristy to go to bed.

The toilet flushed, and then the water ran slightly as she finished her last step before retreating to bed. She pulled her panties off and unsnapped her bra exposing her voluptuous body. She didn't have time to put on her nightgown.

"Guess what tonight is going to be?" Greg asked in a strange voice as he stood there naked with a full erection. "It's time for you to show your hubby just how much you love him. And if you refuse to cooperate…" He hesitated to finish his statement as he grabbed her hard and slammed her body into his. "Well, let's just say it'll be fun for me either way."

She flung her arms at him. "Get away from me you retarded asshole."

"Oh baby, I was hoping you'd be this way tonight. It makes it more intense and pleasurable for me," Greg said in a dark way. He grabbed both cheeks of her butt hard and pulled her against him as he rubbed her with his body.

Kristy felt nauseous and more frightened than ever before in her life. She noticed that Greg's eyes were glazed. It was as if she was staring at the devil himself. She continued to try to slip out of his grasp, but it was to no avail, Greg was too strong. "You're crazy. Take your hands off of me," she finally spoke out.

"Come on Kristy, you can do better than that. Why don't you let it all out? Maybe you should pretend that I'm Brad. That would make it much better for you wouldn't it?" Greg said with fervor.

"Yeah, it would be better because he wouldn't treat me like a dog," she exclaimed with defiance.

He slammed her hard against his body once again trying to cause pain to her pelvic area. "But he isn't as good as me, is he?" Greg asked as he pinned her against the wall, raising her body off the floor.

Kristy just stared at him, which brought more rage to him. She had not recognized the fact that the more she fought, the more aroused he became.

"Answer me damn it. Who's the best?"

Kristy could hardly breathe with Greg pressing his entire body against hers. She was finally starting to realize that the more she fought, the more he liked it. If she defended Brad, he became more violent, enhancing his power. She decided to just relax and not play his dangerous game. She would play a different game. One that would make her sick, but would probably cause her less harm. "You know you're the best Greg. Brad couldn't hold a candle to you when it comes to sex," she lied and followed it with hard kisses to his lips. She just hoped that she could pull this off with throwing up on him.

The plan was working. Greg became less aggressive and seemed to lose some desire. He then tested her as he twisted her nipples hard.

"Oh yeah Greg, that's how I like it. You know how to please me," she replied, hiding her pain.

Greg didn't know how to react as she gave in to him. It made him angrier in another way because he didn't want to be played a fool, so he pulled her from the wall and threw her naked body on the bed. He pushed her over on her stomach and then jumped on her back. "I'll show you how good I am babe. I'm just going to do you like a dog, but use a different passage. I think you'll love it."

He forced himself into her anus and relieved his build up, all the while hearing Kristy moan in pain. It was a great feeling for Greg. Life couldn't get much better he thought.

CHAPTER 19

▼

Brad had spent most of the night going through their belonging in the house. He labeled a few items he would take to Charlotte. He decided to take a few pieces of furniture and some selected dinnerware. It was a hard decision on what to take to North Carolina and what to leave behind. He knew he had to be careful on taking too many things that would say, "This belonged to Anne."

Brianna's personal belongings were just as hard to choose from. Just being in her room suffocated him. He selected some of her most prized possessions and stacked them with Anne's items. He laid himself down on Brianna's bed and went through their nighttime ritual. She would never allow them to leave her room at night until they did prayers and had some small talk. Brad would tickle her sometimes, which irritated Anne somewhat because it would wind Brianna up.

Brad then decided to try to get some sleep, so he went to his bedroom and rested on Anne's side while hugging her pillow. It still smelled of Anne. It took a while, but he finally fell asleep for a few hours, only to be awakened by a bad dream. He looked at the clock and was surprised to see that it was almost six in the morning. That was good enough for him, so he went to the kitchen to prepare a stiff pot of coffee.

After having three cups of coffee, a clean shave, and a shower, Brad dressed for the day and packed his luggage into the Jeep Cherokee. He grabbed the few possessions once belonging to his wife and daughter that he had stacked by the door and loaded them into the jeep. He decided to take a last look around the house in case he missed something.

Satisfied he had everything he wanted, he started out the door. As he turned to close the door, he noticed a drawing in the kitchen. He closed the door and went back into the house to see what it was.

Tears filled his eyes when he saw the finger painting that his beloved daughter drew. Actually it was a combination of finger painting and brushwork. The trail of red, yellow, blue, and green paint from her small fingers revealed a uniquely colored rainbow creating the most beautiful prism of color he had seen. He was impressed by Brianna's work. He assumed Anne had helped her some with the paint brushing because the figures that represented the dad, mom, and daughter were beyond that of a two year old. The three figures in the picture were all holding hands. Up in the right hand corner were blue letters that spelled Brianna. He knew that Anne definitely helped with that.

A smile came to his face as he picked up the colorful artwork and took it with him. It would be hung somewhere in his new home when he settled into his new residence.

Brad left his house and headed for his parent's home. It was a cold sunny day; however the wind had finally subsided making it feel warmer than what it really was. Brad hesitated as he came to the stop sign at the entrance of his subdivision. He wasn't going to do it, but he turned to follow his normal drive to work as he was pulled by an inner force to drive the route that killed his family yesterday. He couldn't turn back.

Brad started breathing a little harder as he approached the curve that killed his wife and daughter. He was surprised to see two sheriff cars at the scene. There was also a tow truck there to retrieve his Audi.

His stomach was churning as he dreaded to see the wrecked car and the physical location where Anne took her last breath.

The sheriff deputies tried to wave him past, but he pulled in behind their cars and got out.

"Hey buddy. You can't stop there. This is an accident scene, so get back in your car and leave," one of the deputies yelled.

Brad could see they were getting irritated as he kept approaching them. He decided to identify himself, so he yelled back at them, "I know it's an accident scene. It was my wife and daughter that were involved."

Both men stopped what they were doing and stared at Brad approaching them, neither one knowing what to say.

Finally one of them spoke as Brad joined them, "May I please see some identification sir?"

Brad introduced himself as he pulled his wallet out of his back pocket. He carefully pulled his driver license out of its window and handed it the officer. He didn't pay much attention to the deputies because he was busy studying the scene.

The deputy handed him back his license and apologized for the inconvenience, but explained that there were too many curious people that would get in the way and possibly cause an accident. "So that was your car?" asked the officer.

"Was, is the correct term," Brad said as he shuddered at the sight of it. He couldn't believe how mangled it was. "I've been worried that someone would go through that opening and down the ravine." But the more he looked, the less dangerous it looked. It wasn't that big of an opening, and the angles from the road would more than likely keep a car from going down the path that his car took.

"I'm wondering the same thing you are," the other deputy said. "It's very strange to me that your car mysteriously hit that opening in the guardrail at the perfect angle and then took the path straight down the ravine. It would almost take someone trying to drive down there or a force that would project the car in that path. But with the weather conditions yesterday, I guess the car could have slid enough to take it down there. It's one of those one in a thousand situations I guess," he added, shaking his head.

Brad looked around more thoroughly trying to replicate the accident in his mind. Something didn't sit right with him, but he couldn't figure out what it was.

Meanwhile the tow truck operator had hooked the cable to his Audi and started to pull it up the steep ravine. It took some doing, but the wrecked car was now back on the surface of the road.

"Do you want to take a look Mr. Preston?" the deputy asked.

"I don't think I could handle it. What are you going to do with it?"

"Since there was a death involved, we have to take it to the county garage and check it out. After that, it's up to you and your insurance company," the deputy answered in a matter of fact tone.

Brad walked up to the two deputies thanking them for allowing him to look around and then asked them to box up any items that looked important.

They informed him that they wouldn't throw anything away and would indeed box up everything for him. It was the least they could do for the poor guy, they thought to themselves.

Brad turned the jeep around and went straight to his parents. When he arrived at their house, he could tell by their looks that they didn't get much, if any sleep last night.

They reviewed the plans for the day while having a cup of coffee. There was a special mass planned at their church at three o'clock this afternoon. From there they would all go to the airport and fly to Charlotte.

The Weatherbys had lined out a funeral director to handle everything from there and had everything set in Charlotte to take care of the bodies of Anne and Brianna.

Brad would have to help out choosing the caskets and deliver the clothes that Anne and Brianna would be wearing. He would then face a challenging time with visitation and the funeral.

Brad was amazed at the number of phone calls they received from friends that heard the news. Several close friends stopped by personally to drop off food dishes. He wasn't surprised when Carol dropped by the house.

Carol broke down crying the second she saw Brad. They hugged for minutes without saying anything. Finally Carol said, "I can't believe this happened. I'm so sorry Brad. I wish there was something I could do."

"Just being here means a lot to me," he said as they broke their embrace. Brad noticed that Carol was bothered by more than his tragedy. She had a concerned look on her face that wasn't related to him. "Hey, what else is bothering you?"

"Nothing," she said lying.

"Come on now Carol. I've known you way too long to buy that. Now tell me what's wrong."

Carol hesitated to say anything. She rubbed her hands together nervously and bit her lip. "It's Kristy. Greg roughed her up last night and raped her."

"Raped her? They're married. Why would he rape her?"

"He's no good Brad. Kristy told me she saw the devil in him last night. He was acting all weird yesterday. She said it was hard to explain what he was like," Carol explained anxiously.

"Why doesn't she leave him or call the police. She doesn't have to put up with that. My God Carol, why does she stay with him? And why did she marry the bastard anyway?"

"She married him because he showed her lots of attention while you were at Duke. And he was fun to be with back then. She thought she loved him, but more than anything she thought it would get back at you. And she won't leave him now because her parents don't believe in divorce, and he promised to kill her if she tried to leave."

Brad stood there shaking his head. He was upset with Kristy for thinking she had to try to hurt him after their split up, and he was afraid for her. He knew Greg was a loose gun.

Their conversation switched to Brad's life with Anne and Brianna. He reminisced about how he met Anne and how Brianna's birth changed his life, as well as Anne's. He told some funny stories about the three of them and explained how close they were.

It was painful for both of them, but necessary for Brad to say in order for him to heal.

Carol recognized that part of Brad was gone. She could see it in his eyes as well as hear it in his voice. Somehow, she was able to remain strong through their conversation. She knew that Brad needed that right now.

Carol promised him that she and John would show up for mass this afternoon, and then she left for home.

They had talked for over two hours, and Brad was grateful for it. He felt a little better. In fact he felt exhausted. He slept until it was time to go to church.

CHAPTER 20

▼

The special mass went well. Brad couldn't believe the number of people that attended the service. It supported his thoughts that his family was well liked in the community. After the service, they went directly to the airport where a private jet was waiting for them, thanks to Bill. He didn't know how he would ever repay Bill for everything he had done for him and his family.

As the jet reached the proper altitude, Brad settled back into his seat allowing him to think about the next few days. He dreaded facing Norris and Grace knowing emotions would be unleashed once again. He felt so sorry for them because the distance didn't allow them to participate in today's mass. He hoped that Grace would be able to cope with the sight of seeing Anne and Brianna dead. He knew the sight of Anne's battered body was imbedded in his memory for the rest of his life.

Brad glanced at his parents and was pleased to see them sleeping, or at least resting. The trauma had taken its toll on them also. He worried about their health and well being through this traumatic ordeal. He had heard stories about people dying of a heart attack from the shock of this sort of thing.

Brad tried to focus on what he was going to do with his life after the funeral was over. What would his life be like, he wondered? The only thing that came to him was the fact that he would never be the same. He lost his passion for life, and his spirit had died leaving a void he felt would never be filled. He couldn't motivate himself to go beyond that. But he didn't really care right now.

The screeching sound of the tires hitting the runway brought Brad back to the present.

The Weatherbys and the Matthews were waiting on their arrival, and it wasn't going to be a happy greeting.

Miles made sure he was the first one off the plane. He would be the shock absorber of the initial greeting that would certainly be full of emotion.

Brad allowed his father to take the lead, thankful for his father's initiative for doing so. His mother was just behind her husband with Brad following directly behind them.

The two fathers shook hands while the mothers embraced each other crying uncontrollably.

Bill ran up to Brad and put his arm around him asking him how he was holding out. The look Brad gave Bill said more than any words could say. It was not the Brad Preston he once knew. It tore at Bill's heart to see this young man that was more like a son to him, so defeated in life. He couldn't blame Brad for being that way though. He couldn't imagine having to face the same tragedy and go on with life.

Norris walked up to Brad and observed the same thing that Bill grasped about his emotional state. He loved his son in law and felt bad for him. But Norris wasn't doing very well himself. He hadn't slept since hearing the terrible news, and he had been experiencing some chest pain. Norris didn't accept Brad's handshake. Instead, he embraced him with all of his might. "I can't believe Anne and Brianna are gone," he said as they held each other.

"Me neither," is all Brad could say.

The men thought it would be a good to time to try and settle the two mothers down. Grace was not quite hysterical, but she was close to it. They were afraid of what would happen when Grace finally saw the bodies of Anne and Brianna.

This was a prelude of what the next three days would be like.

Since it was almost ten o'clock at night, and the Prestons had such a long day, the decision was made to go to the Weatherby's and try and get some rest, allowing everyone to regain their composure. It would also give the funeral director time to prepare the bodies for Norris and Grace to see.

Saturday was a day from hell. It was like starting the entire ordeal all over for Brad. Seeing the two dead bodies again brought back the initial heartbreaking reaction he had experienced in the hospital. At least Anne looked better with her bruises covered up, he thought.

Both sets of parents were near a breakdown when they viewed Anne and Brianna, with Grace taking it the hardest.

After seeing the bodies, they had to choose the caskets. It wasn't as dreadful as Brad thought it would be because it surprisingly took all of your focus off of what happened, and made you think about the matter at hand, with the assistance of an artful sales pitch from the funeral director. He was very good at his profession.

Half of the day was already gone, and everyone was physically and mentally exhausted. With all of the arrangements made, they had nothing left to do but go home and wait until Sunday.

Sunday's mass went well with a special prayer added to the service for Anne and Brianna. The church was filled regular parishioners as well as family and friends of the Weatherby's.

The lunch was as good as it could be under the circumstances. There wasn't much appetite among them, and everyone seemed to just pick at their food.

The viewing was another grueling experience. It was three hours of double torture to Brad. It was so hard on him to be beside Anne and Brianna and not be able to just hold them. It was worse to have to stand there and visit with friends and others he didn't know hearing them say how good his wife and daughter looked. He just wanted to crawl up and die somewhere and be laid to rest with his family.

Somehow the two families made it through the long day.

"I don't know how I have anymore tears to cry," Grace said after the viewing.

Brad knew they all felt the same way, but he knew they had one more rough day to go through.

Monday morning was a cool rainy day in Charlotte. Quite fitting for what was ahead of the Weatherbys and Prestons. Brad knew that God was crying on them as he prepared to bring the last bits of the two beautiful souls to heaven. Ironically, Brad's faith had grown since the accident. Not because of his willingness to have God ease his pain by taking his wife and daughter to a better place, but instead it was some of the strange things he experienced. Like the miracle of Brianna waiting for him to be with her before she let go, or the warm sensation that entered his body as he kissed Anne for the last time. The swirling snow that resembled spirits was another occurrence that was hard to explain. The rainy day being symbolic of Gods tears falling on them only added more credence to his belief.

Brad knew most people would have been angry with God for taking the two individuals that you loved more than life, but he just questioned why he took them. There had to be a reason.

Family members and close friends met at the funeral home for a quick service and to view Anne and Brianna one last time. From there, the bodies were taken to the church for a funeral mass.

The church was at near capacity as family and friends came together to show their respect for the Weatherbys. There were old college friends of both Anne's and Brad's present, as well as several of Brad's baseball buddies attending the service. Coach Culley and the entire baseball coaching staff were in attendance as well.

Brad sat in the front pew along with his immediate family. To his right were Grace, Norris, and Nathan. Bill Matthews and his wife sat directly behind them.

The church service seemed long to Brad and lacked a personal touch towards Anne and Brianna. He was glad it was ending.

Suddenly another strange occurrence presented itself to Brad. It began when sunlight filled the church spraying strong rays of light through the stained glass windows. At the same time, he felt something lifting him up from the pew. He rose to his feet feeling a presence guiding him to the pulpit.

Both families were stunned by Brad's actions. There were no plans for him to talk.

Bill wasn't surprised though as he smiled with glory. He felt the same emptiness as Brad had during the service, and he knew Brad wanted everyone to know how special Anne really was.

Brad whispered something to the priest and then took over. "I didn't have any plans on speaking here today. It's just that something greater than any of us here today had other plans. As I was sitting there just moments ago…" He pointed towards his vacated pew. "I felt something lifting me and urging me to stand. As I stood, I was guided to where I'm now standing. I guess my wife and daughter thought I should speak to each and every one of you here today. I'm not sure what it's about, but I feel confident the words will flow from their hearts, as well as mine."

He stopped for a minute to look at everyone in attendance there today. As he was looking around, he captured the full spectrum of the sunshine showering the room with prisms of beautiful colors. And then something hit him. It was not related to the services, but it was the key to the solution of the computer program they had been working on. The vision came to him as he observed the light coming from all directions creating different shadows. He knew the multi colors and shadows were the key to solving the problem with the CAMM.

He smiled and continued. "My wife and daughter were the most important people in my life." He stopped talking to look at his parents and spoke to them for a clarification, "No disrespect to either of you. I love you very much."

He then focused his energy on everyone again. "To lose them so suddenly and at the same time is something I don't believe I can live with. A big part of me died Thursday. But let me tell you what will keep me going. Of course there will be the great memories of the two I'll cherish forever, but something happened to me more powerful than that."

He paused to catch his breath aware of everyone there leaning forward waiting for his next words. The only sound in the church was the abundance of sniffs from people crying. There was going to be a shortage of facial tissues before the ceremony was over.

"When I arrived at the hospital, the first thing I did was go see Anne. Before I left her, I leaned down to kiss her goodbye. As my lips touched hers, I felt a warmth rush through her lips and into my body. It disappeared almost as fast as it appeared. I know it was her way of touching me for the last time and escaping this cruel world to go to a better place."

Tears were really flowing now from everyone there. Brad had touched every person in the room.

"I was then taken to another area of the hospital where Brianna was fighting for her life. I had no idea at that time just how bad she was. Her doctor explained to me and my parents that it was a miracle she was still alive. Her little body had taken too severe of a blow to maintain life much longer. He said it was just a matter of time. In fact…he was truly surprised she was still hanging on. I rushed into her room and saw my little girl lying there with tubes coming out of her from every direction. It almost killed me to see her there like that. I took her little hand in mine and told her that her father was there…and everything would be all right. It was then that another miracle happened. I felt the slightest squeeze from her hand…and then she gave me a faint smile. I then told her I loved her. With those words, she gave one more faint smile…and then let go to be with her mother. You see, she waited for me in all of her pain…so she could say goodbye. That's the love my daughter had for me and for life. I then laid my body on hers and felt the same warm sensation enter my body as I had experienced with her mother…and then it left carrying her soul to God. I must have been a conduit to heaven for both. One day, I will find out."

Brad was forced to stop as he cried uncontrollably along with everyone else in the church. Brad sniffed the moisture from his nostrils and continued, "I just want everyone to know that Anne was a great person that comes from a wonderful family. We will all miss her so much. And Brianna was Anne made over. There is no doubt about it. Their love for life and their families will live on forever as evidenced from the miracles I just shared with you. We all came here to celebrate their time on earth, and there is so much to celebrate. I can't imagine ever finding the kind of love they both gave me and their families."

He turned to his family and in laws. "I will miss them, and I know you'll miss them also. Thank you Norris and Grace for sharing your daughter with me the past few years. There are no words to express just how much she meant to me."

He then walked up to both caskets and kissed them both saying, "I love you both so much. Please look over me and help me through this."

Both sets of parents got up from their pews and went straight to Brad. They touched the caskets lovingly and then gave Brad an affectionate hug showing their gratitude for the powerful words he just spoke.

Practically everyone from the church followed the bodies to the cemetery. The clouds had completely disappeared as the sun took over for the day. It made it easier for everyone to face the final detail of the ceremony.

The pallbearers had performed their final task as both coffins were set over the gravesite.

Brad was amazed to see so many people there to support his family, as well as the Weatherbys, and show their respect to Anne and Brianna. It meant a lot to him.

The priest did a much better job at the graveside services. Brad evidently put some fire in his soul as Father Mahoney was much more passionate. He made the last act of lowering the caskets down the six foot hole more tolerant.

The tossing of flowers into the hole by family members made Anne's and Brianna's death final.

CHAPTER 21

▼

A week had passed since the tragic event that changed so many lives. The Weatherbys were still in shock from the death of their daughter and Brianna. Grace was taking it harder than Norris could ever have imagined, and he was worried sick from her deep depression.

Brad stayed in Charlotte for the rest of the week and leased a nice apartment close to work that would be convenient because of the short commute. He could even walk to work if he wanted to take twenty minutes doing it. The apartment complex had a nice work out gym in the clubhouse that Brad planned on using everyday. Overall, it would work out just fine for him. He didn't expect to ever have a home the way Anne had made for him.

Brad scheduled an early flight to Indianapolis on Saturday morning to pack up the items he wanted to take with him and then drive them down to Charlotte with his jeep and a u-haul trailer.

Carol had invited Kristy and Greg to dinner on Friday night. She wanted to get Kristy out of the house and buffer Greg's domination over her. She hadn't told John what Greg had done to Kristy two weeks ago because John would not have been able to control himself and would have let Greg have it. That would have been nice, except Greg would have taken it out on Kristy when they got home. Carol just hoped to have a nice quiet evening with the Somanskis.

Greg and Kristy arrived on time for their dinner with their good friends. Greg knew he had to conceal his pleasure concerning the deaths of Brad's wife and daughter. He couldn't afford to have anyone suspicious of him regarding their deaths. He felt too much power now, and prison would diminish that power, so he put himself on his best behavior for the evening.

Carol almost questioned Kristy's story about the way he was a couple of weeks ago, but she knew Greg was a good salesman and she wasn't going to fall for his commendable behavior. Besides, she witnessed the way Greg was at her birthday party, and it wasn't pretty.

The evening was going well, and finally Brad Preston was brought up. Greg asked Carol if she had a chance to see Brad after the terrible loss of his wife and daughter.

Carol and Kristy tensed up from the mention of the accident.

There was silence for a minute before John broke the unpleasant moment. "We went to the special mass on Friday night, but didn't get to see Brad very much since he had to leave right away to get to the airport. Carol did have a chance to visit with Brad earlier that day though."

"Oh my," Greg said like he was concerned. "I bet that was hard on you both."

Carol couldn't allow Greg to control the conversation concerning Brad, so she decided to give a quick view of what happened. She thought that Greg would forget about him if he knew how hard Brad took the loss of his family. "Yes, it was difficult. I cried when I saw him, and we talked for a long time. It hurt me the most to see how lost Brad was. You could see it in his eyes. He even told me that life wasn't worth living. He loved his wife and daughter so much. I just can't imagine losing a child though. They are a part of you."

Greg sat there engulfed in sexual excitement. Brad was powerless thanks to his crime of killing the ones he loved the most, and Greg loved this feeling. He just had to pretend to be sad until he got home. Then suddenly a thought came to his mind that brought a smile to his face. He would get Kristy pregnant. That would give him something he personally took away from Brad. He couldn't wait to let Kristy know.

Greg then hid his true feelings by saying, "That poor guy. He's had some tough breaks in life. You could tell that he really loved Anne when they were here the other night. It's just a shame for his loss."

John agreed with Greg, and they changed the subject.

Greg and Kristy left shortly thereafter, which was a relief to Carol. She felt so uncomfortable around Greg. She was pleased though because she thought she accomplished her task of getting Kristy out of the house for a relaxing evening. She had no idea what Kristy was about to face.

As soon as Greg and Kristy arrived at their modest home, the transformation of Greg was complete. He had been thinking about how Brad had also died from the loss of his wife and child. Carol didn't have to come out and say it, but he knew Brad looked lost. It was thrilling for Greg to hear of Brad's misfortune because of his doings. He was ready for another round of overpowering sex with Kristy, and he would then let her know that she was to get pregnant soon.

Kristy wasn't sure what to expect. She was pleased with her husband's behavior at Carol's, which had her believing nothing would go wrong tonight. They hardly drank any alcohol, so he wouldn't be insanely drunk. She proceeded to get ready for bed going through her nightly ritual. She hadn't noticed Greg standing naked in the bedroom watching her undress.

This time Greg allowed Kristy to get into bed before he pounced on her. He was already in full bloom and anxious to tell his wife the news of there soon to be pregnancy. He was rough at the start with her as he forced himself in her quickly. He was only concerned about his pleasure, and that meant pain for her.

She just tried to lie still without emotion, but Greg wouldn't go for that. He had to inflict pain on her, so he rolled her over again and aimed for a different passage once again. It was a thrill for him knowing this hurt Kristy, and his body released it's fluids to Greg's full pleasure.

"How was that honey?" he asked sarcastically. "It's not nice when you don't participate the right way. One of these days you'll learn. Now, I have good news for you. Starting tomorrow, you'll get off the pill and give me a child. That would please me so much. Do you understand?"

"Yes, I understand. But if you want a baby you're going to have to put it in the right hole. The one you used the last couple of times just won't get the job done," she said challenging him.

He slapped her hard across her butt. "Don't talk to me that way."

Kristy sat up staring at Greg with her own evil look. She knew why Greg wanted a baby, and she held the cards now. "Don't you ever treat me this way again you son of a bitch."

Greg's fist clinched as he raised his right arm at her.

"If you hurt me again, I'll kill the baby inside me if I become pregnant. Do you understand?" she asked staring at him adamantly.

Greg lowered his arm and stared at her in defeat. "Just get your ass pregnant soon."

Brad packed the u-haul as fast as he could. He couldn't take being at his house with all of the memories of Anne and Brianna. He looked at his watch knowing the real estate listing agent would be there any time now. He hated to sell the house in a way, but he knew it was the smartest thing for him to do.

He recognized that he was running away from his past by moving to Charlotte so soon, but he reasoned to himself they had already decided to leave Indiana. This gave credence to his decision to move now. There was no way he was ever going to leave behind his life with them completely. He just had to find a way to live again. His only excitement was his belief in having the solution to the computer program to enable him to pitch again.

Brad finished loading everything up in the u-haul and began to wander around the house as he waited impatiently for the real estate agent to arrive. He already knew what he was going to ask for the house, so signing the papers would be a quick business transaction.

As he strolled about, he noticed small items Anne had placed in the just perfect area of the home making him realize how lucky he had been to have her keep the house so neat and clean. She had been a perfect wife and soul mate to him.

He missed the sound of Brianna playing, and he especially missed the closeness they shared together. With Brianna on his mind, Brad wound up in her bedroom sitting on her bed. Tears fell from his eyes as his loss of Brianna was compounded by his presence in her room. He wanted to run out of her room as fast as he could, but his legs wouldn't move. Finally, the sound of the doorbell stirred him enough to leave her room. Brad reached the door to exit the room before he turned around for one last look.

As he expected, the signing of the contract went by expeditiously. Brad then doubled checked to make sure he had everything he wanted and left his home for the last time. He hoped Norris and Grace would eventually make it up here to go through the remaining items and take what they wanted. Everything else would be sold or donated.

Brad had just finished his two important stops to say his good-byes and was now driving east on I-74 heading for North Carolina realizing this was the start of a new life for him. He had made one stop to his parents and the other to Carol and John. They were the only people that he would really miss here in Indiana. He knew he couldn't replace his close friendship with Carol and John, and he wanted them to know how he felt about them since there might not be many times he would see them again.

He then prayed that he could recapture his passion for life.

Upon his arrival to his new home, Norris and Nathan Weatherby helped Brad unpack his jeep and u-haul. Brad was unable to negotiate some of the larger items into his second floor apartment by himself, so he requested their assistance. It also allowed the three of them to bond more and take the tragic deaths off their minds momentarily. It was good for them, especially Nathan, because he needed some-one to look up to since his sister's death, and Brad filled that need.

After everything was unloaded and put away, they sat back to see their accomplishment.

Norris smiled. "Well Brad, looks like you have some bare spots to fill in, but other than that it looks pretty good."

"It appears I should've brought some more of our furniture. But I'll tell you, I don't think I could've handled bringing the other items. The night Anne died, I went through the entire house and picked out what I thought I could live with at that time, and. this is it," he said, pointing to the few pieces.

Norris patted Brad on the back. "I understand your feelings. I'm sure I would've been the same way. But Brad, don't run away from what happened. You need to face the reminders of your marriage and life with Anne."

"Yes Brad," Nathan said, wanting to add his two cents worth. "You're tough you know. Why don't you get back in the game? I mean, Maybe you should try baseball again. That'll take your mind off of things."

"Thanks Nathan," Brad said. "Actually I plan on working on a program at work that relates to baseball. If it works out, I might just try to play again. We'll just have to wait and see."

"That'd be cool if you play in the big leagues. Can I come and watch you play?" Nathan asked excitedly.

"Well let's not get ahead of ourselves," Brad said with caution. "But if I do play, I'd be more than happy to have you there with me."

"I hope it works out for you Brad. I know that you and Bill have been working on this idea for a few years now. What makes you think it will work now?"

Brad looked a little embarrassed as he prepared to answer the question, but proceeded with his explanation. "When I walked up to the pulpit in the church this Monday, the vision came to me. I know why I was led up there besides tell-ing everybody what had happened to me."

"Oh, and what's that?" Norris asked with a confused look on his face.

"The sun started shining at the end of the service. I felt it, but I couldn't see the beautiful rays of light coming in the stained glass windows behind me until I stood at the pulpit. The rays of sun created a prism of light that surrounded everything in the church. That is when I realized what the answer was to our problem. If we create all of the different colored light rays, and surround the object with them, we'll be able to pick up and document motion. We can use different rays of color to measure different speeds of motion. We then use that theory, and combine it with the vacated light the shadows create to complete the total reading of ones body motion. I know it probably sounds like I've cracked, but it has to be the answer."

"That's an interesting theory Brad," Norris said as he walked a little closer to Brad. "Tell me something. Do you believe those strange occurrences in the hospital really happened, or do you think it was just your imagination?"

Brad didn't have to think about how to answer as he promptly replied, "They were real. It was the strangest thing I've ever felt. It was just a brief moment of warmth that passed through both of them and right through me. I can't explain it. I just believe it was their soul saying goodbye to me."

Norris gave a quick smile. "I believe you Brad. It just makes you believe in the almighty that much more. It's somewhat calming to me to know they were able to touch you."

"They touched me in a lot of ways. I loved them with all of my heart. I just wish it was me in the car and not them."

"You have to stop thinking that way. What's happened can't be changed. If it could be changed, I'd be the first to trade places with them. You have to go on with life now. I know it's hard, so just take it one day at a time. Eventually, time will heal all. Now the first thing you need to do is buy some more furniture," Norris said with a brief laugh.

After the two Weatherby men left, Brad sat down and thought about Norris's words of encouragement knowing there was much truth in them. He just had to remember them so he wouldn't dwell on what happened.

He decided that starting tomorrow; he would follow a strict regiment. He would jog three miles first thing in the morning before work. Upon arrival at work, he would concentrate on the CAMM project for at least four hours. He would review the other departments for several hours and then meet with Bill for at least an hour. When he was done at the office for the day, he would work out in the gym for an hour or so. To end the day, he would study the game of baseball by reading about the great players and great teachers of the game. He would also review film of his days as a pitcher as well as film of the best pitchers in the game to work on his new form.

If it all worked out, he would be playing baseball again better than ever. If not, he would at least be the best versed person on the game. He could even coach with more expertise than he would have had otherwise. But his goal was to play in the big league as a pitcher.

Brad woke up early the next day. He ran his three miles before work, followed by his morning ritual of shaving and a shower, then off to work. When he arrived at the corporate office, he called a special meeting with research and product development teams to coordinate his vision of finally executing the program that Bill had presented to him three years earlier.

There was a mixed reaction from the members of both teams, but the consensus was it would work. The ones that were negative about the plan were just upset because they didn't think of it. Basically, it wasn't as complicated of a solution as they had made it out to be.

Brad performed his other management duties before meeting with Bill. Brad then filled Bill in on the plan to execute the motion readings for the computer program. Brad went on to report his findings to his boss concerning other departments and approaches he took to solve other problems.

Bill smiled at Brad, amazed by the way this young man had taken charge and grasped his job. He was only saddened by the lack of life in Brad's eyes. Bill could see that Brad was different now, not that he could blame him. He knew everybody took a different approach to this type of trauma.

Brad was more of a robot right now. He programmed himself to do this job in a certain way, and he was executing it precisely.

Bill recognized Brad was the best asset the company had, and he knew the company would profit greatly from it. He would have traded the additional profits to have the old Brad back though.

Brad raced home after work and changed into gym shorts, a tee shirt with Duke Baseball written on the front, and a pair of Nikes to work out in. As he entered the gym, Brad took an inventory of the equipment as he set up a work out regiment in his mind. He then went straight to work.

It was a severe regiment that most people couldn't take. His muscles burned as he pushed them to the limit. The pain didn't affect him though. It wasn't anywhere near the pain he felt in his heart as he grieved the loss of the two people that meant the most to him. After completing his weight lifting, he stretched out to keep his muscles loose.

Back at his apartment, Brad called for some carry out food and then showered. The food arrived just shortly after he dressed, and he then sat down to fulfill his last task of the day. Brad ate his food as he logged on to the internet to look up resources for his baseball history lesson. He was fortunate to find some good articles on particular web sites that he was able to download as well as discovering some good books to read. He made his list of books he wanted to read and ordered some on line while realizing he would have to pay a visit to the local library for the others.

He then went to bed exhausted, which was good for him because it allowed him to finally sleep. This was Brad's daily regiment Monday through Saturday, with Saturday's work load being somewhat different because most of the company's employees took the entire weekend off. On Saturday he did minor paperwork and then spent the rest of his time on their special project.

Sunday was spent with his morning jog, which he increased to five miles on this day of the week. He then read the Sunday paper.

Brad tried going to church, but it was too much on him at this time. It brought back too many memories. So he would watch a few sporting events on television or cooking shows, and at the same time practice certain grips on a baseball he had learned to allow him to throw a variety of pitches. He recognized muscle memory, and learning to get comfortable holding the ball in unique ways would be his key to get on top.

This routine went on for six weeks. The only thing that changed after six weeks was the successful execution of the company's specialized computer program they named CAMM, for computer arm motion memory.

There was a grand celebration for all employees involved to reward them for their efforts. Bill spared no expense as he catered a dinner from the best food service in town. He wanted to show his gratitude to everyone involved, so he handed out monetary bonuses to everyone after their special dinner.

He individually acknowledged Brad for his strong leadership role on pushing this project through and for his idea that put the final touch on the program to make it work.

Brad took the praise without any emotion. To him it was just part of his job and a step closer to discover his viability in baseball.

CHAPTER 22

▼

Bill had been impressed lately on how well muscled Brad had become, but today with Brad dressed in gym clothes it really showed. Bill smiled as he saw the powerful legs Brad had developed and the rippled muscle definition in his upper body. Bill thought Brad's arms were solid muscle, but not so as to hinder his pitching.

The robotic mind set of this young man worked a program that created a physique that was perfect. Brad could have played professional football he was so fit.

Jack Ragsdale, the pitching coach of the Los Angeles Dodgers, was equally impressed with Brad. He didn't expect to find the perfect athlete here today. He stared at the stature of this remarkable young man. He could see the determination in Brad by the way he moved and ordered the others on what to do next. Jack felt the excitement starting to stir in his body as he realized Brad was the property of his organization. He sensed this young man would have the perfect disposition to work with and develop into a top level pitcher.

Brad didn't even flinch as Dr. Athinson directed the EMG technician to insert the electromyography needles into selected muscles, while the others in the room squirmed as they watched knowing it had to be painful. This was the final measure to create the perfect pitching motion for Brad.

They would have him use different throwing motions and then read each muscle's stress level. This would enable them to create the mold for a pitching style that would have less stress on his body.

Jack was impressed with the whole concept. He had heard talk about this idea several years ago in the front office, but had reservations of its ability to do what they said it would do. It all made sense now. He knew that only time would tell for sure.

Brad was set up and ready to go. Everyday since his move to Charlotte, he had been studying from pitching manuals written by some of the best coaches and the pitching styles of the most successful pitchers ever, and from that information he created his own style and motion. He had insured his new pitching motion was correct for him by working with it on the computer program.

"This is the throwing motion that I've been thinking about," Brad said as he demonstrated it to the others.

Jack couldn't believe how picture perfect it was. "How was the muscle stress reading on that motion?"

"It appears to be within the proper levels," the doctor answered. "Brad, why don't you try it the way you used to pitch, and let us compare."

Brad had to think back at how he used to pitch. He then went through another motion.

"That's real close to how you once threw," Bill stated.

"This is amazing," Dr. Athinson said excited. "Look at the stress levels on the Tres Majores muscle. It's almost double that of his previous motion."

Bill was getting fired up now. His idea had come to be at last. He was more excited for Brad than himself because it could be Brad's way out of a non existent emotional life and back into the real world again.

Jack asked Brad to perform his first pitching motion again. A smile came to his face after Brad executed the perfect motion again. "Ok, try it this way," Jack ordered as he grabbed Brad's arm and took it through another motion.

Brad tried that motion, but the muscle readings were not quite as good as his original motion. Out of curiosity, Jack asked Brad how he had come up with his new pitching motion.

"For the past two months I've put myself through a strict regiment. I jog everyday and lift everyday except Sunday. Then I researched and studied some of the best pitchers in the game. That is how I came up with this motion. I have cheated some by working on my throwing motion with this same program the last two weeks. I really feel comfortable with it," Brad said straight faced.

Jack couldn't wait to call the front office and tell them about this young man. He stayed around to watch them set the program with Brad, still amazed by its success. He just wondered if his pitching staff had the same resolve to go through this process as Brad has.

"Well Jack, what do you think? Is that a perfect form he has or not?" Bill asked proudly.

"It's perfect. So fluid and simple," Jack answered, glancing back at Brad.

Bill turned to Brad and his project team. "Alright then, let's save this one in the computer and mold his throwing motion to it. Dr. Athinson, please take the readings on this next one to insure we save the right form without adding addition stress to his body."

Brad knew his motion well by now and executed it perfectly one more time.

"What happens now?" Jack asked.

Brad wanted to answer this question, so he turned to Jack. "My throwing motion is now saved in the computer memory bank. I'm now able to set myself up in the sight of all of these light rays and practice my pitching motion. We developed a program to record motion from all of these light rays we projected on me for the computer to interpret. The computer can compare each motion to the motion we just recorded. It'll tell me if I'm out of sync with my designed motion. I'll do this over and over again to work on muscle memory. With enough practice, I should be able to reproduce this motion every time I pitch. Plus, it will be helpful to use periodically to keep a pitcher fined tuned and not develop any bad habits."

"Amazing," is all that Jack could say. "And this will work on anybody?"

"Yes, anybody," Bill said with pride. "Brad, use a different throwing motion this time, so we can see what the computer does."

As directed, Brad used a different form. It was real close to the recorded form, but slightly different. The computer gave a warning that this was an incorrect pitching motion for this individual and displayed data that the arm was two degrees lower than it should have been.

"Brad, when will you be ready to pitch again?" Jack asked.

"I'm not sure. I'd like to work out with this computer for a few months before I actually start throwing," Brad answered.

"Why so long?" Jack asked.

"I've been working on a lot of different pitches. I want the perfect fast ball that cuts in on a right hand batter. I want a fast ball that will tail away from a right hand batter. I want a curve ball, split finger, change up, and a slider as part of my arsenal of pitches. To make this happen, I need to work on each one of these pitches with the computer. When I feel I'm one hundred percent ready to pitch again, is when I'll hit the mound, and that's the only time I'll try," Brad said with authority.

Jack was impressed with Brad's desire to only want to do it the right way. He wanted Brad to start with the team tomorrow, but he knew it would be so much better to wait for this unique talent to join them on his terms. How could you argue with someone that is so determined to be perfect, he thought to himself?

"Hey Coach," Brad said as he gripped a baseball. "How's this for a fastball to run in on a righty?"

"It works for me," Jack said impressed. "Show me the rest of your arsenal."

Brad demonstrated all of his grips on the ball that he had been working on for the past two months, with Jack approving of everyone of them.

Bill approved of Brad's efforts giving Brad a big smile. He was proud of this young man and impressed with his hard work ethics. He knew at that moment that next year Brad would be a major league super star and nobody deserved it anymore than him. His fortitude to rebuild his shoulder and reinvent a pitching style would pay huge dividends for Brad in the big leagues. Bill glanced over at Jack and noticed the coach's interest in Brad. Bill knew Jack couldn't wait to get his hands on Brad, but who could blame him. This was the future star for the Dodgers.

Jack finished his conversation with Brad and said one last thing to him before leaving for Los Angeles, "Before you start pitching call me. I'll fly out to watch." Jack then turned to Bill. "It looks like your idea will work. We'll work out the details when I see the finished product," he concluded, pointing to Brad.

"That works with me. Tell Keith he owes me," Bill replied.

CHAPTER 23

▼

Brad's daily routine had a slight change to it now. He started coming to work an hour early to practice his throwing motion with the computer. He then worked with the research and development team to help adapt their invention in making a better prosthesis device. At night he studied the best hitters in baseball and read hitting manuals.

Bill was concerned about Brad though. It had been close to three months since the loss of his family, and Brad was still unable to show any emotion. Bill didn't like the way he had built a wall around himself. Bill admitted that Brad was still an outstanding worker and manager, but he lacked the emotional passion that employees like to see in their boss. Bill wasn't overly concerned about that negative because everybody liked Brad. He was fair and extremely intelligent making it easy for him to solve problems.

Bill wasn't worried over Brad for business sake. He just thought it was time for Brad to join the real world in a complete way. Bill had witnessed several beautiful women in the office flirting with Brad without him even realizing it. He hoped that something would bring him around. His talks with Brad sure hadn't helped any.

One positive thing developed recently for Brad. The real estate agent had called with an offer from a prospective buyer. Brad countered the offer, and the buyer accepted, leading to the sale of his home. The closing was scheduled in two weeks, so he made plans to fly to Indianapolis for the closing.

The sale of the house brought back vivid memories of Anne and Brianna to Brad. Luckily for him it was a little less painful. He had healed some emotionally, although not enough to bring him out of his robot state of life.

Brad called Norris Weatherby to inform him he sold his house in Indiana and urged him to take Grace there to go through the remaining items. Brad let Norris know that he had taken everything he was going to take, so feel free to remove any and all items of interest to them.

Norris promised that the two of them would go through Anne's and Brianna's things within the next two weeks. He explained to Brad they could now handle the task.

After hanging up the phone from his conversation with Norris, Brad realized he had buried all thoughts about his past with Anne. He had even put his house out of his mind, until reminded by the call from his realtor that he had an offer. My God, he thought to himself. I have to go on in life and face the fact they're both gone. "Get a hold of yourself," he said out loud. But it wasn't that easy. He felt too guilty to allow himself to enjoy life again. It wouldn't be fair to Anne and Brianna.

The following week Brad worked himself harder than ever. Some pain had returned to him from being reminded of his dead wife and daughter, causing him to hide his true feelings by punishing his body.

He decided to call Carol and ask her for some assistance in handling the sale of the remaining furniture and other saleable items. He then asked for her to choose a good charity to donate the clothing and other small items that would be left after the sale. He explained to her he would be there in a week to sign papers and asked her to meet him for a while to go over everything.

Carol agreed to help Brad out and decided to take this opportunity to set up another plan. She hoped that Brad would understand and not be mad at her. Carol prepared her plan carefully because it involved Kristy, and if Greg found out, it could prove dangerous.

Greg had been on the warpath lately throwing allegations at Kristy that she was still on the pill. It had been a couple of months since he decided to have a baby, and she still wasn't pregnant.

Carol had to make sure Greg had no knowledge of Brad coming to town because she believed he would become concerned that Kristy would want to see Brad. Greg would hawk her until Brad left town if he knew.

Brad flew to Indianapolis as planned to sign papers on the sale his house. After executing the closing at a local title company, he agreed to meet Carol at her father's lake house not too far away. It made sense for her to be there because it was unusually warm for May, and she loved it there at the lake, so he just assumed John and Carol were staying there to relax and prepare the house for the summer. Brad was looking forward to some time at the lake since it was so peaceful there.

Brad arrived at the lake house on time. The familiar surroundings brought forth good memories from all the good times they had here years ago. He was anxious to see Carol, so he hurried to the front porch. He knocked on the door, only to be shocked to see Kristy answer the door.

The two of them stared at each other for a minute before Brad said, "Hi Kristy. I'm surprised to see you here. Where's Carol?"

"Carol is playing guard right now. She didn't intend on being here with you. She thought that you and I needed to spend some time together. That's just like her you know," Kristy said as she handed Brad a note from Carol.

He read the note and smiled at the crafty way she pulled this off. "So how did she get you here today?"

"She told me she needed some help here today. Carol dropped me off saying she had to run to the store for a minute, and told me to just enjoy until she returned," Kristy said with a red face.

Brad shook his head and smiled as he walked into the house.

Kristy pointed to a table with cheese, bread, and two bottles of wine on it. "She had this planned out well."

"That's our Carol. She never liked the fact that you and I never married."

"Neither did I," Kristy admitted.

"What do you mean by that?"

"I never stopped loving you. I was so naïve and immature in college that I allowed Greg to lead me down the wrong path. He convinced me you were cheating on me, and I allowed that to affect my judgment at that time."

"I saw you with him at your home during Christmas break. You two were kissing for Christ's sake," Brad stated.

"He just dropped by on his own and caught me under the mistletoe. Come on Brad, you should know how he is. He wanted to take something away from you, and I was one of the only things that he could try to take away. He sure couldn't do it on the playing field."

Brad shook his head in disgust. "So we broke up for no good reason. Why didn't you let me know?"

"I believed his stories about you cheating on me. And when you left my house that day, you were so mad that I knew better than to try and change your mind." Kristy wanted to say more, but she decided to stop for now.

Brad walked over to the bottle of wine and opened it. He carefully poured the wine into the two wineglasses that Carol left for them. "Here, have a glass. It looks like we might need this." Brad held out a glass to his first love.

"Thanks," she replied as she walked over to his side. She took the glass and held it up to his. "To the fool that I was."

Before they clicked their glasses together, Brad added, "To the fools we were." He sipped his wine finally feeling some emotion after three months of keeping it hidden. He stared at Kristy as he took another drink admitting to himself that she was still a beautiful woman. Her blond hair reminded him of Anne, but when he looked into Kristy's blue eyes he saw only Kristy.

"So where were we?" Brad asked.

"I was contemplating telling you about my conversation with Anne at Carol's birthday party," Kristy answered as her heart beat quickened from just being near Brad.

Brad was surprised that Kristy brought up her short talk with Anne. "Anne mentioned to me briefly that you two had a talk that night."

"Then you must know that she informed me you never cheated on me. She was sure she was the first girl you dated after we broke up, and there wasn't anybody you had been seeing while you and I dated. Anne was a great person that I learned to respect. She was good for you Brad. I realize now I could never compete with her for you." Tears filled Kristy's eyes.

"She was a special person, but so are you Kristy. There never was a competition between the two of you. She came along at a time we were no longer dating. What brought this up anyway? I'm sure that you two didn't just initiate a conversation about the two of us."

"When all of the men were out of the room, we all started talking. Anne was asked how the two of you met. She said she was your nurse after your surgery. She read my face knowing I was upset. That's when we talked. Anne knew I still loved you, but she was unselfish and wanted to help me," she answered, reliving the hurt she felt that night.

Brad gripped his wine glass harder. "If you still loved me, why didn't you let me know? I hoped you would at least visit me in the hospital, but you never showed up."

"I was there Brad, but you never saw me. I was getting ready to walk in the room when I noticed a stunning blond holding your hand. I perceived that action the wrong way. I thought she was your new girlfriend, and I felt betrayed by you. It made me believe that Greg had been telling me the truth about you the whole time. All I could do was turn and run away. I drove straight home despising you the entire way. I dated Greg as a way to get back at you. Now I'm paying for it," she said as she started crying.

"Why would you believe Greg anyway? You were the one kissing someone else. I didn't do anything with any woman until Anne," he replied angered.

"You could have tried to talk to me after you saw Greg giving me a kiss under the mistletoe, so I could have at least explained," she added with some anger. "But I should have tried to tell you what happened on my own. How could we have let that happen between us Brad? We loved each other so much, didn't we?

"Yes we did Kristy. I guess we sort of went our different ways with school and all." He slowly approached her.

Brad hugged Kristy, and she returned the favor. The scent of her hair brought back memories of the two of them. For some reason, he couldn't let go of her, which was just fine with Kristy. Brad enjoyed the warmth from her body as his body stirred with excitement for the first time in months.

Kristy felt the same excitement and pushed her body as close to his as possible. She slowly pulled her head from his chest and stretched her body so her lips could reach his lips. She kissed him softly, not sure of how he would respond.

Brad was not sure how to react. The kiss was tantalizing to him. He decided to give her a kiss in return. As his lips touched hers, he felt a hunger from Kristy that wanted more. They kissed long and hard this time while their bodies rubbed together.

"I want you Brad. Please make love to me?" Kristy pleaded.

"But you're married."

"Only with a legal document. I hate Greg. He treats me terrible," she stated as her face turned cold from the mention of Greg.

Brad pulled away from her. "What do you mean?"

"He beats me sometimes, and he's verbally abusive."

"Why don't you divorce him then? God Kristy, you can't put up with that. Just leave him," he said feeling sorry for her.

"I would today, but I can't because he will kill me if I try. Brad, he is crazy! He's so obsessed with competing with you that he loses sight of what is right. Please believe me. I would have left him a long time ago."

Brad was fuming by now. Not with Kristy, but with Greg. He knew Greg had gone off the deep end by the way he acted at Carol's birthday party. "What did he do to you the night of Carol's birthday party?" he asked knowing Greg was drunk and hated the world that night.

Kristy didn't want to answer the question because she was too embarrassed. Brad pressed her for an answer so she answered. "He verbally abused me on the way home and hit me several times." She stood motionless, not sure if she should say more.

There was a brief silence as she contemplated revealing more. She thought now was the best time to bring her suspicion out. She backed away from Brad and clasped her hands tight. "That was the extent of it that night. It was the night of the accident that he was at his worst. When he came home from work that evening, he was in an unusually good mood. He immediately turned the television on to watch the news in anticipation of some news story. It was then I heard about the accident, and I could see he was disappointed when he heard it wasn't you in the car. But he immediately reverted back to a good mood when I pointed out how devastated you'd be from losing your wife and daughter. I knew you'd die inside, and I let Greg know my thoughts. When he realized that it would affect you that way, he changed. In his screwed up mind, he became more powerful because he beat you in some way."

"Wait a minute. Are you suggesting that he had something to do with the accident? How could he have?" Brad asked, confused.

"I don't know Brad. At Carol's party, he really got jealous of you, and he didn't let it go this time. I think he snapped. Anyway, he changed his normal routine the entire week preceding the accident. I didn't know what he was doing. I was just glad he was out of the house. But on the night of the deaths of Anne and Brianna, it appeared to me he was waiting to hear about the accident on the news. He is an evil and dangerous man Brad," she added as a warning to Brad that he might try something again.

Brad was deep in thought. He remembered what the deputy had said at the scene of the accident. "It was like something projected the car in the perfect path to lead it down the ravine," were the precise words the deputy said. Could Greg have been the reason that his car took the unexplained path to death? He poured another glass of wine and sat down to drink it.

Kristy felt bad for him and was almost sorry she told Brad her suspicions. She didn't want to bring her fears up to Brad about her husband. She stood behind Brad and started to massage his neck and shoulders. Her long blond hair brushed up against his face slightly tickling him. He relaxed as he allowed her to dig her fingers into his tense muscles.

Foremost on Brad's mind was the thought on to handle his hate for Greg and how to prove Greg was even involved with the deaths of his wife and daughter? There was no physical evidence. He then closed his eyes and let his mind go blank from the comfort of Kristy's touch.

Kristy was thinking about how much she still loved Brad. Her emotions were leading her back to a course of physical desire for Brad as her massage turned into more of a sexual caress. She could feel him melting in her hands as he relaxed more and his body slouched in the chair. She started touching Brad in places she knew he desired. She hadn't forgotten how to please him as she continued her soft touches, sensing she had him back to their previous level of excitement. Her hands slid to his chest and then up to his face before pulling his head back gently in perfect coordination of her leaning over and touching her lips to his. Kristy then sucked on his lips as she inserted her tongue into his receptive mouth.

Brad returned the favor until the point came to end it or fulfill their desires. He chose the later and led Kristy to the bedroom.

They stood there for a moment staring at each other and then simultaneously stripped off their clothes and fell to the bed. They started off making love in a frenzied way as the rekindled fire between them fueled a reckless abandon of their basic sexual needs, creating an intense climax.

After staring into each others eyes in disbelief of what they had just done, they started all over again at a slow gentle pace allowing each to savor the other. Neither one wanted to let go of each other afterwards, but they knew that their time was limited.

"What are we going to do now?" Brad asked as he held Kristy after they had dressed themselves and made up the bed.

"I don't know. I wish we could be together, but Greg would never let that happen. He would kill both of us. I mean it Brad. He's sick," she said with a lost look on her face.

"I can't allow him to treat you the way he does though." Brad then kissed her.

"I have that under control right now. Trust me, I'll be alright. I love you with all of my heart, and that will keep me going," she said with a reassuring smile.

"Let's keep in touch."

"I'd like that. We can use Carol. That'll be the safest way. Now we better get Carol, so she can get me home."

Brad drove the rental car to the entrance of the lake house to retrieve Carol. He gave her a quick scolding in jest over her grand plan that tricked Kristy and him. He then told her he appreciated it because it was nice to see Kristy again. Brad then asked Carol to keep an eye on Kristy for him and let him know if there were any problems he should be aware of.

After the two returned to the lake house, Brad thanked Carol for everything she had done for him concerning the selling of the house fixtures as well as today. He gave each of the girls a hug and a kiss, and then departed for the airport.

Kristy felt great on her ride home with Carol. She filled Carol in on most of the details, but not the lovemaking episode. Kristy had the satisfaction of believing that a seed was planted today. The timing could not have been more perfect. She knew that Greg would just never have to learn of it.

Brad reflected on today's activities on his flight home. It felt good to him to share closeness with someone again, especially with Kristy because he would always have feelings for her. He worried about her and wondered what would happen between them if she ever left Greg. He didn't see that possibility in the future though. Kristy was frightened too much by what he might do to the both of them.

He then turned his thoughts to the possibility that Greg may have been responsible for the death of Anne and Brianna. What could he do to find out? If Greg knew there was a suspicion of him he might go after Kristy or both of them. He would figure something out to help solve the crime, but he didn't have the answers today.

Thinking of the accident brought forth memories of Anne. He started questioning his decision to make love to Kristy. Did he cheat on Anne by doing it with Kristy? He felt frantic at the thought of it, compounded by the fact that Kristy was married. "What had he done today?" he asked himself as his good mood vanished, and his walls went up again.

He tried to fight with his emotions having felt life again today, but guilt took over leaving him alone inside.

CHAPTER 24

▼

Brad spent the next two months much like the previous three months. He worked hard and stayed to himself. It was a shame he couldn't even enjoy all of the good things he brought to Bill's business. Brad didn't even realize how far he had come with his pitching motion or see how well defined his muscled body had become over the months. His emotional state was still dormant, and he just didn't pay any attention to any progress his body had made. He was still living his life like a robot.

Unknown to Brad, a renewed life was on the threshold for him, and it would begin on this particular July morning. His day started out much like every day. He woke up early to go jogging, but decided to wait since it was pouring down rain. It was Sunday, and he didn't have to work, so he hopped back in bed and fell asleep.

The rain had almost stopped as the sun tried to peek through the clouds unknown to Brad because he was sound asleep. He was awakened by what he thought was someone shaking him. It startled him because there wasn't anybody around. He hopped to his feet and went to the kitchen to make a pot of coffee. As he looked out the kitchen window, he saw the most unusual looking rainbow he had ever seen, except for one time before. It was full of vibrant colors as it towered over his world. He then realized where he saw such a rainbow and ran to the refrigerator.

Brianna's picture was attached to the side of the refrigerator. Brad pulled the magnet off the art piece and carried the painting to the kitchen window to compare it with the real life rainbow. Brianna's picture was practically identical to the prism of colors in the sky this morning. Even the colors blended in the same way.

He thought it was too remarkable of a coincidence and took it as a sign from God and his daughter.

A huge smile came over his face as he felt a darkness leave his body and evaporate into thin air. He finally realized that it was ok to let go of his wife and daughter from the unhealthy way he had held on to them. He posted the picture on the front of the refrigerator and for the first time could look at it without feeling pain. It brought delight to him instead of a deep hurt.

Brad sniffed the air and actually smelled the fresh aroma of coffee. He poured a cup of coffee and opened the patio door and stood on his deck. The fresh smell of the air after a summer rain filled his lungs with new life. He ran inside to check on the time. He suddenly had an urge to go to church. He had time to get to the nine o'clock mass.

After finishing his coffee, he went to the bathroom to clean up. Brad removed his shirt before he shaved. He was shocked at what he saw in the mirror. There was actually a soul in the person in the mirror. He had life in his eyes again. Brad stepped back from his reflection, surprised by the perfect physique he had built the past five months. He turned slightly to allow himself to see the complete picture. It was as if he had just awakened from a long sleep, and found himself in another world. Actually that was the truth of the matter; he had been awakened by a sign from Brianna.

Brad shaved and then showered. He picked out some nice clothes to wear to church and then dressed. He was a different person now, and he felt good about himself. It was time to live again.

Church went by quickly while Brad sat with the Weatherbys in peace, participating in songs, and listening intently to the sermon. He had been fortunate to find an empty seat next to Norris, Grace, and Nathan. It felt good to him to be part of their family again. After the service, the four of them had breakfast and Brad followed them home.

Brad went to grab his glove from his jeep. "Hey Nathan, grab your mitt. It's time for us to finally play catch."

"Really Brad, you're actually going to throw the ball?"

"Yes Nathan, it's the real thing today. Do you think you can handle me?" Brad asked jokingly.

"As long as you don't throw any fastballs at me or a mean curve ball," Nathan replied.

"Not today. I just want to play catch with you."

Nathan grinned from ear to ear. He couldn't believe he was actually going to play ball with Brad. It meant the world to him to have the chance.

Norris and Grace stood outside watching the two warm up. It felt so good to have Brad back at the house. It was especially good to have him involved in their son's life.

Norris watched Brad closely out of curiosity. He had heard from many people that Brad would have been a superstar in the majors. "One thing for sure, there weren't any pitchers built the way he was," Norris said to himself.

"This feels great," Brad said to Nathan as he loosened up. "Hey Nathan, give me a target by just holding your glove in one place. I want to dial in on my control. That is one thing that I couldn't do properly with the CAMM."

Nathan complied with the request by holding his mitt out in front of him while bracing himself.

After about five minutes Brad zeroed in on the target on a consistent basis without Nathan having to move it. He increased his velocity until Nathan said that was fast enough.

Nathan was amazed at how accurate Brad was and blown away by how fast Brad could throw the ball. "Is that your fastball?"

"No Nathan, that was about sixty percent," Brad answered with a lopsided smile.

"You're kidding. There's no way I could handle your fastball then."

"You'll learn," Brad said with encouragement.

They finished throwing the ball after an hour. It was the best day of Nathan's life in some time because Brad was like a big brother to Nathan.

The Weatherbys thanked Brad for joining them today and asked him to be sure and come back anytime.

Brad assured them he would stop by when he could and then headed back to his apartment.

Norris immediately got on the phone and called Bill to give him the good news about Brad.

Bill then called Coach Culley at Duke, and asked if he could have some players get together tomorrow, so Brad could pitch.

The coach was more than happy to do that. He had several players in summer school that he would have ready to play.

The next day, Brad arrived at work as usual, except on this day he was smiling. He stopped to talk to some of the employees and even turned his head when a sharp looking woman walked by. He was taken back when Bill approached him and then led him out to his car.

"What's going on Bill?" Brad asked puzzled.

"We're going to Durham this morning. We have an appointment with some people there. Just relax, it's going to be a fun day."

They talked about business most of the time during their drive, and then Bill finally had to tell Brad how good it was to have him back to his old self.

Brad agreed wholeheartedly. He was surprised when Bill pulled into the sport complex parking lot. "Ok Bill, what's going on?"

"It's time to see what you have. I called the coach last night, and he and several players are waiting for you. Now I want you to start out slow," Bill said sternly.

Brad smiled as he thought about getting on the pitcher's mound again. "Don't worry about me Bill. I've never been in better shape. I studied everything there is to study about the human body and applied that to my workouts. I will pace myself though."

Coach Culley met them at the door. He gave Brad a hug and let him know it was good to see him again. He then led Brad to his old locker where a uniform hung. "Suit up and join us on the field."

After suiting up, Brad trotted out to the field ready to go.

There were quite a few members of the baseball team waiting on him. They were curious to see Brad Preston because they had heard so many great stories about him. They gasped at the sight of his well muscled body.

Coach threw Brad a baseball and told him to warm up.

Brad started out slow and methodical as he eased his way into form.

Coach Culley liked his new throwing motion. It was pure, and simple, and fit Brad perfectly. He let Bill know his feelings about it.

"Batter up." Brad said as he felt ready to go. He was loose and comfortable.

"Nothing fancy now," Bill yelled out.

Brad turned to him smiling. "I'll start out at eighty percent and see where we go from there."

Duke's number two hitter came to the plate a little reluctant to face Brad from not knowing what to expect. He had heard so much about Brad and knew this was the first time he had pitched since his injury. He dug in waiting for the first pitch.

Brad wound up and pushed off hard with his well muscled right leg firing a fastball that cut inside at the last second as the batter swung and missed badly.

Chills ran down the coach's spine by the sight of it.

Bill just smiled.

The batter turned to the coach for a second for some direction.

"Just try to hit the ball son," Coach Culley yelled out.

"What was the speed on that pitch?" Bill asked.

"Eighty six miles per hour," a voice cried out from behind the backstop.

"That's eighty percent," a Duke Player asked. "I sure don't want to face him at one hundred percent."

Brad continued pitching for another twenty pitches. He shook his head and stepped off of the mound.

Coach Culley and Bill ran out to the mound concerned. They were worried he had injured himself again.

"I need to go full bore here. My accuracy is off a tad because I'm holding back," Brad said as they approached.

"Damn Brad, you looked perfect to me," the coach said. "You were hitting the target regularly. Nobody's perfect."

"I can be," Brad said. "I want the ball to hit the target with every pitch I throw."

The catcher braced himself. He wasn't sure how fast this guy could pitch if he hadn't been throwing at full velocity. It seemed fast to him.

The batter was just as nervous. He stepped into the batter's box and waited for the next pitch.

This time Brad threw one hundred percent. He pushed off with more strength from his right leg as his left leg led the way. His arm was cocked perfectly, and the ball released from his hand.

The batter couldn't even get the bat off his shoulder before the ball flew by him making a popping sound as it hit the catcher's mitt.

Everybody there just stared. The coach shooting the radar gun yelled out ninety-nine miles per hour.

"Yes," Brad said when he heard the speed, knowing the ball hit the exact spot that he intended it to hit. He threw another fifteen pitches with the same result and called it a day. He didn't hurt or have any soreness; he just knew that it was enough pitching for his first day.

"Hey Coach, do you have anyone that can throw some batting practice to me. I want to see if I can still hit," Brad asked full of energy.

"Sure Brad." Coach Culley waved his arm at the bullpen. "Tommy get out there and warm up."

Bill and Coach Culley spoke with Brad about his great performance today. They put a deal together to have Duke as a client for the CAMM, with Bill making certain to let the coach know he couldn't expect those same results because there were very few people that would have worked as hard as Brad had to get to where he was.

Coach Culley knew that was the case just from watching Brad and seeing how well conditioned his body was. "Brad, I just want you to know how proud I am of you. You've been through more traumatic events in your life than anyone deserves. You're going to be great in the big leagues one day. Heck, from what I've seen today, you could start now."

"Thanks Coach, that means a lot to me. But let's see how well I can hit. I've made some changes there also." Brad gave his old coach a wink.

Tommy was now warmed up and ready to go. "Do you want me to just pitch batting practice or pitch like it's a game situation?"

"Game situation," Brad said as he dug in.

The pitcher was taken back after the first ten pitches because all Brad did with them was play tap back.

The coach just sat back and smiled from seeing the frustration in his pitcher, so he yelled out to Brad, "Ok, you have the timing down now. Why don't you show these guys how to hit?"

The coach liked Brad's new batting stance. He had opened it up a bit, which a lot of players were doing now.

Tommy wanted to show everybody that he was a good pitcher, so he put everything he had into the next pitch. Brad took a swing at the ball hitting a line drive to within ten feet of the center field fence.

The next pitch was driven into the left field bleachers.

"Is this your best pitcher?" Bill asked the coach.

"One of my top aces," replied the coach, while shaking his head in amazement.

"Good," Bill said, pleased.

Brad continued with batting practice for another ten minutes and then decided he had enough. He felt good about his hitting and pitching after today's performance.

Every Duke player that had been watching today's performance ran up to Brad to let him know what a great job he had done. They wanted to hear some stories about his playing days at Duke.

Brad obliged them by telling several stories.

Bill asked the coach if it would be possible for Brad to continue playing there for the next couple of weeks. He wanted Brad to keep pitching, and he trusted Coach Culley to keep an eye on him to make sure he didn't over do it.

The coach was more than happy and offered to have Brad stay at his home.

It was all set. Brad would stay in Durham for the remainder of the week, only to come back to Charlotte to have his pitching motion analyzed to insure it was still in sync. He would then return the following week to go through the same program.

Brad showered and dressed in his street clothes before taking a walk around campus. It was a good feeling to be there again. His walk ended up in front of Anne's old apartment that they shared after their wedding. Some great memories came to mind as he stared at the place. It made him miss Anne, although his pain was almost gone. He knew what pain was left, would be there for the rest of his life. But thankfully he could live with that.

Bill made a call to Keith Olson the moment he arrived back at his office. When Keith answered he heard the words, "Our boy is ready."

It took Keith a few seconds to realize who the call was from and who the person was that was ready. "Bill, is that you?"

"Yes it is. After all of these years, I wouldn't have thought you had to ask that question," Bill replied.

Keith laughed. "You're right Bill. It's just been very stressful here. I don't know if you check the standings, but we're in last place right now. I assume you're referring to Brad Preston when you say he's ready. Jack made mention to me that he was very impressed with him. He can't wait to get his hands on him."

"That's why I'm calling. I want you to fly out here as soon as possible and see him pitch. Bring Jack if you like."

"And what should I expect to see when I'm there?"

"A phenomenon," is all Bill would say.

"So you've seen him pitch I assume?" Keith asked, shaking his head.

"He pitched for the first time in four years today. And he hit today as well," Bill threw in to add a little flavor.

Keith was becoming curious now. It seemed Bill was playing him by holding out. "Please give me the details my good friend. You have me going now," he said, playing the game.

"He started out at about eighty percent velocity. We clocked him at eighty-six miles per hour on his first pitch. His accuracy was good."

Keith sat up and took notice at the other end of the line.

"He then threw about twenty more pitches at the same level and then stepped off the mound shaking his head." Bill stopped for a moment to allow Keith to feel some of the same anxious moments that he felt earlier.

"What was the problem?" Keith asked concerned.

"He wasn't satisfied with his control. Brad thought his holding back hindered his accuracy. Coach Culley and I were impressed with his control though. This young man is the real thing Keith. He stepped back on the mound and fired a bullet that hit the bull's eye. We clocked him at ninety-nine on that pitch and the next fifteen pitches after that, all of them with the same pinpoint accuracy. It was amazing to see Keith."

Keith was standing up in his office now. He knew Bill was shooting him straight on what happened today. "What do you have him doing now?"

"He's going to stay at Duke with his old coach for the rest of the week and work out with the team members that are there for the summer. Then he'll come to corporate Saturday to reevaluate his motion."

"I'll fly out today and meet you tomorrow morning at the university," Keith said. "Let them know what the plan is so I won't miss the workout. How about ten in the morning?"

"I'll see you then." Bill hung up the phone with a pleased smile on his face.

Keith could hardly contain his excitement. He called Jack to see if he could make it tomorrow morning.

Jack agreed to take a flight out of Cincinnati and then return later in the day for the scheduled seven o'clock game.

Greg had been on Kristy hot and heavy about her not being pregnant. It had been long enough for her to conceive, he thought.

Kristy had missed her last two periods, but had not informed Greg. She didn't want to let him in on any timing issues. She had purchased a home pregnancy test to use tonight. She had it all planned.

Greg arrived home from work as his usual arrogant self. He popped open a can of pop and headed for the bedroom to change into his softball outfit. Greg's sport days were now down to playing slow pitch softball during the summer and some pick up basketball games in the wintertime. Greg was an exceptional player in the park district summer league that he participated in and led the league in homeruns.

Kristy had finished with her pregnancy test just before he arrived home. It tested positive, just as she suspected it would. She knew she was two months pregnant, but would let on like she was only one month. That way she could protect her secret from everyone.

Greg growled from the bedroom, "Kristy, where in the hell's my jersey?"

She carried it in to him freshly cleaned. She let him slip it on before she handed him the test.

"What's this?"

"It says we're having a baby," she replied with a forced smile.

"I knew I had it in me," Greg bragged. "I can't wait to let everybody know."

"I need to call Carol right away," Kristy said, playing along with the whole thing. She knew it was a joke for her to be excited about having Greg's baby. That is why it would be easy to show pleasure while she carried Brad's baby.

"Yeah call Carol. I'm sure she'll let Brad know you're pregnant. Man, that'll have to kill him knowing that I'll be a father," he said almost laughing. Greg felt the power come over him again causing him to become aroused. He started to get rough with Kristy, but he remembered her threat about killing the baby. He knew she would do it, so he decided to stop by the strip bar after the game and take out the hot little Hispanic girl that was hitting on him.

Greg left the house immediately to play softball and then fulfill his sexual desire.

Kristy called Carol to let her know she was indeed pregnant.

Carol was all happy for her, but worried about Greg being a good father. She asked Kristy how Greg had been treating her lately, and Kristy explained that she had it under control right now. That worried Carol because she knew how volatile he could be. She had seen him in his minor anger, and it scared her.

Kristy ended the conversation by asking Carol not to mention the pregnancy to Brad. "If Greg asks you, please tell him you told Brad the news and say no more."

Carol knew something was up when she hung up the phone.

Brad ran his early morning jog around the campus. He cut it back to two miles, so he wouldn't wear himself out for his practice this morning. He and the coach had spent the evening talking about his pitching career, and the coach gave him several tips. Brad wanted to throw a few breaking balls today, and Coach Culley agreed.

Brad was busy warming up as Bill, Keith, and Jack found some good seats allowing them a good view to watch today's performance.

Jack was perturbed that Brad had already thrown without him being there, so he was in an especially critical mood today.

"I will say Bill; the kid has a smooth delivery. How much did you have to do with it?" Keith asked.

"None; he did everything on his own. After his wife died, he ran away from life and was almost like a robot. He executed every job perfectly and set up a regiment for himself that he followed to a tee," Bill answered.

"I'm not sure I like all of that muscle," Keith said. "It takes away some flex."

"He thought of that, so he implemented a stretching program into his routine. Like I said, he was a robot."

Coach Culley yelled up to the threesome to see if they were ready to go, and the three men nodded their heads signaling yes.

"Is he going a hundred percent right off the go today?" Keith asked.

"We'll know in a minute," Bill said as Brad started his wind up to face the hitter.

Brad's first pitch was a ninety-eight mph fastball that blew by the hitter with the ball pounding the catcher's mitt in the exact intended target. The catcher didn't have to move the glove one bit.

Brad executed the next pitch with the same result, but this time it was ninety-nine mph.

Keith and Jack leaned forward mesmerized by what they were witnessing, only to be more amazed by the sinker that Brad threw. They felt sorry for the poor guy out there trying to hit because Brad had him all confused.

Brad then threw a curve ball that changed direction at the last second throwing the hitter off balance.

"Jesus Christ Jack, that kid has a whole arsenal of pitches," Keith exclaimed with excitement. "When can we bring him up?"

"Well, that's a little premature right now Keith. He's only thrown a few pitches," Jack said.

"He can pitch that way all day boys," Bill said with a huge grin. "Just sit back and enjoy. It's worth seeing."

They cut Brad off at forty pitches. He let them know he felt great and could pitch an entire game. Nobody doubted his statement.

"Do you want to see me hit?" Brad asked, anxious to see if he could do as well as yesterday.

"I don't care if you can hit or not son. The way you pitch, who cares," Jack replied.

"I'd like to see it though," Keith said out of curiosity.

Coach Culley had his pitching ace ready to go for them.

Brad slipped on some batting gloves and took some practice swings to loosen up, and then walked up to the plate. This time he didn't play tap back as he drove the fast ball over the center field fence.

All Keith could do was shake his head and laugh. He had never seen anything like it before in his life. It must have been like watching Babe Ruth when he was in his prime, he thought.

They watched Brad drive balls all over the field. He never missed hitting the ball. There were a few foul balls, but he always made contact.

"Where do we go from here?" Keith asked Bill. He respected Bill's opinion, especially since he had been around Brad all of this time.

"I would prefer for him to stay here for two weeks. We can keep an eye on his pitching motion to make sure it hasn't changed by testing him at the corporate office in Charlotte. The rest is up to you two. In my opinion, he could pitch for the Dodgers with no problems," Bill replied.

"I think we put him in one of our minor league divisions today," Jack said.

Keith shook his head no as he pulled his cell phone out of its carrying case. He asked the person on the other end of the line to see when the next home game would be in approximately two weeks for the Columbus single A team. He then wrote a date down and asked to have the general manager of the Catfish call him as soon as possible.

"Ok gentlemen, here's what we're going to do. Brad will pitch for our Columbus single A team two weeks from today. I'll be there along with the big guy to see what we really have. That should give us a good indication of where Brad is at this time," Keith said firmly, not wanting an argument from Jack

"That's a wise choice," Bill said. "When do you want to get together for a contract for our machine and for Brad? You just have the rights to him right now."

"Of course," Keith said. "You draw up the contract on your computerized pitching machine for our pitchers, and I'll work on Brad's deal." Keith then eased up by giving Bill a handshake and a pat on the back. "You did it just like you said you would. And he did it, just like you promised. Now my butt isn't on the line."

"Now let's get us a World Series ring," Bill said smiling.

CHAPTER 25

▼

Brad arrived in Columbus, Georgia on Monday morning at the Catfish home office. He was fitted for his uniform and then taken to the playing field so he could get used to the surroundings. It was a day off for the team as they had just returned from a road trip. They were to get together for practice in one hour, and Brad was looking forward to seeing his new teammates. He had played against a lot of these guys in college. There was even a player from Duke on the roster that Brad had played with for one year.

He walked around the ball field and kicked at the dirt. It was such an over-whelming state of affairs for him after being away from the game for four years. The smell brought back memories of when he played. Brad walked out to the pitchers mound and stood on the rubber while staring at home plate. It was so natural for him, which kept up his confidence level. All he had to do was perform the way he had been doing the past two weeks.

Brad realized how special this was for him because it was unheard of for some-one to work out two weeks and then start a minor league game. But he had really been working for this the past four years. He owed his success to hard work and a great deal of knowledge of the game.

Brad ended up having a good work out today. He threw some, but not hard, and he hit the ball well.

Most of the Catfish team members had heard of Brad and were very impressed with him. They didn't know what to expect, having someone from nowhere arrive one day and be scheduled as starting pitcher the next game, but they were all behind him.

Brad was happy to see his parents again. They made the trip up from Florida to see his debut in the big leagues, even if it was only single A ball. They spent several hours together before Brad had to prepare for the game.

Keith Olson was in the office with the owner of the Dodgers. They were talking with the general manager and the head coach of the Catfish.

There was a great deal of anxiety and excitement in the Catfish locker room as every player wanted to make a good impression. It was rare to have front office personal in the facility, not to mention the owner. It made them all realize just how important their new player was.

After putting on his uniform, Brad spoke with his catcher to let him know what pitches he could throw.

The catcher was shocked by the amount of pitches Brad proclaimed to be able to execute, and questioned Brad about his arsenal as they both departed the locker room to take batting practice before Brad warmed up.

Brad hit the ball extremely well in batting practice. One would have never guessed he was the starting pitcher for this evening's game by the way he hit. He then teamed up with Kurt Hennings, the Catfish catcher, to warm up.

The ballpark was filling up fast, which impressed Brad. He thought it was good to see the team had such strong support from the local people. He then started to get a slight case of the butterflies when he realized that this was for real.

The national anthem finished playing; signally it was time for the game to start.

The coach of the Catfish walked up to Brad and handed him the ball. "I don't know anything about you, so it's up to you to let me know if you feel any tightness or soreness anywhere. You have a fifty pitch limit tonight or there about. Good luck."

The coach walked away as Brad stared at him. "He must be upset that I broke his rotation," he said to himself. Brad trotted out to the mound and kicked at the dirt in front of the rubber. He rubbed the ball vigorously while he looked around the ballpark. He spotted his parents, as well as Keith Olson alongside the owner of the Dodgers. It was show time, and he was ready.

Brad struggled with his first few pitches from being nervous. He then threw a ninety-eight mph fast ball that cut in on the batter for a strike. The pop of the ball hitting the catcher's mitt filled the stadium. He then threw a curve ball, followed by a sinker to strike out the batter. He did the same to the second batter. The number three hitter hit a blooper off the handle of the bat for a base hit. Brad was upset by allowing a hit. He reached deep into himself and struck out the next batter on three straight strikes.

The next two innings went pretty much the same way for Brad, with three more strikes outs, a ground out, and two infield fly balls. Brad was in the zone now, and he felt it. The fourth and fifth innings were six consecutive strike outs for Brad. Everything was working for him, and his accuracy couldn't have been any better.

He had thrown close to fifty pitches after the top half of the fifth inning. It was a scoreless ballgame with Brad scheduled to bat third.

The first batter walked and then advanced to second on a sacrifice bunt.

The coach wanted to pinch hit for Brad, but Keith Olson shook his head no at him.

Brad walked up to the plate and dug in. He took the first pitch for a ball. He had this pitcher's timing down, and he had watched him enough to know what was coming by his motion. Brad waited anxiously for the next pitch as he swung the bat back and forth slowly.

The pitcher reared back and threw a fastball with all he had.

Brad picked up on the ball and hammered it over the center field fence with plenty of room to spare.

The crowd went wild as the Catfish took a two run lead. The crowd then booed when they replaced Brad with another pitcher for the sixth inning.

Keith and the owner of the Dodgers were overwhelmed by Brad's performance. It was a great day for the Dodger organization.

The Catfish's enjoyed it too, winning the game four to two.

After the game, Keith asked the owner of the Dodgers what he thought of Brad.

"Bring him up," the owner said, truly impressed by the performance he just witnessed.

Keith didn't know what to do at this point. He didn't want to push Brad along too fast, but he needed more competition than single A ball. He decided to take him up to AA ball for his next start.

Keith knew there was something special about Brad. He had never seen such dedication and hard work. He was really impressed when he talked about a contract with him, with Brad saying he only needed minimum for whatever level he played in at this time. He told Keith the Dodgers had paid him well without knowing if he would ever play again, and he felt obligated to prove himself like everyone else. Brad said they would negotiate a contract at the end of this season.

Brad was put on the Jacksonville Suns roster and was scheduled to pitch the following Sunday. Jacksonville is the AA minor league team for the Dodgers. The only players that jumped from single A to double A ball in one game were either triple A or major league players going through rehab. The Suns had heard about his dominating performance with the Catfish and were anxious to get a look at Brad.

Brad worked out the rest of the week in Jacksonville and felt more at ease as he stepped on the mound Sunday afternoon for his start. The ballpark was not quite filled to capacity since the Suns were lagging behind this year.

There were a few extra people in the stands with the Preston family there in full force, as well as Norris and Nathan Weatherby, along with Bill Matthews.

Brad dug his cleats along side the pitching rubber to prepare the mound for his throwing style and then threw his warm up pitches. He started the game with a curve ball that hit the outside corner for a strike. He then blew a ninety-nine mph fast by the hitter for a strike two, followed by a mean sinker that the batter swung at wildly. As it turned out, the next nine batters faced the same type of embarrassment. Nobody laid a bat on the ball until one batter hit a weak grounder to the shortstop for an out.

Brad ended his play for the day, pitching six hitless innings and going two for two at the plate, in another dominating performance.

Keith Olson called after the game to get a report. He smiled and pumped his arm up in the air when he heard what Brad had done. He spoke with the catcher about what he thought and was amused by his answer.

The catcher told Keith that Brad's accuracy was so good, he could have held his catcher's mitt and read a book, and the ball would have hit the pocket. The only complaint the catcher had was Brad's fastball stung his hand worse than anyone he had ever caught before.

Keith had a decision to make now. What should he do next with Brad? It was evident that even double A ball wasn't enough challenge for him at this point. But he knew he would be chastised if he put him on the Dodger roster this quick, even though he had no doubt that Brad was ready. Keith knew Brad was already better than eighty percent of the pitchers in the majors. Maybe he was better than all of them.

The mid August heat was almost unbearable as Brad exited the Las Vegas airport. He had been assigned to the Las Vegas 51's, which was the Dodgers triple A minor league team.

"I hope they have air conditioned uniforms here," Brad said to himself as sweat poured from his body. He took a cab to Cashman Field to meet with the team.

Brad recognized immediately this would be stiffer competition. There was a different atmosphere in the locker room. The players were more seasoned, and several had played in the major league. Brad felt uncomfortable being there from the moment he walked in the room. He felt a resentment, which took him by surprise. Not that he expected hugs and cheers from everybody, but he didn't think he would get the cold shoulder the way he had.

After finishing practice, Brad was really concerned. There was a lack of a team concept, and it appeared to him that everybody was just looking out for themselves. Brad met with Derrick Hughes, the coach of the 51's. He seemed like a nice guy to Brad, but it didn't take long for Brad to see the coach had no control over the team. He was a relatively new head coach in the AAA league, and it appeared to Brad he didn't know how to manage this caliber of athlete. Brad wondered what he had gotten himself in to.

When he finally settled into his room, he decided to call Carol. He needed to talk to a friend, and lucky for him Carol just happened to be home. He discussed with her what he had been going through over the past four weeks.

Carol expressed her happiness that he was back in baseball. She wasn't going to let Greg know though knowing it would only add to his hate towards Brad.

Brad then asked, "How's Kristy doing?"

Carol's body stiffened from hearing Kristy's name. "She seems fine, but I don't see her as much as I'd like. We've both been busy lately." Carol decided to see where Brad was going with this conversation, so she returned a question to him, "Do you still have feelings for her? It's ok if you do, you know."

Brad was taken back by the question. He hadn't thought about how he felt about Kristy ever since the episode at the lake house. "I don't know how to answer you Carol. I know she'll always be special to me, but she's married. Kristy made it clear to me she couldn't leave Greg, although it was for the wrong reason. I will admit that it was good to be with her at your parent's lake house a while back. I had forgotten how pretty she was."

Carol had always wanted the two of them to get married and still wanted it to happen. She thought carefully before she spoke, "You know the only reason she's there is because she seriously believes he'll kill her or you if she left."

"I know that. I worry about her being there with that idiot. He's gotten much worse as he has grown older. I just hope she knows what she's doing."

"Brad, I'm going to tell you something that Kristy told me not to tell you, so keep it to yourself. Kristy is about a month or two months pregnant right now."

Brad's mind went to work calculating the time since he and Kristy made love and determined it wasn't his baby. He actually felt bad about it and was jealous of Greg.

Carol waited for a reply, but received none so she proceeded. "She got pregnant to protect herself from him. He had really gotten rough with her again and demanded that she have a baby. Kristy took the opportunity to use it as an offense by telling him that if he roughed her up again, she would kill the unborn child in her if she became pregnant. That's the only reason she agreed to have his baby. Besides, it'll be good for her to have someone she can love."

"Of course," Brad said with his stomach still turning. "I hope it works out for her."

The call ended shortly after that with Carol second guessing herself about telling Brad what she had. She decided that it was best. What if he had strong feelings for her and was hoping for something more from Kristy, she thought to herself concluding that she had done the right thing.

CHAPTER 26

▼

Brad spent the last four days with the 51's and still had bad feelings about the team. He was scheduled to pitch this evening, and he actually dreaded the thought of it. It was so unlike him to feel that way about baseball, but the slight depression was compounded by the hurt he felt by Kristy carrying Greg's baby. It was twofold, as he hated Greg and felt a loss for Kristy. Brad wished he could shake his unhappiness knowing it could have a negative affect on his pitching today.

Brad was dressed in his baseball uniform and ready to take batting practice before the game. He swung the bat while waiting for Tony Coselli to finish hitting.

Tony was the catcher for the 51's. He was a hard nosed Italian that looked like a catcher with his stocky build. Tony had good skills as a catcher and had been expected to go to the majors this year, but the back up catcher for the Dodgers ended up having an outstanding year, therefore keeping Tony in AAA. Maybe that was the reason he went around with a chip on his shoulder. No matter what the problem was, Brad couldn't get along with him adding to more trouble between them.

Brad's performance tonight somewhat reflected the entire teams overall play, although his play wasn't as bad. His fast ball only topped out at ninety-four mph, and his breaking pitches weren't sharp. Brad ended up pitching five innings, giving up five hits, two walks, and two runs. It wasn't a bad performance for most pitchers, but it wasn't what Brad considered good. He was very disappointed in his play. He didn't even get a hit.

The 51's ended up losing five to nothing, and it didn't seem to faze any of the players or coaches. They had given up on this year, and it showed.

Keith Olson surprised everyone when he walked into the locker room. Nobody had expected him to be there today. He walked by the players shaking his head in disgust stopping at Brad's locker.

"Let's have dinner," Keith said to Brad.

As Keith led Brad out of the locker room, several of the players finally realized how important their new pitcher was.

The coach was embarrassed also as he didn't know how close Keith was with Brad.

Keith took Brad to a great restaurant. They both ordered a cocktail before Keith started in on Brad. "Don't be so hard on yourself. You weren't that bad today. Most guys pitching their first game in triple A would have been very satisfied with what you did today. But you're so much better than that. I pondered sending you here because I knew this team had its problems. I just didn't realize they were as bad as I witnessed tonight. I'm disappointed in you for allowing yourself to be brought down to their level though. I thought you were better than that. It just goes to show me you're human." Keith sat back and stared at Brad for his reaction.

The waitress handed them their drinks, and they both took a big sip to ease the tension.

"Look Brad, you're going to have off days here and there in your career. I only expect from you your very best effort. You didn't give that to me or this team today. I knew before the game started tonight what to expect from you when I saw the lack of confidence in your face. Now I'm glad I sent you here because it was a good lesson for you. You'll find when you play in the big league there will be certain players that won't gel with the team. Play over them."

Brad listened to every word admitting to himself that everything Keith said was on the mark. "Yes sir, you're one hundred percent correct. I let all of us down today because I felt uncomfortable the minute I joined the team, and I let it effect me. That isn't very professional is it?"

"No it isn't. Now here's what I want you to do. You take charge of this team. Fire em up. Be a leader the way you've been all of your life," Keith stated with passion.

"What about the coach? He's fairly new with the team, and I'm sure he doesn't want me to get in his way of coaching."

"He'll be fine. He might not like it, but he won't step in your way if he wants to keep his job. I already told him not to stand in your way." Keith gave a quick smile. "One more thing for you to think about concerning this team. Every single player is waiting for his chance to join the majors. You are their competition in many ways, as is every other player on this team. So it's a different atmosphere between players than you were used to in college."

Brad shook his head acknowledging to Keith that he understood what he was saying

They finished their dinner and talked about baseball before Keith returned Brad to his room.

The following day Brad was back to his old self. He became a leader on the field by giving a few of the pitchers small tips that allowed them to throw better. There were a few players really struggling with their hitting, so Brad suggested that they adjust their stance and set their arms properly.

There was some resentment, especially from Tony. He was becoming abrasive with Brad by now, so Brad walked up to Tony and made a bet with him that would change the entire team. Brad bet Tony that he could pitch a one hundred mile per hour fastball and knock a baseball off a stand.

Tony took the bet and offered Brad five pitches to accomplish the feat. Tony then warmed Brad up for the impossible feat.

They found a baseball tee and set the ball on it. The entire coaching staff and team stood around to watch.

The radar gun was set as Brad went through his smooth pitching motion and rifled a fastball towards home plate. The ball was a perfect strike and hit the waiting baseball off the tee.

Everyone turned towards the radar gun to hear the result.

"One, O, one," was yelled out by the person operating the gun.

That was the start of the recovery for the Las Vegas 51's as the entire team surrounded Brad to congratulate him.

The coach stood there stunned.

The 51's won three out of four of the following games. Brad even pinch-hit twice getting key hits that scored valuable runs. The players had bonded and now had a desire to win as a team.

Brad's next start was destined to be quite different than his first time on the mound with the 51's. He now had the backing of the entire team. He and Tony Coselli had become friends, and they were both looking forward to Brad toeing the rubber today.

Tony knew the opposing team well and would be a great help in selecting pitches for each hitter.

Keith Olson showed up again with the Dodgers owner. He had a feeling this was going to be a great day.

Brad didn't let him down as he struck out the side the first inning. His fast ball hit the century mark twice.

Keith watched the team's owner closely wanting to get a true feel for what he thought.

After three innings of no hit ball for Brad, and the 51's scoring three runs, the owner turned to Keith. "I thought this team was out of sync and had a bad attitude. It looks to me like they're playing great together. Why is their record so bad?"

"They just came together four days ago. Brad took control of this team and turned it around overnight. It takes leadership, and that boy has it," Keith said with pride.

"Hell, he has more than leadership," the owner said, displaying a smile that was rare to see this year. "I've never seen a better pitcher in my life, and I've been around some great ones. I want him brought up after today, no if, ands, or buts."

"I thought you'd say that," Keith replied. "He's ready. It's a shame it's so late in the year. We might've had a chance to make the playoffs this year if he had been with us."

"I hate to say this because it sounds like a Chicago Cub fan, but wait until next year. He's the future franchise player for us. We need to fill a few holes for next year, but I'm willing to open the checkbook now," the owner said, pleased with the positive outlook for next year.

They quietly sat there for the next four innings enjoying the performance of their team and the no hitter Brad was throwing.

Brad went seven strong innings of no hit ball. He struck out nine batters and walked none. It was a masterpiece.

The 51's coach looked up to Keith for direction, and Keith motioned to let him hit this inning, but to pull him off the mound. They weren't going to give in to going over the seventy-five pitch limit, and he had already thrown sixty-nine pitches.

Brad approached the plate to a standing ovation from the pleased crowd. They kept to their feet as he pounded the first pitch over the left field fence for a home run and wouldn't stop the roar until he came out of the dugout raising his cap.

The crowd's mood changed when he didn't return to the mound for the eighth inning. They would have booed the entire inning if Brad hadn't come out of the dugout to quiet them down.

The Dodger's owner marveled at the control Brad had over everyone around him. He turned to Keith smiling. "Please remind me to give you a raise." The owner raised his hand towards Keith. "That is, after you sign him to a multi year contract. Now let's go down there and see this young man. I haven't had the pleasure to talk to him."

Keith was pumped up at this point. He made a mental note to do something special for Bill Matthews. It was wonderful to see his boss full of passion again for the Dodgers. Keith had never seen him go sit in the dugout of any minor league team as he was doing tonight.

All of the 51's players appreciated it also and showed it by ending the game with a ten to nothing rout of the league's best team.

After the game ended, the Dodger's owner went out to home plate with a microphone to address the crowd and the team. "I want to thank all of the faithful fans that came here tonight to witness the most dominating performance we have had here. I know you were all disappointed when we pulled this great pitcher in the eighth inning…"

The fans voicing their opinion with some boos and then applause interrupted him. They were all happy for what they just saw. Not only for Brad's performance, but the entire team's. They had been waiting for something good out of this team all year, and they finally got it.

The owner continued with a large smile, "Let me introduce to you the newest member of the Los Angeles Dodgers, Brad Preston." He waited for the crowd to finish their applause. "And I mean the Dodgers, as in the majors."

The crowd agreed by standing, and Brad turned to the owner with an unsure look on his face. It had all happened so fast.

"And let's not forget the performance of the entire 51's team. They played great tonight, and I'm proud of each one of them. Now let me explain why we had to pull Brad out of the game. He just started pitching again after a four year absence from the game, and we had him on a pitch count. I couldn't risk hurting him, so we stuck to our plan of around seventy five pitches. You can see him throw a complete game in Los Angeles."

The Dodger's owner spent several hours with Brad after the game and left with great feelings about his star. He was impressed with the way Brad handled himself, thinking it was refreshing to be around a great athlete that wasn't just interested in his own self interest.

CHAPTER 27

▼

The first order of business for Keith Olson was to get a contract signed with Brad. He knew Brad would probably confer with his father and Bill Matthews first before he agreed to anything. Keith thought Brad would probably use his father in law to review the contract, as was the case four years ago. He put an attractive contract together after receiving approval from the Dodger's owner and corporate attorney, and then called Brad.

Time was of essence for Keith to get this signed for several reasons. He knew Brad would have finished this year for league minimum without hesitation, but he wanted to execute a contract now to be fair to Brad and the Dodgers. Keith had learned a long time ago that you agree on a contract before the other party has a long time to think about it. Besides, he had to have a contract with Brad if he wanted a bonus, per his employer.

Brad arrived at Keith's office. It was comfortable and inviting to him with all of the baseball memorabilia on the walls. There were pictures of Sandy Koufax, Don Drysdale, and Jackie Robinson that really stood out to Brad. Keith's office was fairly neat, but not perfect like Bill Matthew's office. There were things scattered around the room in an organized way. Brad assumed that Keith knew where everything was.

"Well, do I pass inspection?" Keith asked as he walked into Brad's view.

"It feels very comfortable." Brad walked over to Keith's desk. "I like your pictures. Those were the days when baseball ruled the sporting world."

"Yes they were. I'm hoping you can bring that back to the game again. You're a once in a lifetime ball player. I can honestly say I've never seen anyone with the talent you possess. And you have the right attitude to go with it. That's why we want to offer you this contract." Keith handed Brad the contract and sat down at his desk.

Brad took the legal document and started to read it. He was going over all of the legal verbiage and details carefully.

"I thought you might want to go over this with an attorney, agent, or family member. I didn't intend for you to make a decision right now," Keith stated.

Brad glanced up over the contract looking at Keith. "I don't intend on hiring an agent. I had several business classes in college, in addition to learning a great deal working with Bill about business contracts. If I have any problems, I'll contact an attorney. It basically comes down to this Keith. I trust you. I can tell by what I've read that you wanted to cover my interests as well as the Dodger's interest. Besides, I want to play baseball, and this is the team that took the gamble on me four years ago. The money you paid me to sign with the team has made my life much easier, and I thank you for that."

Brad started to read again, but then quickly added, "I know you thought I'd have the three men I admire the most check this over, so you covered everything in advance. Oh, you're being added to that list, and you're now the fourth man that I admire the most."

Keith sat back and started laughing. He wished that all professional ball players felt the same way. It would make life more enjoyable for him and the fans.

Brad read every word of the contract, asking Keith a question here and there about some of the clauses. He felt like the Dodgers went out of their way to sign a multi-year agreement. He put the papers on Keith's desk and stood up.

"What's wrong Brad?" Keith asked, perplexed from Brad's action.

Brad just walked over to Keith and shook his hand. "I'll sign these now if you allow me to buy you dinner tonight." He then gave a big smile that made his eyes glimmer.

"I wouldn't expect anything less from you," Keith said as he calmed down. "Well you're a rich man now. What are you going to do with the money?"

"Invest it. It isn't about the money for me. Maybe I thought about it years ago, but not since I lost the most important things in my life. This is my life now, and I promise you I'll work as hard five years from now, as I have the past four years getting here."

Keith just stared at a young man far wiser than his years.

The Dodger's baseball team treated Brad very similar to the way he was treated when he arrived at the Las Vegas locker room. There seemed to be resentment from some players while others stared at him trying to size him up.

Brad remembered what happened with the 51's, and he wasn't going to allow that to happen to him again. This was serious business now. He was being paid millions to play a game he loved.

Harry Elders was the coach for the Dodgers. He had been in the game for thirty years before he finally made it to the top job. There was much work to do in this organization, and he was the man to get the team back in contention. That is why he greeted Brad with open arms. He had heard about this young man and had seen film of his minor league play. He was extremely impressed and had prepared a strategy to build this team around Brad.

"Gentlemen," Coach Elders stated. "I want you to meet Brad Preston. He's our new addition to the pitching staff. His numbers in the minors were outstanding."

A couple of the players went up to Brad to shake his hand. They had heard about him and respected his record.

Brad's Major League Baseball dream had finally become reality as they headed for the playing turf in Dodger Stadium for pre-game warm ups.

They lost the game as well as the next two games, before flying out to Colorado for the start of a seven game road trip. Brad was scheduled to start the first game with the Rockies, which was a big challenge. Coors's Field is known as a hitter's ballpark

Brad was allotted eighty pitches for his first couple of starts, and that was enough to get through seven innings. He gave the Dodgers what they wanted from their newly signed pitcher, giving up just four hits and one run. He struck out twelve and didn't walk anyone. At the plate he went one for three, leading the Dodgers to a three to one victory, ending their three game losing streak.

Since both teams were not contenders, there was only a small television audience. However, ESPN made a big news story about this great up and coming pitcher for the Dodgers that caught the eye of Greg Somanski. He watched the news clip in disbelief as his power faded. This couldn't be happening he thought to himself. "I took him out," Greg said to himself.

Greg kept track of the Dodgers for the next few games to see when Brad would pitch again. It really struck a nerve in Greg when he found out Brad would be pitching against San Francisco in the game of the week.

San Francisco was leading their division and trying to gain home field advantage in the playoffs, so it was an important game for them, not to mention the rivalry between the two teams.

The big game had arrived as Brad warmed up in the bullpen for his start. He felt good and had the confidence of a veteran as he loosened up. He had no clue this game was featured on national television.

However, there was one individual in Indianapolis that was aware of it, and he was sitting in front of a big screen television in a local bar to watch the game. It really rubbed Greg the wrong way when he saw all of the interest the locals displayed towards their local hero, Brad Preston, so he pounded the drinks hard to ease his pain.

The ball game turned out to be a fantastic pitching dual. There was no score after five innings, with only three hits in the game.

Brad had only given up one hit and it was a blooper. He was in total command of his control today and his fastball was untouchable. Brad was scheduled to bat first in the bottom of the sixth. He hit the ball solid in the third inning, but the center fielder made a great catch to rob him of a hit.

Brad stepped up to the plate totally focused.

The Giants' pitcher was intimidated by Brad's look and determination, so he threw a fastball inside to Brad to try to shake him up.

Greg was sitting in the bar being the only one there not rooting for Brad. He just prayed the pitcher wouldn't throw him a curve ball. He knew all too well that Brad loved a curve ball. Well, at least his anyway.

Brad waited for the next pitch. He guessed it would be a fastball on the outside corner or a curve ball. He was right on his second choice. The curve ball started out inside, but then broke down and away a bit before Brad drove it over the left-center field wall for a home run.

Brad's homerun ended up being the difference in the game as the Dodgers won the game one to nothing on a complete game from Brad.

They cheated some on his pitch count and let him exceed it by ten pitches. A star was born in the Dodger's organization, as well as throughout the country.

Kristy had watched the game at home and was excited for Brad. She called Carol to see if she had seen the game.

Carol told her that of course she and John had been watching. It was amazing seeing their best friend on television performing so well.

Kristy asked Carol if she could stop by one day this week, so she could try to call Brad and congratulate him. They both knew Kristy couldn't call from her own house because Greg might discover the call if he looked at the phone bill, so it was no problem for Carol because she wanted to talk to him also.

A short time later Greg stumbled into the house totally drunk. His eyes were glazed from drinking. Kristy knew something was up. He had seen the game, she thought to herself.

Greg angrily yelled, "That son of a bitch never dies. Did you see Brad Preston on TV today?"

"Why no I didn't," she lied. "What was he doing on television?"

"He's pitching for the Dodgers," Greg said slurring his words. "He must be a cat. He seems to have nine lives," he said drunkenly as he approached Kristy.

"What are you doing?" she asked frightened.

"I have to get my power back and you're one way I can do it." He grabbed her hard.

"I'm pregnant with your baby," she screamed. "Leave me alone or I'll…"

"You'll do what, kill the baby? You can't do it Kristy." He threw her down on the couch and pulled at her shorts.

With all of her might, she pushed him back and threw her right fist into his face. Blood exploded from his nose as he was temporarily stunned.

"You're dead bitch!" he yelled as he pounced on her again.

"Kill me now, and get me out of this misery. Life isn't worth living with you in it. And take the baby's life also," she said with a determined look on her face. She didn't care about life at this point. It wasn't worth living with Greg in it.

Greg backed off of her a bit realizing she didn't care if he killed her. He lost most of his power over her, but he knew he could have some control of her and make her life miserable.

He was about to let her be when she said, "I'm leaving you! I'll divorce you tomorrow, and you will not hurt me again!"

Greg threw a punch into the side of her head that knocked her unconscious. He was going to take her sexually, but he couldn't get himself up for her. He left her there and took off to find another sexual prey that would satisfy his hunger and instill power in him.

The following day Kristy had started to pack her things. She had to get away from Greg before he killed her. She had to take it easy though, because she became dizzy if she moved too fast. She knew Greg had seen her bags out before he left for work, and he didn't say a word, which left her unsure of his intentions. She just wished she could have left yesterday, but her head hurt so much after she regained conscience, making her inept to do so.

As Kristy was packing her last suitcase, the phone rang. She answered and heard her mother on the other end crying.

"Somebody shot at your father's car today during his lunch break. I told him not to drive through some of those areas."

"Is he ok Mom?" Kristy asked with a sunken feeling.

"Yes, just badly shaken. Evidently someone fired three shots into the car, but missed your father, thank God," her mother said settling down a bit.

Kristy's head dropped as tears filled her eyes from knowing that she was stuck in this relationship until one of them died. She was ninety-nine percent sure Greg shot at her father's car as a warning, and next time he would kill one or both of her parents.

After finishing the phone call, Kristy unpacked her bags and put everything away. She was defeated in one way, but she would somehow gain some control again. Her head hurt too much now to think about what that might be.

CHAPTER 28

▼

The last month of the Dodgers season ended on a positive note. The team pulled together winning over sixty percent of their games in September. Brad finished the season with six wins and no losses. Next years season tickets for the Dodgers were selling fast because the fans felt good about the team, especially with Brad Preston on the roster.

Brad took a flight back to Charlotte after the last game. He had things to finish up with Bill's company after his abrupt departure this past summer. He would then help set up the CAMM in Los Angeles for the Dodgers. It was a full schedule again for Brad, and he loved it.

As he entered his apartment, he was startled by the lack of furniture in it. He couldn't believe he had lived that way during his grieving time. Brad walked up to the refrigerator and stared at the painting Brianna had drawn. He smiled appreciating the artwork. He thought back to the day Anne and Brianna died realizing he was fortunate to be where he was today. He missed them both dearly, but he could now handle his loss with the faith the two of them were still with him in spirit.

Brad walked around the small apartment making notes to himself on what he would keep or discard when he moved. He was going to have to move to Los Angeles in a week or so, and he thought now was the best time to prepare for it. As it turned out, he decided to keep almost everything. He would just have someone truck it out there when he found a place to live.

Brad was instantly reminded to check his messages when he saw his phone sitting on the desk. It had been a few weeks since he called home to pull them.

There was a message from Kristy from two weeks ago, and she sounded rattled. After pulling the other messages, he immediately dialed Carol's phone number to see what was going on back home. The phone rang until the answering machine kicked in, so Brad left a message for Carol to call him in Charlotte as soon as possible.

He then tended to several more calls and left for the office. It was two o'clock in the afternoon, and he thought he could get a few things done with Bill.

The entire office staff surrounded Brad as he entered the building. They congratulated him for his outstanding play with the Dodgers. There was a sudden moment of silence when Bill Matthews walked off the elevator to meet his favorite employee.

"What are you doing here?" Bill asked as he gave Brad a hug. "I can't believe you came here today. The season just ended, and you should be relaxing."

"I missed everybody, even you," Brad said, kidding. "I felt guilty after leaving here so quickly. I have work to do."

"You've been replaced," Bill said with a laugh. "Look Brad, you have a big job ahead of you in LA. We can handle things here. Maybe not as well as when you were here, but we will survive." He tried to play along like Brad's absence from his company was minor, but he was serious about the loss of Brad's organizational skills in the company.

The employees went back to work allowing Bill and Brad to go over business details for the rest of the afternoon.

Brad made notes on a few things that stood out to him in need of immediate attention. He discussed the shipment of the CAMM for the Dodgers with Bill and selected the personal he would work with in Los Angeles to help set it up.

Bill felt a sense of relief having Brad around again. He forgot how much worry Brad had alleviated from him.

They went for a nice dinner to catch up with each other and before long they talked baseball. It was a wonderful evening for both of them, especially for Bill because it was the first time since Anne's death he really got to see Brad back to his old self with just the two of them together.

The two finished their drinks and departed for home.

Brad entered his apartment to the sound of his phone ringing. He hustled over to pick it up and heard a voice that was pleasing to his ears. "Hey Kristy, how're you doing?"

"Brad, I'm glad you're home. I've wanted to talk to you for some time now. I'm ok I guess. How've you been?" she asked, being polite as well as interested in his well being.

"Things have gone well for me lately. Everything has happened so fast that I haven't been able to think about it."

"Yes, it has. I watched you play on television. You were great. I understand that Carol told you I was pregnant."

Brad was surprised by her forward approach of the subject and wasn't sure how to answer her. "Well, she did mention it to me, but she swore me to secrecy. I hope you're happy that you're having a baby," he said to be nice.

"Yes, I'm pleased," she replied, sensing that Brad wasn't too happy about it. "Look Brad, I had to do it to keep Greg away from me…"

"If I remember correctly, getting pregnant takes getting real close to someone."

Kristy was happy to hear the jealousy coming out of Brad. It gave her some confidence that he still had feelings for her. She decided to change the course some. "Brad, it sounds like you don't agree with my decision, but let me explain. Greg has become more psychotic as each day passes. He beat me, raped me, and threatened to kill me. Getting pregnant gives me an advantage over him. I promised him I'd terminate this pregnancy if he ever hurt me again."

"Just leave the loser Kristy," Brad replied bitterly. His face turned red as he visualized Greg beating and raping her.

"And do what? Are you going to take me?" Kristy stopped for a few seconds, and Brad didn't reply, so she continued. "I'm sorry Brad. I'll bare my soul to you and tell you I wish you'd take me for your wife. God, I'd love for that to happen. But it isn't going to happen because it's too dangerous. Besides, you have your life now, and I'm not your problem. I screwed that up years ago, and now I'm sentenced to life over it."

"Kristy, don't be so hard on yourself. Neither one of us know what would happen between us if you left Greg. I can't think about it because you're married and you have no plan to get divorced. So don't play that card. What else is wrong besides your problem with Greg?"

"Nothing…he's the problem. Look Brad, this is hard to communicate to anyone without somebody thinking I'm crazy, but I'll try to explain. Greg is an angry man with severe mental problems. He feels inferior now because his life hasn't amounted to much in his eyes, and he wants power to make him feel like something. That's what he strives for and that's why he comes after you. You're a powerful person that is so much better than he is, and he thinks you stole everything you have from him for your personal gain."

"Jesus Kristy, is he that bad?" Brad asked, realizing just how far Greg had regressed.

"Worse than that. It seems to have affected his sexual appetite. The more crazed he gets, the more turned on he gets for rough sex. I've been researching some news stories about call girls getting raped and roughed up by some white male that fits Greg's description. He wears a sock hat, so they can't recognize him. I put the dates together, and they're times he wasn't home or had left home in a rage."

"Why don't you call the police?"

"He'd know it was me that turned him in, and he'd kill me or torture me. Look Brad, I tried to leave him about a month ago. He knocked me unconscious and ran out. That is one of the dates there was a rape and beating."

"Why didn't you leave him then Kristy? You can't let him hit you," Brad said, clinching his left fist.

"I had my bags packed and ready to go until my mother called and informed me dad's car had been shot at three times during his lunch break. I knew it was Greg, but I had no proof. It's only speculation, which won't go anywhere in the courts," Kristy said, pleading her case.

There was silence on both ends of the phone for a minute. Brad finally said, "What can I do to help?"

"I'm not sure yet. I'm going to play private eye, and catch him doing something bad, and then blackmail him so he'll leave me alone," she said in desperation.

"That's too dangerous Kristy. Why don't we just hire a private eye and let him do the work. I'll even pay for the service."

"I thought about that, but it has its bad side also. It's best if I catch him and then kind of blackmail him to leave us all alone. I'll even play the bluff that I have proof about his involvement with your family being killed or my father being shot at. I know he was involved in both incidents."

"You told me that before, and I wasn't sure I believed you then, but I'm starting to believe he might have been involved. I just don't see any way to prove it though. God Kristy, I don't like you going out on the limb this way. If you get caught, he'll do something terrible to you. Isn't there anything else to do?"

"I've thought about it, and this is the best solution for now. I might take you up on the private eye offer, but I'll pay you back discreetly. It would be too obvious if he saw checks written to a private eye or you."

"Don't worry about the money. I'll do whatever it takes. Please be careful and don't take too many risks." A frown covered Brad's face and he worried about her decision.

"I'll be careful. Now, who do you trust that I can send a package to in confidence? I only want it opened if something happens to me," she said, referring to any hard evidence she might come across that she could use to blackmail Greg with.

"Bill Matthews," he said without hesitation. He gave her the address to send the package to and Bill's phone number, as well as phone numbers where she could reach him.

"Thanks Brad. I love you with all of my heart and I always will." Kristy hated to hang up, but she had to get home.

Brad put the phone down and tried to put everything she had said in order. It was difficult to think about how Greg had disrupted his life, as well as others. He thought about contacting the police to investigate Greg, but he didn't have any concrete evidence to give them. He decided to keep in touch with Kristy and not get involved right now unless something else happened to him or his family.

Brad started the following day as if he had never left Charlotte. He ran three miles, showered, and went to work. When he arrived at the office building, he went to research and development for a few hours. He then reviewed all of the department manager's performances while making suggestions to increase their output before he met with Bill to talk about what he discovered.

After his meeting with Brad, Bill sat back in his chair amazed by the dedication Brad had for his company. Here was a young man that was now worth millions coming to a job he didn't have to work anymore. Bill was even more impressed on how quick Brad picked up on small details in his business that needed addressed. He decided it was time to offer Brad a chance to leave the company for now, so Brad could live a life he deserved.

Bill was relieved of his thoughts by the ringing of his phone. "It's your sister for you Mr. Matthews," his secretary said.

"Thanks," he replied as he picked up his phone. "Hi stranger. Is there anything wrong?"

"Of course not. Why would you think that?" she asked.

"Probably since we hardly talk. So what's up with you for you to call me, Michelle?"

"Well, Peter and I were talking to Keith yesterday, and we mentioned we were leaving the country for six to nine months to work on a film and play a little bit also. We commented on how nice it would be to have a reliable person stay at our house to make sure it was cared for properly. We have a good staff you know, but we thought we should have someone else there to oversee things," she ranted.

"I can't stay at your house for all of those months. I still have a business to run," Bill said, kidding, but making the point he wasn't interested.

"I know you'd never come out here. We were thinking about Brad Preston. Keith said he didn't have a place to stay here yet, and he wasn't sure Brad was that keen on buying a house."

"Keith is probably correct about Brad not wanting to buy a home there. But he does need to find a place to live out there right now. I do appreciate your thoughts about Brad and offering him your home. I think it'd be a great idea, and he would be the perfect guest. He's a remarkable young man," Bill added.

"Well that's why I called you. You know how Keith is sometimes. He's all sports, and I don't want just anybody in my house," Michelle said.

"Look Michelle, Brad isn't just a jock. He's very intelligent and has the manners of royalty. Do you want me to ask him if he wants to stay at your house?"

"Would you please? It would mean so much to Peter and I to have someone like that here to take care of things."

"I'd be glad to. I'll call you shortly and let you talk to Brad."

"Alright Bill. I'll wait for your call. Thanks a bunch," she said as she hung up.

Bill sat there and smiled to himself. This would be a real treat for Brad.

The rest of the week flew by as Brad prepared to leave for Los Angeles. He agreed to stay at Bill's sister's house for a while, thanks to the push by Bill. It made sense to stay at the Olson's house for now, allowing Brad to keep his residence in North Carolina, and not have to worry about moving the few things he had. He knew he could afford to buy a nice place anywhere, but it wasn't that important to him at this time.

CHAPTER 29

▼

Brad had been on the road for two days now on his way to California. He took care of the last of his tasks in Charlotte, stopped to visit with the Weatherbys, and then visited the gravesites of Anne and Brianna before he departed on his long trip.

He was driving his trusty jeep to California with the few personal things he wanted to take with him, as well as much of his clothing. It was a beautiful drive enabling Brad to see the versatile scenery of the country. With the fall season in full bloom, the colorful trees highlighted the different landscapes, from the beautiful mountains, to the flat plains, making the trip breathtaking at times.

Brad enjoyed the journey to California, but found the worst thing about a long drive was all of the time you had to think. He was trying hard to keep from thinking about Kristy, but what she was planning to do was dangerous, and he didn't want anything to happen to her. There was a strange feeling he had that made him feel closer to her than he should. He admitted to himself he would always have a place for her in his heart, but didn't know how she would fit in to his life. It was just a peculiar feeling for him to have. But there were many strange things that happened this year that were hard to explain, so why should this be different.

Brad wondered if he would ever find someone special enough for him to marry. He missed Anne and Brianna, and he wanted that same family bond again. He made up different scenarios of his life with some women he knew. The only one that sparked an interest was Kristy. "Just forget about her," he said to himself out loud.

He changed his thinking to baseball because he had more control over that part of his life. He started to talk to himself to allow his thoughts to advance fluidly. "What can we do next year to bring us a championship? There were a few players on the team that ended the season with a sour attitude that should be replaced, and I'd like to see Tony brought up from triple A. Now we need to find a new short stop. I'll have to talk to Keith about that when we get together."

With Brad so heavy in thought, he had driven so long that it didn't make sense to stop for the night. He continued driving and thinking about life until he was just fifty miles outside of Los Angeles. He had just merged with I-15 and was now heading south towards LA for the final leg of his long trip. It was five-thirty on a Saturday morning, and there were very few cars on the highway.

Brad was driving about eight miles over the posted speed limit when a Mercedes SL 500 blew by him almost hitting the front bumper of his jeep as it cut in front of him. He just shook his head in disgust by the lack of respect the driver had.

He dug in the console under the armrest to locate the directions to Bill's sister's house while keeping an eye out for traffic. He wanted to be prepared to know where he was going since he was not very familiar with the area yet. In fact, it was strange for him to be driving around Los Angeles because he had always been bused around town or taken a cab. He studied the directions for a few seconds and then looked up at the road and then back to his map, repeating the task until he was satisfied he knew where he was going.

Brad wanted to relax, knowing he was close to his destination, but he denied himself that pleasure since he had driven all night and was somewhat tired. He drove another ten minutes before spotting a car off on the side of the road just up ahead. He slowed as he approached and noticed a woman standing by the car staring at the tire. A smile came to his face when he recognized the car as the Mercedes that sped by him a short distance ago. He drove by the disabled vehicle, and then suddenly hit his brakes, and pulled over to the side of the road. Brad then carefully backed his jeep up until it came within fifteen feet of the Mercedes.

He exited his jeep and walked up to the lady. "Do you need any help?"

"I have a damn flat," she said rudely.

Brad wanted to turn away and leave, but he was too much of a gentleman. "I see that. I'll ask you again. Do you want some help?"

The young woman looked up at Brad for the first time and was taken back by his good looks and kindness. But she quickly regained her crabby composure. "What can you do to help?"

Brad bit his lip and then replied in an exaggerated hillbilly tone, "Well ma'am, I'm not sure. I guess I could change that there tire if you have a spare somewhere to put back on your car."

"Don't make fun of the situation. What are you, some wanna be movie star. Do you think with good looks and a nice body you can make here in Hollywood?" the attractive woman asked in a persnickety tone.

"You have a nice day," Brad said, turning away. His patience had already worn out. "God, I hope the rest of the people out here aren't like this," he said to himself softly as he headed to his jeep.

"Hey, where're you going? And I heard that by the way," she yelled back at him.

Brad opened his door and was about to get in when she cried out, "Come back here please. I don't know how to change a tire."

"Call triple A. They can help you," Brad shouted back.

"I lost my cell phone. I had a bad night, and I just want to get home and sleep," she said as she softened up a bit.

"Are you going to be nice?" Brad said, playing her. "Because I've been driving all night, and I'm tired too."

"I'll be nice. You don't know who I am, do you?"

"I haven't a clue. Have we met before," Brad asked, not knowing if she was someone he went to school with or met in LA during his short stay there. "Did we go to school together?"

She laughed. "I don't think so."

Brad walked around to the back of her car. "Is it alright if I open your trunk? I want to see if your spare tire is in here."

"Help yourself." She stared at him trying to figure him out. She noticed his strong body and great looks, but was taken back when Brad turned towards her, and she caught a glimpse of his powerful eyes. "So did you come out here to be a star?"

"No, I have no interest in that," Brad replied with a short laugh. "Your in luck, it appears your spare is brand new and full of air. I'll change it for you, and then we can both get on our way."

"Thanks," she said as she started to get a complex from his lack of interest in her.

Brad moved fast and had the tire changed in a matter of minutes. He put the bad tire in the trunk and slammed the lid closed. "That should get you home. Just don't get another flat, or you'll have to walk. These things only have one spare." He gave her a quick smile and walked away towards his jeep.

"Thank you," she yelled at him as he opened his door.

Brad just waived back and drove off, leaving the hottest movie star going wondering what happened.

She wasn't used to being treated like everybody else.

The haze over Los Angeles was mild this morning allowing Brad the beautiful views of the city. It was hard for him to get too excited though with the of maze highways he negotiated that took away from the elegance of the city. The scenery improved immensely as he exited the main highway and drove through the palm-tree ridden streets. He drove through wonderful neighborhoods that portrayed the elaborate Los Angeles lifestyle that he envisioned.

It was almost eight o'clock before Brad found the right house. It was located in a very ritzy neighborhood where every home was extravagant in design and size. The styles of the homes were so much different than the mansions in the south. Brad was debating what styles he liked best, only to come to the conclusion that he liked them both because they had their own unique look and personality, although the southern homes did seem to be more welcoming.

The jeep came to a halt at the front gate, and Brad pushed a button to alert the Olson's he had arrived. A voice came from the speaker asking the nature of business, and Brad told the unknown voice his name, and the gates opened. He drove up to the side of the house and was met by the butler.

The butler opened the driver side door of the jeep to allow Brad to get out. "Good morning Mr. Preston," the older gentleman said. "We were expecting you here tomorrow, but we are pleased you made it here early. I am Nelson, and I will be here to serve you."

"It's a pleasure to meet you Nelson. Please call me Brad," he said as he shook Nelson's hand. "You don't have to serve me either. I'm used to taking care of myself," Brad said politely.

"That would not be allowed here sir. Don't worry; I will only be there when needed. Now please follow me, and I will show you around."

"I should unpack my things first," Brad said as he started to unload a suitcase.

"Please sir; let us take care of that."

Brad kind of shrugged his shoulders not knowing how to take the personal service. "This is a beautiful place Nelson. How long have you been with the Olson's?"

"Yes, it is beautiful, but you haven't seen it all yet. I have been here five years enjoying my job, as the Olson's are wonderful people," Nelson replied sincerely.

Nelson had been right about not seeing everything. It was a grand place that was more than impressive.

Brad guessed the house to be around ten thousand square feet. The foyer had the original black and white checkered marble floors representing the style when the great structure was built. A massive chandelier with oversized crystals illuminated the entire foyer. There was a rounded staircase lined with museum quality artwork that led upstairs. Almost everything in the house was either a valuable piece of art or a rare artifact. The furniture was a mixture of early to mid nineteen hundred styles in the formal areas, to ultra contemporary in the more casual areas.

Brad peeked in to Peter's den. It was light and airy with a marble fireplace on one wall that featured six Oscar's on the mantle.

Much to Brad's surprise the entire house had a very comfortable environment making you feel welcome. He had expected it to be artificial, so he was taken back a bit. By now, Nelson had shown him the entire part of one wing of the home, except for the Olson's bedroom. Brad was especially pleased to see a professional gym filled with weight machines and other exercise equipment he planned on using extensively.

Nelson guided Brad to another stairwell that led to another wing of bedrooms. After climbing the flight of stairs, Nelson opened a door to a large bedroom that had an attached sitting room. "This will be your room Mr. Preston. I hope this suits you."

"It's just fine Nelson." Brad walked up to the windows to capture the awesome view. With the house sitting high above the city, Brad could see the beautiful sites of Los Angeles giving him more of an appreciation for the city. He also made notice of the swimming pool surrounded by lush landscaping. It was a house to be envied, and Brad felt he could be quite comfortable here.

"I will get your luggage now. Is there anything I can get you first?" Nelson asked before he left the suite.

"Just allow me to help with my things. I'm capable of that Nelson. Nothing against you, it's just that I feel bad about having you do it," Brad pleaded.

"That is part of my job sir," Nelson replied with a smile. He liked Brad already, so he decided to give in to his request. "Come on then, but hurry. I don't want Mrs. Olson seeing you carrying your baggage."

The two men worked fast unloading Brad's jeep. When they finished, there was a plate of fresh fruit and sweet rolls in his room.

Brad thanked Nelson and explained to him that he was tired from driving all night and needed to get some sleep.

"Shall I draw your drapes now?" Nelson asked.

"No, I'll get them. I think I'll have some of this fruit first. It looks delicious."

"Have a good rest. The Olson's want you to feel like this is your home, so just relax and come down when you want to. Oh, by the way, there is a going away party for the Olson's tonight in the ballroom that you should plan on attending," Nelson said before he departed the room.

Brad slept for about six hours before he woke up still feeling a little tired. He shaved, showered, and then dressed before going down stairs to meet Peter and Michelle. He was curious about what they were like. As he reached the lower level, he saw the hustle and bustle of staff and others preparing for the party.

Nelson was directing some workers when he saw Brad standing alone. He excused himself and then walked up to Brad. "Did you sleep well Mr. Preston?"

"Yes, but I could use some more sleep, although I have tonight to catch up on that. You mentioned a party tonight. What should I wear?"

"You will see a wide variety of fashion tonight, I assure you of that. I noticed some clothing you have that will work out just fine. We can go over that later. Would you like something to eat? I can get the kitchen to prepare you something," Nelson offered.

Brad looked at his watch and did some calculations in his mind. "What are the plans this evening? I wouldn't want to spoil my appetite."

"I suggest that you eat something now. It will be a late dinner tonight. There is always an extended cocktail hour on these occasions."

"I hate to put anybody out right now with everyone so busy."

Nelson gave a brief laugh. "You will have to get used to this service. We get paid to take care of the guests in this home, and we pride ourselves in doing it in the utmost professional manner. Why don't you go out by the pool and introduce yourself to the Olsons, and I will bring you something to eat."

"Yes sir," Brad replied with a pleasing grin on his face.

Brad made his way to the pool. It was a beautiful day with the sun's rays filling the air providing comfortable warmth. He noticed two people resting on loungers that he assumed were Peter and Michelle Olson. He then walked up to the well tanned couple. "Hi, I'm Brad Preston. Are you the Olsons?"

The man stood up and extended his hand to Brad. "Well, yes we are. I'm Peter, and this is my wife Michelle. We've heard a lot about you, and it's all been good."

Michelle lowered her sunglasses a bit in order to get a better look at Brad. "My God!" she exclaimed. "Bill didn't tell me you were so handsome. Look at him

Peter. We could've used him in our last movie. He would've made it sell." She rose to her feet to shake Brad's hand and welcome him to their home.

Michelle couldn't get over Brad's looks and body. She hadn't seen many bodies like his. She finally made it up to his eyes, and was taken back by how beautiful they were and by the way they spoke to her.

Michelle wasn't quite what Brad expected either. He guessed her to be in her upper fifties, but she had a younger look in many ways. She had short red hair that he assumed was colored and friendly hazel eyes that belonged to a pretty face. Her body was of medium build, but firm. Brad guessed she used the work out room regularly. He looked more closely at her, seeing a few features in her that Bill had inherited also.

Peter looked more like his brother Keith, except he sported a well groomed beard. His hair was slightly thinner than his younger brother's and more of a blondish red in color, but you could tell they were siblings. He had a slight stomach bulge, although not bad for a man approaching sixty. His body was well tanned that left several lines in his face. Overall, Peter was a good looking man portraying a life of success.

"Well, it's good to meet the both of you. I think the world of each of your brothers. They mean a lot to me."

"It goes both ways," Peter said. "Keith praises the earth you walk on, and that's a rare feat. How was your long drive out here? I can't believe you decided to drive when Bill would have been more than happy to fly you here."

"I was really looking forward to my drive here because I needed to see the world again in person. It was a long drive, but really beautiful and worth the effort. Besides, I wanted my trusty jeep here. It's one thing that belonged to my wife that I can use and not tear away at me."

"You're right about the beauty of this special country. You can't see the sights when you're thirty-five thousand feet in the air. I'm sorry for your loss earlier this year. Both Keith and Bill filled us in on the tragic accident," Peter replied.

"Thank you," Brad replied with a saddened look on his face.

"By the way, Nelson told me he informed you about the party tonight. We do want you to join us. It'll be a fun evening with lively people, all having different personalities that you'll enjoy."

"Yes, thank you. I will join you tonight. I just hope I don't stand out in your crowd. I really don't have much in common with them."

"I wouldn't be too sure about that," Michelle broke in. "You'll fit in just fine. You aren't as different from most here as you might expect, so prepare yourself to meet many guests that you'll click with just fine. Besides, Keith will be here, so that might put you at ease. And we have a few sport enthusiasts that should be here, most being avid Dodger fans."

"You might even see a few very beautiful women tonight. They've been known to hit these parties," Peter said.

"I'm sure I'll have a good time tonight. It's been a long time since I've been to an event like this." Brad replied as he watched Nelson approaching carrying a serving tray with a fresh sandwich accompanied by a salad.

"Your lunch Mr. Preston," Nelson said professionally.

"Thank you Nelson," Brad replied graciously.

Brad ate his lunch while he talked with the Olsons. He took a liking to them both immediately and was disappointed by the fact they wouldn't be around during his stay here.

CHAPTER 30

▼

Brad was impressed by the way Nelson put together his attire for the evening. He wouldn't have thought to put this outfit together the way Nelson had. Brad looked in the mirror to make sure everything was in place before he went down for the evening festivities. He had no idea what he was in for tonight, but prepared himself for every possibility.

As Brad joined the small crowd, he observed Nelson giving him a nod of approval over his appearance. He looked around to see if Keith had made it there yet, but to no avail. He realized it was still early and there were many people that had not made it to the party yet.

Brad walked outside to capture the pleasant evening air. The palm tree leaves were dancing slowly to the light evening breeze. Brad smiled as the breeze brushed against his face, reminding him of the night Anne asked him if he would prefer a warm breeze blowing against him or the cold northern wind. He preferred the warm breeze without a doubt.

He captured the fresh fragrance filling his senses from the well manicured garden. It was a life he could get used to, but probably wouldn't have the time to enjoy at this time. Brad was startled when he felt a tap on his shoulder. He turned around to see Keith holding out a champagne flute to him.

"Are you lonely out here?" Keith asked as he sipped his champagne.

"No, I was just enjoying the great evening. Your brother has a beautiful place here. I appreciate your efforts to have me stay here for a while. It'll work out perfect for me."

"Don't thank me. You're doing them a favor by staying here." Keith replied. He tilted his head back and drew a deep breath through his nose to capture the bouquet of scents that surrounded him. "They have a wonderful garden here don't they?"

"Yes they do. In fact, I was taking in the ambience just before you arrived. So, do you resent your life in baseball when you could have had this?"

"No way. This is nice, but I love what I do better. I mean, how can you beat the smell of a locker room?" Keith laughed hard. "Come on inside. There are some people you need to meet. After all, we have to promote our organization, and there's going to be a lot of people here that love the game of baseball."

Keith led Brad around the ballroom introducing him to most of the guests. Brad was astounded by the number of compliments he received from everyone on his pitching. He didn't realize he had made such an impact in such a short period of time.

On the other side of the room stood a young lady surrounded by a baronage. She wasn't giving them her full attention. She was trying to get a better look at an exceptionally handsome man on the other side of the room. She thought she recognized him, but wasn't sure where. She continued to talk to the group around her while catching glances of the mystery person. It finally hit her. He was the guy that changed her tire this morning. What was he doing here? He told me he wasn't in the movie business, she thought to herself. She wanted to ask someone who he was, but she didn't want anyone to think she had an interest in him.

The attractive dark haired lady with bronzed skin from the California sun, started to mingle around the room trying to get closer to the unknown man. The closer she got, the more intrigued she became, as she was able to get a good look at him. She thought his eyes were so beautiful that they could hypnotize those around him. He was tall and broad shouldered, appearing dominion to those around him, although it was not because of his actions. He just carried himself in a way, whereas people around him became mesmerized by him, or so it seemed to her.

She finally couldn't stand it anymore and suddenly walked up to him. "So do you recognize me now?"

Brad looked down at her and took a minute before recognizing her as his lady in distress earlier today. "Oh yeah, you're the lady with the Mercedes that almost took off the front bumper of my jeep this morning and then ended up getting a flat tire that I changed."

The attractive lady was so taken back by the fact he didn't recognize her as a famous movie star that she could only ask, "So you really don't know who I am?"

Brad was starting to lose his patience with her. "No, I haven't a clue who you are. Why is it so important to you?"

"Are you from another country, or have you just gotten out of prison?" she pressed on, thinking his mind had to be diminished since he did not recognize her.

Brad stared at her in disbelief. It gave him a chance to take in her good looks, but they were no competition to the beauty of Anne, although Brad did find her pleasing to look at. Her eyes were a darker brown than Anne's, but didn't possess the kindness of his deceased wife's eyes. He finally responded, "I assume you're someone important, or at least you think you are in your eyes."

The fireworks were about ready to blow when Michelle walked up to the pair. "Oh, I see the two of you have already met. I was hoping I could get the two of you together. You make such a nice couple."

They both broke out in laughter at the same time.

Michelle felt hurt. "Did I say something wrong?"

Brad raised his hand to Michelle. "No, it's fine. Actually we met this morning."

"My God Brad, you sure do work fast," Michelle said, surprised by his answer.

"It's not what you think," Brad protested. "I don't even know her name. We were in a heated discussion about my ignorance because I didn't know who she was."

"Well, I can solve that problem," Mrs. Olson stated. "Brad Preston, meet Lisa Collins. Lisa is currently the hottest star in the movie business. And Brad plays for the Los Angeles Dodgers, and he's the hottest star in baseball right now. Now you two get along. I had plans for the both of you," she said scolding them both before walking away to mingle with the guests.

"Well, that was fun," Brad said sarcastically.

"You don't like me, do you?" Lisa asked.

"Let's just say that I haven't been overly impressed yet," Brad stated bluntly.

"Are you gay?"

Brad did a double take and looked at her as his eyes narrowed. "Why would you ask me a question like that? Are you that pompous?"

She pouted. "You don't seem to care about me or show any interest, and I find that weird."

"I believe you think way too much of yourself." Brad briskly walked away.

Lisa stood there speechless.

Brad worked the room after he left Lisa. He found some very interesting people there, but he ended up chatting with Keith about next year giving him some suggestions about personnel changes to help the team. They were discussing the best prospect to bring in for short stop when Nelson announced dinner.

There were several tables set to accommodate all of the guests. Michelle kept up with tradition by having pre assigned seating, with Brad seated next to Keith at a table with a good mix of personalities. Brad was irritated when Lisa Collins ended up sitting beside him.

He looked at her with contempt, and then decided he should act like an adult. He forced a smile on his face and leaned over to her and whispered, "If we can't say anything good to each other, we will not say anything at all, so everyone at this table can have a nice dinner."

Lisa nodded her head yes and acted like he wasn't there.

Keith noticed the tension between the two and was curious about what the rift could be with them. They hardly knew each other to have a lover's quarrel, which is what it looked like.

Ben Hennings was sitting directly across from Brad. He was the president of the largest bank in Los Angeles, and he financed many of Peter's movies. Ben was a long time Dodger fan, and had been very impressed with Brad's play. They talked about some of the glory days with the Dodgers and then switched their conversation to the upcoming season.

Ben was very knowledgeable about the game and enjoyed reading about all sports. He had read an article in the Los Angeles Times about Brad and was curious about a few things. "Brad, if you don't mind me getting a little personal, I'd like to ask you a few questions that came to mind when I read the article on you in the Times?" he asked politely.

"Sure Mr. Hennings, I don't mind," Brad replied.

"The article said you hadn't thrown a pitch for four years because you had an injury. That seems to be a rather long time to heal."

"Four years is a long time to lay off because of an injury, but I wanted to come back with an entirely new motion. We had an idea at Pro Tech to design a computerized program to help establish a proper throwing motion to enable us to monitor a pitcher to keep his motion consistent on every pitch. We named the program CAMM. The program allows you to practice your pitching motion over and over again while monitoring your motion for consistent form. The monitored repetition of the proper motion then allows muscle memory to create the same motion out of habit. We didn't put the final touches on the computerized program until this past spring," Brad explained.

"That's a very interesting concept. Who came up with the idea?" Ben asked intrigued by the program.

Brad sipped his champagne. "Bill Matthews, he's Michelle's brother."

"What brought about the break through?" Ben asked, truly intrigued with the invention.

Brad was a little uneasy having to talk about this part because he hated to bring up the funeral. He looked around the table and noticed everybody leaning forward to hear his answer. Even Lisa was paying attention. "The problem we were having was not being able to record the motion properly. We tried many ideas that didn't work, until finally a miracle of sorts happened…"

"What was the miracle?" an older gentleman at the table asked.

"This is hard for me to talk about. I don't want you to think I'm some crazy guy from Indiana with too much religion, because I'm not. However, I do believe in God," he prefaced. "I don't know how much you know about me, but I lost my wife and daughter in a car accident in February of this year."

Keith put his hand on Brad's arm as a comfort to him.

"Oh Brad, I'm sorry to hear about that," said an attractive lady at the end of the table.

"Thank you. It was the hardest thing I've ever had to go through. It took me five months to join life again in an emotional capacity. But I'm getting ahead of myself," Brad said wanting to stay focused on his answer. He took a quick sip of his drink and cleared his throat. "The funeral was held in Charlotte. It was raining hard the morning of the last rites, but right before the service ended, the rain stopped and the sun came out. I was seated in the front pew with my family when I felt like I was being lifted up from the pew and then guided to the pulpit. As I turned to face everyone to speak, I saw the most brilliant prism of light rays flooding the church. They seemed to be coming from every direction. I smiled when I realized the answer to the problem with the program."

"What was the answer?" Ben asked, leaning forward while sitting on the edge of his seat.

"We used different colored light rays each traveling at different speeds to record the motion and combined that information with the shadows, and came up with a perfect recording of the body movement. That solved our problem, and allowed me to start using the CAMM on a daily basis. I had also been studying great pitchers and coaches every night to develop a format for my new style of pitching. And what you saw this past September is the finished product."

"What brought you back to life Brad?" Lisa asked, curious to see what made Brad what he was.

Brad turned to her and noticed a tear in her eye. "It was a rainy Sunday morning, and I woke up to jog, but decided to wait until the rain stopped. So, I went back to bed, only to be awakened by a feeling like someone was touching me.

The rain had stopped, so I got out of bed and went to the kitchen. As I looked out the window, I saw the most beautiful, unique looking rainbow I had ever seen. The colors were vibrant. It was identical to a colorful painting of a rainbow with three people my wife and daughter painted for me the day before they were killed. I knew when I saw the rainbow on that Sunday morning that my wife and daughter wanted me to join the real world again. I felt alive again and even pitched the following day for the first time," Brad finished as he wiped tears from his eyes.

Every guest at the table had been captivated by his story. There weren't any dry eyes at Brad's table after his explanation.

Ben lifted his glass and toasted Brad for the way he handled the ordeal, and everybody followed with a, "here, here."

Brad was surprised to see Lisa's seat vacant when he turned her way.

Michelle came over to Brad's table with a concerned look on her face. "What's going on over here. This table is too quiet."

"Brad just told us an amazing story. It touched all of us," Ben said.

"Well, let's enjoy ourselves tonight," she said before she went back to her table.

"You know Keith; I believe that my bank needs to buy more season tickets for next year. It's going to be a very interesting year," Ben said.

"Yes it is Ben. And here is the key to make it happen," Keith said, patting Brad on the back.

The food was served as everything returned back to normal at Brad's table. But not everyone was back to normal, because Brad touched some of them in a way they had never experienced before. He changed some minds about living life tonight, although that wasn't his intention.

The rest of the evening went by quickly with Brad thoroughly enjoying himself. He was thankful he could enjoy life again in so many ways. He excused himself from the party before all of the guests had left because his lack of sleep was catching with him.

Brad had just turned off the lights to his comfortable bedroom and laid himself down on the bed when he heard a knock at the door. He got up and opened the door with just his bottoms on thinking it was Nelson to see if he needed anything. As he pulled the door open, he saw Lisa standing there in the doorway.

"May I come in for a minute?" she asked.

He could see by the look on her face she wasn't there to antagonize him, so he allowed her in his room. He turned on some more lights while she walked around the room being noisy.

She picked up a picture of Anne and Brianna and turned to him. "They're both very beautiful."

"Thank you. They were beautiful in other ways too," Brad replied to suggest to her looks weren't everything.

Taking the hint Lisa asked, "Is that why you don't like me, because of the way I act?"

"I never said that I didn't like you. But what you said has some truth. Anne, my late wife, was the most beautiful person I've laid eyes on. She went through life downplaying her beauty so much that she hid her inner beauty. When we became close, her inner beauty blossomed making her irresistible. I'm not judging you, so don't take me wrong. You're a beautiful woman. Just don't let that run your life."

"You're right. I have been too caught up in my success. The story you told tonight. That really did happen to you didn't it?" she asked in a whisper.

"Yes, that and more."

"One of these days, I'd like to hear the entire story, if that's ok with you?" Lisa asked with a smile that brought out her full beauty.

"We'll see what happens," Brad said as he walked her to the door.

Lisa stopped at the door and turned to Brad. She slowly raised her hand to his face and gently touched his left cheek, and then left the room.

CHAPTER 31

▼

Nelson waited patiently at the airport for Brad, per their plan to retrieve the young man from his return trip from his parents. Brad had spent the Thanksgiving weekend in Florida for a much needed rest and time with his family, and his plane had just landed in Los Angeles.

"Did you have a good holiday?" Nelson asked as he opened the car door for Brad.

"Yes I did," Brad replied. "And what about you, did you have a good Thanksgiving?"

"Well yes I did, thank you. I have family living here, and we all got together for the day. You had a few calls while you were away."

"Anybody important?" Brad asked before realizing it was a dumb question to ask Nelson.

"I'm not sure sir. Lisa Collins called, and a Kristy called. The later call seemed somewhat urgent. She said she would try to call you back today some time," Nelson answered in his professional manner.

"Thanks, Nelson," Brad replied, wondering what was going on with Kristy and her scheme. "I hope that everything's ok with her."

"If you don't mind me saying sir, one woman at a time is more than enough," Nelson suggested.

"I agree Nelson. One woman is plenty, but as of right now, I have zero women in my life. I don't know why Lisa called me. I thought I made it pretty clear to her that I have no interest in her. The other woman is an old friend of mine that is experiencing some personal problems. I'm not sure how I can help her. She's married to an abusive husband," Brad added, defending his position on wanting to talk with Kristy.

"I suggest you steer clear of that situation. That can bring nothing but problems to you if you get in the middle of it," Nelson emphasized.

Brad laughed. "Yes father."

"I am only looking out for your best interest's sir," Nelson said, laughing to himself from Brad's parenting comment to him.

"I know Nelson. And call me Brad. You're too formal with me. The Olsons aren't around to discipline you."

"It's just many years of habit. I am sorry because I do feel close to you. You are a true gentleman, and I have grown to respect you."

"Thank you sir," Brad said as he looked at Nelson with admiration.

Upon arriving at the Olson's house, Brad changed into his workout clothes and went to the gym to lift. He hit each station extra hard today since he was unable to get a good workout in during his visit to Florida. He had just finished his stretching routine when Nelson informed him of a phone call.

"It is the married one," Nelson said, shaking his head in disagreement.

Brad took the remote phone from his friend. "Thanks Nelson."

"Brad, this is Kristy. How are you doing?" the sweet voice on the other end of the phone said.

"I'm fine Kristy. How are you? I heard you called for me the other day and sounded rattled."

"Well, I finally got some evidence on him," she said proudly.

"On Greg?" he asked, surprised.

"Yes, I caught him in the act, or at least enough of the act that would get him in trouble with the law. It's definitely strong enough evidence for me to use to make him leave me alone," she said excited. "Especially with him knowing he was the guilty party."

Brad paced nervously. "What do you have, and how are you going to use it?"

"Ok, I'll start from the beginning. We had Thanksgiving at his house with all of his family. They have no idea how much of a problem Greg has with you. I don't even think they know that Greg hates you. Anyway, we were having dinner when your name was brought up. They were all bragging on you and expounded on how proud they were to have a local boy make it. Greg started to argue a bit, but his family kept going on about you being the next super star and how glad they were to know you."

"So what happened?" Brad asked, intrigued by the dinner conversation.

"Greg started drinking heavily, just like he always does when he's angered. His face was beet red from hearing all of the stories about you. They brought up incidents when you beat Greg out in a certain position, and marveled on how good you were as team captain. It was like someone throwing jet fuel on a fire. I tried to change the subject, and they finally did out of respect for me, but the harm was done to Greg's ego. His mother told me after dinner that she was sorry for bringing you up since the two of us dated so long. She didn't want to hurt me. They have no clue how sick their son is," Kristy said as she ran out of breath.

"The Somanskis are good people, all except Greg that is. Why can't they see his evil ways?" Brad asked, befuddled by their blindness towards their son.

"He's never shown them how bad he gets. He does a pretty good job hiding his feelings. I think he's afraid of what his parents will think. Now back to the reason I called. I take that back Brad because I called to hear your voice more than anything. Maybe I'm selfish getting you involved in this, but I want to talk to you."

"I understand Kristy. I do like to hear your voice also. I just wish it was under different conditions. And I mean several different conditions," he said, trying to hammer home the fact she was married.

Kristy understood his point, but ignored it at this time. "I don't have much time, so I better get to the details. He dropped me off at home and then left. I was able to catch up to him and follow him. I had a bag prepared that had a camera, and video camera, along with some binoculars. He parked his car in a rough area of Indy and walked about six blocks. I was scared for myself, but I knew this was my best opportunity to get something on him, so I followed him in the car the best I could. I was video taping him the entire way. He pulled a sock hat out of his jacket and put it over his face before he came to a corner. He must have been around the area before, because there was a girl working that particular street, and he seemed to know she would be standing there. He peeked around the corner after he pulled the sock hat over his face, and then ran up to the girl, and dragged her off to a vacant building. He took her inside and then came out of the building a little later by himself. I drove off to get home, so I don't know what else he might have done that night, if anything."

"God Kristy, that was too risky for you to do. If he doesn't kill you, someone else will," Brad said, scolding her.

"I'm fine. Nothing happened to me," she said in defense.

"You were lucky this time. Look Kristy, I don't want to lose anymore people that mean a lot to me."

Kristy smiled to herself from hearing his words stating she was important to him. "Brad please relax. I shouldn't have to do this again. I have enough to scare him and make him leave me and my family alone. I checked the newspapers and the regular news the following days. There was a prostitute that was beat up and raped in that same building, on the same night, at the same time that I was there to witness. There wasn't too much made of it since she was a prostitute, but it did happen. Greg's smart enough to attack the right type of people. If that was a young school girl or a mother, the police would be all over it, and they'd work hard to find the guilty person. Being a prostitute will probably make it a low priority."

"So what are you going to do now?"

"I took the tape, along with an affidavit to an attorney. He dated the tape and had his secretary notarize my affidavit. I left a copy with the attorney to put in my file, plus I have a copy to send to Bill Matthews, per your suggestion. I want you to let Mr. Matthews know what is going on please. That way, I can cover myself pretty well. What do you think Brad?" Kristy asked, praying that Brad would think it would work.

"I'm worried for you. Are you sure this is the best way to go? Why not go to the police?" He had some doubt about her plan working.

"Two reasons. There's no guarantee he would be convicted, and if he was convicted, he wouldn't be in prison very long. When he got out, I'd be dead. Or he would get out on bail and take me out then. I need him to be dead or life in prison to be rid of him. And I will not kill him no matter how bad he is, unless it was self defense," she added.

"So what's your next plan of action?" Brad asked, feeling more at ease with her plan.

"I'll show him the copy of the tape and tell him what I've done. I will not mention any names though. Then I'll say that as long as he leaves me and my family alone, nobody will know what he has done. It's simple blackmail in a way, except there's no money involved."

"Call me and let me know what happens after you present this to him please. But never call from your house."

"I'll always call you from somewhere else, don't worry. Wish me luck. And Brad, take care. I wish I could see you. I could really use a hug from you right now."

"That'd be nice. Now make sure Carol knows what's going on. Greg will back off of you some if he thinks you'll let them know how bad he is."

"I'm not sure I want to involve her. Look Brad, this is a gamble worth taking. I really don't want to live my life this way, and if he killed me over this, then it's best for me. Just nail him if that happens. Now I have to go, but always remember that I love you," Kristy said, ending the call.

Brad had mixed emotions from his conversation with Kristy. He admired her for her gutsy plan, but worried about the outcome. He wished there was something he could do, but struggled with all of his choices. He said a quick prayer for her and then went to his room to shower.

Brad was preoccupied all night thinking about Kristy. He couldn't wait to hear from her again, so could be assured that she was ok. He started to question what his true feelings for her were. Did he still love her? He concluded he still did have strong feelings for her, so he decided to put his thoughts about her aside because they couldn't lead to anything good.

Brad had just returned from his morning jog when Nelson informed him of another phone call from Kristy. Brad anxiously took the phone. "Are you alright?"

"I'm ok. Just a couple of bruises, but it was worth it," she said as she gingerly touched the bruises on her face.

Brad's blood pressure elevated and his body tensed. "Bruises, how'd you get them?"

"Well, he turned on me from the start and hit me several times. But then he stopped right away when I showed him the video tape of his escapade the other night. I informed him of what I had done with the original tape, as well as the letter I attached with it," Kristy explained.

"Did he agree to leave you alone? Did you try to leave him?" Brad asked, hoping in his heart that she would leave Greg.

"He realized he has to leave me alone now. He won't allow me to leave though. That gives him his power over you, which is what he seems to live on more and more. I wish I could tell you otherwise, but he told me he would kill me if I tried to leave him. I'm sorry Brad."

Brad's heart pounded his chest rapidly. "You don't have to apologize. So you're fine, and you believe he'll not harm you as long as you stay with him?"

"The sad truth that it is...Yes...I believe he'll leave me alone. It's the only thing that will keep me going. I hope you don't look down on me over this abuse I take. I don't like it, and I'm doing everything I can to not take it, so please don't judge me," she pleaded.

"Kristy, I'm not judging you, and I'm not looking down on you. In fact, I've been searching my soul on how I really feel about you. At least we have become friends again."

Her heart beat faster as she listened to him. She assumed he still had stronger feelings than just a friendship, but she wasn't going to press the matter. What good would it do anyway? "At least it's good to hear you say you think about me. That will help to keep me going," she said in a loving way.

"I wish I could hold you right now." He wanted to say more, but held off. The conversation was getting a little deeper than he intended it to get.

"That would be wonderful. I wouldn't let you go this time."

There was a brief silence as neither one knew what to say next. They knew it would only lead to disappointment, and they couldn't afford that right now.

Kristy broke the silence by saying, "Well, I better get going. I have a few things to get done yet today. Don't forget to call Mr. Matthews about the package I just put it in the mail to him today. And Brad, I love you so much. I'm sorry I had to drag you in this mess."

"Don't worry about dragging me into anything. You be careful and call me anytime. I do miss you Kristy," he said as he closed his eyes to see her beautiful face in his mind.

Brad immediately called Bill at his office to let him know what was going on with Kristy. He explained the entire scenario, and gave Bill directions on what to do with the package.

Bill asked Brad if he still thought Greg had something to do with Anne's death, and Brad stated he now believed Greg was involved.

They finished the conversation by reviewing the initial set up of the CAMM for the Dodgers.

CHAPTER 32

▼

A week had elapsed since Brad returned from his family Thanksgiving get together in Florida. He had not heard from Kristy for five days now, which he took as good news.

Brad had just finished lunch when Nelson informed him of a phone call from Lisa Collins. Brad made a sour face to Nelson, but took the call anyway.

"I called you over a week ago and haven't heard from you, so I thought I'd try again," she began her conversation with Brad.

"Yes, Nelson mentioned to me you had called. I didn't know you expected a call back. I apologize for that," he said in defense.

"You don't sound like you're very comfortable talking to me."

"I'd say I'm just cautious about you. We really didn't start out on a positive note you know," Brad stated without any emotion.

"I thought we were better when I left that night, but maybe it was just me. So, where were you off to when I called?" Lisa asked nervously

"My family resides in Florida now, so I flew down there for Thanksgiving." He looked at Nelson and made another sour face while pointing to the phone.

"That sounds nice. How was it?"

Brad wasn't sure why he was having a conversation with her, and he didn't understand how she could think they were friends. He decided to answer her question anyway to at least be nice. "It was ok. The landscape and weather didn't make it feel like Thanksgiving, but it was good to see my family again. So, what's on your mind? This is twice in about ten days now that you've called."

"I was just thinking about you. Evidently, I came away from the party with stronger feelings for you than you did towards me. I'm sorry if I started out like a pompous bitch. Unfortunately, many celebrities take stardom the wrong way. But to defend those that do, I'd just like to say that when you're constantly barraged by everyone wanting your autograph or picture, you change. Please take that into consideration before you toss me out," she stated sincerely.

"I'm not sure about your stronger feelings comment because I thought we both pretty much despised one another from the start. My rebuttal to your last statement would only be, you think too much of yourself, and that has nothing to do with fan reaction," he said firmly.

"You're dead right, and I realized that after seeing how beautiful your wife was and then you telling me she was more beautiful from her inner beauty. I came to see things in a different light from those wise words. I definitely see you as a kind and sincere person, and I like you in a few ways. So, can we start over again from the beginning like nothing ever happened?"

"Lisa, I really don't work that way. You showed me your true colors. Besides, I'm not interested in any kind of a relationship right now, be it innocent or full-blown. I don't have time for it," he said holding firm on his desire to stay away from her, although she did soften him a bit.

"Do me one favor please? Next weekend, I want you to come with me to the mountains for a weekend get together with some friends. It's a cozy log cabin with plenty of room. It'll be fun, and it might put you in the Christmas spirit since it will be colder up there with beautiful forests all around. We can have a big fire. It should be a great time where you can meet some new friends, and I want you to come with me as a friend," she pleaded.

"Who will be there besides us?" Brad asked as he actually considered her offer.

"Some good friends of mine, and they aren't even in the movie business. They're more down to earth like you. It's just a weekend to enjoy the season. That's all, and I promise that I'll behave myself around you. I learned my lesson."

"Why me Lisa? You must know a lot of other guys to take along with you."

"Because they aren't like you. I've found you to be special, and I'd like to get to know you better. In fact, I've never met anyone like you before," she said as honestly as she could.

"What are the dates we would be away, and how long does it take to get there?" Brad asked to see if it would fit into his schedule.

"We can leave this Friday afternoon, and return Sunday afternoon late. It's about a four hour drive, but it's a beautiful trip there. So are we on?" Lisa asked anxiously, trying to close the deal.

"These other couples, are they married and how old are they?"

"One couple is married, and the other couple is not quite engaged as of yet. They're all close to our age. You'll like them. I know that Jim is an avid Dodger fan. Come on, be a sport," she begged.

"Ok, I'll go with you. Maybe the mountain air will get me in the spirit of the season. Why don't you call me Friday morning early, so we can set a time to leave?" Brad stared at the floor in disbelief that he was going to spend time with Lisa.

"I'll do that Brad. Make sure you pack some warm clothes. It'll be cold up there this weekend. We might even get a little snow," she said excitedly. "Oh, and thanks for giving me a chance."

"I'll be sure to pack some winter things. Call me Friday." He hung up the phone, shaking his head.

The week went by quick as things were progressing well with the new CAMM. Brad had been working close with Jack and the entire pitching staff, but there were two pitchers that were not cooperating with the system. However, the others were true believers, and working with the program with hundred percent efforts.

They talked about bringing a select few minor league pitchers to get them on the program also.

Brad was feeling good about the entire Dodger organization. They were preaching and practicing the team concept. He felt they could be serious contenders next year making him more anxious to get out on the mound and start playing. But first he had to get through the winter and spring workouts. There was a lot to do before the season started.

Brad worked out early on Friday, so he could allow time to drive to the mountains for the weekend. He was actually looking forward to it. Not because of being with a big star, he just looked forward to be around other people his age for some fun and good conversation. He just hoped he could get along with Lisa. At least she was kind when she asked him to come with her this weekend. He would find out very soon, as he was to pick her up at noon because they wanted to be able to relax and enjoy their drive.

Brad arrived at Lisa's home at 11:45 a.m. She came out of her house wearing low rise jeans with a tight green sweater that came to her waist allowing a clear view of her belly button when she raised her arms the slightest bit. Brad took notice of her tanned bare skin in her mid section and admired the remainder of her body, as it was provocative.

She only wore a hint of makeup to accentuate her fine features and not take away from her tanned face. Brad had to admit to himself that Lisa was a very attractive woman.

Brad put her few bags into the back of the jeep and opened the passenger door to allow her to get in. Once she was seated, he closed her door and walked around the front of the jeep to the driver side and hopped in. "You look nice today," he said in a pleasant, complimentary way.

Lisa looked at Brad closely still taken back by his looks. "Thank you. You look good yourself."

Brad was wearing blue jeans and a crew neck short sleeve shirt. He had a sweater in the back to match the shirt if needed.

"Do you know where we're going?" Brad asked. He hated to get lost, so he always prepared a route for a trip.

"Don't worry," she said, waiving a sheet of paper with directions and a phone number. "I don't want to get lost in the mountains either."

Brad drove away from Lisa's house and headed north out of the city, while sharing small talk trying to break the ice between them.

Lisa fished through some CD's and found one with songs from ten years ago. "Do you mind if I play this?" she asked with an infectious smile.

"I don't mind. I forgot they were in here." He realized how much Lisa had changed.

They were silent as they listened to the music. Finally Brad broke the silence. "These are all songs from my high school days."

"Yeah, me to." Lisa started to sing along. She had a great voice that impressed Brad. "Come on, sing with me. I bet you know the words," Lisa added as she started to sing again.

Brad laughed and shook his head as he joined in with her. It felt good to him to enjoy life this way, even if it was with someone he wasn't sure he trusted completely.

They went through a couple more CD's before they came to Fresno. Brad decided they should pull into a grocery store to buy some food and drinks. He hated to go somewhere empty handed.

The two of them purchased fresh fish, beef tenderloin, fresh vegetables, and other items. They then picked up some beer, wine, and a variety of cheeses and breads.

Before checking out, Brad picked up a cooler and ice to keep everything fresh. They paid for their purchases and hustled out of the store to load the cooler.

Satisfied that they had plenty of food and beverage, Brad sped off to their destination.

The weather was noticeable colder in the mountains. As they drove further up the mountains, the scenery became magnificent, highlighted by landscapes of pine tree forests that were accented with snow flakes. In fact, the snow had become steady and plentiful the more they drove.

"I should've checked the weather before we left," Lisa said. "I saw the forecast earlier this week for this area, and they didn't mention a snow storm."

"It's not bad. We shouldn't be too far from the cabin," Brad said as he stretched out his right arm and laid it down on the arm rest.

Lisa took his hand with her left hand and then rubbed him from his fingertips to his forearm. "Are you a little tense?"

"I'm not tense, but my hand was cramping a little bit. That feels great." He gave her a friendly smile. 'Thanks for asking me to come this weekend. I think we'll have a good time. Don't you?"

"Yes, that's why I wanted you to come with me. I'm friends with Jim and Molly, and fairly acquainted with their friends they invited along for the weekend. But I'm not real close to them since I'm gone so much, although I do enjoy being around them. It's a shame I don't have time to lead a normal life. It makes it hard to have real friends," Lisa said sadly.

"I know the feeling. My best friends live in Indiana or they're the people I work with. Most of them are my bosses."

Lisa pointed to a side road just up ahead. "I think we turn up here Brad. Yes, that's it. Turn right and follow that road for about five miles, and then there should be a narrow road to the left that leads us to the cabin."

Brad followed her directions, and eventually turned onto a narrow road that was not much better than a logging road. They drove through the heavily wooded area into a clearing and saw the log cabin. It was like a miniature lodge featuring a full-length porch that was very inviting with a beautiful view of the mountains in the background. Brad wasn't sure where to park because the snow was getting deep enough to cover the ground completely. He picked what seemed a likely spot for a parking area and stopped the jeep.

"Looks like we're the first ones here," Brad said.

"Jim said we'd probably beat them here. He told me where the key would be though, so we can go inside and unpack." Lisa pulled her jacket on and hopped out of the jeep. She put her face up to capture the snowflakes on her tongue.

"There is some firewood over there," Brad said, pointing. "After we unload, I'll bring some wood up to the house and start a fire. With the snow coming down the fire will make it cozy."

Lisa shook her head in agreement and gave him a big smile showing off her perfect teeth.

They unpacked the jeep and walked up to the cabin. Lisa located the key and unlocked the door before they entered their weekend quarters. The rustic interior of the house enveloped you with a feeling of warmth, but gave way today to the cool temperature outside.

Brad immediately started a big fire in the fireplace to get some heat going. He then found the thermostat and turned it up to kick in the furnace. He looked around the large cabin admiring the craftsmanship it took to build the log structure. It had the fresh smell of cut wood to give the home an outdoor flavor.

Satisfied with the accommodations, Brad went back outside for the rest of their belongings. He then carried in plenty of additional wood to take care of them for the night before loading the log holder on the porch. After finishing those chores, he finally went inside to relax.

Lisa had two glasses of wine with some cheese and bread spread out on a platter for the two of them. She cuddled up next to Brad to keep warm since the furnace wasn't warming the house up fast enough.

Because the softness of her body felt good, Brad didn't mind her sitting so close to him. Besides, he had caught a chill while outside from the cold air being stirred by a ferocious wind, and her warmth felt good to him.

The wind was still blowing hard, making a whistling sound as it made its way into the house through the window sills. The sound of the wind made it feel colder inside the cabin than it actually was.

"This is nice," Lisa said as she sipped her wine. She admired the color and savored the fruits of the wine. "Good choice."

"I hope the others make it here alright. The weather is getting bad out there. It looks like a snow storm."

"Maybe we should check the weather," Lisa suggested as she went over to the television. She pushed the on button, but there was only fuzz on the screen. "The dish must be down with all of this snow and wind."

Brad lifted himself from the couch. "I'll find a radio."

"Here's a radio," Lisa said, opening the lower doors of the entertainment center. She turned the radio on and channel surfed until she found a weather forecast.

The recorded broadcast was repeating a winter storm warning for the mountain areas. They were to expect strong winds and heavy snow accumulation, with blizzard conditions at times through the evening and early night.

"I wonder if anybody else will make it today?" Lisa asked, concerned. "I hope they're alright."

The lights in the cabin flickered before Brad could reply to her concerns. "We better look for some candles and a flashlight. There's a good chance we'll lose power tonight." He headed for the kitchen to look through the cabinets and pantry for emergency lighting.

"At least we have a warm fire to sit by," Lisa said before she started her search. "Do you want me to call Jim to see if he's on his way?"

"We should, just to let him know that we made it here, if nothing else," Brad replied as he entered the utility room. "Looks like they've lost power here before." He carried two lanterns and a large flashlight out of the storage room.

They now felt like they were prepared for the worst. Brad thought they should go through the entire house, so they would be familiar with everything should they lose power.

Lisa agreed, and they walked the house thoroughly getting a good feel of the place. Lisa then tried to use the phone to call Jim, only to find the phone was dead. "I doubt if my cell phone will work up here, but I'll try," Lisa said while she dug her phone out of her purse. "Just as I thought, there is no signal."

"Well, let's just relax and let the snow fly while we soak in the heat from the fire. At least the furnace is working right now and warming the place up," Brad said as he sat back down.

Lisa gathered the bottle of wine and filled their glasses before she joined him on the couch.

They both sat cross legged on the couch facing each other.

"Well Brad, it's just you and me, and we're actually getting along. Why don't you enlighten me about yourself, and I'll do the same with you."

Brad told Lisa about his family and explained how close he was to his parents. He went on to tell her about his high school days with Kristy as well as his early college years dating her. He left nothing out as he gave details of their breakup, putting most of the blame on Greg. With the mention of that individual, Brad explained how Greg ended his college baseball career. He talked about Anne and Brianna telling Lisa just how much they had meant to him and how devastated he was from their untimely deaths.

Lisa had listened to Brad intently, taking in every word. "I told you I wanted to hear about the other miracles that happened when they died."

Brad then explained his experiences in the hospital and at home that evening. The more he told the story, the stronger his convictions were that the events were truly what he perceived them to be.

"You know Brad; you said that Thanksgiving this year felt weird to you because it was so different in Florida. What would be a perfect Thanksgiving for you?" she asked trying to learn as much about him as she could.

"I was born and raised in central Indiana. Although we lived in the suburbs of Indianapolis, there were many farm communities close by. Every fall, I'd drive around the countryside to see the trees changing colors, and I'd see these nice old farmhouses with the large front porches. You know the type of porch where an entire family could sit in the summer time while they drank their ice tea. Well, I always thought it would nice to spend Thanksgiving with one of those families in their old farm house and see what Thanksgiving really meant to them. Maybe it's because it's symbolic of what the day is all about. Thanksgiving was originally a holiday to thank God for their harvest that was supposed to feed them through the winter. Does that sound funny to you?" he asked as he sipped his wine.

"No, it sounds great. You're a romantic, aren't you?" she said as warmth filled her body.

"I don't know about that. What about your life? Why don't you fill me in on it."

"Mine's not near as interesting as yours. In fact, I lived my entire life more as a grown up. My mother pushed me into beauty contests when I was only five years old. I wasn't allowed to be a kid when I was young. I took voice lessons, dancing lessons, and everything else that goes with it. I guess it paid off because I'm now a star," Lisa said in a sarcastic way.

"There's more to your life than that. What did you like to do when you were younger?"

"I don't know. I never had a choice to do anything. My mother pushed me to the limit on being a star. The worse thing is, I never really worked hard enough to become a great actress. I always relied on my looks because my mom always said they'd get me anything in life that I wanted. I cheated myself by thinking that way. I have you to thank for making me recognize that because I never realized it until I met you. You're lucky by the fact you don't have to work hard to be successful," she said, trying to compliment him.

"That's where you're wrong Lisa. I've always worked harder than anyone around me. I learned in life that there's always someone out there working hard to take your place. Whether it be with hard work or cheating, someone is out to get you. The only reason I could play baseball as well as I did this year after being away from the game for four years was from hard work. I studied the game and the great players. I found out what made them successful and instilled that in me. For anyone to be at the top, it takes a lot of work. There might have been some luck along the way, but skill and hard work is what got them there. Don't sell yourself short on that fact. You worked hard, and now you're at the top of the list of actresses." he said passionately while staring straight into her eyes.

"Thanks, but I could be better." Lisa felt the power that Brad transmitted and it gave her a warm feeling inside and a longing to be with him.

"I've never seen one of your films, so I can't judge you or give you advice, but I suggest you do something similar to what I've done. Study films of the great stars and see what made them great. Go back to the forties, fifties, and sixties. Those were the days they didn't have all of the special effects that could make up for a lack of talent. Watch the films you're in and grade yourself. That will make you better." Brad sipped his wine and studied her reaction.

"That's good advice. I never thought about doing those things. I want to apologize for behaving like a conceited brat when we first met. That was nice of you to change my tire, especially after you'd driven all night. I had no right to treat you like dirt." Lisa leaned towards Brad and kissed him on the cheek.

"I accept your apology. Now tell me what you want out of life," Brad replied before taking a long sip from his wine to help absorb the hot spot on his cheek.

"I don't know exactly. I thought that being a star was it, but it only brings a void into my life. I never thought about marriage or raising a child. Life to this point has been all about me," she said, shrugging her shoulders.

"What about your relationship with your parents?"

"My father left us when I was ten. He married someone else and forgot about me until I was a big star. My mother still lives in LA, but I rarely see her. I ended up resenting her for the way she pushed me all of those years and stole my childhood," she said with spite.

The lights started to flicker off and on again as the wind was gusted ferociously.

"It's getting late," Brad said. "It doesn't look like anyone else will show up tonight. Should we cook some dinner?"

"That sounds good. The cheese didn't satisfy my hunger totally," Lisa replied, rubbing her belly.

Brad got up and went to the kitchen. "You sit back and relax. It's my treat to serve you. Would you prefer fish or beef tonight?"

"I'll have whatever you want. They both sound good to me." Lisa dug her knees into the back of the couch and hung her elbows over the back, so she could watch Brad.

Brad was checking out the kitchen thoroughly to aid in his decision on what to prepare. He didn't like his steak prepared in the oven or in a pan, so he decided on the fish.

"I can prepare fish two ways. I can put the veggies and the fish in aluminum foil and put them in the oven to steam them all together, or I can blacken the fish in the frying pan and prepare the vegetables separate," he stated after finding enough spices to make his choices work.

"Just steam them. That's easier and less messy." She smiled to Brad while enjoying his efforts to gather everything he needed to cook her dinner.

Brad went to work on dinner like he knew what he was doing, with Lisa watched intently, admiring his good looks and fantastic body. He should have been a movie star, she thought to herself.

Brad looked up at her and winked and then went back to preparing their dinner. He folded the aluminum foil carefully before putting both pouches in the oven.

"Well that's done. At least the oven is gas, so if we lose power, it will still cook our dinner," Brad said as he rejoined Lisa on the couch.

They sat sipping wine and watching the fire while they absorbed the information they had previously exchanged between them.

The wind gusted fiercely once again, and the lights flickered off and on. A few minutes later the lights dimmed and then went off for good. The cabin was now without electricity.

"Brad, what are we going to do now?" Lisa yelled out nervously.

"Not much we can do now. Let's just enjoy the fire. The lights will probably come on soon. Besides, dinner is almost ready." Brad moved his body next to Lisa to comfort her.

The food was delicious as the two enjoyed the dinner and each other's company. The ambience of candlelight and the blaze of the roaring fire added a special flavor to their dinner. It would have been a perfect prelude for a loving couple before they headed to bed for nighttime activities.

Lisa felt the desire in her, but she wasn't sure Brad felt that way. She stared at him lovingly after she finished her meal, wanting him, but knowing it was not the right thing to do at this time.

"You haven't told me that much about yourself," Brad started in again after finishing eating and noticing her stare. He leaned back in his chair to hear her response.

"There isn't much left to tell you. I've been through several men. None of them meant anything to me though. I just went through the actions with them. My life has been so artificial. When you're in the film making business, nothing around you is real. I think we all, and I mean we, as in theatrical workers, find it hard to know when the real part of our life starts. You get to a point where your personal life is like your stage life. You choreograph how you want your life to be, and then try to control everything. I couldn't do that to you though. You broke me in a way. Not for the worse, but for the better," Lisa said sincerely.

Brad took in her pleasant looks. "What do you want to happen now?"

"I want to continue to find out who I am and discover what I want out of life. Making movies is fun, but it's hard work. The money is great, but comes so easily it doesn't mean that much. You can only buy so much stuff. You know Brad; I'd like my life to be the way it was today. I had a chance to look at things differently than before. I'd parallel my life with yours after your wife and daughter died, in the way it was more robotic, with lack of emotion. And then you came along and showed me the rainbow of life." She gave a big smile.

"I wish I could have all of my emotions back," he said quietly.

"Are you talking about love? I think we both have some work to do on that. I'm confused about love right now. I feel like I'm falling for you, but I can't be sure it's the real thing because I have never truly experienced it."

"Just remember that love comes naturally. It can't be forced. It starts from the inside and works its way out. Then there's an ever telling glow about you letting everyone around you know, including the one you have fallen in love with," Brad replied with confidence. He then left the table quickly and walked to the front door and opened it slightly to see what the weather was doing.

"Well the snow is letting up some, but the wind is still blowing strong," he said, returning to the table to clear the mess.

Lisa helped Brad clean up the dishes and then hurried to the couch to get warm.

"Is there anything I can get you while I'm up?" Brad asked before he joined her.

"A piece of that cheesecake sounds good right now. Would you have any interest in starring in the movies? You'd be an instant hit with your great looks and the way you handle yourself. I believe that you'd be a good actor." She felt a chill and her body shivered.

Brad saw a blanket by the fireplace and went over to pick it up. He then gently laid it on Lisa to keep her warm. He looked down at her. "No, I wouldn't be interested in doing movies."

"I though that's what you'd say. Thanks for the blanket, I did feel a chill," she said while snuggling up in the blanket.

He walked back to the kitchen and cut two pieces of cheesecake and then looked over at Lisa. "Nothing against you, but acting isn't the kind of life I want to live." He put the cheesecake back in the refrigerator before he carried two pieces to the living room.

"Thanks," Lisa said as he handed her the plate. "I didn't take your answer as an insult to me. I hope you don't think I'm shallow for making my living that way,"

"I didn't mean to imply all actors or actresses were bad. I just don't want that lifestyle. I feel it's artificial in some way. It's hard to explain what I really want to say, but I don't look down on you at all for being a star. I just don't respect people that are too full of themselves," he said, trying not to put his entire foot in his mouth.

She gave a quick laugh. "The way I was when we first met?"

"You said it, not me," Brad said, returning her laugh.

"Don't you consider yourself a celebrity? I bet if you walked down the streets of LA, pedestrians would recognize you, and you'd instantly be mobbed by autograph seekers. You're an entertainer also you know."

"I don't look at myself that way though. I know what you're saying, but I approach my profession differently. I've witnessed athletes in all sports take an entertainer approach to the way they play, and then live a selfish life off the field. God, I made myself sound like I'm better than the others and that's not what I meant. Let's get off this subject." Brad then dug into his cheesecake.

"You're the one that switched the subject from emotion and love," Lisa said, smiling. "So do you have feelings for someone right now?"

"No," he said defensively.

"I'm not sure I believe you…so I assume you're holding out on me." Lisa sat up straight.

"I still talk with Kristy every once in a while, but it isn't what you might think. She has severe problems with her husband…"

"So she calls you for help. Come on Brad, she still wants you. Why doesn't she just leave him then?"

"Because he would kill her," Brad said straight forward.

Lisa's body shot back into the couch. "Do you believe that?"

"Yes, I truly believe her. She has told me things that seem to fit as facts. My good friend, Carol, has told me the same things also. But could Kristy be playing me? Maybe, but it isn't her style. We have become friends now."

Brad got up and refilled his wine glass. After taking a sip of wine, he leaned over the kitchen counter with his elbows on the countertop and his hands under his chin. "Look, Greg Somanski is an evil person. I have witnessed things he has done, and they aren't good."

There was silence for a minute as Brad thought hard on how much he wanted to tell her. Brad was not sure how he felt about Kristy or Lisa at this point, and he didn't want to chase Lisa off completely. He stood up and paced slowly in front of the fire.

"Well, why don't you just tell me what's on your mind. It's evident I've hit a sensitive subject here, and I apologize if it bothers you," Lisa said in a consoling tone.

Brad turned from the fire to face Lisa and said, "There are some facts I can't tell you right now, but they're irrelevant to my feelings for Kristy. I've questioned myself recently on how I really feel about her. I just can't define it. She's pregnant with his baby, which stirred a little jealousy in me when I heard about it. Maybe it's because I lost my little girl. But I can honestly say that I don't think I could be with Kristy if she divorced because it would be too hard seeing that child every day and be reminded it came from a worthless being such as Greg. I hope that doesn't make me sound shallow."

"It doesn't," she replied, somewhat relieved.

"Besides, with a child involved, it'd allow Greg a presence in my life, and he'd butt in all of the time causing trouble. It would make life miserable for me," Brad added, trying to convince himself there would be problems with that scenario.

"I agree with you. The additional stress would make your life with her terrible," she added, wanting to pile on the negative aspect of his life with Kristy.

"And a few weeks ago, I didn't know you the way I do right now. I don't know if anything will happen between the two of us, but I don't want to close that door with you now." Brad was becoming mildly infatuated with her.

Lisa stood up, and walked over to Brad, and put her hands on his broad shoulders. She stared into his warm eyes. "I don't want the door closed on me either. I appreciate your honesty. Very few people would be as open as you've been with me. At least I've climbed the ladder from a conceited brat that you loathed, to someone you don't want to close the door on. I'd say I've come a long way today." She lifted herself up on her tiptoes and gave him a soft kiss on his lips.

"Since I'm being so open, I'll tell you that felt good," Brad said, staring into her mischievous eyes.

"Is it just me, or has it gotten colder in here?" Lisa asked as she leaned into Brad's body for heat and comfort.

"It feels like the temperature has dropped a little. That cold wind doesn't help things in here. What're we going to do about sleep tonight?"

"I'm not tired yet, so I haven't thought about it. I bet those bedrooms are cold though," Lisa stated, knowing the rooms weren't close enough to the fireplace to get warm.

"Let's go see how cold they are." He really just wanted to end their conversation about relationships.

They strolled through the house and checked each bedroom's temperature.

"Oh man, these bedrooms are freezing," Lisa said as they entered the last one. "Looks like we'll be better off in front of the fire all night." She leaned up against Brad's firm body. She enjoyed the feel of his body and used every excuse she could to touch Brad.

"Well, I think the couch is a hide a bed. We can both sleep in it together, unless you'd rather sleep by yourself and freeze."

"I think I'll let you keep me warm Brad," Lisa replied, surprised by his suggestion.

They sat in front of the fire talking about themselves in more detail and revealing some of the funny things that happened in their pasts. It was a great evening for both of them allowing them time to relax for a change and be their true selves.

Brad actually found Lisa more interesting than he would have thought.

They hadn't realized how long they had been sitting there together, until they both yawned at the same time.

Lisa glanced at her watch. "Oh my God! I had no idea it was this late. With the wine and the drive today, I'm beat."

Brad laughed hard and his cheeks turned pink. "You just want me in bed with you."

Lisa smacked him on the leg. "I'm not that kind of woman. Well, maybe a little, but only with you," she said, joining him in laughter.

They both felt anxious thinking about sharing the same bed.

Brad had a desire to lie next to her marvelous body all night, but he admitted to himself that was all he wanted to experience at this time.

Lisa had changed, and she knew that having sex on the first date would be a major mistake. She sensed his feelings and didn't want to push things with Brad because he was too important to her to risk losing right now.

Brad set forth to make up the bed while Lisa prepared herself for bed. He then gathered more firewood from outside and laid it by the fireplace. He just finished his tasks when she entered the room wearing flannel bottoms and a tee shirt. He swallowed hard to keep from choking, knowing he was going to be next to her all night. He thought Lisa looked great even though she wore flannels, but he not been around women since Anne's death, except for the one time with Kristy, and it was wearing on him.

"I hope I don't look too messy for you. I didn't bring a nice nightie with me," she said, wishing she had something sexier to wear.

"I prefer what you have on. I never liked those lace nighties. They're too scratchy," he replied, staring at her.

Lisa jumped in the bed to keep warm. She got a chill from changing her clothes and walking back to the living room with just pajamas on, but she knew it would be much more comfortable than sleeping in her clothes. "Go get ready, so you can keep me warm."

"I hope you don't mind me wearing my footed pajamas tonight," Brad said, laughing.

Brad came back from his bed time routine still fully clothed. He blew out the candles and then piled a couple more logs on the fire before sitting down on the uncomfortable bed.

Lisa wasn't sure if he was going to wear his clothes to bed or not and was feeling slightly embarrassed for wearing her pj's. Lisa breathed a sigh of relief when Brad undressed, stripping down to everything except his briefs and a Dodgers tee shirt.

Lisa made a pretend pout. "That's not fair. You're almost naked."

"I don't recall reciting a dress code to you for tonight." He pulled the covers over his body and snuggled up against her body. "Besides I'll put out more warmth for you without much on."

Lisa gave a naughty smile. "That makes sense. Now put that body heat to work, and warm me up. I'm cold," she replied, pulling herself closer to him.

Brad raised his body slightly to allow himself to put his left arm under Lisa's neck, and then pulled her over towards him even more with her taking his lead by laying her head on his chest.

"Is that alright with you?" Brad asked, not wanting to be too forward.

She rubbed his chest gently and wiggled her butt a few times. "Ah, that's better," she said as a different chill ran through her body.

They talked for a few minutes while he rubbed her back, and she continued caressing his chest and arm. It relaxed both of them tremendously and brought forth a closeness that neither expected.

Lisa then gave him a long passionate good night kiss. For the first time in her life she realized this is what a relationship was all about. She was aroused, but the cuddling and caressing was enough for now. Sex would just ruin the loving moment.

Their bodies touching highlighted the warmth and softness between them, but also gave Brad a sexually charged feeling and a strong desire for her, but he restrained from doing anything. His guilty feelings from making love to Kristy abruptly came to mind. He read Lisa's body motion, stating this was satisfying enough and then relaxed.

They both gave each other slight moans of pleasure when one or the other would find a sensitive part of the body from their caresses. The tension in their bodies evaporated with each touch.

Brad combed his fingers through Lisa's thick black hair, making her body go limp, but giving him a pleasure he welcomed.

Lisa fell asleep first while Brad kept rubbing her body. The feel of her soft smooth skin felt wonderful to him. It brought back good thoughts about being married to Anne. He really missed this part of his life. He fell asleep dreaming of Anne, Kristy and Lisa.

Brad didn't sleep as well as Lisa because he kept getting up to add more logs to the fire to keep it going for the much needed heat. He would then cuddle up to Lisa to recapture the pleasure of her body. He figured he could sleep anytime, but moments like this were rare for him. He finally fell asleep in a hard way while holding on to Lisa the entire time.

Brad woke up to the smell of fresh coffee. He had to squint to shelter his eyes from the daylight.

Lisa was able to brew a pot of coffee after she found a stove top percolator. There was still no power and Lisa had put additional logs on the fire to help heat the cabin.

As Brad's eyes focused, he was disappointed to see her in a sweat shirt and pants.

"I slept wonderful last night thanks to you." Lisa handed Brad a cup of coffee and sat down next to him on the makeshift bed. "I could get used to that you know."

Brad gave her a smile and took the hot coffee cup between both hands to warm them. "It was nice. I guess I finally crashed. I didn't hear you get up. I woke up when I missed your body next to mine."

"You needed to get some sleep. You must have rubbed my body almost all night, and it was so soothing. I haven't slept that well in years. And thanks for keeping the fire going last night. It would have really gotten cold in here if you hadn't tended to it." She kissed his cheek softly.

"Well it looks like the sun is trying to come out today," Brad declared as some light rays of sunshine rippled through the snow-coated windows. "I wonder how much snow we got last night?"

"I don't think we got enough snow to keep us stuck here for a week," Lisa said in a disappointing tone. "I just wonder if the rest of our party will show up later today?"

"I guess it depends on how far they got yesterday, if they in fact left LA to come here. They might have checked out the weather forecast before they left," Brad said in a playful way. "And yes, I could have checked the weather just as easily as you. I just didn't think about snow in California."

Lisa laughed hard, causing her to pat her chest so she could speak. "Well, I guess you learned your lesson. I wouldn't expect this in Los Angeles though, but you can never tell what will happen when you get up in the mountains. It is beautiful up here and so peaceful. Too bad it's so far from home."

"I'll see how pretty it is here when I go out there and shovel snow," he said as he got to his feet and put his clothes on. "It's the least I can do to help the others if they show up today."

"Do you want some breakfast?" Lisa asked, disappointed that he was going outside for a bit.

"Not yet. I'll just have another cup of coffee before I shovel snow." Brad finished dressing by latching his belt. He walked over to refill his coffee cup and sat down close to the fireplace.

There was about ten inches of snow on the ground with snowdrifts in excess of three feet. Brad plowed the big drift off the front porch with the snow shovel he found in the utility room. It wasn't a real heavy snow, which made the removal easier. He cleared the front porch and pathways to the woodpile and his jeep. He then plowed out an area for another car to park, if need be. Brad stopped shoveling and allowed himself to see all of the beautiful views around him. The tree ridden mountains decorated with the sparkling snow brought chills to Brad. The cold air was refreshing and reminded him of the winter weather back in Indiana.

He felt alive and full of energy, so he took a walk down the long driveway to the main road. The main road was still snow covered with just a few tire tracks from other vehicles traveling up or down the mountain, but that was the only sign of life around them.

Brad turned around, surprised to see Lisa approaching him. She gave him a big wave and ran the last hundred feet to him. As she came within three feet of Brad, she lunged her body into his body while wrapping her arms around him.

"I haven't been out here that long," Brad said, smiling. "What's up?"

"Nothing, at all. I just missed you, and I was a little worried about you. I didn't know where you went. I thought you just left me all to myself," she said, acting like a damsel in distress.

Brad reached out and grabbed Lisa, then whirled her around in circles until they both fell softly into the snow. The winter weather was putting him in the holiday spirit, and playing in the snow added to it. They both stared at each other for a minute, not noticing the coldness from the snow.

"God, you're too good looking," Lisa said, staring into his eyes. "Plus you have to be the nicest person I've ever been around. Don't you have any faults?"

"I'm sure I have plenty of faults." Brad studied her face without taking a breath. "And you're very attractive yourself."

They lay in the snow for another minute before Brad stood up and pulled Lisa from the snow. "Are you in for a short hike?" he asked Lisa, while he brushed snow off her body, and then wiped himself clean of the white stuff. Before she could answer, he grabbed her hand and led her towards the wooded area.

"As if I have a choice," she replied, skipping through the snowdrift. "What's on our agenda today? We pretty much covered the history lesson on each other yesterday, so that leaves what we want in the future to talk about, and I doubt neither one of us really knows at this point."

"Let's just enjoy the day and each other, and let the rest happen. Or if you're bored, I can drive you home," he said as a joke.

"I think I'll stay here and see what the day brings." Lisa's eyes revealed she only wanted to be with Brad.

They walked through the woods back to the clearing in front of the house.

"Let's walk that way," Lisa said, pointing toward a mountain.

"I'm not walking to that mountain, I can tell you that right now," Brad said wryly.

Lisa gave a warm smile. "You have a dry sense of humor don't you?"

"One of my faults." He returned her smile and held her hand harder.

They returned to the log house after a long walk. With the sun now at full strength, the temperature had warmed up a bit, bringing about a sweat to each. They kicked the snow off their boots and threw off their jackets the second they entered the house.

"How about that, we now have electricity again," Lisa stated, after seeing the lights on.

"At least I can take a shower and not freeze," Brad said, delighted.

"Let's do breakfast first. I'm starving!" Lisa walked over to the refrigerator to see what there was to eat. Unsatisfied with her choices there, she walked to the pantry to see if there were any breakfast items to choose from. "Well, there isn't much of a choice here. I guess we should've picked up some breakfast food at the store."

The front door opened abruptly, startling the two, before Jim yelled, "Hello, we finally made it. Thank God for the snow plow that led the way here from our hotel. Thanks for shoveling the porch and a parking spot," he added as he dropped some bags on the floor and held the door open so his wife Molly could enter.

"Hi Jim, hi Molly," Lisa said as she walked towards them. "Where did you guys stay last night?"

"There's a motel about a half an hour from here that we spent the night in," Molly replied, while watching Brad walk their way.

"Hi, I'm Brad Preston," Brad said, extending his hand out to Jim and Molly.

The two men shook hands. "Good to meet you. I'm Jim Milnick, and this is my wife Molly," Jim stood motionless as he stared at Brad in awe while sizing him up.

"You're bigger in person." He felt dwarfed by Brad's broad shouldered body and above average height.

Brad made a quick assessment of the two and guessed them both to be about thirty years old. Jim was a nice looking man with a look success, and Molly was attractive, but seemed to be more reserved. "Are your friends going to make it?"

"They should be right behind us. They stayed at the same motel as we did," Jim answered, still staring at Brad. "I can't believe it's you. I saw you play once in person and watched you on TV, and you were amazing, especially for a rookie."

"Let me help you with the rest of your things." Brad put on his boots and started walking out towards their car.

Jim hustled outside to catch up with Brad. He didn't want Brad carrying everything in. He straightened his arm and pointed his finger to a car pulling up to the house slipping and sliding as it approached. "There's Tommy and Lynn now. They aren't married yet, so don't call Lynn his wife. She gets upset about that because Tommy is dragging his feet on marrying her," Jim stated as a fair warning to Brad.

"Gotcha," Brad replied, thinking that was an unusual thing to say.

Brad hustled over to the new arrivals and introduced himself to Tommy and Lynn when they got out of their car. He judged them to be in their late twenties, thinking they made a nice couple.

Lynn was a very attractive woman with a slender build. She was dressed in a trendy ski outfit and appeared to be comfortable with the mountain environment that surrounded them.

Tommy had the look of the stereotype California man, with floppy blond hair and a trim muscled body. He looked like a surfer boy, and carried himself in that free and easy way.

They all unloaded the cars of the goods and suitcases, and headed for the house.

Lisa was snacking on a coffee cake when Brad walked in with the last of the bags. "I couldn't wait," she said, gulping down her big bite of coffee cake. She swallowed the food, then wiped a few crumbs from her mouth, and ran up to Brad to give him a big hug. Playfully she said, "I'm sorry honey."

Lisa saw the newly arrived couple and didn't want to be rude, so she walked towards them. "Hi Tommy and Lynn."

Tommy and Lynn turned to each other with a curious look on their faces. They thought Lisa was a different person than before. She was a much nicer version than her previous self.

"So you two stayed her last night?" Molly asked curiously as her imagination started to generate images of a night of fun for the two.

"Yes, we arrived here before five and spent the night in front of the fire trying to stay warm. The power went out last night and just came on," Lisa explained proudly, knowing why Molly asked.

"It's a nice place Jim," Brad broke in. "I appreciate you having me here this weekend. We both needed the down time."

"My God," Tommy said. "I can't believe we're here with two huge celebrities."

"Tommy, we're just normal people," Brad said modestly.

They all ate breakfast together chit chatting about one another, so each could get to know the others better. It appeared to all that there was going to be a good combination of personalities.

Brad excused himself, so he could shower and put on clean clothes, leaving the others to talk among themselves. He was inclined to believe that they would drill Lisa about the two of them. At least he was confident she would tell them the exact truth about last night.

Molly wasted no time and was the first to comment. "Don't get jealous Jim, but he's so good looking. How long have you two been together?" she asked Lisa.

Lisa explained their relationship to this point, telling them everything from start to present.

"You two are a gorgeous couple," Lynn said. "Is he always this nice?"

"Yes, he's the sweetest person I've ever met. He really doesn't have a clue how he affects those around him, and that's refreshing," Lisa answered honestly.

"I can't believe how fit he is," Jim broke in. "Most baseball players aren't built like that, especially pitchers." Jim knew what he was talking about because he was a baseball junkie and kept up with the sport profusely. "Oh, and by the way Molly, I don't mind you saying he's good looking. I know you'd never leave me," he said, laughing.

"So what is the plan for the day?" Brad asked when he entered the living room all cleaned up. He was wearing blue jeans and a cream colored crew neck sweater, giving him a casual appearance.

"Have you considered modeling," Lynn asked, impressed with his looks.

"I'll stick with baseball," Brad replied as his cheeks turned pink. "Actually, I'd go back to my job in prosthetics if something happened to my baseball career. And let's all remember that I was only in the majors for a month. That doesn't make me a superstar."

"Oh you're going to be a superstar Brad. I know baseball, and I've never seen anyone pitch like you. And haven't you read all of the sport magazines? They're all predicting you to win twenty-five games next year," Jim stated, demonstrating his astute knowledge of the game.

"He doesn't pay much attention to that," Lisa stated. "He actually spent a lot of time studying the best players of the game before he started pitching again."

"Alright, enough about me. Jim, you read all of the sport magazines, and I assume you watch all of the sporting news. Who do you think we should get to fill some positions?" Brad asked.

Jim put on a serious face, thinking hard on how to answer the question. "I'd like to see us go after AJ with the Red Sox. He's the best shortstop in the league in my opinion. Lenny needs to go because he hasn't been getting the job done in center field. His fielding is suspect and he sucks at the plate now."

"Well, I agree with the weak fielding, but I wouldn't say Lenny sucks. But, you're right, we need to improve those two positions," Brad answered.

"It wouldn't hurt my feelings to practically replace the entire team and build a new one around you," Jim said to Brad.

"What do you think Brad?" Tommy asked, interested in Brad's take on the team.

"I'm going to keep my opinion to myself. You have to understand this is a team effort, and if I were slamming the other players on the team, it would be detrimental to what we need to accomplish. Besides, they've all worked hard to get here, and they have assets to work with to put them on top again," Brad added, being very diplomatic. "Let's talk about something else that the girls might enjoy joining us in."

Lisa had been listening carefully to the baseball talk, finding it intriguing. She got a glimpse of a bottle of orange juice on the kitchen countertop, so she poured Brad a fresh glass and brought it to him.

It was hard for the two couples to not be in awe over Brad and Lisa. They noticed how much more pleasant Lisa was, and they were tickled by the way Lisa was brought down to earth by Brad. Not that he made her act that way by telling her to be nice, she just wasn't as powerful of a presence as Brad, and she didn't even try to be the center of attention, which was unusual, but welcomed.

The sun was starting to set, painting the sky a beautiful pinkish orange color. The three couples had spent the afternoon talking about their lives allowing Brad to get to know them very well. Brad answered everyone's questions honestly, shedding a few tears now and then when he talked about Anne and Brianna. It was therapeutic for him to be able to openly talk about their tragic death.

Dinner was brought to the forefront, and Brad volunteered to cook for everyone. The weather changed for the better allowing the use of the outdoor grill, so

Brad could now cook the filets and fish the way he desired to bring about the best flavor.

Molly insisted on making a salad, and Lisa volunteered to cook the vegetables. It would be cooking by committee tonight

Jim uncorked two more bottles of wine while Brad had the main course going on the outdoor grill. Jim thought it was weird to see a baseball star preparing dinner for him. "How did you learn to cook," Jim asked, when he caught up with Brad.

"After my wife died, I had a daily routine. I usually made time to watch a cooking show to learn how to cook. I really didn't realize how much I learned, until recently. I actually enjoy it." Brad pulled a steak off the grill and cut it slightly to see if it was cooked enough. Satisfied, he removed the rest of the filets from the grill and piled them on a plate.

It was quiet at the dinner table. Everyone was too busy eating the great food to talk too much. Lisa had been watching everyone at the table while she ate. She felt different now than before. She realized how important it was to have friends around her, and she now felt a need for that in her life. She turned her attention to Brad, and a smile overcame her pretty face. Lisa became more enamored with him the more she witnessed his charms and skills. For the first time in her life she questioned herself being good enough for a man. It was somewhat unsettling to her. She watched the others being captivated by Brad's presence and the way he was interactive with everyone's conversation. She hoped she could change her way of life to fit in with his.

After dinner was cleared, Jim brought out the trivial pursuit game. He loved the game and was very good at it. The couples formed teams, which paired Lisa and Brad.

This game was taken seriously by the other two couples, raising Brad's competitiveness. He had played the game years ago and was knowledgeable on many of the subjects in the game.

The first game ended rather quickly as Brad and Lisa blew them all away. They each covered each other's weaknesses well, which was the strength of their relationship.

"Is there anything you can't do well," Jim asked in an amusing way.

"Lisa answered as many questions as I did," Brad answered, while grabbing her hand.

They played several more games to allow Jim and Molly a chance to win one, as well as Tommy and Lynn, and then gave it up for the night.

They all paired up with their partner around the fire and enjoyed a nightcap before heading to bed.

Brad had decided to stay on the couch tonight because he didn't want the others to think he and Lisa were that close. It would only take one slip of the tongue to the wrong person and the two of them would be in the gossip papers, and he wasn't prepared for that right now.

Lisa understood his thoughts without asking him and headed off to her bedroom alone.

Brad sat on the couch in private sipping his unfinished drink when someone sneaked into the room. He assumed it was Lisa, but was surprised when he saw Jim standing there.

"I hope you don't mind me intruding on you, but I'd like to talk to you about a few things if you don't mind?" Jim asked.

"I don't mind at all. It is your house after all," Brad replied graciously. "What's on your mind Jim?"

"I have something I want you to watch that might be of interest to you." Jim went to the television and inserted a tape into the VCR. "I was at the San Francisco game when I took this footage. Tell me what you see here."

Jim played the tape and kept quiet while Brad studied the film.

"Reverse that back some Jim. Right there is good enough."

Jim held the remote to the VCR, prepared to rewind it again if necessary. He could see that Brad was very perceptive and picked up on Jim's suspicion.

Brad stared at the television. His body stiffened and his face turned red. "Jesus, my own teammate was letting the opposing batters know what each pitch was going to be. Is that why you said we needed a new shortstop earlier today?"

"That's one reason, along with the fact he made too many errors and hardly ever came through at the plate when we needed him to," Jim stated, piqued.

"Do you mind if I take this with me? I'd like to show this to someone that has the authority to do something about it."

Jim smiled with satisfaction. "Help yourself. That's why I brought it along with me. Are we going to win this year Brad?"

The door to Lisa's room opened slightly with her sticking her head out the door just slightly. She was about to come out to see Brad before she witnessed Jim sitting there talking to him. Her curiosity took over, so she listened in on their conversation. Lisa knew Jim respected Brad, and she wanted to know what he had to say to him.

Brad had been in deep thought about the prospect of next year before he answered Jim's question. "We have a few positions to strengthen before we get there. I believe management will make the right decisions to get the job done, but it's hard to say if we can pull certain trades off to bring in the right players. We do have some great talent in our farm system that I think we should tap into during spring training to see if they have what it takes."

"What about Tony Coselli as catcher? He has a lot of talent," Jim said confidently.

"You must study baseball very thoroughly."

"I told you earlier, I'm a baseball aficionado. I love the game, and I don't want to see the players feel like they're greater than the game. The players almost ruined baseball years ago you know."

"That can be a problem in any profession. It happens in all sports, movie celebrities, even real estate people."

"I know that," Jim admitted. "Speaking of movie celebrities, what are your intentions with Lisa?"

"At least you don't beat around the bush," Brad proclaimed. He stood there for a minute in silence trying to size up the situation. "I don't know for sure, is the only truthful way I can answer you right now about her."

Lisa was zeroing in on this conversation now. She wanted to know how Brad really felt about her.

"I don't know her that well yet, but I've become fond of her this weekend. We didn't get off to a great start, so anything is an improvement. She's attractive and smart, which is a plus," Brad noted.

"You know Brad, I've never seen her carry herself in the way she has today. I believe her being around you has changed her. I really like Lisa, and I like her even more after today. Just be cautious. She's had some turbulent relationships previous to you, and I don't want you to get caught up in that kind of situation. I just hope she's changed for the good. I'm not saying she was really bad, she just had room to improve, so don't take me the wrong way,"

"Thanks for your concern. I can only say that when I'm ready to be with someone, she'll have to be an outstanding person that is very kind and unassuming. Lisa was raised in a way that made her believe her good looks are all you needed to survive, and only time can change that in her if that is what she chooses."

"Good," Jim said, satisfied with Brad's answer. "I'm not trying to force the two of you together, but why don't you stay in the bedroom with Lisa and get some rest. If you stay out here you won't get enough sleep."

"Thank you, but I don't want to send the wrong signal about the two of us. We aren't an item, and I don't want the word out that Lisa and I are having an affair."

"I assure you that none of us would breathe a word to anyone. We all respect both of you too much for that. Besides, we all want to be together again. It was fun today. Now go get comfortable in a nice warm bed with a very attractive woman," Jim said, before he went to his room.

Lisa closed the door to her room very slowly so it wouldn't make any noise and climbed into bed. She was angry with Jim for what he said about her, but her anger faded as she thought back about her past relationships. He was right, they were messy, and she realized she had an affair with someone in the cast every time she made a movie. How could she have allowed her life to be so screwed up? She had always lived for the moment, which she now recognized was the wrong way to live. "What a self revealing weekend," she said to herself.

Brad remained in the living room digesting the facts Jim had brought forth. He was upset about a player on his team intentionally trying to sabotage his performance as well as the team's performance. He thought about what Jim said concerning Lisa and it worried him a bit, but he knew he wouldn't allow himself to fall for someone that was not the real thing. He had been spoiled by Anne and he wouldn't consider any woman that would not come close to providing him a great life as she had.

Lisa decided to go relieve Brad of the couch by offering the bed to him while she slept on the hide a bed. She startled him when she touched him on the shoulder. "I'm sorry. I just wanted to offer the bed to you tonight, and I'll sleep out here."

Brad put his right hand on her left shoulder "That's ridiculous. I won't allow you to sleep here tonight."

Lisa smiled kindly. "Do you always have to be the hero?"

"I wasn't trying to be," he defended himself. "It's just the way I am."

"I know that, and there's nothing wrong with it. But I can be that way too you know, or other people can be the hero also. You have to learn to receive some good things also. Now get in there and get some sleep," she demanded.

"You're right; I need some good sleep tonight, so I'll take you up on your offer to sleep in a good bed." Brad grabbed Lisa's hand and led her to the bedroom.

"I don't recall saying anything about me being part of the package," she said, and then thought for a minute before continuing. "I have a confession to make. I was coming to get you earlier to share the bed with me when I witnessed you talking to Jim. I heard what he said about me, and I was hurt and angry, until I reflected on my life. I haven't led the kind of life you'd tolerate, and I don't blame you. I have things I need to change in my life to be the person I now want to be as well as what other people expect from their friends."

"You don't need to change your life because of me."

"I know better than that for two reasons. One, you'd smell it out and not stay with me, and two, I understand how I've been, and I want to change." She stopped talking and took a deep breath, and a tear came to her eye. "I'm not playing a game with you."

"Good, because you're right, I wouldn't put up with it. I learned that inner beauty is natural and only surfaces when it's real. We have time to see how things work out. I'm in no hurry to start a relationship, so I'm not shopping for someone at this time. Now I'm tired and I need some sleep, so get in bed, and I'll join you in a minute," he said with authority.

"Are you ready for bed?" Lisa asked with a bashful smile.

"I just need to brush my teeth."

"I'll get the bed warmed up for you. Please hurry, I need you by my side," Lisa said, realizing how important he was to her.

Brad finished his nighttime routine and slipped into the bed snuggling up against Lisa. They were silent tonight and just gently rubbed each other before they quickly fell asleep.

They both slept hard through the night and woke up at eight o'clock in the morning. They decided to lie next to each other for a while and enjoy their last night together a little bit longer. Temptation was at hand, but they withheld their desires. They finally joined the others to a round of applause as they entered the living area.

Lisa started laughing and her cheeks turned red. "Alright guys that's enough. I want you all to know that we actually slept and didn't do anything else. And as of this weekend, a new Lisa Collins has arrived. Please let me know if I go back to my old ways because I don't want to revisit that way of life again."

They stood there stunned for a few seconds before realizing she was serious about what she said.

"I don't want you to think that I didn't like you before Lisa, but I can tell you already that you are much more likeable now," Jim said boldly.

"Thank you Jim. I like myself better too," Lisa said, proud of her transformation.

Brad gave a short laugh. "I like you better too honey. Because the first time I met you, I wanted to hurt you."

Everyone else joined in with the same sentiments, ending with a round of laughter. None of them would have guessed this would have happened with Lisa, but they all knew strange things do happen sometimes.

Brad poured Lisa and himself a cup of coffee and carried it over to her.

Lynn stood there watching with a pout on her face. "I'm jealous. They've only been together for a few days, and they're tuned in to each other better than we are.

Maybe I should find me a Brad," Lynn said, verbally pounding Tommy. She had developed a crush on Brad and was jealous of Lisa.

Everybody had picked up on it over the short time they had all been together.

Brad sensed and uneasy situation and winked at Tommy. "Tommy's a good man Lynn. I think he'll be better from now on about recognizing your feelings. Won't you Tommy?"

Tommy took the hint that he needed to focus on Lynn more. He even realized for the first time that she could be interested in another man, which had never crossed his mind before. He made a mental note to buy the ring she wanted and ask her to marry him when they got back to LA.

Brad thought this was a good time to change the subject knowing the message to Tommy had been delivered and received. "Hey Jim, do you know anything about a Brian Hendrix? He's a shortstop, and I'm not sure where he went off to."

"Brian Hendrix? I haven't heard of him," Jim answered.

"He played ball with me at Duke and was loaded with talent. I always thought he had it in him to play ball in the majors. He just needed to work on a slight flaw in his swing," Brad said.

"I get your drift," Jim said, referring to their conversation last night. "I'll research him for you when I get home and give you a call on what I find out. It'll only take me a few minutes once I get on the computer."

"Good, I think it'll be worth looking in to." Brad was working on a plan in his head to fill the positions that they were talking about last night.

"What are you two up too?" Molly asked.

Brad turned to Molly with a big smile. "Just a big plan."

Lisa looked up at Brad wondering what he was up to. She could never keep up with him on what he was thinking. She was determined to get to know him well enough to read his mind. Then she remembered listening in on their conversation last night. It was hard to hear everything they said, but she remembered them talking about the Dodgers shortstop in a negative way. Just to let Brad know she was on to him, she gave him a pinch on the butt, and grinned at him when he looked down at her.

As they all settled down to have breakfast, Brad noticed Tommy giving Lynn addition attention that Lynn was lapping up. What a weekend he thought to himself. He felt like he was going to come away from it with a few new friends and a good friend in Lisa. He didn't have to wonder what she was like before because he saw her at her worst, or so he thought.

The rest of the day flew by as they had a big lunch and then went outside for a hike and a snow ball fight. Brad made sure he held back on the velocity since the snow was heavier now and packed well. He didn't want to hurt anyone with a fast-ball.

When they were done with the outdoor activities, they went back in the house to relax before they headed home to start another week.

Jim pulled out a bottle of champagne and popped it open to toast a nice week-end and a new friend. They all clicked their flutes together promising to keep in touch and do this again sometime. Jim told Brad he was welcome to stay here any-time he wanted. All he had to do was call to make sure nobody else would be there.

It was time to pack up their things and head south to the big city to participate once again in the fast pace life of Los Angeles.

The ride home was quiet for Brad because Lisa wasn't saying too much. She was not her bubbly self.

"Is something wrong?" Brad asked, concerned.

"I just hate for this weekend to end. I won't be around you all of the time, and it actually makes me crabby thinking about it." She took his hand in hers and held it tight. "You know I have a movie coming up that we are going to shoot in New York."

"You mentioned that to me before, but it didn't mean that much to me then, but now it does and I'll miss you. Please keep in mind I don't know what I can offer you except to be a very good friend right now."

"I've recently learned that good things are worth waiting for. Instant gratifica-tion doesn't work out in a loving relationship because there was never love. I learned a lot more from you this weekend. The way you work with people and get them to respect you within minutes was fun to watch. What do you bet Tommy asks Lynn to marry him this weekend? He noticed the crush she has on you and took your advice seriously," Lisa remarked from her astute observation.

"She didn't have a crush on me," Brad said, thinking Lisa was crazy for thinking that.

"You're so naïve Brad. That's one thing that's so charming about you. You need to pay more attention to those things though, or you might get in trouble some-time. Don't trust everyone."

"I don't trust everyone Lisa. Not picking up on some woman's infatuation is dif-ferent than picking up signs of someone who is about to harm you. But I'll listen to your street smart advice anytime," Brad replied as he gave her a quick glance.

"I hope I get the chance to coach you. What are you doing for Christmas this year?" she asked, realizing that it was less than two weeks away.

"Flying back down to Florida to be with my family. What about you?"

"I don't know. I should spend it with my family, but I'm not sure I can handle it. They're what made me what I am, or was," Lisa said, remembering that she was leading a different lifestyle now.

They both were quiet for the rest of the ride home.

Brad finished off the weekend with Lisa by giving her a warm kiss as he dropped her off, and Lisa held on to him not wanting to let go.

They promised to call each other and have dinner later in the week.

CHAPTER 33

▼

Brad had only been home an hour when he received a phone call from Jim Milnick.

"Ok Brad," Jim started off excited. "Brian Hendrix played with an Arizona farm team in South Bend, Indiana last year. You were right about his batting average being low, but his fielding percentage was great."

"You work fast Jim," Brad complimented. "Why don't you research other players for me if you don't mind? You know our weaknesses, so go after those positions."

"I'd love to," Jim replied, feeling like he had died and gone to heaven.

"I'm not sure we can do anything with our ideas, but it won't hurt to try."

"It'll be fun for me either way," Jim said, excited about the project. "I'll get back with you later this week with my findings."

"Sounds good, and thanks again for the use of the house this weekend. I really enjoyed it." Brad was glad he gave in to Lisa's request.

The wheels were turning for Brad now. The video tape exposing his shortstop passing on signals was burning him deep down, and he was going to address the problems with Keith.

First thing Monday morning, Brad played the video tape for Keith.

It didn't take long for Keith to pick up on the problem. "That's ridiculous!" Keith yelled out. "I can't believe our own team members are trying to help out the opposing team. He's gone."

"Keith, I know that I'm only a regular team member and personnel is not my job, but I'd like for you to do two things for me. Bring Tony Coselli up for a chance with the team, and get Brian Hendrix from the Diamondbacks," Brad asked with resolve.

"Who is Brian Hendrix?" Keith asked, perplexed.

"He played shortstop with me at Duke. He has plenty of talent, but needs to be worked with on his swing, and I now know how to fix it," Brad answered with determination. "I'm not saying we bring him up here now, but I'd like to see us work with him. Trust me on this one."

"I understand Tony, but I question this Brian guy," Keith stated as he looked at Brad with a confused look. "Where did he play last year?"

"South Bend team in single A. It shouldn't cost us too much," Brad pleaded to help his cause.

"I'll look into it Brad. What else do you have working?" Keith asked, knowing how Brad was.

"I have a friend researching players for our weak areas. I hope you understand what I'm trying to do. It's just the way I am," Brad said with a huge smile.

Keith smiled back. "I know that by now. Let's just keep this between us. You know what would hit the fan if the others knew about this."

"How well I know," Brad said, accepting the go ahead.

Brad went back to work full force working with the CAMM and working on his game. He put Lisa on the back burner unintentionally.

Jim met with Brad concerning the players that impressed him and gave their complete resume to Brad.

Brad gave each resume a thorough examination and did a little research of his own with Jim's assistance on certain players. He added his own comments and suggestions, and then filed them in his briefcase.

Keith was surprised when Brad entered his office and pulled out a thick set of paperwork that he laid on Keith's desk. "I don't know where this came from," Brad said with a wink of his right eye. "But I believe these might be of interest to you."

Keith just stood there shaking his head. "Don't you ever relax Brad?" Keith looked down at the stack of papers and then back at Brad with a big smile. "By the way, we traded for Brian Hendrix."

Things were starting to move along the way Brad wanted them to. He started to think they might make a run at the pennant this coming year.

Brad and Lisa had dinner that Saturday night, and she informed him she would be heading out to New York right after Christmas. They had winter shots to take in her upcoming movie making their departure from each other start earlier than she thought. They talked about how difficult it would be for them to build on what they started because Brad would be going to Florida for spring training in a few months. They did the best thing they could and promised each other to call when they could, and to communicate any problems.

Lisa knew it would be difficult on her for two reasons. She would miss Brad in the worst way, and she wasn't used to being single. She had almost always had some guy around to keep her company.

At the end of the night, they made it a point to try to get together before Christmas day and exchange gifts.

They weren't able to keep that promise though because Lisa had to fly out to New York on the twenty third.

Christmas day had arrived and was starting out to be extremely hard on Brad. It was his first Christmas without Anne and Brianna. He missed the excitement that Brianna brought to this special day. She loved opening all of her presents and did so with exuberance.

The rest of the family was also feeling the loss making this day difficult.

David and his fiancée were there to celebrate while Rebecca was spending the day with her boyfriend's family.

They had all just finished their morning coffee when the doorbell rang.

Margaret went to see who would be visiting them on Christmas morning. She opened the door, only to see a beautiful woman standing in the doorway that looked familiar.

"Merry Christmas," the young woman said. "I hope this is the Preston home?"

"Well yes it is," Margaret answered, trying to place the face.

"Is Brad here by chance?" the smiling woman asked.

"Yes he is. Oh my, you're Lisa Collins," Margaret said, finally putting a name to the pretty face. "Come in please. Do you know Brad?"

"Yes, I do. Not as well as I'd like though," Lisa replied. "If you don't mind I'd like to get a package out of my cab."

"I don't mind at all. And please let the cab go. We can drive you where you want to go if need be," Mrs. Preston said.

"Oh, I have my luggage in there also. I don't want to intrude on your Christmas anymore than I already have," Lisa answered politely.

Margaret turned around and yelled for Brad. As he approached, she said, "Go help this young lady with her bags."

"Lisa," Brad said, surprised by her presence. "What are you doing down here? I thought you were stuck in New York."

"Merry Christmas," Lisa said as she gave Brad a big hug. "I'm sorry to bother you, but we never got together before Christmas to exchange gifts, so here I am."

"Well you're staying here then," Brad demanded to the delight of Lisa.

Brad and Lisa carried in her things and then went to meet the rest of the family that was anxiously waiting to see her.

Lisa took an instant liking to Brad's parents. She was surprised to see how different looking David was compared to Brad. She thought David's personality was not as outgoing either, which complimented Brenda, his fiancée, because she was more subdued.

"So when did you leave New York?" Margaret asked.

"I took the first flight out this morning. I hope you all don't mind me being here. I wasn't invited," she said with disappointment.

"You are more than welcome," Miles replied with a welcoming smile.

Lisa sat down close to Brad and grabbed his hand.

Margaret's curiosity heightened seeing the closeness between them. "So how long have you two known each other?"

"We met the day I arrived in LA," Brad answered, preparing for more questions.

"Oh, and how did you two meet?" Margaret continued as she leaned forward a bit to hear the story.

Brad and Lisa looked at each other and let out a short laugh. The two of them told the others their entire history between them while both added things from their perspective. Brad even mentioned the fact they had slept together in an innocent way.

When they finished, the Prestons sat there flabbergasted.

"Brad, you never cease to amaze me," David said, shaking his head at his younger brother's good fortune with good looking women and his baseball career. He was a little jealous of Brad's success in life with what he thought was little effort, although Brad always reminded him when it was brought up that he had worked hard to get to where he was in life.

"So, are you two serious about each other?" Margaret asked.

"Mom, it's like we said, we haven't known each other long enough to say one way or another," Brad tried explaining with a blush on his face.

"I can tell you from my point of view," Lisa broke in. "I'm serious about Brad. I've never met anyone like him before, and I'd like to see more of him."

Brad's face turned from pink to a bright red color from hearing her say that to his family. He thought Lisa liked him, but he didn't know it was as deep as she seemed to make it. Brad wasn't sure about getting real serious about anyone at this time, especially after being reminded on this special holiday about Anne and Brianna. But he still liked Lisa at his side, which added to his confusion.

Brad's parents could read his body language and felt sorry for Lisa in a way. She seemed like a nice person that truly had strong feelings for their son, but they both knew Brad was having a rough time on this particular Christmas day. Miles and Margaret knew that a good relationship with another woman would help fill the void in Brad's life that the departure of Anne and Brianna left.

Lisa had been looking around the living room admiring the beautifully decorated tree with all of the presents still underneath, which brought delight to her. She hoped she could be involved when they all opened presents. She yearned for a life with many special family memories like this. She couldn't remember the last time she had an enjoyable moment with her family.

"I hope you haven't had breakfast yet," Mrs. Preston said to Lisa. "I have a breakfast casserole in the oven with fresh biscuits."

"I'm starved," Lisa said. "May I give you a hand in the kitchen?"

"Why thank you Lisa. Yes, I could use some help," Margaret answered with a smile.

The two of them headed for the kitchen, only to be detained when Lisa spotted some pictures on the wall of Brad, Anne, and Brianna. There were several pictures of Brianna at different ages there also.

"We miss here so much," Margaret said sadly. "She was our only grandchild and very special to us all."

"She was beautiful," Lisa said softly as she studied the little girl. "She looks like her mother with a touch of Brad, don't you think? I really didn't pay that much attention to the picture in Brad's room."

"Yes, she did favor her mother. Anne was a beautiful woman in every way, and Brianna was following in her mother's footsteps. You know, this Christmas is really hard on Brad. He misses his little girl running towards the tree to open her presents and screaming with delight over what she received."

"I thought he was not quite himself today, but I assumed that was the reason. I can't imagine having to face life with the loss of my child, not to mention my spouse. Do you think I'll ever be able to compete with the ghost of Anne? I don't mean that in a bad way," Lisa said apologetic.

"Time heals all," Margaret said wisely. "Just keep in mind that Brad has always been somewhat different with women. He has only been with two women, and one is now dead. I'm not sure what Kristy is up to except for the fact she's married. She was his high school girl friend. I guess I'm trying to tell you to be patient with him and never give up. You must always love him and be sure to show it to him because he has always been too busy with sports, school, and even work to seek romance."

"Thank you for the advice. You must be a great mother to have raised such a special person. He's well mannered and the nicest person I've known. He doesn't even realize how good looking he is."

"Brad is a special man Lisa. It's been so hard on Miles and I seeing him go through the grieving process and having to face life with the loss of Brianna. That is an emptiness that nobody can fill. He seems to have come along pretty well though. Maybe you have something to do with that," Margaret said, trying to build Lisa's confidence.

"I appreciate what you're trying to do. It'll be difficult to do what you say when I'm away making a movie and he's gone playing baseball."

"It wouldn't be any different for any other woman," Margaret added.

Lisa smiled as Margaret took her arm and led her to the kitchen.

"You're much different than I thought you'd be," Brad's mother said.

"I wasn't this way before I met your son. I was the bratty star that got everything she wanted. My mom pushed me into stardom from my childhood days until I was old enough to be on my own. I guess I should thank her for my success, but I can't because I resent her too much," Lisa stated with a slight frown on her face.

"Well, things change. Like I said, time heals all and that goes for most everything," Margaret said in a motherly way. She liked Lisa, but felt sorry for her sensing something had been lacking in her life.

The two of them put everything on the table and called the others in for breakfast.

With everyone freshly showered and dressed, it was time to open the presents. Brad was thankful that by accident he packed Lisa's present along with his family's, especially when Lisa pulled out presents for his entire family. She definitely surprised him at times.

Margaret was very pleased with her presents. Lisa had given her the movie script to the film she was working on signed by most of the cast and the director. She also had purchased a rare book on American Literature. Lisa had remembered Brad telling her about his mother's love for theater along with the fact that his mother had been an English teacher in school.

Brenda received a delicate gold necklace that Lisa had purchased for Rebecca, but quick thinking on Lisa's part allowed her to switch the name on the present to the upcoming new member of the Preston family.

Brad gave Lisa a uniquely designed necklace with three layers of intertwining gold that accented her long thin neck. He also gave her the matching bracelet. The gold stood out on Lisa's bronze skin, and the design of the necklace was striking.

Lisa then handed Brad his present, which was a stylish one of a kind solid gold watch with "Love always, Lisa" engraved on the back of it.

Miles was excited about his oil painting of the New York Stock Exchange by a renowned artist, while David marveled over his new Rolex watch.

Lisa had done very well in her choices of presents, and she received great pleasure in giving them to Brad and his family.

"I feel so bad," Miles said to Lisa. "You brought us these great gifts, and we have nothing to give you."

"Yes you have," Lisa said genuinely. "This is a wonderful Christmas for me, and I have all of you to thank for it. Plus, I have this guy here to share some time with, which makes me so happy. Do you ever sing Christmas songs together?" she asked, eyeing a piano in the corner.

"We used to, but we haven't sung any carols for a few years now," Margaret answered as she walked over to the piano. "How about I play the piano and you sing?" she asked Lisa.

"I'd love to," Lisa said, racing over to the piano. "Come here by my side and help me out," she signaled to Brad.

The rest of the family formed a circle around the piano as Margaret played mistake free, and Lisa sang with her wonderful voice. It was star quality highlighted with so much passion that it brought goose bumps to everyone. The rest of the family finally joined in on the fourth song, which was Jingle Bells, so they couldn't mess it up too bad.

"You are talented," Mrs. Preston said to Lisa with much praise.

"Thank you," Lisa replied. "It's easy to sing when you enjoy the songs. I always enjoyed singing Christmas carols. I just never had a chance to do it with a great family."

Brad pulled Lisa close to him and stared into her brown eyes. He definitely saw something different in them now compared to the first time he met her. She was winning him over a little bit at a time.

The rest of the day passed them by quickly with everyone thoroughly enjoying themselves. The turkey dinner and fresh homemade pies were delicious and a real treat for Lisa.

Lisa was overwhelmed by the whole close family concept the Preston family possessed. She thought the entire house was filled with love and respect for each other. No wonder Brad was such a great person, she thought to herself.

Lisa and Mrs. Preston built a strong relationship between them making Lisa wish Margaret was her mother. Lisa cried when she had to leave for New York the next day. She had finally participated in a real family holiday and learned what it was all about, making her reluctant to leave it behind.

Brad drove her to the airport in silence and gave her a long hug and kiss before she left his side to catch her flight.

Things had calmed down at the Preston house with Lisa, David, and Brenda gone. Brad wanted to stay with his parents one more day before he took a flight back to Los Angeles. He dreaded the long flight.

Miles and Margaret decided that it was a good time to talk with their youngest son. They hadn't been around him enough since the death of his family and wanted to make sure everything was going the way he wanted it to go. So after dinner that night, they started in on him with questions they felt were necessary for Brad to think about.

Mrs. Preston addressed Brad first. "You've been through a lot this past year and seem to be headed in the right direction to heal you from the terrible loss of Anne and Brianna. What plans do you have right now to allow another woman in your life?"

Brad knew that she was referring to Lisa. "I haven't made any plans for anyone and that includes Lisa Collins. You should know me well enough that I don't require a woman to be at my side everyday. I do enjoy the company from Lisa and the warmth she brings along with her, but right now I'm focused on my baseball career. I acknowledge the fact that I don't have the time and energy required to take a relationship from point A, to marriage. Besides, I believe that if there is the right woman, the relationship will make its way to the ultimate end of marriage on its own," Brad explained his position, as if it were memorized.

"You may be single for the rest of your life then," his mother said in a strong tone. "Anne was one of those once in a lifetime romances. There are very few people like her out there, so don't try to clone her into someone else. Lisa has some of those traits, and only time will tell if she has them all, so be patient and be careful…not only for your well being, but for hers also. I came away from meeting her liking what I saw, so please don't hurt her or lead her on," she added sternly.

"Yes Brad, and don't allow that to happen to you either," Miles added.

"I appreciate you both trying to look out for me, but I'll be alright. I admit I'm perplexed over this situation, but I will do the right thing. It just isn't my number one priority right now, so please understand that. I do still talk with Kristy every now and then, which gives me mixed emotions," Brad explained.

"That's not a very good idea Brad. She's a married woman and is about to have a child."

"I know that Mom, but you don't know the whole story. Greg has beaten her and threatened to kill her if she ever left him. Kristy even suspects that he had something to do with the deaths of Anne and Brianna," Brad proclaimed to them for the first time.

"Oh my God!" Margaret said.

"What makes her think Greg was involved with the accident?" Miles asked, getting to his feet.

"He's always been jealous of me, and it gets worse with time. Kristy said he had been acting weird the week of the accident. On the day of the accident he was in an unusually good mood. As soon as he walked in the house, he turned on the television to watch the news, which he never did. He was looking for a particular news story and was disappointed when he heard it was Anne and Brianna in the car and not me," Brad explained as he directed his attention to his father.

"Have you notified the police of this?" his father asked, concerned.

"What can I tell them? There isn't enough to go on right now," Brad explained. He purposely held off telling them about the other information he knew about Greg. He didn't want them to worry any more than they had to.

"Would you want Kristy as your wife?" his mom asked with concern.

"I don't think so. It would be tough having to live with Greg's child. I dislike him that much. I do believe Kristy when she said that Greg would kill her if she left him, so I really don't see her as an option. But I still get tingly when I talk to her. I'll just have to wait and see if that goes away with Lisa in the picture. Right now baseball is foremost on my agenda. Let's just leave it at that for now please," Brad stated, wanting to end the talk about his love life, or lack of it.

"Well, I agree with you Brad on the fact that your baseball career is number one right now. You have wanted this all of your life and the opportunity is in front of you to take it and run with it," Miles said, reinforcing Brad's desire of playing in the big leagues. "By the way, your investments are doing just fine, so don't worry about money."

"That is one convenience I really do enjoy," Brad replied. "With my contract with the Dodgers, and your help investing my money, I should be set for life money wise."

CHAPTER 34

▼

February 19, had come to mark the anniversary of the death of Anne and Brianna. Brad woke up early in his Charlotte apartment to start off his day with his normal routine of jogging. The day had an eerie feeling to him, but he believed it was only in his mind.

Much had happened since the first of the year with the Dodger organization and Brad's personal life. He had been working with Brian Hendrix on his batting while throwing to Tony Coselli on a regular basis. The Dodgers made a bold trade to get a strong center fielder to replace Lenny. Things were coming together with spring training just weeks away.

Lisa was still filming in New York, but called Brad almost daily, or he called her. Their relationship had not elevated, however it had not diminished either. It remained at a comfortable level for Brad, while Lisa was growing impatient. She wasn't used to living alone for such a long time, and Brad hadn't tried to expand on their relationship.

Kristy still kept in contact with Brad letting him know she still loved him more than ever. Her pregnancy had been perfect so far, and she was excited to hold her newborn baby in her arms. She worried a little about the baby looking too much like Brad because Brad and Greg looked nothing alike. She thought that Greg was so wrapped up in his perverted world that he probably would never notice. Things had been going fairly smooth for her as far as Greg was concerned. He had kept his distance from her since the day she presented the evidence she had on him.

Brad finished his early morning run and had just gotten out of the shower when the phone rang. It was Lisa checking up on him to make sure he was ok. She knew he had flown to Charlotte yesterday to be there on this particular day to visit the gravesites, and she wanted to make sure he was handling it all right.

He told her it was an awkward day for him with different emotions pulling at him, but he needed to face these feelings head on to be able to go on with his life in a positive way.

Lisa agreed totally because she wanted his ghost to leave forever. She only prayed this would be one step closer for him to leave Anne behind and allow him to pursue their relationship further. She didn't understand the overall picture of what Brad had been going through.

They finished their conversation on a positive note with Brad promising Lisa he would call her if he needed any emotional support after visiting the gravesites.

It was just past nine in the morning when Brad felt something strange. It was like a warm wind blew through his body.

At the same time in Indianapolis, Kristy felt a warm glow in her body. It was so strange to her because she had never felt anything like it before. She passed it off as another freak thing that pregnancy did to you. She was nine months along, but others thought she was only eight months. Kristy looked down at her big belly knowing at this point in a pregnancy it was hard to tell the difference in a month.

Kristy went on with her day as usual, but felt the strange stirring in her body increase. She was fully aware of what happened a year ago today not so far from her home. According to the report, the accident occurred at about this exact time and Anne died on impact. Kristy started to freak out when she put the time lines together. Her strange feeling had come on her at the exact time of the accident. She was close to crossing the line of becoming panicked. "What was happening?" she asked herself. Kristy packed her suitcase just in case it was time to go to the hospital.

Brad arrived at the cemetery to visit the gravesites of Anne and Brianna. He told them both he missed them dearly and wished they were still here with him. He set fresh flowers on each grave and kneeled down to rub his fingers over their tombstones. He said a prayer for each of them and asked God to take care of him and lead him in the right direction.

As he got up to leave, a fresh breeze raced past his face, and he felt the strange stirring that ran a warm current through his body. He had no idea what was going on, but didn't question the peculiar event. He had been through it before and assumed it was either Anne or Brianna. Brad had no idea that Kristy was experiencing the same feeling hundreds of miles away.

Two hours later, Kristy started having contractions. They were mild, but they were consistent. She called her mother to come over to drive her to the hospital, but refused to call Greg. She didn't want him around on this special day and spoil the joy of her baby's birth. It wasn't his baby to start with. She wished Brad could be there at her side to participate in his child's birth.

When Kristy arrived at the hospital, she was angered to see Greg waiting there for her.

"So, it looks like you're a little early," Greg said coldly. His eyes narrowed. "Your dad called me to let me know you were on your way here. Weren't you going to tell the father of your baby?"

Kristy almost blurted out that he wasn't the father because Brad was the real one, but she held off. She held her big belly up with both hands and timidly looked at Greg. "We were going to let you know. I just wanted to make sure this was the real thing," she said, lying to him.

They checked her into the hospital since her contractions were consistently three minutes apart. It was easy going for Kristy as she barely experienced any pain. The labor was a smooth process for her, which disappointed Greg.

Greg wanted her to be in a lot of pain like he had seen on television. The pain would have added to his pleasure, but nothing could ruin this day for him. He would soon have something that Brad didn't have and on the same day that he killed Brad's daughter. It was a sign to him, but not a sign from God.

Kristy was getting closer to delivering and still not experiencing much discomfort. There was still that warm glow stirring around in her belly. Maybe that was helping her out, Kristy thought to herself. Could this have anything to do with Anne or Brianna? Was one of their spirits in her body to help deliver a new brother or sister for Brianna, Kristy wondered?

Kristy continued to coast through her labor. Greg even wondered if this was the real thing because it was so easy.

Suddenly, as if it was on a time line, the baby was ready to be born. The hospital staff moved quickly trying to keep up with the rapid pace of the birth because the doctor wasn't prepared for it to happen so abruptly.

Kristy delivered the baby girl with ease while having very little pain. It couldn't have gone any better.

Greg was disappointed it wasn't a boy, but a smile soon covered his face when he realized that a girl would be a much better way to out do Brad because his little girl was dead.

Greg held his trophy for a few seconds and then handed it back to the nurse. He was pumped up and had things to do so he could cap off his day. It had been a while since he had felt this way, and he didn't want to waste it.

Greg had already departed when they brought the adorable baby girl back to her mother all cleaned up and dressed in a small nightgown.

Kristy marveled at her newborn baby and was stunned by the resemblance of Brad, or so it seemed to her. Kristy asked what the official time of birth was and would have bet the farm it was the same time that Brianna died. A miracle had happened today, and an angel was born. There was only one name to call this precious little girl, so Kristy named her Angelica because she was her little angel as well as Brad's.

The warm glow left Kristy's body at the same time she held her newborn baby girl in her arms safe and sound. She acknowledged what happened to her today was nothing less than a miracle from up above. Questions surfaced as Kristy thought about today's events, making her wonder if there really had been an angel working with her today, and if so was it Anne or Brianna? Believing it to be the later she said a long prayer thanking God for sending an angel to get her through the delivery without any problems or pain. She pleaded for the strength to raise this child in the terrible conditions of her marriage, and asked for God to bless her and the newborn baby and protect them both from her awful husband.

Kristy knew a new life had started for her today with the birth of Angelica. It would be a life with just the two of them, each having to protect one another in their own way. But that was fine with Kristy. The only thing that would complete her life would be the addition of Brad, which was next to impossible.

Carol and John arrived at the hospital that evening to see the baby. Carol was stunned to see how much Angelica resembled Brianna as a baby. She looked at Kristy with a quizzical look questioning the baby's father.

Kristy didn't know how to respond to the nonverbal question because she wasn't sure she wanted anyone else to know at this time who the father was. Nobody else would question it anyway. She decided to tell Carol the truth giving her a slight up and down motion with her head. Kristy only did it so Brad could be informed of the truth if anything happened to her. She never knew what could happen with Greg's sickness.

Carol gave a big smile in return and took Angelica from Kristy and held her tight. She would love this baby like her own knowing Brad was the natural father.

John looked on not catching the hidden conversation between the two women. He grabbed Angelica's tiny little hand. "What a miracle a baby is." He looked up at his wife with a smile. "Maybe we should start our family. It will make them close enough in age to be good friends."

"I'm ready when you are," Carol answered, beaming with joy over the idea.

"That would be wonderful for you two to have a baby," Kristy added. "Get started right away, so they won't be too far apart."

They all laughed with joy from the arrival of Angelica and the plan for Carol having her own baby.

As the two left Kristy and Angelica, Carol bent down to give Kristy a hug and whispered, "I won't tell a soul."

"Thank you. But promise me you'll let Brad know if something happens to me," Kristy stated.

"I would have done that without your permission anyway," Carol replied with a gentle smile.

CHAPTER 35

▼

Brad and the rest of the team were in Florida for the start of spring training. He had become restless from his time off and was ready to start playing again. There were high hopes for the Dodgers this year with the addition of key players due to the off season trades that took place.

The media had been focusing most of their press towards Brad as they were labeling him the key to the Dodgers success for this upcoming year. None of the other team members could argue the fact as they recognized his skill as a player, as well as his great leadership skills. He was bringing everyone around him up another level.

The only thing not in perfect order for Brad was his personal life. He was still torn concerning how he felt about Lisa while he still questioned his feelings for Kristy. He heard that Kristy had given birth to a beautiful little girl. It made him jealous of Greg, which really made it worse on him. He could see Greg going around playing on the fact that he had a little girl and Brad Preston did not, with the mother being Brad's high school sweetheart to double the impact.

So Brad did what he had done in the past. He dug into his work one hundred percent and put the other thoughts to the side. It was his survival instinct taking over, although it would create problems down the road because Lisa wouldn't like being put on the back burner. His phone conversations with Lisa had already dwindled to one call per week.

It was the last week of spring training, and Brad was scheduled to pitch in today's game. He was having breakfast when he looked down at a newspaper with a picture of Lisa and a good looking man apparently having a good time together.

The caption under the picture read, "Lisa Collins has a new boyfriend, she and her co-star of her upcoming movie are an item."

Brad felt anger overcome his emotions unlike he seldom experienced. How could he have been duped by her? "I guess that some people never change," he said to himself.

The whole episode bothered Brad more than he thought. He gave up three runs in the game, which was highly unusual for him. He made a mental promise to himself that he would never allow a woman to effect his performance on the playing field again.

There was a message from Lisa for Brad on his phone mail, but he did not return the call. He had cut her out of his life, so he wouldn't have to face the hurt he was subject to. Brad had his mind on one thing now, and that was to have the Dodgers win it all this year. Nothing else was as important to him as that, or so he instilled that thinking in himself. He had built a fence around himself to protect him from others that could possibly hurt him and also to keep the emptiness inside of him hidden.

Lisa was a wreck knowing she had lost Brad. She didn't blame him for not returning her phone calls or not wanting to see her. Lisa realized she messed up big time since Brad was not the type to put up with that kind of lifestyle. She only wished he would at least talk to her, so she could explain to him that nothing happened because Lisa stopped herself from going too far with her co-star, although the photograph would make you believe different. She knew she should never have let things go as far as they did, but she was lonesome and in her old days she would shack up with the best man available at the time to keep her company.

Now Lisa was lost and didn't want to go on with her career. She had about a month more of work to do before the filming would be complete, and she would then take time off to pull herself back together and try to persuade Brad to give her a second chance. Lisa wanted him back in her life more than ever because she now realized she loved him more than she thought, and it was killing her.

Kristy was as happy as she could possibly be. She devoted her life to her daughter and hid behind that fact. She only communicated with Carol and visited her often now that Carol was pregnant. It was a blessing for both of them because Carol had wanted a baby for some time, but John wanted to hold off until they were more financially sound.

For Kristy, it gave her a way to help out her best friend. It was fun to see someone else go through the same thing she had just gone through.

Carol was already three months along and starting to show as her stomach had a rounded plump look.

They had both talked at length about Angelica being Brad's daughter. Carol didn't think it was fair for Brad to go through life not knowing that he had another daughter, especially one that looked so much like him. But Kristy always talked her out of telling Brad the truth.

Carol knew Greg would do something awful, and she didn't want anyone to get hurt or killed. She always thought there had to be a way to let Brad know the truth. She knew in her heart that someday the truth would come out, and she couldn't wait for that day to arrive.

Greg Somanski had been living a very incomplete life. His wife hated him and wouldn't allow him close to her. Plus, he had to watch himself now because he never knew what Kristy might do to put him away. Greg wanted to kill her, but he knew she meant what she said that night when she showed him the video. He wasn't sure what other information she might have sent to the unknown person.

Greg also thought that having a daughter would make him more powerful, but that wasn't happening. Even his abusive sexual encounters with prostitutes, or easy to get women didn't fuel him anymore. But how could anything give him power when all he read in the newspapers or saw on the sports shows was how Brad Preston was the second coming of baseball.

Brad had dominated the game of baseball winning thirteen games by the all star break. Brad's .93 earned run average was remarkable and would have been lower had he not pitched three games with a slightly sprained ankle.

Greg had to do something soon before he lost it. He felt like he was superman, and Brad's success was like a dose of kryptonite to him dwindling his strength to nothing. The only way he could regain all of his power was to take Brad out once and for all, and that is what he was going to have to do.

Greg wasn't even looking forward to going down to Frankie's Bar to watch the all star game with his buddies because they all loved Brad and cheered him on. He knew they had no idea that Brad had stolen his life from him and it should be Greg Somanski out there starting for the National League instead of Brad. He believed everyone would realize what Brad had done and congratulate him for killing the thief when the real truth was revealed.

Greg went straight to Frankie's after a worthless day at work. He didn't come close to selling a car today with his mind elsewhere. Brad was killing him one day at a time by stealing Greg's life to make him a better and stronger baseball player. Greg ordered a couple of drinks before the rest of the gang showed up. He needed to be drunk this evening, so he wouldn't have to hear all of the cheers for the hometown boy.

Brad was in the bullpen warming up for his first start of an All Star game. The fans demonstrated their love for him by giving him the most votes for a pitcher. His ankle was healed, and he was throwing around one hundred miles per hour again. He was at the top of his game with the other arsenal of pitches he mastered making him almost untouchable to the hitters. He had also been learning to move his pitches around better, which added to the aggravation of every hitter he faced. Not only did the batters have to guess his pitch, they now had to guess the location.

Brad was the cornerstone of the Dodgers, and the other players rallied around him, thus making the Dodgers the first place team in the west. It had all come together just the way Brad wanted it to. Brian Hendrix was now the starting shortstop for the Dodgers and playing great defense while batting .282. Tony Coselli earned the job as starting catcher and was a great team leader. He made every Dodger pitcher better, including Brad.

Tony and Brian were among the sell out crowd to watch their best friend make his All Star debut. They were all there in anticipation of seeing whether or not the American League hitters were just as defenseless as the National League players against Brad?

It only took minutes for Brad to let everyone know how dominant he was. He struck out the side in the first inning. In the second inning he struck out two and forced the other batter to hit a weak ground ball to the first baseman for an easy play.

The National League had a rally going in the bottom of the second allowing Brad to bat with the bases loaded. He drove the second pitch to the fence in left center missing a home run by a few feet, but drove in three runs with a stand up triple. He was the real thing, and the fans appreciated his hard play.

Greg was drunk when Brad hit the triple scoring three runs for the National League. Everyone in the bar was shouting and cheering for their local hero, except Greg. He only tolerated the others because he knew they had no idea that all of Brad's skill came from him. He just shook his head at their ignorance and vowed that one day soon they would all know the real truth. Then they would be carrying Greg Somanski around the bar on their shoulders and cheering for him while they spit on Brad's grave with disgust.

Brad went to the mound for the third inning pumped up after hitting in three runs to give the National League the lead. He had the confidence and the skills to blow every batter away, and those were his intentions. The first hitter went down with three straight strikes. The second hitter was able to hit a foul ball that the third baseman caught at the wall by the dugout. Another three pitches, and the third hitter was out on strikes ending Brad's performance for the night. He left the field to a standing ovation from every fan in the ballpark. He later was named the most valuable player.

One week after the all star game, the Los Angeles Dodgers traveled to Cincinnati to play the Reds. Brad was scheduled to pitch the third game of the series. Cincinnati had been coming on strong lately and was in contention for their division title, so the hometown fans were all fired up for the series. They split the first two games making the third game critical for both teams.

Brad was feeling exceptionally strong today as he warmed up in the bullpen for the rubber match of the series against the Reds. He had everything working for him, and even Tony realized this would be a special day. As they both walked together towards the dugout, Tony made mention to Brad he had never seen him as sharp as he was today.

After five innings, the Reds and the rest of the country were seeing the truth in Tony's words as the Reds were hitless, and not one of their hitters had made it to first base. People were used to seeing Brad dominate the other team, but not the way he mowed them down today.

Brad came to bat in the top of the sixth and hit a two run homer to give the Dodgers a four run lead.

The next nine batters of the Reds went down in order. Through eight innings, Brad had struck out seventeen batters, walked none, and had not given up a hit. It was a perfect game in the making coming into the bottom of the ninth intensifying the drama on the playing field.

The Dodgers scored one run in the top of the ninth inning, setting the scene for the most difficult feat for any pitcher, throwing a perfect game. Everyone in the stands was now on their feet clapping, some wanting a hit while others wanted to see a perfect game.

Brad had thrown his last warm up pitch and was ready to go. Just for fun Brad's first pitch was a change up that dropped out of sight making the hitter look ridiculous as he swung at the disappearing ball. Brad's next pitch was a hundred mile per hour fast ball that cut in on the batter and called a strike, leaving the count 0 and two. The third and final strike was another fast ball that the batter chased for the first out.

A pinch hitter approached the plate as the Reds tried to get a base runner. It was a lost cause though because he swung at three pitches without laying a bat on any of them.

Brad felt comfortable and still had all of his stuff. He knew what was on the line, but he felt cool about the situation. Brad knew he was almost impossible to hit today, and he planned to challenge this batter the same way he challenged the first batter.

As the fans clapped their hands together, Brad started his windup and threw a bullet for a strike. The stadium became louder as some fans were chanting, "perfect game" over and over again.

Brad missed with a curve ball on the second pitch to even the count. He then threw a rare slider that surprised the batter for strike two. By now the fervor from the fans was overwhelming as they waited anxiously for the third and final strike of the game.

Tony signaled for the pitch, and Brad nodded his head in agreement and then threw a hundred mile per hour fastball right past the hitter for the third strike and a perfect game.

The entire Dodger team ran out to Brad and carried him off the field as they all enjoyed participating in the masterpiece.

The crowd was going wild, and even the Cincinnati fans were jubilant over the game even though their beloved Reds lost.

Brad Preston had become a hero in the baseball world, and today he added the punctuation mark to that status.

Not every fan in Cincinnati was happy today by the result of the game. Dressed in a colorless outfit with a high powered rifle at his side, from an empty room in a building overlooking the stadium, a disturbed person laid waiting. The rifle was in place and loaded with high caliber rounds that would surely kill someone from this distance. Well hidden, the assassin held the binoculars to his eyes while aiming them at an exit door of the stadium.

The door opened as the Dodger team filed out still laughing and having a good time from today's victory and perfect game. It brought more anger to the killer in the vacant room. His heart started beating faster when he saw Brad Preston walking through the doorway. Taking the rifle in his hands the killer set the scope on Brad, waiting for a clear shot. There were several people swarming around the target which was to be expected since he pitched a perfect game, but it aggravated the shooter more. He wanted to take the shot and vacate quick.

Time was starting to run out on the assassin as Brad was now fifteen feet from the bus. With his finger on the trigger he squeezed slightly knowing that he would have a clear shot in a second. The time was now as the shooter pulled the trigger, but at the same time Brian Hendrix had called out to Brad causing Brad to stop and turn to see what Brian wanted.

Brad heard the gun fire and instantaneously felt the breeze of the bullet brush his face. He ran as hard as he could for the bus.

The killer was not prepared for the sudden stop of his target and became flustered, but still squeezed off three more rounds at the now difficult target. He then packed up everything and vacated the area without leaving anything behind for evidence.

Brad felt a burning sensation in his left leg as he fell into the bus. He felt like his leg was on fire and then felt the warm blood flowing down his leg. He looked up at Brian with an anguished look on his face from the severe pain he was experiencing.

Brian saw the red stains come through Brad's pants and then quickly pulled his tie off to use as a tourniquet by wrapping it around Brad's leg just above the bullet wound.

It was chaos on the bus as the other team members were worried about more gun fire. They didn't know their best player had been shot.

"Get an ambulance," Brian yelled out as he pulled hard on his tie to try to stop the bleeding in Brad's leg.

That was the last thing Brad heard before he passed out.

CHAPTER 36

▼

Every news network was running the same story about Brad Preston. They were reporting the gem he pitched that turned into a rare perfect game, but celebration turned into a nightmare as Brad was gunned down by what police suspect was an angry fan. He is in serious condition in a Cincinnati hospital.

Kristy started crying as she watched the report on the news. She suspected Greg right away since she hadn't seen him in a few days. Tomorrow she would check out the local newspapers as well as Cincinnati's papers to see if anyone was beaten and raped. She knew that was his M.O. Kristy wanted to get down to Cincinnati to see Brad and tell him of her suspicions. She called Carol to see if she had heard the news yet and to make arrangements for Carol to go with her to the hospital.

Kristy wasn't naïve enough to think she could just walk into Brad's room. She knew security would be tight since someone tried to kill Brad. She had to try to contact Brad's parents or Bill Matthews for help. One way or another, she was determined to talk to Brad in person. She wanted to take Angelica with her and announce to him she was his, but it was too dangerous. If Greg tried to kill Brad today for no apparent reason, he would surely try to kill all three of them if he knew the baby was not his, but indeed Brad's.

Kristy went to work making her phone calls to arrange a meeting as soon as possible with Brad. She was being selfish for wanting to see him because she missed him in her life so much.

Miles and Margaret Preston were already in flight to Cincinnati. Keith Olson had called them shortly after the shooting to let them know what happened and gave them the name of the hospital where Brad was taken. They were worried sick about their son in two ways. They were concerned about his gunshot wound, but they were more concerned about someone trying to kill him. How anyone could be so shallow as to try to kill someone over a sporting event was beyond their perspective, they thought to themselves.

They both agreed to make a demand to the Dodger organization to give better security to Brad. But first they wanted to see Brad alive and well.

The nurses wheeled Brad out of the surgical ward into the recovery room. He was doing fine after they replenished his blood volume and performed surgery on his leg. Brad was lucky in one way; the bullet missed the bone, but exploded threw his thigh muscle in his left leg. His extensive bleeding had been caused by a severed artery caused by the bullet slicing through it. Thankfully, Brian Hendrix acted quickly and wisely by controlling Brad's blood loss.

The hospital was full of police to add the additional security they felt was needed to protect Brad from anyone bothering him or trying to finish the job the original shooter started. Only security cleared hospital staff or visitors approved by the Dodgers were allowed near Brad's room.

By the time Mr. and Mrs. Preston arrived, Brad was conscious and happy to see them. He didn't know what to think about the ordeal earlier today that could have ended his life. It gave him a chance to reflect on his life and the emptiness Anne and Brianna left him with. He felt selfish by wishing he had someone special to him there by his side. He knew it was time to open his heart up again to allow that special person to be involved in his life.

He conversed with his parents about his feelings, and then brought up the thought that Greg Somanski might have been involved.

Miles thought Brad was reaching though, but he didn't know everything about Greg that Brad knew. Miles agreed with the theory that it was an upset fan trying to take Brad out for pitching a perfect game against the Reds.

"You know Dad, every time I get close to a perfect game or pitch one, I end up getting hurt. Doesn't that seem unusual?" Brad asked as he huffed out a sigh.

"That appears to be true, but Greg was present at the last event, and there isn't any evidence he was around Cincinnati today, so I go by what the facts are and believe it was a disgruntled fan. If we can tie Greg to the area today, I might change my thinking," Miles stated firmly.

Keith Olson entered the room wanting to see his star player and his good friend all in one. He was upset about the attempted murder, not only from the perspective of losing their best player, but having someone he liked and respected so much nearly killed.

Keith read the Preston's minds. "We will look into this act of violence today and find out who tried to kill Brad. We will also provide a top notch security force around Brad and the rest of the team."

"Thank you for that," Miles said. "I was hoping I wouldn't have to make a demand to you to provide more security for my son."

"Brad's well being is at the top of both of our lists Mr. Preston," Keith replied. "I've grown rather fond of your son, and I'll look after him as if he were my family."

"Well Keith," Brad said. "What's the deal with my leg?"

"You're done for this year," Keith stated apologetically. "A few more inches and your femur would have been cut in half, so we are lucky there. The muscle will heal, but it takes time. It could have been worse Brad," Keith said, knowing he could have been killed or crippled.

"We have some great players on this team Keith. They can win without me, so don't let them lose their momentum," Brad said wisely.

"You'll be in the dugout again soon to help lead this team as you have done all year. Don't think you have the rest of the year off just because you got shot," Keith said with a quick smile.

Kristy missed the Prestons when she tried calling their home phone yesterday. She had a call in to Bill Matthews, and she was waiting impatiently at Carol's house for his return phone call. She also had found a story in today's Cincinnati's newspaper about a young woman being raped and beaten last night. She felt confident it was Greg that pulled the trigger yesterday and then following the shooting found a victim and beat and raped her.

Kristy reflected on her life with Greg and couldn't believe how dumb she was to have married such a loser and sick man as Greg. Somehow, she had to get out of her pitiful marriage. She thought of ways to have him killed, but she couldn't do it no matter how much she hated him. The only other plan was to run away with Angelica, but life on the run and having to look over your shoulder every minute was not the kind of life she wanted to live, plus it wouldn't fair to her baby either. So she just prayed that something would happen to change her life.

Thirty minutes later, the phone rang. Carol answered the phone after the first ring. She was just as nervous about things as Kristy. Carol signaled to Kristy that it was for her, and announced it was Bill as Kristy took the phone from her hand.

"Hello Bill, this is Kristy Somanski. Thank you for returning my call," she said anxiously.

"Hi Kristy. From your message I couldn't resist not calling you. Tell me what you have please, so I can help you and Brad out," Bill requested.

"I sent you a package last year that had a letter and a video tape concerning my husband's deviant behavior. The tape ties him to a rape and battery case while the letter explains how I suspect Greg was responsible for the deaths of Anne and Brianna Preston," Kristy stated.

"Do you really think he had something to do with their deaths Kristy? There was nothing stated in the report that would make anyone think it was nothing more than an accident caused by the bad weather conditions," Bill questioned as he swiveled his chair in the opposite direction.

"You weren't around to see how he acted that day. Greg anticipated the report when he turned on the news that evening. Look Bill, I don't have any concrete evidence on that accident or yesterdays shooting, but I'd bet the farm that Greg was involved in both incidents. He was away on a fishing trip a few days before the shooting as well as the day of the shooting, and some woman was beaten and raped last night in Cincinnati, which is Greg's behavior pattern."

"Why do you stay married to the man Kristy?" Bill asked in disgust.

"He'd kill me if I left him. He's beaten me half to death and raped me just like the woman in Cincinnati. Look Bill, I'm only calling you to see if you can help me see Brad in the hospital in Cincinnati. I need to talk to him and let him know what I suspect, plus I want to see him. I love him, and I always will love him, so please help me," Kristy pleaded as she looked at Carol a look of desperation.

"I'll see what I can do to help you, but I'm not sure I have enough pull to make it happen," Bill explained. He was concerned about Greg Somanski more than ever now since Brad had brought him up before. "In your honest opinion, do you think your husband was actually the shooter yesterday?"

"I have no doubt Bill. Greg had been acting strange again lately, and it seemed to center around Brad's success. I believe he gets a surge of power when he feels control over Brad, and then loses the power when Brad has success. Greg is a sick individual Bill, and it all centers around Brad. He's the one that lied to me and made it look like Brad was having all of these affairs while I was dating Brad. It's hard to explain, but it's a truth we have to face. Greg will try to take Brad out again. He won't be satisfied until Brad is dead or crippled. We have to do something to stop Greg from doing one of those things to Brad," Kristy said, exhausted from her long dialog.

"Alright, I'll do what I can for you and call you back. What number should I call to reach you?" Bill grabbed a pen and piece of paper.

"Just use the same number you just called. Carol can get in touch with me. And thanks Bill, I owe you."

"Thank you for your concern and for the information. I promise you I'll seek additional information on your husband," Bill said as he ended the conversation.

Bill immediately called for Keith Olson and then called a private investigator that had done some work for him in the Indianapolis area before. The man was very reliable and private about who hired him, which worked out perfect. Bill told the man to keep an eye on Greg Somanski and use whatever means he had to let Greg know they were on to him, plus let him know that from now on someone would be on his tail at all times. He left it at that hoping the acknowledgement of Greg's involvement in Brad's misfortunes would keep Greg at bay.

Lisa Collins had been working full days trying to finish the filming of her latest movie that she was starring in. It was lunch time on the day after the shooting of Brad Preston before Lisa learned what had happened to Brad. There happened to be a newspaper lying on the table where she sat to eat when she saw the headlines, "Brad Preston, Shot, After Perfect Game."

She immediately grabbed the paper and read the article that followed the headline. She couldn't eat her lunch because she was so upset. "Why would anyone try to kill Brad?" she stated out loud.

"Yeah, that's a real shame," one of the cast members said, irritated over the incident. "That guy could really pitch. I started watching baseball again because of him. He brought a touch of class back to the game."

"He is a classy person," Lisa replied.

She left the lunch area with her cell phone in hand and made a call to Keith Olson. She left a message for him to call her. She then called Nelson at the Olson estate and asked him if he had heard anything.

Nelson told Lisa he hadn't heard from Brad as of yet, but hoped Brad or Keith would call with his condition.

She asked him to have Brad call her, and Nelson said he would.

The rest of the day was horrible for Lisa. She forgot her lines, and lost her passion for her part, and finally left the set early. She sat by the phone for the rest of the day hoping that someone would call her.

Brad was tired from the surgery and from the drugs he had taken, but was able to make a few phone calls to some important people to him. He called Bill Matthews, the Weatherbys, Carol, Nelson and Jim Milnick in that order.

Bill told Brad about his conversation with Kristy, and Brad agreed with her that it was a good chance Greg was the shooter. He told Bill to try to contact Kristy again to have her come see him. Brad really needed that right now.

The Weatherbys were happy to hear from Brad and relieved to hear he was ok. They talked a minute about his perfect game, and then ended their conversation.

Brad then called Carol, and she informed him that Kristy was working hard to come see him. He told her to have Kristy call Keith Olson, and he would work it out. Brad insisted that Kristy should come in a disguise because he knew the press was there at the hospital, and he feared Greg might see her walking up to the hospital on the television news.

Brad then called Nelson to let him know he survived the shooting.

Nelson was relieved to hear that Brad was ok and insisted on Brad staying at the Olson's estate during his recuperation so he could take care of him when he was released from the hospital. He then told Brad that Lisa called and was truly upset. Nelson urged Brad to call her.

Jim was happy to hear from his newest and most respected friend. Although the two of them didn't have much of a chance to socialize together, they tried to talk with each other once a week on the phone.

Brad had become fond of Jim appreciating his insight on the game and respecting Jim for not going around town telling everyone that he was a good friend with Brad.

Jim also tried to persuade Brad to call Lisa. He told Brad he had talked to her a few times since the fling, and she was devastated that Brad wouldn't see her or talk to her.

Brad was tired after the phone conversations, but he dialed Lisa's number to fulfill his promise to Nelson and Jim.

"Hello," Lisa answered in a meek voice.

"Are you alright?" Brad asked concerned. He had never heard her that sad before.

"Brad, is that you?" she asked in a more enthusiastic tone. "Are you ok?" She started to cry violently.

"I'm fine, but you don't sound like you're doing well. How've you been?" he asked, feeling sorry for her.

She regained her composure. "Terrible. I haven't been worth much since our last conversation months ago. I've tried to bury myself in my work, but I don't think I'm as good at that as you are. What happened yesterday that someone would try to kill you?"

"It's almost impossible to say," he replied truthfully since the police found no evidence anywhere. "I have a gut feeling Greg Somanski had something to do with it though."

Lisa was stunned. "Kristy's husband? What makes you think that?"

"Kristy called Bill Matthews and told him that Greg had been acting strange lately, and he was away on a fishing trip the day before and the day of the shooting. I don't know what makes him hate me so much. He's the one with a wife and daughter," Brad said with a touch of jealousy.

"Brad, I want you to know nothing happened that one night. Yes, I was lonely, and I almost fell back to my old ways, but I couldn't go through with it. I didn't want to do anything, so please don't hold that against me forever," she pleaded.

"I know I've pulled away from you, but I promise we'll get together soon after I get out of here. I don't want you coming to the hospital right now with all of the press here, so please understand that."

"I can live with that. We don't need the wrong thing being written about us. I should be done here in New York in another week or two. Maybe we can get together then?" Lisa asked, sporting a full fledged smile.

"That will work out with me. Thanks for being concerned about me," Brad added.

Lisa felt revived after the phone call and approached life and work with a better attitude.

The following day, a black haired nurse walked into Brad's room. Brad didn't pay any attention to her until she took off her glasses, pulled a wig off her head, and blond hair fell revealing Kristy.

She went up to him and gave him a long hug and then kissed him on his forehead.

"You don't look as good in black hair as you do as a blond," Brad said, kidding her. "I wondered what time you'd show up today. Keith informed me of his conversation with you."

"I'm glad you allowed me to see you," Kristy replied. "You didn't have to since I'm a married woman. I'm sure you have a flock of women wanting to see you," she said, testing his dating status.

"Quite the contrary. I haven't had time to put up with a woman right now." He gave Kristy a quick smile. "Besides, I've always been stuck on two particular women in my life."

Kristy's face turned red and she looked down at the floor bashfully. "I wish I was the only woman for you and married to you."

"That would definitely change things between us wouldn't it? So, you think my old buddy Greg did this to me?" Brad asked with sarcasm.

"Unfortunately yes, I do think he's responsible. I have no proof though, only weird circumstances."

"What do you have Kristy?" Brad reached for her hand.

Kristy gladly let Brad take her hand as she melted from his touch. She had to concentrate to answer him. "Not much, except the fact he's been acting psycho again and wasn't around for a few days before and during the day you were shot because he was supposedly fishing. I studied the newspapers and found a rape and battery case in Cincinnati on the night you were shot. It all adds up to me."

"I can't believe you live your life the way you do Kristy. How do you get by with that kind of marriage? I mean, the guy cheats on you and is rarely at home, that's not a life," Brad stated bluntly.

Kristy's face became redder in color and warm to the touch. "I'm embarrassed to live it also. I hope and pray that one day he'll be gone, so I can live again. Just don't judge me on this situation Brad. I would change it this minute, but we see what he's capable of doing. He tried to kill you," she replied as she looked down at his bandaged leg.

"Well, we aren't quite sure of that Kristy, but I have to side with you on that possibility." He pulled her close to him allowing him to take in the fresh scent of her hair, which he always enjoyed. His body sensors reached out from the touch of her long hair brushing against his face and neck. He couldn't help it when he pulled her face to his and gave her a long passionate kiss. It had been too long for him, and he needed to experience those feelings again.

Kristy held on to Brad tight trying to take in as much of him as she could. A tear trickled from her eye falling on Brad's face.

He left the fallen tear on his face, but ever so gently wiped the moisture from her face.

"I'm so sorry Brad that I screwed up years ago. I know it's not right for me to ask you this, but please hold off marrying someone until I can work my way out of my worthless marriage. I promise you it would be worth your while. There is more to me than you now know," she said, trying to give him a hint about her daughter.

"I have no plans to get married Kristy. But I could never promise you a life with me right now, even if you divorced Greg. We have grown older and have changed, and there is no sure guarantee we still have enough in common between us to live our lives together. We can't rely on the special love we had years ago. Don't take me wrong though, I still have feelings for you, but I'd want to make sure they're the real thing and not a comfort from my past."

"I understand what you're saying Brad, and I'm not taking it the wrong way. I love you and I always have. I guess there is a minuet possibility that the strong feelings I have for you comes from my terrible relationship with Greg, but I doubt it. I wish I could express everything I need to, but I can't at this time. Please trust me when I say that I'd make you a very happy man and give you something no other woman can," Kristy said, skirting around the issue again concerning Angelica.

"I'm not sure I understand what you're saying, but I'll keep it in mind. I have to because you really kicked up my curiosity. Besides, I still have feelings for you, and I'm vulnerable right now," Brad said while trying to fit all of the pieces together.

"I have to go Brad. Carol is with Angelica, and I don't want to keep her waiting. Did you know Carol is pregnant?" Kristy was delighted by the fact that Carol would soon have her baby, and her enthusiasm showed.

"Yes, I heard the good news. I'm happy for them." Brad had a sad look on his face from feeling left out of parenthood. He thought how things change because at one time he and Anne were the only ones with a child, and now he didn't have a daughter while Kristy did, and Carol had either a son or daughter on the way. The fate of life was unbearable at times, he thought to himself.

Brad thought about Kristy's daughter and wondered what she was like. "I like the name Angelica. What made you name her that?"

"She was my little miracle baby, and she looked just like an angel. I'll tell you more about why I named her that later though," she answered nervously.

Brad pulled Kristy back to him as she started to walk away and held her one more time before he kissed her hard. He knew it was not a good thing to do, but he couldn't hold back. She had a power over him he couldn't ignore. Maybe he did truly love her, he thought to himself.

Kristy turned to him as she walked towards the door when Brad asked, "Can we get together sometime for an hour or so?"

"I'd love that Brad. Just work everything through Carol, and I'll do the same." She gave a happy smile that lit up her beautiful blue eyes. She put her wig and glasses back on and left.

Brad was flown to Los Angeles and taken to the Olson's where he had been living for the past nine months. He would recover there for a few weeks and let Nelson take care of him, per the insistence of Nelson.

It was an ideal place for Brad to recuperate with all of the security already in place and a staff to wait on him. Nelson was pleased to have the opportunity to help him out since Brad had always been so nice to him, and Nelson appreciated it.

Brad had asked Nelson for total peace and quiet from the outside world for the first few days unless it was a dire emergency. Brad had so many things to think about, and he wanted the time to reflect on where he was in his life, plus he wanted to open the doors to a path for his future.

He couldn't seem to keep Kristy off of his mind. He recalled holding Kristy and giving her the long kiss in the hospital, filling him with lust for her. She made him feel like no other woman could, giving him a zest for life and a craving for marriage. He knew a relationship with her was probably never going to happen unless Greg ended up in prison for a long time or died and went to hell. But Kristy was trying to tell him something important that he felt would change everything. He just couldn't put it all together.

Brad had promised Lisa he would get with her to talk about any possible relationship they might have together. He liked Lisa, but didn't have the loving feelings for her that he had for Kristy. He rationalized the situation admitting that Lisa was single and available, making her stand out. He thought that his brief past with her was the cause for his lack of love towards her. He wasn't sure how he felt, but he promised himself he would keep an open mind about her.

Brad's thoughts turned to Anne. He had truly loved Anne and still missed her. She was the most beautiful person he had ever met with her great looks and sincere kindness. She liked everybody and let everybody know she liked them in such a natural way. Maybe that is why he still had strong feelings for Kristy. She was equal personality wise, but not quite as pretty in looks, which didn't matter to him. Anne just had a classy look about her that was so natural to her. Perhaps it derived from the good bloodlines she had on each side. Kristy was classy, although it was in a different way.

There was no denying it to Brad, Anne and Kristy were very close in every aspect except for Kristy's lack of judgment years ago. Brad's final conclusion came to be that Anne and Kristy were very much alike; explaining why he fell for Anne so fast and the reason Kristy was on his mind so much and in his heart forever.

Brad finally recognized he was lonely and wanted someone in his life again. It actually felt good to him to have those feelings. He knew he needed to proceed with caution though because he did not want to make the wrong choice.

CHAPTER 37

▼

Lisa finally finished her filming in New York and had arrived at her home in Los Angeles. She called Brad as soon as she was home, asking him if she could come over and see him.

He agreed to have her come over for dinner tonight since he was lonely and wanted some company. He did miss Lisa and was anxious to see her again.

Nelson had the chef prepare a special dinner for the two of them as he wanted Brad to have a good time tonight. He could see the hollowness in Brad from the lack of that special person in his life. Nelson thought that if anyone deserved the best in life, it should be Brad.

Lisa arrived at the Olson's house perfectly on time. At one time in her life she would have been fashionably late, but not now because this was too important to her. She gave Brad a long hug when she saw him and started to cry from seeing him hobble around on crutches. The reality of the shooting hit her hard when she finally saw the results from it.

"My God Brad, I can't believe you actually got shot in the leg. You could've been killed," she cried out as she put her hands on each side of her face.

"I believe that's what the guy was trying to do. It's lucky for me Brian called out as he approached me at the same time the shooter pulled the trigger because I stopped to turn around as the bullet breezed right past my head. I could feel the air blow by my face." Brad shuddered from reliving the incident.

"So what are you going to do about it?" Lisa asked, wanting some action on Brad's part to keep it from happening again.

"Bill Matthews informed me he hired a private investigator to follow Greg around to see what he was up to. Bill said Greg would receive some kind of a message from the guy he hired and let Greg know we're on to him. We'll see how that works out. I don't know what to think about the suspicion of an unhappy fan of an opposing team trying to kill me though. That thought doesn't appeal to me at all."

"It doesn't bold well with me either. There are a lot of strange people out there you know, and we can't monitor every one of them."

"Unfortunately you're correct about that. I just never thought about it though because I never expected it to happen to me. I'm only a baseball player, not some-one like the president that makes decisions that effect people's lives," Brad said, shaking his head in disbelief.

"You're now a high profile individual, so you better get used to it."

"Well let's change the subject to one that isn't so negative. How was your filming in New York?"

"Long, hard and lonely for you. It feels good to be home again. New York is a great city, but somewhat suffocating. I like it much better here on the west coast."

They sat outside by the pool while Nelson brought them a glass of wine. They didn't say too much as they sipped their wine and stared at each other trying to understand their relationship. They were both lost on where they stood with each other.

Brad finally broke the silence. "Look Lisa, we aren't going to solve our differ-ences overnight, so let's just relax and enjoy the evening together. Things will work out naturally, and it will take some time to get caught up with each other. If we are meant to be together, it will happen."

"You're right. I guess I'm worried you won't forgive me and just walk away from me. I don't want that to happen," Lisa replied as her eyes pleaded for for-giveness.

He gave her a quick smile. "I'll never walk away from you, unless you force me to because we'll always be friends."

"I think I want you more than just a friend Brad. But I won't push myself on you. I realize you have so many things to work out in your life. You've lost your wife and daughter, and you were just shot. My God, how much more should you have to go through in life?"

"I'm fine Lisa. One thing I realized after I woke up in the hospital was the fact that I have an emptiness in me I wanted filled. I want someone in my life again, and I just need to stop hiding behind all of my energies of work or whatever and allow someone in my life. I have to take down the walls I've built around me. I'll take them down one by one," Brad stated firmly. "But I want a relationship to form naturally and innocently. I don't want someone trying to force her way into my life feeling like she needs to change to conform to what she thinks I want in a woman."

"Well said. So what do you want to happen?" Lisa sipped her wine.

"Nothing...and everything in the end," Brad said, trying to let Lisa see how he felt about a relationship.

Lisa digested the short answer. It took her a few minutes to figure out what he was saying, and then it hit her. She hadn't thought about life the way Brad did. But she had never experienced love the way Brad had with Anne. She wished she could have met that special woman, so she could have learned from her.

Lisa was learning about what real life was all about, but she decided to not think about it for now. She would just relax with Brad, and enjoy his company, and stop trying to get him to love her, which is exactly what Brad wanted.

Alex Friedman was the private investigator that Bill had hired. He had been following Greg around for weeks taking notes and learning Greg's habits. Alex had already learned that Greg was a weird sort with a distasteful sexual appetite. He could see this guy was capable of pulling a trigger on someone and not think anything about it. Alex wanted to keep his distance from Greg, but recognized it was time to inform him they were on to him. He came up with a plan he thought to be safe.

Alex disguised himself with a mustache, wig, and sunglasses and showed up one day at the car dealership where Greg worked. He had parked his car a mile away and taken a cab just a block away from the car dealership. He walked around the car lot until someone came out to wait on him.

A salesman strutted up to him introducing himself as Greg Somanski. Greg felt fully energized again since the shooting of Brad and was very full of himself.

Alex explained to Greg that his car had been totaled from an accident and he needed something to replace it.

Greg jumped at the chance to sell him a car and asked Alex if he wanted to take a test ride in a particular car Alex had been eyeing. Of course Alex agreed, and they drove off on what Greg perceived as an innocent test drive.

Alex drove the car communicating to Greg that he really liked the car. He only had one concern, and that was the backseat had to have plenty of leg room. He needed it to be comfortable since his teenagers were good sized and they needed the additional room.

Greg offered to drive the car while Alex sat in back to see for himself if it would work out.

Alex agreed to his proposal since he was about to suggest that himself. Alex asked Greg to drive down a particular street that was in close proximity to his car, explaining to Greg it was a rough road, therefore allowing him to see just how comfortable the car rode.

Greg had bought into the whole hoax feeling like he had a lay me down buyer. Greg was about to ask his potential buyer if he was ready to purchase the car when his passenger put a gun to his head.

"I want you to know we're on to you. You leave Brad Preston alone and everyone else you do harm to, or you're dead. We'll be watching you at all times, so behave yourself. Do you understand?" Alex asked as he pushed the gun harder against Greg's head.

"Yes, I understand," Greg responded as he shook his head yes.

"Good, now pull over, and don't say a word to anyone about this. You don't know who you pissed off, but I hear he has little patience for a guy like you," Alex stated and then exited the car.

Greg left his passenger and then drove around for a while to gather himself. Who would have hired this guy, Greg wondered? And how much did they know about him? He concluded they had no proof of anything, or the police would be involved. He questioned the possibility of Kristy having anything to do with this, but thought against the likelihood knowing it wasn't her style. Greg was angry, but he was more afraid of being caught, so he decided that he better behave on all fronts for the time being.

CHAPTER 38

▼

It was game seven of the World Series as Brad found his seat just behind home plate. It was a classic series between the Yankees and the Cardinals. Brad had been hoping to see his Dodgers in this year's October Classic, but with his injury as well as a few other players' injuries, it just didn't happen. His ball club played hard after he was shot, but they lost their team leader and found it hard to rebound. The team was also affected negatively from the shooting. They were more skittish after that traumatic day.

Brad was present tonight to see two great teams compete for the world championship and was intent just to be there and witness the game. He admired the Cardinals for their hard scrappy play and for the way their pitching staff played above their true ability. The Yankees were the best team that money could buy and a hard team to beat. They were also well managed as you'd come to expect with the demands of their owner. It takes a great coach to get the top athletes to unify as a team.

Tonight would be different for Brad. He would have to be just a fan of the game while sitting with his good friends Brian Hendrix, Tony Coselli, and Jim Milnick.

The news media instantly found Brad and did a quick interview with him.

Brad was polite to them, but deferred on personal questions by answering, "Tonight I'm just another fan of the game. These two teams deserve one hundred percent of the attention, and I'm here to witness a good game." Brad then answered a few questions about the big game, and then he gracefully excused himself to join his friends.

It was an exciting game to watch with the Yankees taking the crown once again, winning by only one run. The Cardinals could have won just as easily, but the Yankees capitalized on one more opportunity than St. Louis, giving New York the championship.

"Well guys," Tony said. "That's the team we'll probably have to beat next year if we're going to win the World Series."

"You're probably right," Brian agreed. "What do you think Brad, can you beat those guys? It looks like they can hit anybody."

"I should be one hundred percent by then, but that might not be enough. They're a great team and will more than likely be better next year with a few off season trades that they're notorious for," Brad stated.

"You guys play better together," Jim broke in. "I like your chances next year if we can stay healthy."

"All we need to do is have Brad wear bullet proof clothing, and he'll lead us to the big game," Tony stated with some humor thrown in. Tony admired Brad and knew there wasn't a pitcher alive that had anywhere near the talent Brad possessed.

Brad, Tony, and Brian made a vow to make sure the Dodgers would be playing in the World Series next year with Jim as their witness.

Brad went back to Los Angeles, fired up to make it to the playoffs next year. He had enjoyed the atmosphere of the playoff games. They were so much more intense because one mistake could end your season. It was the best verses the best, and that was the way Brad liked it.

Brad was now able to train and work out at full strength, so he started his vigorous weight training and worked with the CAMM daily to get back in tip top shape. He had a mission, and he was determined to fulfill it.

Lisa had left for the heartland of her beloved country just ten days before Thanksgiving. She told Brad she had to help prepare for some filming on her upcoming movie and asked him if he would join her for Thanksgiving this year to keep her company.

Brad agreed since his family had made other arrangements this year. They were joining David's in-laws for Thanksgiving.

Brad was looking forward to making a stop in Indianapolis to see John and Carol, and hopefully see Kristy. He would then meet up with Lisa, wherever she ended up being at the time.

Brad had made arrangements to visit with John and Carol on Tuesday evening. They had a great time together while they caught up with each other's life.

Brad teased Carol for being so big and asked her if she was expecting twins.

Carol slapped him on the arm while John sat back and laughed at the two of them.

John always knew Carol and Brad were best of friends, and he was never jealous of the fact. He respected Brad and appreciated him as a friend.

"How's Kristy doing?" Brad asked out of the blue.

"She's making the best of her life," Carol answered. "She wants to meet you tomorrow, if that is all right with you?"

"I was going to ask for you to arrange a meeting with her, so yes, I'd love to see her," Brad answered with excitement.

"Brad, what are your plans concerning your future with a woman?" Carol asked, so she could work him the right way. Carol knew with all her heart that one day Kristy would be free of Greg, allowing Brad to know about his daughter.

"I don't know how to answer that question Carol. I've only had two women in my life, Kristy and Anne, however I've been seeing Lisa Collins here and there as a friend," Brad admitted.

"Lisa Collins?" John asked, blown away by Brad bringing her up. "She's a huge star. How did you meet her?"

"It was quite simple," Brad explained. "I changed a flat tire for her the first day I arrived in Los Angeles, from my long drive from Charlotte, and then she came to a party at the Olson's the same night I arrived. I hated her at first, but she grew on me."

"Brad, please take your time and don't rush into things before you know for sure that your love for Kristy doesn't exist," Carol said, scolding Brad in a light way. "I know you two are meant for each other and one day you two will be one. There's too much between you."

"I know I have feelings for Kristy, but she's married, and she made it clear she can't leave Greg. What am I to do Carol?" Brad asked, hoping Carol could help him out.

"Give it some more time Brad. Greg has lost interest in her and is only holding her back from you, but that seems to be a lost cause for him now, and he knows it. Fate will bring you two together again. I guarantee it," Carol stated with confidence.

"What do you know that I don't know Carol?" Brad asked. He had been fielding statements with hidden meanings from both Kristy and Carol, and he wanted a translation.

"More than I'm willing to say at this time Brad. Just ask yourself a simple question. Do you truly love Kristy?" Carol's eyes twinkled with delight from trying to get her two best friends together.

"I wish it was a simple question to answer, but it isn't. How am I supposed to keep reinforcing any feelings I have for her when she's married? And she's married to a psychopath that she's afraid to leave because she believes he'll kill her and whoever gets in the way. It doesn't sound like a good life. Plus, I'd have to put up with the guy on visitations with his daughter. I can't see it ever working out," Brad stated firmly, throwing his arms up in the air from frustration.

"Yes, it appears like a lost cause, but something will happen to change the situation. I feel it in my heart," Carol answered.

"I'll promise you one thing Carol, and that is, I won't rush into anything with anyone right now. Besides, it doesn't work that way with me, except with Anne, and she was a once in a lifetime woman for me," Brad replied.

"Well tomorrow morning you can see for yourself concerning your feelings for Kristy. She'll meet you at the lake house again," Carol stated with a mischievous smile.

John just sat back amazed by the fact that Brad could have anyone he wanted, and yet he stood by his first love waiting for an opening while he could have a knock out like Lisa Collins. What a life to lead, he thought to himself.

Kristy was waiting for Brad when he arrived at the lake house. The sight of her took Brad's breath. She was slim, but fit, and wore the slightest amount of mascara to accentuate her beautiful eyes. He thought of his conversation about her with Carol last night, and realized that Carol might be right about the fate of him and Kristy being together one day.

"Well aren't you going to say hi?" Kristy asked as she stood there waiting for him.

"I'm sorry Kristy, but I was overtaken by your beauty. You've always done that to me you know."

"No I didn't know that Brad, but it's good to hear it come from your mouth."

Brad and Kristy walked towards each other. They stood inches apart staring into each other's eyes trying to get a read on each other's thoughts.

Brad gently put both hands on the sides of her face and caressed her cheeks with his thumbs.

Kristy put both arms around his neck and reached up to give him a long kiss. "It's been too long," Kristy said, after their lips departed. "I've missed you so much. How's your leg doing?" She looked down at his leg to inspect the progress. "My leg has healed well. And yes, it's been too long. How've you been?" He felt energized and happiness surged through his entire body from just being with her.

"As well as can be expected, under the circumstances. I pretty much live my life as a single parent. Greg is hardly ever around, thank God. If and when he is around, he leaves Angelica and me alone. We don't even sleep together, which is great. He knows I won't have sex with him, so he doesn't bother. I'm sorry," Kristy said with a look of embarrassment. "I shouldn't be telling you these things."

"I don't mind," Brad said, finding her statements easing his guilty feeling for meeting with her. "So what else do you do to stay busy besides raising your daughter?"

"That's about it. I thought I should do something with my college classes in literature and music, so I've tried to write some poems and put them to music. Unfortunately, I haven't had any luck as of yet getting anyone's interest to record them. I also think about you all of the time which helps me through life." She hugged him harder. "What about you?"

"I work out everyday and work on my pitching form. I have to get back in shape again, so I can play next year," he answered as he rubbed her back softly.

Kristy felt his firm body. "You feel like you're in great shape to me."

They were both so glad to be with each other again that they just fell back on the couch and cuddled up to each other while making small talk between kisses. Their talk became less while their passion grew more intense, leading them to the bedroom.

They undressed each other between kisses and then made passionate love for the next couple of hours. It was two hours of passion and uninhibited sex that they both needed. It filled a huge void in both of their lives, especially the void of the love they had for each other that they couldn't express or admit openly to everyone.

As they were about to leave each other, Kristy said, "I hope you don't think I do this just for the sex. It's the best way I can show you how much I love you under these circumstances and the best way that I can be close to you. However, I do love the way you take me to a different world as we make love."

"I feel the same way Kristy," Brad said, knowing that he would not have done it if she had not mentioned the fact she no longer had sex with Greg. "Are you ever going to get out of your marriage?" he asked, hoping for a positive answer.

"One of these days I will. I just hope you're still available when it happens. But I can't expect you to wait for me forever. You have a life to live, and I respect that. But remember, there isn't anyone that can give you the things that I can," she said, without revealing her secret.

They gave each other a long hug and passionate kiss before they left, and then went their separate ways again. But this time something was different. For the first time, they both left with a strange feeling that something just might happen to allow them to pursue their love for each other.

Brad drove away without having guilty feelings for making love to Kristy. He admitted there was a magnetic current between them that drew them to one another when they were close to each other. It was a feeling he could not deny, so he decided he would not try to refute the good feelings at this time.

Brad had driven to the Bedford, Indiana area to meet with Lisa on Thanksgiving morning. He was somewhat puzzled by her request, but happy to be able to spend the day in his old state. It felt more like Thanksgiving to him as he drove through the countryside seeing the bare fields and naked trees, as Mother Nature proclaimed it was soon to be winter time and the start of the holiday season.

He found the little gas station where he was to meet Lisa and was pleased to see her already there waiting for him. He could see she was glowing with pride from seeing the big smile on her face when he got out of the car to meet her, making him suspect she was up to something.

"So what's the big plan for today?"

"I'll show you in a few minutes. Just follow my directions please," she said, after giving him a quick kiss on the cheek.

They drove off together into the rural areas as Brad followed Lisa's instructions. They were in a beautiful hilly area with farmland on every side just like Brad remembered from his drives in the country years ago.

She directed him to turn into a driveway that led to a two story farm house with a wrap around porch. There were several old barns with faded red paint in need of some major repairs. An old farm tractor rested beside a tall oak tree. It appeared the farm had almost been abandoned, except for the fact that someone had farmed it this year leaving the cut corn stalk stubs just inches above the soil.

"So, this is where we're having Thanksgiving this year?" Brad asked, admiring Lisa for going the extra mile to fulfill a dream he had.

"This is it, just like you painted it for me last year," she said, pleased with herself.

"Well thank you. It's just like I wanted it to be. Is anybody else here with us today?"

"Yes, there's a nice family here," she replied, flashing her wonderful smile.

They both eagerly walked up to the front porch and carefully went up the old steps. Brad turned around and gathered in the sights of the small pond with about twenty head of cattle standing around it. He could see the bare cornfields that intersected with large wooded areas, accentuating the feel of the country. Brad could visualize hunters in the fields walking through the thick brush to bring home some fresh game to eat. It was definitely a different lifestyle than he was used to and probably a more relaxed one.

Lisa gave a quick knock on the door and then opened the door. "Hello, it's Lisa and Brad."

They entered the old farmhouse feeling like they had been taken back forty years. The furniture was dated, but in very good condition. There were old family pictures hanging on the wall dating back to the Civil War. The house had a stale smell to it, however it was clean.

Brad saw an older man that he assumed lived here. He guessed the man to be between seventy and eighty years old, but it was hard to say with the leathered skin from working outdoors all of his life.

The older gentleman still had some spunk as he easily lifted himself out of the chair he was sitting in and walked up to Brad. "I'm Leonard Miller." The older man approached Brad and shook his hand. "I want to welcome you to our home on this special day. Your kind friend explained to my wife and I your desires to spend Thanksgiving Day on a farm. As you can see, it ain't much to look at, but it's our home. Has been for my entire life."

"Well I appreciate your hospitality of sharing your home with us on this special day. It means a lot to me," Brad replied.

Brad's senses picked up the aromas of the turkey in the oven, and the smell of the freshly baked pies. He felt it was going to be a special day for him and he turned to Lisa with a thankful smile.

Mr. Miller took Brad into the kitchen to meet his wife Mamie. She looked to be somewhere in her seventies, but it was hard to know for sure with her hair being pure white. She had a pleasant smile to her and seemed pleased to entertain two guests for her special Thanksgiving dinner.

Brad saw a man sitting in one of the kitchen chairs just staring. He was about fifty years old, but it appeared there was something wrong with him. He could see by looking into the man's eyes that he was not all there.

"That's my son Henry," Mr. Miller stated as he read Brad's mind. "He was involved in a farm accident about thirty years ago that left him that way. He was driving the tractor on a steep incline and the tractor rolled over on him. Darn near killed him, but the good lord spared his life for us."

Mrs. Miller poured Brad a cup of coffee and then handed it to him. "Would you like sugar or cream with it?" she asked with a friendly smile.

"No thank you ma'am, black is just fine," he replied, taking the coffee from her. "The food smells delicious."

"Why thank you Brad," Mamie said. "It's been a long while since we had company on Thanksgiving. I forgot how much I used to enjoy cooking up special food for everyone. Our oldest son left here angry twenty years ago, and we haven't heard anything from him since. I don't even know why he left." A tear ran down her face.

"Now Mamie, we've been through this before. He just wasn't meant to be on the farm," Leonard said to his wife.

They all sat down at the table to get to know each other before the Thanksgiving dinner would be served.

The Millers then broke out a deck of cards, so they could all play pinochle.

Brad and Lisa had played the game years ago, but they weren't very good at it.

Mr. and Mrs. Miller were serious about the game, criticizing any mistakes they made against the younger couple, but only playfully.

Brad felt good about bringing the older couple enjoyment. He could see the thrill of playing the card game in their faces. He guessed it had been some time since they had the pleasure of playing cards against another couple.

Following four straight wins for the Millers, they put the cards away and prepared the dinner table for their special feast.

After saying a special Thanksgiving prayer, Mr. Miller cut up Henry's food and directed him to eat. Then they all piled their plates full and indulged on the great tasting food.

Dinner was outstanding as the food was prepared the old fashion way with plenty of rich gravy spilling over the mashed potatoes onto the turkey and dressing. The dressing was perfect and highlighted with the flavor of oysters. The bean casserole was delicious, especially with the homemade onion rings on top to give it an extra kick.

They all ended up stuffed after having at least two servings of everything, putting dessert on hold temporarily.

The rest of the day was spent hearing stories of days past from Mr. Miller. He had some good tales to share that brought laughter to everyone and a few tears to the eyes of Brad and Lisa.

Brad admired the Millers for the way they had lived their lives, with hard work on the farm and a dedicated mother and father to Henry. One thing Brad noticed was how the Miller's life was centered around their farm and old house that gave a life of its own. There were so many memories there that the Millers could never leave it behind. Brad just wished that his entire family could have participated in this special day with the Millers.

Brad found Mr. Miller to be a very intelligent man that truly appreciated their company, as did his wife Mamie. It was a day of visiting the past for all of them and making them appreciate what they had. But it also left them yearning for life the way it used to be.

Brad and Lisa made their departure from the old farmhouse with a different perspective on life. It was a very enlightening experience for them. Brad drove off knowing how important it was for him to have a family again. He didn't want to grow old by himself and not share his life with a wife and children.

Brad dropped Lisa off and thanked her for a special day. He knew she must have spent a great amount of time and effort to find the Millers and then ask them to allow the two of them to join them for Thanksgiving.

Lisa was proud of her feat and expressed it through her eyes. She told Brad she wanted him in her life more than ever, leaving him with many feelings to sort out.

Brad flew back to Los Angeles more confused than ever before concerning his feelings for Kristy and Lisa. Lisa showed a side of herself that Brad truly admired, and he felt like she had grown wiser over the past year. He still didn't have the feelings for Lisa that would make him want to marry her. They had never made love together, which Brad thought was good and bad. He just didn't have as much desire for Lisa as he did for Kristy, but that could be because of his past with Kristy, both in bed and on a one on one relationship.

He felt more of a belonging to Kristy, but realized he couldn't take their relationship any further. He thought back to Wednesday when he made love to her, and for the first time not experience any guilt from their actions. He only felt an excitement in him as he thought back to that wonderful morning.

He reviewed his conversation with Carol in his head and went over Kristy's comments trying to bring the true meaning of what they were both trying to say to him. "One day it will come to me and it will solve the whole problem," he said to himself.

CHAPTER 39

▼

Brad spent the next four months still perplexed over Lisa and Kristy. He had spent more time with Lisa building on a relationship more than just a friendship. But he felt something was still missing. Maybe it was the little time they had to share with each other. Their careers were definitely time consuming for both demanding all of their energy.

Things had not changed on Kristy's front either. She was still married to Greg and living an abnormal life with him. He hadn't been bothering her at all, and she assumed he had a girlfriend hidden somewhere. Kristy still talked with Brad on a few occasions to stoke the fire between them, but it was getting old for Brad. He wanted more than that from Kristy. All she could do was promise him that someday they would be together.

Opening day had finally arrived for the Dodgers. They were picked the team to beat in the National League after dominating the spring training games.

Brad's hard work over the winter paid off and he regained his form from before he was shot in the leg. He was next to impossible to hit once again, and the other members of the pitching staff had bettered themselves during the off season making the Dodger staff the strongest in the league.

Tony Coselli and Brian Hendrix had taken their game to another level over the winter and spring keeping to their promise to go to the World Series this year and win it.

By mid June, Brad was undefeated and had seven shutouts under his belt for the year. He had earned the respect from every player in the league. In fact, the opposing teams based their play on how many hits they could get off of Brad instead of runs because his era was .63. With his domination, the Dodgers held a five game lead in the western division.

The shocking front page article highlighted with a revealing picture of Brad and Lisa together finally exposed their relationship. The picture told the story by showing Brad and Lisa coming out of a luxurious hotel in New York, portraying them as lovers.

The Dodgers had just finished a three game series with the Mets and were off the following day allowing Lisa to spend the night with Brad. They had a nice dinner together in privacy, but they were spotted by the paparazzo as they left the establishment and followed to their hotel.

The celebrity couple went to Brad's room for an evening together. It had been about three weeks since they had last seen each other and they had a need for each other.

Brad's feelings for Lisa had grown to another level with the changes she had made in her life over the past year. Lisa had become comfortable with having him around when the chance arrived, instead of having to be with someone everyday. She wasn't pushing for anything more with Brad at this time, allowing him to feel at ease with her.

Lisa had developed similar traits to Anne in the way her inner self had blossomed, making her a very likeable person portraying warmth, sincerity, and a good humor. Even Lisa liked herself better now.

On this particular evening Brad was much more loving than usual towards Lisa. He pulled her close to him while sitting on the couch, and gently rubbed her back, or stroked her long hair.

Lisa was looking exceptionally beautiful tonight with her tanned body scanty clothed body in a revealing black dress, showing off her perky breasts and pleasurable backside.

Brad had been admiring her beauty all night, and Lisa's actions and dress were appropriate for her to seduce Brad.

By the time they got in bed together, the mood was set for more than cuddling each other for the night. Brad pulled off all of his clothing before he joined her in bed, and Lisa was prepared for him as she was completely naked and full of desire.

Their previous nights spent together were trumped by the aggressive nature they approached each other tonight, with long wet kisses, and caresses of all body parts. They were ready for a night of passion after enduring over a year of foreplay between them.

When Brad finally entered her, they both knew they could never refrain again as the pleasure it brought them both tipped the scales. They both exploded together as their bodies dispersed a year's worth of sexual tension between them. By morning, they were exhausted from a night of sex that was glorious to both.

But now their secret was out, and the whole world knew about their affair. Lisa was used to it, but this time she resented the breach of her privacy. What she had with Brad was special and not open to the public.

Brad didn't know what to think about the situation because this had never happened to him before. He couldn't deny the article since he did indeed have a night of pleasure with Lisa. He then became concerned over Kristy's reaction to the news release, but decided he had a right to love someone in his life without her. It was no fault of his that she was in the quagmire with Greg.

Kristy immediately called Carol when she saw the newspaper article. "Well Carol, I guess he couldn't wait much longer for me." Kristy was torn up inside over the article.

"It doesn't mean anything right now Kristy, so stay calm. If it gets more serious, you can use your trump card if that is what you want. You're going to have to decide what you plan on doing about your screwed up marriage though," Carol scolded. She had changed her feelings about Kristy staying with Greg since the birth of her baby boy. She resented Kristy in a way for not letting Brad know he had a daughter of his own that he would surely love and enjoy having in his life. She also thought it was unfair for Angel not to be with her real father.

"The timing isn't right yet Carol," Kristy said, being agitated over the whole thing.

"It will never be right Kristy, so you need to decide to live your life the way you have been for the past four years or change it and follow your heart. It's that simple. Greg hasn't shown any signs of hurting you this past year, and he leaves you alone for the most part, so take advantage of the situation and get the hell out," Carol stated with irritation over Kristy's reluctance to get away from Greg.

"I'm working on it Carol, but there's no guarantee Brad will be there for me, so I have to have plan B available." Kristy now realized she may have gone to long in her marriage with Greg.

"If you procrastinate he won't be there for you because he'll have a new family going. I know Brad well enough to know that he would not walk away from you and Angel. So don't play that game with me," Carol said firmly.

"I'll work on ending my marriage harder and speed up the process then." Kristy felt the clock ticking with time running out as far as her chance with Brad.

"Look Kristy, I apologize for getting cranky with you, but you have to realize that you and Brad are my two best friends, and it's hard for me to sit back and see you guys suffering over this screwed up mess. I love you both, you know."

"I know Carol, and I really appreciate you for being there for me and keeping quiet about our secret. Give me a little more time please?" Kristy pleaded.

After their conversation, Kristy sat down and cried. She then walked to Angel's bedroom where her precious daughter was knapping and laid down beside her. Kristy stared at Angel acknowledging how much she looked like Brad. She brushed her daughter's blond hair with her fingertips as she thought to herself how unfair it was for her daughter to be brought up in a home with no love between the parents. Kristy corrected herself by adding the fact that Greg was a fake father that cherished Angel only as a trophy. She knew Angel deserved the love and devotion Brad would give her, so she decided it was now time to do something that she should have done years ago. It was time to leave Greg once and for all.

Kristy just wanted to make sure Greg would not do something dumb when she left him. She also hoped someone would buy her latest song that she recently sent out that some of her critics gave her a great review on. If the song worked out, it would give her some money to work on a secondary plan. If not, she would have to go to Brad and fess up that Angel was his daughter, and hope Brad would provide the protection needed to keep Greg away from them all.

A week later, Carol called for Brad. It was almost impossible to call him direct now with the baseball season in full swing. Carol had to communicate to Brad the importance of him refraining from getting to serious with Lisa, but wasn't sure how to be the trumpeter for Kristy without telling him about his living daughter.

A day later, Brad returned her call. "Is there something wrong Carol?"

"Yes and no, Brad," she started out saying. "I saw the newspaper article about you and Lisa Collins, and it concerned me."

"Why Carol? It's been well over a year now since Anne and Brianna died. I think it's time for me to get on with my life, and Lisa is a great person," Brad said, defending himself as well as Lisa's reputation.

"I'm not questioning your loyalty to Anne, and I'm not saying Lisa isn't good enough for you, but there are other things out there you're unaware of that would change your thinking," Carol replied, hoping that she didn't reveal too much.

"What are you talking about Carol? I've tried to decipher some references from you and Kristy stating the same thing, but I have no idea what you're talking about. Why don't you just come forward and be honest with me by giving me the facts. Stop the what if bull please," Brad said, exasperated.

"Brad, I love you as my best friend, as I love Kristy. I'm not trying to play cupid with you two because the situation won't allow me to, but I'm trying to do the right thing. Please trust me on this matter. I have knowledge of things you don't know about that would change your entire perspective of your relationship with Kristy." Carol closed her eyes hoping she was getting through to him.

"If it's so important to me, then why won't you tell me what it is?" Brad was aggravated by the entire circumstance of the situation.

"I can't right now Brad, but if I have to I will tell you." Carol walked around her home nervously trying to figure out the right way to accomplish her feat.

Brad was silent for a moment trying to determine the meaning of the message Carol was trying to say without her breaching some promise. He just couldn't figure out what the hidden message was. "I promise you I will not marry Lisa or anyone else without talking to you first Carol. I know you too well to question your motive here because it must be something very important. Please promise me you'll let me know someday for everyone's sake." Brad had a confused look on his face.

"When the time is right, I'll tell you everything if Kristy doesn't. All I can say to you now is she's working hard on leaving Greg, so she can be with you. She loves you more than you know Brad, and I believe in the fate of the two of you getting together again," Carol said, pleased that she got through a little bit to Brad without telling him the real story.

"I hope you both don't believe I'll come running to her if she does leave Greg because I'm not sure I would."

"You will Brad. I guarantee it," Carol stated full of confidence.

"I hate it when you do that to me. By the way, how's she doing?" Brad hoped everything was alright with her.

"She's stronger than she has ever been before. Being a mother has been good for her on regaining some self esteem. At least now she feels like she's worth something after Greg took everything away from her. Basically, she's living her life for Angel and the hope that you come back into her life again. That's what keeps her going day in and day out."

The words hit Brad hard in a couple of ways. He felt sorry for Kristy for being married to Greg and having to raise their child by herself, and he felt bad she lived her life in hope he would be there for her. Did she really expect him to wait forever for her? He had many questions that always ended in unanswered insinuations. How much more of this could he take, he thought to himself?

"I don't have a time frame on getting married again, if I ever do marry again, so don't worry right now. But do push Kristy to get out of her marriage soon for her sake alone. Let's keep in touch more than we have been lately. I miss you guys, and I'm anxious to see that little boy of yours," Brad said as he finished their conversation.

CHAPTER 40

▼

The regular season was half way complete, and the Dodgers had extended their lead to seven games in the western division. They were playing like a team destined to win as everyone was playing to their full potential. The Dodgers had four players participate in the All Star game, but Brad out shined all of the stars being voted the MVP for a second straight year for the mid-season spectacle.

Greg had to relive Brad's dominance as a pitcher as he once again watched the All Star game with his buddies at the bar.

Everyone in the smoke filled place was praising Brad for his great play, as well as his choice in women. They were talking in their drunken slurred speech about the picture of Brad and Lisa Collins, envious of Brad for sleeping with the sexy, beautiful movie star.

It upset Greg that Brad once again had a beautiful woman at his side. But it wasn't just any woman. He had the hottest woman on earth.

Greg sat back and listened to their praises and once again felt a loss of power in himself. He didn't know how to regain it again. He knew someone was still following him around, but he wasn't sure how often and when it was he was being followed. He had the urge to take his anger out on someone right now, but had to refrain since he could get caught by some unknown person that was on to him. Life was not pleasant for Greg at this moment in time, and he was determined to change that scenario soon.

Greg thought about his relationship with Kristy and his daughter and decided he would be better off without them both. Kristy could no longer supply him with enough power to put up with her attitude anyway. He didn't really know his daughter Angel, and he hated her name, so she wasn't any good to him either. He had a much better life with his mistress. They were even trying to have a child together, although to no avail.

He decided it was time to move on and try to enjoy his life. But what could he do with Brad Preston? What did he have to do to expose Brad as the imposter he was and show everyone that Greg Somanski was the real athlete? It was time to come up with a scheme to kill Brad, so he could become the all powerful again and be the hero to his buddies.

The Dodgers were on the last leg of a grueling road trip and looking forward to a home field crowd again as well as the luxury of sleeping in their own beds. It was the later part of August and they were facing a tough Houston team.

Brad was still unbeaten for the year, but he felt the wear and tear on his body from the long season. He knew the Astros were coming on strong with great hitting and a powerful pitching staff and they would test his stamina.

It was Brad's turn in the rotation to pitch on this windless sultry day in Houston Texas. Brad struggled from the beginning of the game, but pitched well enough to make it a pitching dual from the start with both pitchers having a no hitter going into the fourth inning.

The Dodger hitters were lethargic today with their star pitcher on the mound. They had gotten worse over the course of this year about scoring runs when Brad was on the mound, and this was a day Brad needed some offense. He was challenging some hot hitters, and he didn't possess his best stuff today.

Brad worked hard all game long, but lost two to nothing. It was a wake up call for the rest of the team though as they got to see for the first time this year that Brad was indeed human. They still had to play hard even though they held a ten game lead in the western division.

When asked by the press what happened, Brad simply answered, "They were better than we were today, and I was out pitched by a great player." He made no excuses for his play and took the loss hard, but as another learning experience.

Brad thought about his loss all night trying to diagnose his below par performance. He didn't have his usual velocity today, and his curve ball was not working. He finally wrote it off as a bad day, but made it a point to get on the CAMM when they got back to Los Angeles. He pledged to get some rest to allow his body to recharge before the playoffs.

Brad then reviewed his life with Lisa over the past three months in search of something there that would have caused his poor performance. They had certainly become close, but he felt something was still missing on his part to go further. There was no reason to believe she was responsible for his less than par game.

He dug deeper into their relationship realizing they had a great sex life together, but the true love was missing on his part. He then recognized his feelings for Kristy were stronger than he had imagined. She was the person that caused him to withdraw from taking the big leap with Lisa. "But why was she so important to him?" he asked himself out loud. It had been many years since he had dated her, but yet there was this overwhelming feeling in him to wait for Kristy. It was like someone up above kept the fire stoked and wouldn't let the flame go out.

He kept trying to understand what Kristy and Carol had been trying to tell him. He knew Kristy didn't want him to know what it was that would change everything for him, therefore being the turning point for him to decide to spend the rest of his life with her. It had to be something simple and something that stood out for everyone to see. But what was it that he had not seen, he wondered?

He stood up all at once filled with energy at the thought of her daughter. He had never seen her, which seemed to be a purposeful act. He started computing the timing from the day in Carol's parent's lake house when he made love to Kristy three months after the loss of Anne and Brianna.

Could Angel be his little angel? He made it a point to find out more about this little girl he had never met.

Brad arrived in Los Angeles from his road trip and immediately hired a private investigator in Indianapolis. He directed the private investigator to find out more information on Angelica Somanski and to watch over her and Kristy. He also wanted to know what Greg was up to because he felt like something was about to happen. It was a gut feeling he had as well as the inside knowledge that Kristy was going to leave Greg that made Brad decide to put a tail on him.

Brad then went to the complex where the Dodgers kept the CAMM and worked out with it to make sure his pitching mechanics were in sync. He wasn't going to allow himself to falter again.

After analyzing his pitching motion, he found out he was just less than two degrees off when he threw his curve ball, so he worked on that particular motion for an hour before he felt comfortable with his form. He would then do the same thing every day for the rest of the home stand.

Brad's hard work paid off as he threw a one hit shut out during his next outing while he drove in three runs, leading his team to a seven to nothing victory over the division leader in the east. The Dodgers were set for the final full month of the regular season and ready for the playoffs. With the big lead they held, the Dodgers were almost certain to make the playoffs.

After receiving a message from Randy Winters, his private investigator, Brad dialed the phone to see what Randy had found out.

Randy picked up the phone on the second ring and went on to explain to Brad that there wasn't much he could find out about Angelica Somanski, other than what was on the birth certificate. "It reads, Angelica Somanski, born on February 19, of last year. Mother is Kristy Somanski and the father is Greg Somanski," Randy stated, thinking the information was trivial and little to go on.

Brad's heart seemed to stop for a minute when he heard February 19. "What time was she born?" he asked with urgency.

Randy looked down at the copy of the document and finally found the information that was requested of him. "It says here she was born at 3:04 p.m."

Brad nervously thought back to the exact time Brianna had died. He knew it had to be close in time, if not the exact time. "Do me a favor Randy and pull the death certificate of my daughter, Brianna Preston, and call me back with the exact time of her death."

"I can do that Mr. Preston," the private investigator replied, not sure about the relevance. "Any thing else I can do right now?"

"What have you discovered concerning Greg Somanski?"

Randy glanced down at the notes he jotted down in his notebook from his surveillance of Mr. Somanski. "Not too much as of yet. He seems to never be home, and he spends his nights with this stripper, but I haven't been on the job long enough to find out much more than that."

"Stay on him for now," Brad demanded. "I want to know a whole lot more than that."

"I'll call you with the time of death of your daughter and stay on this Somanski guy for you," Randy stated.

As Brad hung up the phone, he wondered if Randy was competent enough to handle this job. Brad hadn't researched him at all since he didn't think it would be much of a job, but now he had some concerns.

His thoughts about Randy evaporated into thin air when he thought of Angel's birthday and her exact time of birth. This had to be the fact that both Carol and Kristy were hiding from him. They both had to realize the true miracle of Angel being born on the day his daughter had died, and about the same time of her death. He wanted to talk to Kristy about his discovery to see what she felt that day. He recalled her mentioning that her baby was a miracle, which brought on the name Angel.

Brad also recognized the fact that this could be his baby. It was almost nine months from the day he had made love to Kristy. What would he do if Angel was his baby? He knew he could not walk away from her. He wished he had a photograph of Angel, so he could see if she had any of his characteristics.

Brad sat back and thought of the sudden changes in his life. He had opened up his heart this year to the opportunity of having another woman in his life, and now things seemed to be in turmoil. He had mixed feelings for both Lisa and Kristy, but in different ways. Maybe he should have stayed in his cocoon the rest of his life, so he wouldn't have to face the emotional challenges that life dealt you, he thought to himself.

The following day Randy left a message on Brad's phone stating Brianna had died on February 19, at 3:04 p.m. He then made a comment about what were the chances of Angel being born at the exact time as his daughter's death, and ended his message.

CHAPTER 41

▼

Greg had been building up to a mental breakdown, bringing him to the point where he had to react soon to get his power back. He had been dreaming about his real life of being a star baseball player. Brad was nothing in his dreams because Greg had always fought him off and not allowed Brad to steal his skills from him. These dreams were a reality to Greg as he truly believed Brad had taken his life from him.

The first thing Greg had to do was take out this private investigator that had been following him over the past year. He had noticed someone on his tail every-day recently, and it was hindering his plans. Greg needed to recharge his power source with a strong dominate sex act as he had done in the past, but he couldn't do it with a witness. Raping someone wouldn't make things right for him com-pletely, but it would help temporarily.

Greg then had to formulate a plan to take Brad out for good in order for him to get his power back from Brad. He couldn't wait for the day when he would finally look Brad in the eyes and see his reaction from hearing that Greg knew Brad had stolen all of his skills, and Brad was only living his successful career at the expense of him. Greg knew Brad would be shocked by the fact that his old dumb friend figured it out.

Greg would then go out on the mound and pitch better than Brad ever pitched, showing the world the real truth. He couldn't wait to expose his arch enemy and experience the power surge it would give him. The thought brought forth an arousal that flooded his body with sexual energy.

There were many things for Greg to do now because he also had to have a plan to dispose of Kristy. He knew that would be tough to do since she had to die in way as if it was a natural act, so the person she sent the video to wouldn't execute her order to expose him as the rapist in that one case.

Greg was now excited about life again. He was only disappointed he had waited so long to get these two things taken care of. He was mad at himself for allowing them to hold him back for a year while they enjoyed their lives. But that was going to change soon.

Brad pulled his messages and his insides imploded as he listened to Randy's findings about the time of Brianna's death. It was the exact minute that Angel was born. It was too strange of an occurrence to be just a random freak of nature. Brad had experienced too many miracles to believe that.

He called Carol to see what she knew about it, but there was no answer, so he left a message on her answering machine to call him as soon as possible. Brad then thought about how he planned on finding out the truth about Angel.

That night he dreamed about Brianna miraculously being brought back to life. He was so glad to hold her again and look into her beautiful eyes. He looked for Anne in his dream, but all he could see was Kristy at a distance watching his reaction of seeing his little girl again.

Brad was disappointed when he woke up the next morning and ending his dream. He walked around his apartment looking to see if Brianna was indeed back, but he could not find her. His dream was so real that it worried him. He wondered if Brianna was reaching down to him trying to tell him something. After what he had experienced at her death, he thought it could be possible.

The ringing of the phone interrupted his thought for a second, until he heard Carol's voice on the line.

"Is there something wrong Brad?" she asked concerned.

"I'm not sure." Brad squeezed the phone hard. "I just found out that Kristy's daughter was born on the same day and at the exact time that Brianna died. Why wasn't I informed of that?"

"I didn't know it was the exact time," Carol replied, shocked by the fact.

"But you knew about the same day, didn't you?" Brad asked, fully charged with emotion.

"Yes Brad, I did know about that. Kristy didn't want you to know though." Carol's mind thought fast trying to stay ahead of the impending questions that were sure to come her way. "I think she thought you might take it as a sign this child was mysteriously yours,"

Brad's body stiffened and he closed his eyes tight. "Is it my child?"

Carol knew the question was coming, but it still hit her hard. "How should I know?"

"You two are as close as friends get Carol. She tells you everything. Now don't play with me, you and I are too close for that," Brad said, determined to find out the truth.

"You're going to have to ask Kristy that question Brad," Carol said, wiggling her way out of answering the question truthfully.

"Have her call me please. And look Carol, I don't mean to be pushing you on this matter, but this is something I need to know. If I have a child, I want to know about it.

"Brad, I didn't know you did something with Kristy to be involved with her baby," Carol said, playing even dumber.

Brad's face became warm and turned red. "Well, we made love that day in your father's lake house."

Carol gave a brief laugh. "That's nice to know."

"Sorry I used your father's house in that way," Brad said, embarrassed.

"I don't care as long as you two had a good time."

"Ok, enough of this talk. You're too good at changing the subject when it comes to Kristy. Just have Kristy call me. I'll be in town for a couple more days before we start another road trip."

"I'll tell her to call you. Good luck on your road trip, even though you don't need it. It appears the Dodgers have it wrapped up," Carol replied, demonstrating once again how good she was at changing the subject. But she also wanted to let Brad know that she and John were following his great career.

"Thanks, and I'll talk to you later," he said as he hung up the phone.

The night before Brad had to leave on another road trip he had an unexpected guest at his apartment. He saw Lisa standing in his doorway, and she appeared to be all shook up. As he let her in, she stormed by him trembling with fear.

"What's wrong Lisa?" Brad asked as he approached her.

Lisa put her right arm out motioning him to stop. "I think I might be pregnant."

Brad stopped in his tracks stunned by what she just said. "You think you are, or you know you are pregnant?" Brad asked, anxiously.

"I think I am." She put her hands on her hips. "I don't know if I'm ready for a baby Brad. We aren't even engaged, and I still have a career ahead of me." Lisa wandered aimlessly in Brad's apartment trying to gather herself.

Brad could see that she had not considered getting pregnant and wasn't sure if she wanted a baby. He had been through this before, but he wasn't as willing to work it out this time. Maybe it was the way Lisa commented about her career that bothered him.

"What makes you think you're pregnant?" he finally asked as a frown took over his face.

"I am way late! I'm almost always on time, and now I'm two weeks late. This can't be happening to me," Lisa said, not realizing she was digging a bigger hole for herself with Brad.

"Have you ever been late before?"

"Yes, but it was a long time ago. God, I have so much going on right now," she complained.

"Have you taken a home test yet?"

"Yes, I took one last night, but it came out negative. It's probably too early for it to be correct," Lisa said, pacing. "What'll we do if I'm pregnant?"

"That'll be more up to you than me Lisa. I don't think you want to be hindered with a baby right now," Brad said, bluntly.

"I don't want one right now Brad. The time isn't right," Lisa stated, coldly.

"When will the time be right?" Brad was trying to learn more about her on this subject. He would like to have another child to love again, and it was important for him to learn her desires if he was to go further in their relationship. He knew he might not have a choice if she was indeed pregnant and decided to have the baby.

"I don't know Brad. I just know that right now is not the best time to start. I don't even know if you love me enough to want to spend the rest of your life with me." Lisa was perplexed over everything involving her life with Brad.

"I understand. If you're pregnant and decide to have the baby, I will be there for you for the rest of your life," he said without any emotion.

"That's mighty noble of you Brad. But is it for the right reason?" she asked, perceiving his intentions as a solution to a problem, rather than a true desire for her as his wife.

"I love you Lisa. I just haven't felt like we were far enough along in our relationship to think about marriage," he said, stretching the truth some. He did indeed have feelings for her he thought to be love, but they weren't strong enough to propose for marriage.

"Well, I apologize for ruining your evening with this news, but I thought you needed to know. I have an appointment with a doctor in two weeks, so we'll know then for sure. I guess we both have a lot to think about right now," she said, pouting.

"Yes, we have a lot to think about. But you need to be sure that having a baby at this time is what you really want. Don't do it if you aren't committed one hundred percent on being a mother. It's a big job, and it will change your life forever."

They hugged each other, and then Lisa went home to think about her predicament.

After closing the door, Brad leaned his back against the wall and said to himself, "One day I have no children, and the next day I might have two." He wondered what he would do if that was indeed the case.

Brad started the second game of the road trip. He had been thinking about Kristy and Angel quite a bit, as well as Lisa and her possible pregnancy. At one time he would have fallen apart at the mound, but this time he put all of his excess energy into his game. Brad pitched a no hitter with what seemed like little effort, laying the foundation for a strong October.

CHAPTER 42

▼

Greg had been toying with his newly assigned private investigator. He concluded that this guy must be new at the business since he wasn't very good at staying out of sight. Either that or the man just didn't care. Either way, it was going to make Greg's job that much easier to put a stop to it. He just had to get all of the timing down to carry out his plan to regain his power.

Greg had even started to work out again supplemented by the help of steroids, so he would be prepared to play baseball in the major league. He didn't want to look like a slouch out there pitching.

He had been spending more time at home recently, so Kristy wouldn't be too suspicious when he would finally put an end to her life. He wasn't sure how to cause her natural death, but he had been researching ways to do it for some time coming up with three different approaches to consider. He thought his college chemistry classes might be useful after all.

It was now just a matter of time for Greg to achieve his goals and take back his life.

Kristy had tried to call Brad, but wasn't getting through to his live voice. She didn't want to leave a message for him over this sensitive subject, so she would hang up when his voice mail kicked in.

Things had been starting to turn around for Kristy, except for Greg spending more time at home lately. She wasn't sure what he was up to, but she knew it was not good. He had even been spending more time with Angel lately, which really worried Kristy.

The best news for Kristy was the actual recording of her latest song she had written. She finally had a recording company accept it, and it was now about to be released to the radio stations. She was very excited about being able to celebrate an achievement she performed herself. Kristy would wait patiently for her song to be accepted by the public, before she would truly rejoice over her first success.

She had been nervous about Brad's discovery of Angel's birthday, with him now questioning the possibility of being her natural father. She wasn't prepared for him to know the truth at this time, if indeed he would ever know Angel was his daughter. Kristy would only tell Brad if she thought it was safe for everyone.

The Dodgers were the hottest team in baseball at this point. Brad was unbeatable once again, and Rex Campbell was closing in on a twenty win season as the second best pitcher of the Dodgers.

It was the final game of their road trip, and Rex had been pitching a great game by only giving up one run on four hits. It was the bottom of the eighth inning when the batter hit a ground ball to the right hand side of the first baseman. Rex ran to first base to cover the bag and collided with the runner after forcing the batter out.

Rex didn't get up off of the ground after the collision. He lay there on the ground with his knees bent slightly while holding his left arm.

The doctor ran to Rex and immediately turned to the coach shaking his head. He could see right away that Rex's arm was broken. The only good news was it was not his throwing arm that was hurt.

The entire team felt the loss as they surrounded Rex. They all made eye contact with one another acknowledging the need to elevate their game. Every player ended up laying their eyes on Brad, knowing he would have to carry them through the championship.

Brad felt the stares knowing the pressure was being put on him to pick up the loss of Rex. He returned the unspoken message with a determined look letting the rest of the team know he was up for the challenge.

The stage was being set for a dramatic October.

The regular season only had two weeks left, and then the playoffs would start, so Coach Elders pulled Brad aside for a talk. "Brad, you're the catalyst of this team. We have a great chance to win it all this year, but it will be much harder on us with Rex injured. Our bullpen is in decent shape right now, but it isn't as strong as I'd like. Since we have won our division, and look really good for home field advantage, I want to rest you some. You'll still pitch, but it'll only be for five innings tops. Hell son, you've already won thirty two games this year. That's a record that will stand for a long time, if not forever. We just have to look towards the playoffs now, and resting you is important. Keep working with the other pitchers, and be the team leader the same way you have all year."

There was a moment of silence between the two before the coach added, "I witnessed the rest of the team looking to you to carry us since Rex is out for the year. You have what it takes to take us to the top," the coach said with a quick smile.

"You know Coach, you're one of the reasons we're on top right now." Brad felt strongly that he was only one player on a well-balanced team and the coach is what brought success to the team. "I feel strong, but the rest might do me good. What do you envision my role to be in the playoffs?"

"With our number three and four starters struggling a little right now, it's hard to say. You might have to win eight games in October," the coach replied, revealing a lack of confidence in the rest of the starting pitching staff.

Brad swallowed hard at the task ahead. "We can get Mike pitching better than he has been lately. He has it in him. Let's get him on the CAMM when we get home and fine tune him. Even if he misses a game in the rotation, it'll be good for him," Brad suggested.

"Brad, I need you to play your best and keep your head in the game. We can't allow any outside problems to hinder your performance."

Brad realized the coach had great insight. He had not been totally focused on his game lately with all of the distractions going on. Brad hated to do it, but he told himself to put Kristy and Angel on the back burner for now as well as Lisa. It would only be a little over five weeks and the season would be over.

A week later, Lisa called Brad to let him know she wasn't pregnant. She started her period the same day as her doctor appointment. She informed Brad her doctor prescribed a different birth control pill and to not have sex for a month to be safe.

Brad asked Lisa if she was ok with the fact that she wasn't pregnant, and she admitted it was the right thing at this time. He then told her about what was going on with the team and the next month or so would be extremely demanding, so he would not be able to spend much time if any with her right now.

Lisa understood, but also sensed Brad pulling back from her. She would give him his time over the next month and a half knowing that was the right thing to do, but she would then ask him for some kind of commitment.

It was the final weekend of the regular season, and Greg had a plan drawn out. He was at his favorite bar with his friends to celebrate the eventual death of Brad.

He and his friends had just finished watching the Braves beat the Marlins. That was the only baseball game worth watching because with just one more game left on the schedule, all other divisions were decided. After today's game the Braves had a one game lead over the Marlins leaving tomorrow's finale the deciding game.

Greg and the gang now sat back to enjoy some college football. They were all fired up to see the Fighting Irish of Notre Dame playing Purdue for state bragging rights.

After a long afternoon of exciting college football, Notre Dame beat the Boilermakers by a touchdown in a well played contest. Half of the bar patrons were upset, and the other half were celebrating Notre Dame's victory after the two Indiana teams played a hard fought game.

Greg was one of the upset people in the bar since he loathed Notre Dame. They had the gall to fight hard to sign Brad and offer him a scholarship, which he eventually turned down. But any connection with Brad Preston wasn't going to bold well with Greg.

Greg pounded down a few more drinks that put him over top. He had been making all of these plans on taking Brad out of this world, and he was feeling aroused in his old sick way. Greg left his buddies and somehow drove himself to his favorite strip bar. He was not too drunk to notice the lackadaisical private investigator following him.

Greg entered the bar to waste some time and sober up. He had enough of this guy and wanted to find out who had hired him. It was about eleven o'clock at night when Greg finally felt he was sober enough to pull off his scheme. He walked out of the strip bar and went to his car. He then looked around after he closed his door and spotted his tail.

Greg drove his car to a run down part of town with old warehouses and slum looking apartments. He checked to see where his tail parked and came up with a plan. He then put on a pair of gloves, grabbed his sock hat, along with his hunting knife, and got out of the car. Nobody was around to see anything, so Greg circled the block and came up to his unknown stalker from behind.

It was a warm night, and Randy mistakenly had his window down.

Greg sprung up from the side of the car, putting the knife to Randy's neck. "Unlock the back door and then put both hands on the dashboard," Greg demanded as he pressed the sharp utensil against his pursuer's neck.

Randy didn't have a clue who it was forcing himself in his car, but he was in no position to ask. He was totally caught off guard. "You can have all of my money, which isn't much," is all Randy could say.

Greg positioned himself in the backseat and kept the knife to his shadow. "What the hell are you doing here?" Greg asked gruffly. "You don't look like you belong here."

"I was just following this guy in that car over there." Randy was visibly shaking as he pointed to Greg's car.

"Now why would you follow someone in a car into this neighborhood? Don't you know better than to come here all alone?" Greg asked, playing with the guy. He knew this person was very inexperienced from the way he handled himself.

"I was hired to follow him. What do you want with me?" Randy asked as perspiration beaded up on his face.

"I want to know why you're in my neighborhood," Greg said, not wanting to let the guy know he was the target. "Who hired you to follow someone?"

Randy gripped the steering wheel even harder. "I can't say. It shouldn't matter to you anyway since you're not involved."

"Oh, but I am involved. The guy that drives that car is a friend of mine, and I don't take to someone following him around." Greg applied more pressure to Randy's neck with the knife. "Now tell me, who hired you, and what does he want?"

"Brad Preston hired me," Randy said, trying to save his own life. "He wanted me to check on a young girl named Angel, or Angelica."

"Now why would someone want to know about a little girl?" Greg asked, gripping the knife harder and clinching his other fist so hard it turned red.

"He had me find out when she was born and who the parents were. He acted really strange when I told him the time and date she was born. It seems it was the exact time and date that his little girl died a few years ago. I think he believes this Angel might be his," Randy said, accidentally letting those words slip out of his mouth.

The anger in Greg grew stronger. "Why would he wonder that? That little girl is my buddy's daughter pure through."

"I haven't a clue." Randy knew he made a mistake telling the guy what he had.

"Do you have a wife at home waiting for you?" Greg asked in a threatening tone.

"Yes, and a young child also." Randy thought the guy wouldn't kill him if he knew someone was waiting for him at home.

"My friend doesn't like you following him, and I don't like you in my neighborhood, so I'm going to give you some advice. Stay away from my friend, or next time you won't be so lucky. What else did you tell this Brad?" Greg asked, trying to learn as much as he could.

"Not too much. He just seemed to want to know about this little girl. He also asked me to look after that guy's wife and to be sure to follow him around to make sure he doesn't do anything to her or anyone else." Randy relaxed a bit. He didn't care about his employer at this moment. He only wanted to save his life.

"So, did you find out anything interesting about my friend? I'd like to know, so I can kid him about it."

"I didn't find out too much. He likes to drink, and he went to a strip bar, but that's about it."

"Here's what you do then. You call this Brad, and tell him you don't feel any need to follow my friend, and tell him you're off the case. I really think it'd be a good idea to not say a word to him or anybody else about tonight. I know where you live because I have your license plate number. That sweet little wife of yours would taste awfully good to me. Do you understand what I'm saying?" Greg asked in an evil tone.

Randy stared straight ahead hoping this would end soon. "Every word."

"Then you'll forget about this whole job that you were hired for." Greg eased the pressure of his knife from Randy's neck.

"What job?" Randy said feeling more confident.

"Get the hell out of this neighborhood then and never come back. And leave my friend alone, or you're dead." Greg got out of the car and ran off.

Randy made the tires squeal as he sped away.

Greg made sure his shadow was long gone before he retreated to his car. He didn't know what to think right now. His anger was at a level where he wanted to kill Brad and Kristy at this very minute, but he had to wait. He needed to know more about the possibility of Angel being Brad's daughter. Why would Brad believe that Angel could possibly be his? He would have had to have sex with Kristy to think that. "That son of bitch is screwing my wife now," Greg yelled out.

Suddenly a maddening calm came over Greg. He was crazed, but in a very controlled way. The jobs ahead would be done precisely and on Greg's terms.

CHAPTER 43

▼

The Dodgers won their first playoff game with a great pitching performance from Brad. He threw seven shut out innings while the Dodger offense hammered eight runs, blowing out the Braves in the first game.

Game two was a much tighter contest having to go into extra innings, but a pinch hit double in the bottom of the eleventh by Brad gave the Dodgers their second victory in a row taking the series to Atlanta.

The Dodger players were serious about getting to the World Series this year. They felt more at ease now after getting some good pitching from Mike and their relief pitchers. They didn't want to rely solely on Brad to pitch them to victory, so every player stepped up a notch elevating a great team to a super team.

Greg walked into the doctor's office on Wednesday morning for his appointment with the specialist to see if he was fertile. The more Greg had thought about Brad and the possibility that Angel could be his, the more he worried about the possibility of being sterile. Greg knew he abused steroids in high school and college, which can have the side affect of making one sterile. He remembered it taking Kristy a while to get pregnant, and added to that the fact his mistress had not become pregnant yet, and he concluded he could be sterile. He told himself he would stop taking steroids after he bulked up.

Greg explained to the doctor that he and his wife had been trying for some time to have another baby, but couldn't get the job done. He then admitted his steroid use to the physician telling the doctor he was worried it might have left him sterile.

The doctor confirmed that steroid use could cause infertility and stated a sperm test was necessary to verify his suspicion.

Greg went into his assigned room to produce his sample and then left it with the nurse.

The nurse told him that it would take a day or so for the results since the lab was backed up, but someone would call Greg with the results.

Atlanta, Georgia was the site of the third game. Coach Elders really wanted to win this game, so Brad could start the first game of the next series. He knew it would give Brad a chance to start game seven of the National League Championship Series if it came down to that.

Jose Jimenez, the number four starter in the normal rotation, was scheduled to start. He was a hard throwing pitcher with a mean slider and a decent curve ball. His worse problem was he would become too emotional at times and over throw the ball causing him to get wild.

Coach Elders kept a tight rope on Jose during the game. His efforts paid off, with Jose going through eight innings with a three to two lead.

The Braves were playing good ball tonight in a must win game for them. The game was down to the bottom of the ninth. The Dodgers still had a one run lead, with only two outs left for the Braves to score a run or two in order for them to extend their season to one more game.

Brad had been sent to the bullpen earlier to warm up, just in case he was needed to pitch to a batter or two.

The Braves then put two men on base with a double followed by an infield single. With runners on first and third, Coach Elders called Brad out to finish the game.

It was an odd feeling for Brad to come in as a relief pitcher and throw warm up pitches with runners on the bases, but he was ready for the challenge.

Brad threw three bullets for strikes to sit down the first batter. That brought up the Braves best hitter in a do or die situation for Atlanta. Brad threw a ninety-eight mile per hour fast ball right by the batter for strike one. He then threw a slider that just missed for a ball. He threw the third pitch inside for ball two, to set up a mean curve ball that started inside and angled across the plate for a strike. The Brave's batter then chased a split finger fastball for strike three to end the game and the series.

It was an important win for the Dodgers and a good test to see how well Brad could pitch in relief. The coach and upper management knew that Brad was going to have to be capable of starting and working as a reliever in order for them to win the World Series this year.

It was Friday, and Greg had grown impatient waiting to hear from the doctor's office concerning his test results, so he made an unannounced visit to the doctor to see what the results where. The nurse directed Greg to a private room, and about twenty minutes later his doctor entered the room.

"Well Mr. Somanski, your instincts were correct about your infertility. Your test showed that you are indeed sterile," his doctor stated with a sadden look.

Greg's fists pounded the doctor's desk as his eyes narrowed. "How long do you think I've been sterile?"

"That's impossible to say. You evidently were fertile when your wife conceived your first child, so it could have been a slow process. You must be thankful you were able to have a baby when you did," the doctor replied nervously.

"I want to know if you think I became sterile during my college days when my steroid use was high," Greg asked in a demanding voice.

"I can only guess at the answer, but I'd say that's the most likely time your infertility occurred, except for the fact that you got your wife pregnant. Look Mr. Somanski, just be thankful you have a child. That's better than most patients I talk to everyday," the doctor stated frankly.

"Thank you for your candor," Greg said bitterly. He walked out of the office numb.

Greg sat in his car and felt almost sick at the news. He was more upset by the possibility that Brad might actually be the father of Angel, therefore stealing something else from him. The discovery that he was sterile bothered Greg also. It made him feel like less of a man. But then a huge smile came over Greg's face as he realized that he would become fertile again when he killed Brad.

He drove directly to an attorney friend of his and then walked into the small office that was less than professional.

This particular attorney was not very respected in the legal world. He was known for his borderline illegal actions. He actually broke the law in most of the cases he represented. If it wasn't for the fact his cases were so trivial, he would surely be disbarred by now.

The office was cluttered with magazines, and there were a few inexpensive pictures hanging on the wall in a disorderly fashion. There were two doors off of small lobby, one that led to the main office and the other door leading to a restroom.

A chubby man walked out of the main office dressed in an out of date suit. He recognized Greg and quickly approached him.

"So Greg, what brings you here? Did you finally get caught with one of those hookers?" the attorney asked with a short laugh.

"Not funny Jeremy," Greg answered sorely. "I need your help with something, and you won't even have to break the law to do it."

"Come on back to my office Greg, and tell me what you have for me." Jeremy led Greg into his private office and offered Greg some coffee before they sat down and proceeded to get down to business.

"What's this situation you want me to handle for you?" Jeremy asked as he took out a legal pad and a pen.

"I want you to set up a paternity test for me and my daughter," Greg replied with a calm look on his face. "I have reason to believe she may not be mine, and I plan on divorcing my wife. I believe that it would be smart on my part to know up front if I'm the father, so we can keep child support off the table in the legal war."

"What makes you think you may not be the father?" Jeremy asked, surprised.

"I just left a specialist, and he found me sterile," Greg said without any emotion.

"That'd be a good reason to have this test then. Why don't you just take your daughter to a clinic and have the test done?"

"I don't want my wife to know anything about it right now. I need to do this in a way that nobody knows what's going on, except you, me, and of course the doctor. There isn't anything illegal about me having this test done without my wife's permission, is there?"

"No, there isn't. I can arrange this with a quick phone call. When do you want this done?"

"Tomorrow would be fine with me. I can take my little girl out on a one on one with her father and then sneak her into the doctor's office. I can even cause her to have a small accident that will produce a small cut so we don't have to stick her with a needle to get the blood," Greg said as he already had a plan in his head. His thinking was clear now with his calm craziness.

Jeremy lifted the phone from the cradle. "You're sick my friend." He dialed the phone and held his pen to a piece of paper. "Dr. Langford please?"

Jeremy made the arrangements with his doctor friend to take the paternity test on Saturday morning. He informed Greg it would take several days for the results, which Greg expected.

Greg hustled off to work, so he could maintain his normal life. He didn't want to draw suspicion with a change of routines, although he knew Kristy would question his desire to spend a day alone with their daughter, or Brad's daughter, whichever be the case. But he had to find out the truth because it could add one more fatality to his hit list.

Kristy was very nervous about Greg's change lately. He was behaving like a real man now, and she knew it was a put on. He had to be up to something that was not good, but she couldn't figure out what it could be. She almost wouldn't allow Greg to take Angel alone for the morning, but she had little choice. Kristy was worried sick now, so she left to visit Carol to lean on her for support.

Carol was perplexed over the situation. She had witnessed Greg's distant relationship with the adorable little girl knowing that an overnight change of heart was not normal. He had to be up to something, she concluded.

"Have you ever talked to Brad since he left the message for you to call?" Carol asked.

"You know, I've called many times, but he's never home. I'll try him now. But what should I say to him Carol?" Kristy was nervous thinking about talking to Brad and she paced back and forth trying to prepare herself for what to say.

"He deserves to hear the truth Kristy, but I'm not sure this is the right time. Greg is acting too weird, and he'd react violently if he found out he was not the father. Especially if he knew the real father was Brad. Buy some time if you talk to him."

"You're right, I'll skirt the issue and make Greg's change of behavior the main subject and concern," Kristy said, relieved that Carol wasn't pressing her to tell him the truth.

Kristy dialed the phone nervously having to concentrate on pushing the right buttons on the phone since her hand was shaking. She almost wished he would not answer, but it was too late because Brad answered the phone on the second ring.

"Hello Brad," Kristy said shyly.

"Hello Kristy. Why haven't you called me back before now? It's been weeks since I left a message for you to call me."

"I've called many times, but you're never home. I don't want to leave a message on your voice mail. How've you been?" she asked, trying to dominate the conversation.

"Very busy," he answered in a frustrated tone.

"Brad, I think I may have a problem here."

"What is it Kristy?" he asked as frustration turned into concern.

"Greg's been acting strange lately. He's actually been a kind person and doing odd things, like staying home more lately. This morning he even asked to take Angel to the park to play. Just the two of them."

Brad could hear the fear in her voice. "Something's up then. I had a call the other day from a private investigator that I hired to keep an eye on him and to find out something on your daughter. By the way, why didn't you tell me about her birth date?" he asked in an irritated tone.

"Let's not go there right now Brad," Kristy said firmly. "We have an urgent matter to address right now."

"You're right Kristy, but sooner or later we will address that issue. Now as I was saying before I changed the subject, this private eye I hired called me all of a sudden leaving a message on my voice mail stating he didn't feel the need to follow Greg anymore. He said Greg was a decent guy that spent time at home, and he didn't want to waste his time or my money on following him anymore."

"You hired a private eye to look out for us?" Kristy asked, surprised.

"Yes, I'm concerned about you."

"I'm more concerned about us now. I was planning on leaving him soon, but now it'll be more difficult. He'll try to hurt me now. I know it because something is fishy about your private detective all of a sudden pulling off this case and the sudden changes in Greg's behavior."

"I hadn't thought of it that way Kristy. My God, what can we do?" He was now confused and worried about what Greg might do. "Why in the hell did you let him take Angel this morning? That doesn't make sense to me," he yelled out.

"I felt like I had no choice in the matter. Look, we both need to be extra cautious right now. Greg is a sick man mentally. I took enough psychology classes in college to recognize that. He's so caught up with the belief that you somehow ruined his life, and your success came from him, depleting him of his so-called power. Just as your failures or losses in life give him power."

"Why would he think I took something from him Kristy? It doesn't make sense to me." Brad thought it was absurd for Greg to feel that way.

"Because he's a failure in his mind, and rather than blame himself, he sees you as the one that put him there. You have to admit it Brad, that next to you most people feel less important and inferior. You were always the best athlete, best student, and a very popular boy in school. These are things Greg wanted, but lacked the fortitude to obtain. And he didn't have the natural ability that you have. But who does?" Kristy stated like a professional.

It all made sense to Brad now, but he didn't like what it all meant. Maybe Greg's change of behavior meant he was on to something, or maybe it meant he was now ready to change his life. Either way, it didn't look good for them.

"So how do we handle the situation?" Brad finally asked. "And does Angel have anything to do with this matter?

Kristy froze when she heard Angel's name mentioned. She wasn't prepared to be confronted by that issue now. Kristy swallowed hard. "We both keep our eyes and ears open. There's no telling what Greg might do. And of course Angel is part of this equation. She's my daughter, and he'll try to use her against me."

Brad knew better than to go any further on the subject of Angel at this particular time. He focused on the problem at hand. "Are you sure you can fend for yourself against Greg?"

"I don't know Brad. It all depends on what Greg has planned for me. Look, I don't want to put any undo pressure on you with the playoffs going on, but you'd better watch yourself right now. In case you didn't notice, you are the talk of the town in the baseball world. You almost single handedly beat the Braves. That's the sort of thing that angers Greg. Why don't you hire a bodyguard to watch over you for now."

"Are you serious?" Brad asked, stunned.

"Brad, he tried to kill you twice before, and he'll try again. It's the only way he can go on with his mediocre life. Don't be naïve about the situation, or it will get you killed. And one more thing, good luck in the playoffs. Oh, I love you, and don't ever forget it."

"I won't forget Kristy." He wanted to tell her the same, but decided it wasn't the right time. "You be extra vigilant with him right now. Don't trust anything he says or does!"

"I never have trusted him completely, and I'll definitely keep my eyes and ears open around him," she said, ending their conversation.

Greg drove Angel to the doctor's office that Jeremy had made arrangements with. As he had hoped in his plan, Angel fell and scraped her hand allowing him to take her to the doctor as a concerned parent to have her checked out. The doctor took a blood sample from her cut hand for the paternal test, and then cleaned the small wound and put antibiotic cream on it.

Meanwhile, Greg had blood pulled from him to allow the lab to complete the paternity test to see if he was the natural father. The plan went perfect and within a week he would have his answer.

CHAPTER 44

▼

The National League Pennant was on the line with the Dodgers and Astros prepared to face each other for the right to play in the World Series.

Brad was scheduled to pitch the first game of the series, and he was ready to go both mentally and physically. He tunneled all of his emotional turmoil concerning Kristy, Angel and Greg into his game. He was determined to not let Greg beat him mentally or physically, so he took Kristy's advice and hired a bodyguard as a safeguard measure.

It was now game time, and Brad toed the rubber to start the National League Championship Series. He wasted no time in sending the Astros a message by setting the first three batters down in order. He was determined to not allow the Astros to beat him again.

As the game progressed, Brad's fierce competitiveness increased becoming infectious to the rest of the Dodgers. They followed Brad's intensity with great hitting and flawless fielding.

Brad threw seven scoreless no hit innings before giving up one hit in the top of the eighth.

The Dodger's eight to nothing drubbing of the Astros had the baseball world already proclaiming the Dodgers as the World Champions.

The locker room had a quiet air of confidence with every Dodger player looking at each other with an unspoken, "We will not be beat."

The three team leaders, Brad, Tony, and Brian spoke quietly to each other concerning the rest of the series with the Astros. They knew Houston would not go away easy, so they discussed strategy on how they would pitch to the Astros potent offense.

The threesome had become best friends over the last two seasons, and Brad was thankful to have them in his life because they filled much of his lonely time. They had become the foundation of the Dodgers with their hard work and superb play and were instrumental in raising the bar for the entire team.

Later that night Brad spoke with Jake, his new bodyguard, about why he had hired him. He explained the entire scenario of everything that had happened since Anne and Brianna had been killed. Brad was impressed with Jake's professional approach of his job.

Jake took notes and asked pertinent questions that Brad would not have thought to ask. After the question and answer session, Jake requested a picture of Greg, but Brad had none to give him.

Brad thought Carol and John might have a picture of Greg, so he called Carol and asked her if she had any photos of Greg Somanski.

She took several minutes, but came back to the phone and said she had a few good pictures of him that she agreed to next day mail without bothering to ask what they were for. She already had an idea, and she thought it was about time Brad was finally reacting to Greg.

Jake gave Brad instructions on how to react to any confrontation and how to avoid contact with an opponent. Jake then told Brad how he was to stay at Jake's side at all times when out in public and to allow him to take on any attacker.

Brad led Jake to the spare bedroom where Jake unpacked his suitcase. It was a weird feeling for Brad to have a guest in his modest apartment. He hoped it would only be for a short time.

Greg had been working on a recipe for a deadly poison that would leave no traces in the body when the victim died. The poison would break down the blood in the victim's body and eventually kill them in about a week of the first dose. It was a potion that he would give Kristy daily, once he had it made up. But first, he had to get all of the ingredients, which wasn't going to be an easy task.

Greg was totally psychotic now. His rage was controlled by his belief that he would regain everything he lost when Brad was dead. This gave him the opportunity to design and execute his evil grand plan. He wasn't sure what he would do with Angel, but he considered poisoning her along with Kristy if she was indeed Brad's daughter. That way he could let Brad know what he had done to both of his daughters, giving him a higher level of satisfaction. He could feel the arousal in his body again, and he couldn't wait to finish his plan, so he could indulge in a violent sexual encounter. He had already picked out his victim.

Kristy didn't know what to think about Greg's behavior lately. She really thought it was odd that he brought her coffee in the morning, which he had never done before. She was even more shocked when he told her about Angel's scrape on her hand and how he took her to the doctor for him to inspect the minor cut. It wasn't making sense to her. He had to be up to something bad, but she couldn't be sure. Maybe he was finally maturing and changing into a man with responsibilities, she thought.

Kristy decided to keep her guard up and watch Greg closely. She was glad he hadn't tried to make love to her, which she wasn't about to let happen again, especially with all of the other women he had been with over the past two years. Besides, she couldn't do it with him again because she hated Greg and loved Brad.

The Dodgers won their next game against the Astros giving them a two to nothing lead in the series. They then traveled to Houston for the next three games, if indeed game five was needed.

The Astros came to life on their home field with their offense exploding for seven runs. The Astros' pitching staff clicked well holding the Dodgers to just one run, tightening the series to two games to one in favor of Los Angeles.

The next day the Dodger locker room had a totally different attitude. They had been embarrassed the day before, and it really bothered them. Every player on the team knew they were a championship caliber team, and nobody was going to take them out of the playoffs. It was much easier for the Dodgers to be confident today with Brad scheduled to pitch.

The team recognized there was something strange going on with Brad. They thought it was so much out of character for Brad to hire a bodyguard to escort him around everywhere he went. But it just made them want to play harder because he was their man, and he treated each one of them with great respect and fairness. He had never made the game about just him like some other superstars had, which only disrupted their respective locker room.

Game four started with a bang for the visiting team as they had three players cross home plate in the top of the first. That was a death wish to a team with Brad pitching because he would use that lead to his advantage. He moved the ball around on the hitters all night, hitting the corners, and making the batters swing at balls well outside of the strike zone. Brad ended up pitching a two hit shut out that could have just as easily been a no hitter. A blown call at first base allowed a questionable infield hit and a broken bat blooper was just out of Brian's reach for the second hit.

The Houston fans never had a reason to cheer for their beloved home team, and the Astros knew they were in serious trouble being down three games to one to a superior Los Angeles team.

Greg's attorney called Greg on Saturday morning to inform him that the doctor had the results back on his paternity test. Jeremy made the call to Greg's place of work, so there would be no chance for Kristy to know what was going on.

Greg knew he was about to carry through on a well laid out plan, and he wouldn't do anything to draw suspicion on himself. He had thought of everything and wasn't about to fail this time. He was even patient enough to wait for his lunch hour before he would go to the doctor's office.

As he was driving to the doctor's office, Greg was nervous about finding out the truth about Angel. He didn't want to be outdone by Brad again. He knew it would be the final straw if Brad had indeed stole his daughter from him. No man could handle that, he thought to himself.

Upon arriving at the medical center, the nurse immediately took Greg to an office and informed him the doctor would be with him in a few minutes.

To Greg's surprise, the doctor promptly entered the office in two minutes.

"Mr. Somanski I have your results here," the doctor said as he lifted an envelope from his desk. The doctor pulled some paperwork out of the envelope and read through it briefly, as he had done earlier. "I'm sorry to say that you are not the father of your wife's daughter. There is no possible way you could be according to the lab results."

"I appreciate what you have done for me Doc," Greg said as his fists clinched and his face turned red. His madness was contained by a controlled anger though, keeping him from trashing the office out of rage. "How much do I owe you?"

"I don't know for sure, but my receptionist will have the amount when you leave. Is there any other assistance I can provide for you?" the doctor asked out of respect.

"No that's all I needed to know." Greg got up from his chair and stared at the doctor. "It's just a shock to hear the news after I loved this little girl since her birth," Greg threw in to make him look like the victim.

"How's that cute little girl's hand doing?" the doctor asked kindly.

"It's just fine." Greg walked out of the small office unconcerned about her health, but he didn't go directly to the front desk. He snooped around the place and discovered the supply room. He found the last ingredient for his potion and then walked to the front desk and paid his bill.

Game five of the Dodgers and Astros series was a thriller of a game. It started out as a pitching dual until the fifth inning. That's when the bats broke out of their slump and turned the game into a slugfest. The Dodgers took a ten to nine lead into the bottom of the eleventh, and to the surprise of everyone, Brad Preston was on the mound.

Brad had only thrown ninety-four pitches to win yesterday's game, and had no stiffness or soreness, making him ready to go.

The Houston hitters looked defeated at the sight of Brad on the mound, and their mind set prevailed because it took only eleven pitches for Brad to strike out the side sending Los Angeles to the World Series. It was quite a feat for a pitcher to win three games in a five game series.

The champagne was not popped in the Dodger locker room. The players refused to celebrate the National League Championship with the bigger and more important series ahead of them. This was a team focused on one thing, and that was winning the October Classic.

Brad's bodyguard, Jake, was impressed by the business like manner the team portrayed, and he knew that neither the Yankees nor the White Sox were going to be able to beat them, especially with Brad on the team. Jake had already developed a high level of respect for Brad, and he knew his job would be much more intense with the table set for the big contest.

Meanwhile, the New York Yankees and the Chicago White Sox were battling hard for the American League Championship. It was a grueling series that was taking its toll on the players. There had already been two extra innings games, one game going fourteen innings before the White Sox came out as the victors.

It took seven hard fought games, but Chicago beat the Yankees to advance to the World Series for the first time in many years. They would fly cross country from New York to Los Angeles for the first game, and face Brad Preston on full rest, along with his fearless team.

C H A P T E R   45

▼

Greg had finished his deadly poison. Today would be the first dose he would inject into Kristy's coffee and Angel's milk. He decided to kill Brad's daughter since she was no use to him alive. Killing her would give Greg that much more power and provide him with a way to torture Brad, which he couldn't wait to deliver.

Kristy's coffee was waiting for her much like it had been lately. Angel was drinking her tainted milk when Kristy entered her small kitchen. Kristy noticed Greg's behavior being just slightly different. She perceived his actions and manners as being dastardly as he could not completely hide the zeal he had for his scheme.

Greg was indeed having trouble hiding his enthusiasm to kill Kristy, Angel, and Brad. He had come to the point where he couldn't take any more talk about how great Brad was and that he was the answer to the Dodgers winning the World Series this year. That was all they talked about on the sport channels and printed in the newspapers, and he just couldn't take it any longer. He wanted to go take Brad out this very minute, but he had to wait for about a week before that would happen in order to slowly kill Kristy and Angel. He could taste the victory.

Brad had a chance to spend most of the day with his family. His parents were in town to watch the first game of the World Series. They had been to most of the playoff games, but today was more important because this was something their son had always dreamed of.

Brad had purchased a block of seats for all of the home games and two of the away games. He wanted Bill Matthews, the Weatherbys, Jim and Molly, and of course his family at the games for their support and for their enjoyment of the special event.

The Prestons and the Weatherbys arrived at Dodger Stadium along with Brad and Jake. It was early for fans to arrive, but they allowed the special guests into the stadium without hesitation.

Brad took Nathan to the locker room for a quick look around and to meet some of the players.

Nathan appreciated Brad's graciousness and marveled at the calm approach he took towards such a big game. In fact, he noticed the entire team carried the same calm businesslike manner about them. Nathan would have thought the locker room would be filled with a high fervor of a "Go get em," attitude. But instead, he saw a team that had a feeling of destiny, and they weren't going to allow anyone to take that away from them.

Game time had approached quickly, and to Brad's surprise, Lisa Collins sang the National Anthem to start the game. Brad enjoyed her beautiful voice as did the sell out crowd that gave her a standing ovation at the end of the song.

Brad threw his last warm up pitch setting up the start of the series. From the first pitch of the game it was apparent that Brad was going to be a dominate force in the series. He struck out the first three White Sox hitters on ten pitches.

The Chicago White Sox players were still worn out from their hard fought series with the Yankees. They looked tired and out of sync. To make matters worse, they weren't confident facing Brad, and they showed it at the plate as they struggled all night against him.

The television announcer was already claiming the Dodgers as the World Series champions by the eighth inning, since Los Angeles was overpowering Chicago in all areas of play. The announcer ran out of words to demonstrate how good LA was.

Words were not needed tonight to show the world how good the Dodgers were playing. The Dodgers said it all with their superior, flawless play. Brad had a no hitter going, while the Los Angeles offense had tallied six runs, one being a solo home run by Brad.

The game came to a fitting end, with the last Chicago batter hitting a lazy fly ball to short right field that was easily caught, giving Brad a no hitter and the Dodgers a one to nothing lead in the series.

Greg had watched the game at Frankie's Bar with his friends. Normally Greg would have been angered to the point where he drank himself into a blind stupor from witnessing Brad's dominating performance and all of the praise that came with it. But not tonight, because Greg relished in Brad's superior play knowing he would soon possess the skills and athleticism Brad had stolen from him.

Greg was disappointed in himself for being so upset by Brad's success since it was really him out there pitching, and not Brad. A big smile overcame his pudgy face knowing he would soon unveil the truth about his rival and claim the fame that Brad stole from him. It was only days away for the finale, and Greg was building up to it slowly.

The next morning Greg put another small amount of his potion into Kristy's coffee and Angel's milk. He purposefully started out with small amounts because he didn't know how potent he had made his poison, and he didn't want to take a chance in the poison showing up in their system when an autopsy was performed.

Greg was totally prepared now to execute his dastardly plan. He packed up his personal car with a change of clothes, a high powered rifle, and a pistol, along with enough ammunition to get him out of a tough situation if he was corned. He even made up some homemade explosives just in case he needed them.

The series moved to Chicago after Mike followed Brad's feat with a six hit, two run performance of his own against the White Sox. The Dodger bats were hot, scoring six runs to secure the victory of game two. Following an off day for traveling, game three was rained out, which was a bad sign for Chicago. It would bring Brad back to the mound on three days rest. It appeared the destiny of Los Angeles was at hand.

After much speculation concerning the weather, the rain finally stopped an hour before the game was scheduled to start allowing the game to be played, but making the playing conditions miserable with a wet field and temperatures in the upper forties.

As Brad took to the field, it reminded him of his playing days in high school in early spring when there were many times it was this cold. It did not dampen his spirits or take away from his game, but instead allowed Brad to reach further into himself.

True to form, the Los Angeles Dodgers took control of the series with Brad pitching a two hit shutout, while the Dodger offense scored five runs to win game three.

The Chicago fan's spirits were dampened even more as a steady rain began to fall again just ten minutes after the game ended.

Brad just smiled and said to himself, "Nothing like the fall classic in Chicago to bring on the adverse weather conditions."

The weather man could not guarantee the start of game four since there was a cold front approaching Chicago from the west and a warm trough sliding up from the south. It would be a matter of timing on when the two fronts would collide; to determine whether or not game four would start as scheduled.

Jose was scheduled to pitch game four even though he wasn't used to playing in the cold wet weather conditions predicted for tonight's game. Coach Elders secretly prayed for rain, so he could come back with Mike. He didn't have the confidence in Jose at this time, but he was the best available starter for tonight.

As game time approached, the winds were gusting twenty to thirty-five miles per hour, and the temperature was dropping to a predicted forty-two degrees. There was no rain delay for game four this evening, and the game started in the cold sloppy conditions.

It was an advantage to Chicago, and they jumped at the chance from the start of the game.

Jose never had a feel for the ball and started off wild from the beginning. The weather wasn't particular good for the batters on either team, but the White Sox were able to score three more runs than the Dodgers to save themselves from being swept in the series.

The weather gods were still not cooperating with the baseball championship this week as heavy rains delayed the series two more days. Game five felt like game seven with all of the delays that had come along. The early morning weather forecast was for clear skies and a cool night to allow game five to finally occur.

Greg realized he needed to get to Brad and take him out tonight. He felt confident making the hit in Chicago since he knew the area well. He calculated that his wife and Angel should die sometime today or tomorrow with the strong dosage he would give them this morning, along with the doses he had given them over the past seven days. The timing would be perfect.

Angel had become sick from the poison she had taken, and Kristy was showing physical signs of being sick as she looked pale and complained of being tired, which indicated to him the poison was working on her also. Luckily for Greg, Kristy just assumed she and Angel were coming down with the flu making her reluctant to go to the doctor.

Kristy noticed Greg moving around the house in a rapid pace on this particular morning and acting rather strange. She thought it odd that he was irritated with her for drinking her coffee so slow. She had no idea she had been slowly poisoned all week and today's double dose could possibly kill her by evening.

Kristy's suspicions accelerated after seeing Greg's reaction to her spilling her coffee this morning.

Greg became raged by her act and demanded that she clean up her mess while he refilled her cup.

Kristy wiped up the spilled coffee and peeked into the kitchen, only to witness Greg pouring something into her coffee cup from a glass bottle. He then slipped the bottle into his jacket before she sneaked back into the dining area acting like nothing happened.

Kristy apologized to Greg for being so clumsy, instilling a false security in him that his secret was safe. Greg seemed reluctant to leave the house until Kristy finished her coffee as he stared at her with his beady eyes.

She knew he wouldn't leave, so she drank her fresh brew so fast it burned her mouth.

As soon as the empty cup hit the table, Greg picked it up and took it to the kitchen to wash it thoroughly. He then left the house to drive straight to Chicago.

Kristy immediately ran into the bathroom and made herself vomit. She dressed quickly, and took the soaked paper towel out of the garbage and put it in a sandwich bag. She carried Angel to the car and drove to the hospital while she called Carol from her cell phone to let her know what was going on.

Carol told Kristy she would get to the hospital to help her out when she could. She explained to Kristy that she and John had to drive to Chicago later in the day to go to the game. Brad had given them a special invite to sit with his family and friends, and they didn't want to miss the opportunity.

Kristy understood Carol's need to go to the game, not knowing the severity of the situation with her and Angel.

The hospital gave Kristy a run around about her suspicion of being poisoned by her husband. They weren't willing to test the sample she brought with her in the plastic bag.

She didn't know what to do, so she dialed Bill Matthew's office.

He was out of the office for the day, is all the receptionist would say.

Kristy gave the receptionist her cell phone number, and told her to tell Bill it was a life or death situation concerning Brad, and to have him call her immediately.

Kristy was finally able to get Angel in to see a doctor after waiting a few hours. She pleaded with him to do a test on the spilled coffee sample that she brought with her.

338   Journey To Fate

He didn't take her seriously at first, but changed his mind about the matter when he examined Angel. She was going down hill fast. He ordered blood tests on Angel and Kristy, and requested an immediate test on the sample Kristy had with her.

Carol finally arrived at the hospital just after the blood had been drawn on Kristy and her daughter. She felt bad seeing how shook up Kristy was, and worried even more when she heard that Angel had been sent to the intensive care unit because her vitals were getting weak.

Kristy explained the circumstances to Carol, and they both cried over the critical status of Angel.

An hour and a half later, the lab called down to the doctor with the results of the sample Kristy had brought in. The lab found the liquid to contain a toxic and deadly poison. They explained how it would break down the blood in someone and eventually kill them.

The doctor told the lab to look for the effects of the poison in the two blood tests that he sent up. He then ordered a blood transfusion for both Kristy and Angel in preparation of the worse scenario, followed by a directive to the front desk to inform the police of a possible attempted murder.

After the call to the authorities, the police arrived at the hospital to interview Kristy about her husband. An arrest warrant was soon issued for Greg Somanski, but he was nowhere to be found.

The decision was made by the coach and favored by management to start Brad tonight. He would be pitching again on three days rest, and that seemed more than enough for their superstar.

Brad was called to the coach's room and informed of the decision. He agreed with the coach's judgment, telling him he felt great and was ready to go tonight.

Brad felt the moment take him over as he started his mental preparation for the big game. He was glad he had made arrangements for family and friends to see the game in a warm stadium luxury box. He only hoped that tonight would be the final game of the series. He wanted the World Series Championship more than ever. Not just for him, but for the other teammates that worked so hard this year, and for the front office that put so much faith in Brad, and last but not least for the faithful Dodger fans that filled the stadium almost every game this year.

By three o'clock in the afternoon the lab had located the problem with Angel and Kristy. Kristy's blood was not nearly as tainted as Angel's blood, making the doctor believe a blood transfusion should be enough to correct Kristy's problem with the addition of special drugs. He knew Angel needed more than a transfusion. He came to the conclusion that she needed a stem cell transplant to give her a chance to live.

A search was on for a good donor for the now failing toddler.

It was then that Kristy told the doctor who the real father was.

The doctor was flabbergasted when he heard it was Brad Preston.

She explained that Brad had no clue he was the real father, but she knew he would donate his stem cells to save his daughter. She also possessed a strong feeling that Brad would be a perfect match for Angel, and expressed it to the doctor.

The doctor wasn't overly excited about Brad's prospect of being a donor and explained to Kristy there was a very slim chance the parents would even match their children for a stem cell transplant. He informed her that a sibling of Angel's would be the best chance of matching her daughter, so he prepared her for the worst since there were no brothers or sisters.

At six o'clock that evening, Bill Matthews returned Kristy's call to her cell phone. Luck was with them, because Bill was in Chicago and he was with Keith Olson at the time.

Kristy told them about Angel and went on to explain what Greg had done to the two of them. She advised them that Greg was probably going to try and kill Brad because Greg couldn't be found. She then gave the phone to the doctor to let him explain the situation and what was needed from Brad at this time.

Bill and Keith were stunned by the news and agreed with Kristy to not say anything to Brad at this time about what was going on. They assured the doctor they would produce a blood sample from Brad as soon as possible.

An hour later, Keith Olson, accompanied by the team doctor advised Brad that the league had ordered a random drug test on a few players. They told Brad that he was one of the chosen few selected, given that some people were suspicious of him because he was playing at such a high level and dominating the game. They told him not to worry since it was just a random test. They expressed their opinions to Brad that they knew he had worked hard to get where he was without drug enhancement.

Brad was confused by the request, but gladly allowed the doctor to pull his blood since he had never used any performance enhancing drugs in his life.

The sample was then sent directly to the Chicago Hospital to see if it would match Angel's blood. It would take some time to verify the results since it was to match his daughter for a stem cell transplant, which should allow Brad to finish the game.

Carol left the hospital earlier to meet John and then drive to Chicago. Since Carol would be with Brad, it was decided that she should be the one to tell Brad about Angel, if and when the proper time came up since she would be there with him. They had a long wait to see if Brad would even qualify to be the donor for Angel. They hoped that a match could be found somewhere, but it was a very slim chance and too early to know.

Kristy was feeling better physically, but she was not in the clear yet. They planned on pulling blood from some of her family and use it to purge Kristy's system again. They felt the treatment plus the drugs they were giving her should clear Kristy up one hundred percent.

Angel was a different story though. They had given her a blood exchange that would give her temporary help, but without a stem cell transplant she would more than likely die.

Kristy's family couldn't believe Greg had tried to kill the both of them, and asked Kristy why she hadn't said anything to them.

She told them she tried several times, but they were too caught up in the "Until death do you part," that they wouldn't listen. She had lost a lot of respect for her parents the last couple of years.

Greg had scouted the U.S. Cellular Field in Chicago to find his best advantage for tonight. He wore a disguise after hearing from his attorney that he was wanted for the attempted murder of his wife and daughter. "That damn bitch," he yelled out when he heard what she had done. He wished he would have used the nine millimeter on her in the same way he was planning on using it on Brad later tonight, but he thought she would die from his poisoning anyway.

Greg came up with what he thought was a fail safe plan and prepared everything to execute it. He set plastic explosives in another area to throw security off track to allow him to pull off his execution. He was beaming with pride from his hard work, and getting caught was not going to be an alternative tonight.

The coaching staff, along with Keith Olson tried to decide how they should handle the delicate situation unfolding as they spoke.

Kristy had made it clear to them she didn't want Brad to know what was going on until after the game or if and when he was found to be a perfect match for Angel.

They knew Greg was missing and concluded he was out there somewhere planning on killing Brad.

They also had to agree on whether or not they should let the other teammates know what was going on. There was a small chance Brad would have to leave the game early if he was the perfect match as his daughter's donor, and they didn't want the other players wondering during the game why he left all of the sudden. They thought if they did tell the team in advance, it would be a distraction for them during the game, so they finally agreed to not say a word to the players. Besides, they thought it wouldn't be fair for Brad to be the last to know about his daughter. He should be the one to know if anyone was going to be told.

From all indications from the laboratory, it would be later tonight at best before they were finished with the blood work, so the coaching staff went into this game not knowing what to expect. They considered starting Mike on short rest, but knew that Brad would not be able to play for a while if he was the stem cell donor for his daughter. This was not the way they wanted to approach a game that could end this year's World Series.

The entire team felt an eccentric air in the locker room tonight. Besides the extra heavy security, the coaching staff seemed to be hiding something and appeared reluctant to fill the players in on what was happening, raising their curiosity.

Brad felt the tension, but it made him take the leadership role that much more.

They all went through the warm up drills and batting practice in a normal fashion. The cool weather made it more difficult to loosen up, but they were determined to obtain their destiny tonight, so each player worked that much harder. They had to with Brad as their example. He was the main reason they were in the position they were in right now. He had been pitching the last few games on three days of rest, plus he had thrown a few innings of relief. If he could work that hard, they could all do the same.

There still wasn't much change with Angel. They had somewhat stabilized her, but the poison had done too much damage. There still weren't any qualified donors for her. Kristy was never in the picture as a donor since she had also been injected with the vial poison, plus she was not a match anyway. They needed a benefactor with perfect blood.

Kristy was back in Angel's room after completing a blood exchange. The hospital would keep pulling her blood every hour to verify she was indeed under control of the poison in her bloodstream. Kristy looked into the face of her beautiful daughter seeing so many of Brad's features. The older Angel became, the more she looked like her real father.

With Angel in serious condition, Kristy now had more of a sense of what Brad had gone through when he lost Brianna. She knew his ordeal had to have been worse since she died in his arms just after he saw his dead wife. Tears filled Kristy's eyes as she thought about what he went through that day, and the strong possibility that the both of them might go through it with Angel. The doctor had not given her any guarantee that the stem cell transplant would save her life; highlighted by the fact the transplant is a dangerous procedure that could kill her in itself.

The waiting game was killing Kristy, but she knew she needed to get strong because there were many more hours or days of the wait and see with her daughter. She wished Brad was there beside her to give her the strength to face the situation better, but she wanted him to fulfill his obligation to the Dodgers and realize his lifetime dream of winning the World Series. She hoped Brad would understand her decision to not let him know about Angel at this time.

Kristy placed her two hands together and looked up to heaven. She said a prayer for Brad, Angel, and the three of them as tears fell from her eyes.

The Dodgers were ready to take the field for game five as they prepared to depart the locker room.

Brad closed his locker and felt a warmth enter his body. He had experienced this same warm feeling before, so he stopped for a few seconds to see if it would pass, but instead it enveloped his entire body.

"Hey guys," Brad yelled out before they exited the room. "Tonight is the night we've worked all year for. It's ours to take, and each and every one of you deserves it. I can tell you right now this is going to be a special night. Play your hearts out, and let's win the big championship that everyone dreams about, but only a few get to experience."

His words hit home with everyone in the locker room.

Coach Elders stood there and smiled because Brad made his job so easy.

Brad walked onto the field and looked around the stadium soaking in the true excitement of the fall classic. He could see the ball park was packed with fans from both teams creating the special exhilaration that only the World Series can produce. He found the luxury box that held his most cherished friends outside of baseball, along with his family. He noticed that Lisa was not there with the rest, which was no surprise to him. He felt she knew there was no future for the two of them. He saw them all waving down to him, so he nodded his head towards them to acknowledge their presence. He then closed his eyes and dug deep into himself. Flashes of his past stampeded threw his brain. He then pulled out every ounce of strength, knowledge, and determination within him and then dispelled all emotion. That was all he would remember after the game started.

The media went out of its way to hype this game. They really stressed the fact that if Brad won tonight, it would be the first time a pitcher started three games in a five game series and won all three of them. It was also noted that it had been a long time since a pitcher batted with the designated hitter in effect in a World Series game. They also went back to last season when the Dodgers were in contention until the shooting of Brad, and how his remarkable comeback was the reason Los Angeles was knocking on the door to the World Championship.

The hype and commentary meant nothing now with the game ready to start. It was two great teams on the ball field playing for the greatest prize in baseball, on a cool, but dry Chicago evening with a brisk wind. The television commentators gave the cool weather as an advantage to Chicago.

For Brad, it meant nothing because he was filled with a warmth that the forty five degree weather couldn't penetrate. He threw his last warm up pitch to start the bottom half of the first, after his team stranded a runner in the top of the inning.

Brad was totally lost in the game, and the Chicago batters could see it in his face and see it in his pitches. His fastball was one hundred and one mph and it cut in sharply on the right handed batters, or tailed away from the batter with just a slight adjustment of his grip on the ball. His change up dropped out of sight making the hitters look bad after they swung at it wildly. Everything was working for him tonight better than ever.

Tony knew after the first inning that this was going to be a pitching masterpiece. He didn't have to do anything but hold his glove where he wanted the ball to go, and that is where Brad put it. Tony smiled walking back to the dugout as he thought about the day when Brad bet him he could throw a hundred mile per hour fast ball and knock a baseball off of a tee. He knew that moment changed his life for the better.

Brad was the first hitter in the top of the second. The Chicago pitcher was almost afraid to pitch to Brad when he saw the determined look on his face that said, "I can hit any pitch that you throw me." The pitcher ended up walking Brad on four straight pitches.

Brian was the next batter, and he bunted Brad to second to set him up to score on a single. A long fly ball allowed Brad to tag up and move to third with two outs. He ended up stranded on third after a great play by the Chicago shortstop for the third out.

The stage was now set for a great game, with neither team willing to give an inch tonight.

Brad mowed down the next three White Sox batters ending the second inning with no score and no hits.

The game was fiercely played by both teams. The White Sox knew this was a do or die game for them, and they played with an intensity that reflected that attitude.

The Dodgers felt this was their year, and this game would cap off all of the hard work they put into the season. It was their game to win, and they were playing error free. They knew with Brad pitching, they only needed to score one run to bring home the trophy.

The top of the fifth inning was ready to start with the game still tied. The weather conditions were dry, but it was colder than the start of the game. The fans could see the players breath and the steam rise from there jerseys.

Brad was scheduled to bat second this inning. He waited in the on deck circle watching the opposing pitcher throw to Tony while he worked on his timing by swinging at every pitch. Brad felt confident he had the timing down.

Tony hit a long fly ball to right center field that excited the fans, but ended up being a long out.

Brad walked up to the plate receiving applause from the Dodger fans. He held his right hand up signaling time out, as he adjusted the dirt around the plate so he could dig in. He waited patiently for his pitch by taking a fastball that was low and away for a ball.

Brad dug in again and eyed the pitcher carefully. He saw the ball coming at him and put his body weight on his back foot while cocking the bat back. The pitch was a curve ball that hung just a bit. Brad took a powerful swing at the ball making a nice souvenir to a lucky fan in the upper deck of left field. Without emotion Brad circled the bases to give the Dodgers the lead.

Angel had lost some color as death seemed to be dancing around her. She was due for another blood transfusion in another hour.

The doctor was experimenting with different drugs to help her body fight off the deadly toxin in her body and buy her some time, so they could search for a match for her stem cell transplant.

Kristy sat at Angel's bedside holding her precious daughter's hand in hers while she prayed for a miracle. There was a small window of hope in her that

Brad would be the miracle. She felt it in her heart and soul knowing how strange occurrences follow Brad.

Angel laid in her hospital bed half conscious, dreaming about a small child much like herself. The child would take her hand telling her she was taking her to her father, and not to worry about anything.

The game was clipping along at an extremely fast pace as the pitchers controlled the game coming into the top half of the eighth inning. There was only one run and three hits given up in the entire game. The cold weather had really affected the batters in a negative way tonight.

The ballpark became quiet since the home run in the fifth inning. Every fan was mesmerized by the great pitching dual they were witnessing tonight. The silence was temporarily broken by applause when Brad stepped into the batters box for his third appearance at the plate for the night.

He stared the opposing pitcher down, waiting for the first pitch. Brad watched a curve ball go way outside for ball one. He then hammered a fastball off of the left center fence for a double to wake up the faithful Dodger fans.

Brian was up next and singled Brad home on a line drive to left center field to give the Dodgers a two run lead. By the time the inning was over, Los Angeles scored three more runs, which practically drove a stake into the hearts of the Chicago players.

Brad went out to the mound in the bottom of the eighth and threw like a machine. He struck out the side on nine pitches. There was a quiet murmur in the stands as the fans whispered talk of a perfect game. Brad had not allowed one Chicago batter to reach first base.

Not a soul left the ballpark early on this crisp October Chicago night.

The Dodgers went down in order in the top of the ninth, pleasing Coach Elders and the rest of the staff. They wanted this game over in a hurry just in case the call came in to get Brad out of there.

Brad walked to the mound without thinking about a perfect game. He still felt the strange warm glow in him as he went out there throwing bee bees to the Chicago batters.

There wasn't a fan in the entire stadium that wasn't standing on their feet with the last out at hand, after the first two batters struck out without laying a bat on the ball.

The third batter anxiously swung at a mean slider for the first strike. Brad followed up the slider with a fastball cutter that hit the inside corner for a called strike two.

It was deafening in the ballpark as the fans were clapping and yelling perfect game.

Brad was the only one in the stadium that could not hear them. He wound up and threw a nasty change up that the batter swung at too early, giving the Dodgers the World Series Championship and Brad a perfect game.

It was a historical series for Brad, throwing a no hitter in game one and a perfect game to end the series.

His parents were beaming with pride and gave each other a hard long hug. They took a deep breath to refresh their bodies with oxygen because they hardly breathed the last inning.

Bill Matthews had tears in his eyes and eagerly shook hands with Norris Weatherby in celebration of the victory, as well as Brad's triumph in life.

Jim and Molly were going crazy over the victory and Brad's grand performance, while John and Carol were cheering, but worried about what was coming up next for Brad.

Brad's celebration turned to instant confusion when he entered the locker room and was herded away from the rest of the players.

Keith congratulated him, but then told Brad that something serious was going on and he needed to get dressed right away.

Brad didn't ask why from seeing the serious look in Keith's face. He quickly showered and dressed.

Jake and another man were patiently waiting for him, but both men seemed nervous from Brad's perspective. He then noticed the unusual amount of police and security personnel hanging around the locker room, and wondered why.

Jake whispered in Brad's ear to be alert and to get between him and Stan, the new additional bodyguard.

They whisked Brad out of the locker room and out of the stadium towards a well lit parking area.

About a half a minute after the door closed, an explosion went off several blocks away.

Jake reached for his pistol in his pocket just in case he was confronted.

The three of them were heading for a landing area where a helicopter could take Brad away, but they ended up taking an alternate route after the explosion. Suddenly there were two gunshots fired, and Stan fell to the ground, followed by two more shots taking Jake down.

Brad ran away from Jake disregarding his previous orders. He had seen a place to take cover and his instincts sent him in that direction.

"Stop running Brad, or I'll shoot you too," a familiar voice rang out to Brad.

Brad stopped and turned around to see a silhouette of a man in the darkness he knew to be his enemy. He watched Greg put one more round in Stan for safe keeping.

Greg looked over at Jake, who was further away because of Brad fleeing from him, and then quickly turned his attention to Brad being satisfied Jake was also dead.

"You're a hard person to kill Brad. How is that thigh of yours anyway?" Greg took a few steps closer to Brad.

"So you really were the one that shot me. Why me Greg?"

"You know why Brad. Don't play these games with me," Greg said with glazed eyes.

Brad was trying to buy some time, but he also wanted to know the real reason Greg had tried to kill him twice before and was intending to finish the job right now. "No, I have no idea what you're talking about. Why don't you enlighten me, so I'll know what I died over," Brad said calmly.

Greg stood there smiling with the pistol aimed at Brad's chest. "You stole my life Brad. I was always the best athlete, but you stole that from me. The only reason you're so good is because of me. Your skills were taken from me. I should have been the one out there pitching the perfect game, not you. Don't you see what you've done Brad?" Greg said with a crazed smile.

"You're crazy, is all I know Greg. I'll admit that you were good at sports, but you never had the fortitude to be better. I raised my level of play from hard work and a lot of pain. That's what it takes to make it in the higher levels of the sport world Greg. You just didn't work hard enough to take your game to the next level," Brad replied, challenging him.

"Don't disrespect me," Greg yelled as his finger applied more pressure to the trigger.

Brad's eyes narrowed. "Or what Greg, you'll kill me? I think you've already made that determination."

"Yes, that's right Brad. I am gong to kill you, and by doing so, I'll have shown the world you were an imposter, revealing me as the true athlete. I'll be starting for the Dodgers next year and break all of your records in one year," Greg said with a hallow laugh.

"You couldn't pitch American Legion ball Greg," Brad replied having lost his patience. Brad looked for any weakness Greg might have, so he could take him out before Greg shot him.

Brad's criticism made Greg furious now. His plan wasn't going as smooth as he would have liked. He had visualized Brad on his knees begging not to be shot.

He didn't expect to be challenged by him. "My patience with you has worn out." The gun shook slightly in his hand. "It's now time for you to join Kristy, and Anne, and your daughters."

Brad didn't pick up on the plural in daughters because he was stunned by what Greg said about Kristy being dead. His body tensed and his hands turned to fists. "What the hell did you do to Kristy?"

"Ah yes, your little Kristy," Greg said, finding delight in hitting a sore spot with Brad. "She should just about be dead right now. I poisoned her in a way that nobody will know that I did it. It seems that I enjoy killing the women in your life. You know, I actually thought it was you in the car that snowy morning, but it was Anne and your precious daughter Brianna that I plowed into and sent them down the ravine to their deaths. And now I've killed your girlfriend and your other daughter, and there is nothing you can do about it."

A blind rage overcame Brad at the mention of Greg killing Anne and Brianna. He didn't even pick up on the statement that Greg had killed his second daughter. Brad stared at Greg for a few seconds and then screamed, "You son of a bitch," as he suddenly charged him.

Three rounds went off as Brad violently approached Greg, and a body fell to the ground. Brad turned to look at Jake and saw him lying there with his pistol still aimed at Greg. Brad then walked up to Greg's body and kicked the pistol away. He checked for a pulse, but could not find one.

"It's a good thing I bought this special vest and wore it tonight," Jake said weakly. "My homework paid off on him. Every indication led me to believe he would use a special round to kill you."

"Are you ok?" Brad asked, concerned, but elated that Jake was alive.

"Yes, I probably have a couple of broken ribs, but other than that I think I'm fine. I guess it's a good thing you didn't follow my advice." Jake slowly got to his feet.

"Sorry Jake, but my instincts took over and I raced for cover." Brad walked over to check on Stan.

"Is he dead?" Jake asked.

Brad shook his head yes. He felt bad that Stan had to lose his life trying to save him.

Jake read his mind. "That's what we get paid for Brad. You saved my life by running off. These bullet proof vests don't protect your head." Jake pulled a walkie-talkie out of his coat and called for help.

In a matter of seconds there were several police there to take over the scene. They had heard the gunshots and were already on their way.

Jake prodded Brad to start walking, leading him towards the landing area for the helicopter. The rumbling of the unique flying machine could be heard as it approached.

"You have to get on that helicopter and get to airport to catch your flight to Indianapolis. I'll stay here and clear up the killings," Jake ordered.

"What's going on Jake?" Brad asked, not sure what he was doing flying to Indy.

"Didn't you listen to that psycho? He told you enough for you to put the pieces together," Jake replied.

"I only heard that he killed Kristy, Anne, and my daughter," Brad said, trying to think back to the conversation with Greg.

Jake smiled. "You'll know everything in a few minutes. I don't have time, and I don't know enough to try to fill you in."

The helicopter landed in its designated area as Brad spotted Carol and his parents there waiting to board it.

Mrs. Preston gave Brad a long hug and asked him if he was all right.

Brad let them all know he was fine, but Greg and a bodyguard were dead.

Jake made sure Brad and his family had safely boarded before he went back to the crime scene.

CHAPTER 46

▼

After their jet took off from the Midway Airport, Carol was finally able to inform Brad and his parents what was going on in Indianapolis. It had been too noisy in the helicopter to talk, and this was the first time she had a chance to explain the situation. "I'm sure you're wondering what this is all about," Carol stated.

"I assume it has something to do with Kristy," Brad replied, hoping she was alive and well.

"Why don't you give us all the facts Carol," Miles requested as he looked at his wife in a way that said he had no clue what was going on here. All he knew was the fact that his son pitched a perfect game to win the World Series, and instead of celebrating with his teammates, they were on a private jet to Indy.

Carol sat up straight and clapped her hands together. "As you all know, Kristy and Greg have had a terrible marriage. In fact, I'd describe it more as a non-existent marriage over the past two years. Kristy had always thought that Greg was the one that caused the deaths of Anne and Brianna…"

"And that turned out to be the case," Brad broke in. "He told me tonight when he confronted me that he had plowed into the side of my car to push it and me down the hill. I say me because he thought I was the driver."

"Oh my God," Margaret said as she turned to Miles in disbelief.

Miles grabbed his wife's hand and held it tight. He wasn't sure what else they would learn tonight.

"Well, Kristy wanted to be the one to tell all of you this news, but under the circumstances she's not able to do it," Carol said sadly.

"Is she dead?" Brad asked, terrified by the thought that she was dead.

"No, Kristy is doing ok. The poison that Greg gave her hadn't progressed enough to kill off her blood. But Angel is in serious condition. Greg tried to poison her also, and with her being so small her little body couldn't fight it off the way Kristy's could. Or maybe the doses that Greg had given her were not proportionate to her body weight and he overdosed her. It's too hard to say, but the fact is, she'll die without a stem cell transplant. That's why Brad is being rushed to Indianapolis. He's Angel's natural father."

The news hit Brad unexpectedly and he just started crying.

Miles and Margaret were stunned by the news. They were elated for having a granddaughter, but upset about the news that she could die. They didn't want to lose another granddaughter, and they couldn't bare the thought of Brad losing another child.

"Brad, I know you asked me point blank about her being your daughter, but I couldn't tell you the truth. Only Kristy and I knew the truth, and we were afraid of what Greg would do if he found out. Now we know what he would do." Carol now wished she had told him anyway. She thought if she had mentioned the fact to Brad, Angel might not be in the hospital on her deathbed right now.

"I don't blame you or Kristy," Brad replied, knowing the two of them were only trying to protect everyone. He saw the look in Greg's eyes tonight, and he meant business. Greg was mentally sick.

Carol reached into her purse and pulled out some pictures. "Here's your daughter Brad." She handed him a few pictures of Angel.

"She looks a little bit like Brianna," Brad said as he viewed the photographs of the beautiful little girl. "By the way," Brad said, directing his words towards his mother and father. "She was born on February 19, at three o four in the afternoon. That's the exact time and day that Brianna died."

"That is a miracle," Miles said as he sat there stunned.

Brad then handed the first picture of Angel to his parents for them to see.

Margaret began to cry when she studied the picture closely. "Yes, she does resemble Brianna, except she looks more like you than Brianna did," his mother said between sniffles.

"So you had a suspicion that this little girl was yours?" Miles asked, shocked by the fact.

"I started to figure things out from all of the hints that Kristy and Carol threw at me. But I really didn't know what to think when I found out her birthday. I made love to Kristy when I closed on the sale of my house. We met at the lake house, and talked about a lot of things, and became close. With a little wine and our past relationship, it led to this beautiful little girl," he said, handing the other pictures to his parents and then wiping the tears from his eyes.

"The blood test I took just before the game was to see if I'd match as a donor?" Brad asked Carol as he thought about the unusual request.

"Yes, that's why they pulled your blood. I hope the results are back. We hadn't heard anything yet when we left Chicago," Carol answered.

There were several minutes of silence as the Prestons digested the news and kept staring at the pictures of their surprise gift.

Carol proceeded to fill the Prestons in on Angel. She told them about her favorite things and her cute little mannerisms.

It made Brad and his parents much more anxious to meet her. They prayed she would be all right.

Their jet hit the Indianapolis runway with no problems and taxied towards an area where another helicopter was waiting. They boarded the helicopter for their final leg to see their newly discovered little girl. Minutes later, the helicopter landed at Riley Hospital, and they were all escorted inside.

The anxiety level was high in the Prestons as they were being led to Angel's room. It was a strange feeling finding out you had a daughter, or granddaughter in Brad's parent's case, which they had never seen once in the two plus years of the little girl's life.

As they approached Angel's room, a doctor met them to inform Brad they had just received news verifying he was a perfect match for the transplant for his daughter.

"I want to see my daughter first," Brad replied.

"Of course," said the doctor. "In the meantime we'll prepare for your stem cell harvest. We're going to take it from your bone marrow. It'll be a little painful for you, but it will hopefully save your daughter's life."

The words, "Your daughter," sounded strange to Brad, and he had to fight off tears.

The doctor requested that only Brad see his daughter for now. He said she was still in critical condition and too many visitors might upset her. The doctor said he would explain everything he could to Brad's parents about Angel's condition while Brad visited with Angel.

Brad first saw Kristy standing beside the bed. She turned around to see who entered the room overwhelmed with joy to see Brad in the doorway. She walked up to him slowly. "I'm sorry I could never tell you the truth about her, but after what happened today, I think you understand my reservations to tell you."

"I understand Kristy. I had started to figure it out though from all of the hints you threw my way." Brad pulled Kristy close to him and gave her a hug. "I'm so glad you're alive. Are you doing alright?"

Kristy stared into Brad's eyes as tears filled her eyes. "I'm fine now, but your daughter is in serious condition. Now come and meet Angel…your daughter."

Brad walked up to the bed holding Kristy's hand. As he peered down at the little girl that laid lifeless on the bed, his knees buckled causing him to almost fall to the floor. He thought she looked more like Brianna than the picture revealed. But what bothered him the most was seeing all of the tubes attached to her delicate little body. It brought back memories of Brianna in the hospital just before she died. The pent up emotions that Brad had put aside since the start of the game erupted all at once. Brad cried uncontrollably while staring at the lifeless little body that lay on the bed below.

Kristy put her arm around Brad and laid her head on his shoulder. Tears filled her eyes and she couldn't help but cry along with the man she loved more than life. Kristy's tears were twofold though, as they were brought about by fear of losing her daughter and a happiness that Angel had a father that truly cared for her.

Brad wiped his face off with the sleeve of his arm, and bent over the bed, and gently stroked Angel's blond hair.

"This is your father," Kristy said to Angel. "He's your real dad, and not the other man who was mean to you."

A weak smile came over Angel's face as she recognized him from television. You could barely understand the word, "Baseball," as she tried to talk to them in her weakened state.

"That's right honey, he's the man we watch all of the time on television playing baseball," Kristy replied softly.

"Why didn't you tell me earlier today that she was my daughter?" Brad asked, slightly irritated.

"For a few reasons Brad. I thought you'd be safer at the game with all of the security there, and I knew that this was a lifetime dream of yours to pitch the winning game of the World Series. I hope you understand," Kristy stated with sad eyes.

"I don't hold anything against you Kristy, but I should have been here with you and Angel. We have a beautiful daughter to take care of." He returned his focus to Angel.

Brad was beaming with pride from having such a sweet and cute daughter. He felt bad he was not able to see her being born and grow up from the baby stage.

But this was such a cute age also. He then looked up and said a prayer to save her life.

The door to the room opened and the doctor walked in. "It's time Mr. Preston. We're ready for you."

There were several other nurses there to take Angel to another room where they would transplant Brad's stem cells into her.

As Brad turned to leave, Kristy pulled him to her and kissed him on the lips. "She'll be ok once she gets your blood in her body Brad. I know it in my heart and soul," she said as she let him go.

The doctor was correct about the pain, but Brad didn't mind. In fact he put it out of his mind altogether as he thought of Angel and pictured her in his mind.

"By the way," the doctor said. "That was one remarkable game you pitched tonight. I've never seen such a performance in all of my life. At least what I could manage to see of it," he added, not wanting Brad to think he was neglecting his daughter.

"Thank you. I almost forgot about the game with everything else happening tonight." Brad fought of the pain, hoping they were almost done with him.

"That's it; now let's get it to your little girl. You'll feel a little weak and your pelvic bone will be sore, but other than that you should be fine. Now pray for your daughter, and I'll try to work the medical miracle on our side of things," the doctor said before leaving Brad.

Kristy entered the room when the doctor left. They wanted Brad to lie down for a short while, which would allow some time for the two of them to talk.

"They sent me away, so I thought I'd visit the other person who is most important to me. I can't believe he tried to kill you again. You must be blessed to have escaped death once again," Kristy said as she sat next to him.

"I guess I must be. Greg was standing about ten feet away aiming a gun at me. He admitted to shooting me in Cincinnati, and he told me about the way he plowed into my car that Anne was driving killing the two of them," Brad said as rage filled his body once again. "I can't believe he was so obsessed with me. He thought I stole his life from him or his playing skills anyway."

"That's what I tried to tell you the past couple of years. But the important thing is you're all right. We just have to pray that Angel is too."

"I have been."

"It's just hit me," Kristy said, feeling a sense of freedom she had been longing for. "Greg is dead now, and he can't bother us again. Oh my God, I can't tell you how good that feels." Tears rolled down her beautiful face.

Brad grabbed her soft hand. "So that leaves you single now. And you're the mother of my child."

"Right on both counts," Kristy replied with a big smile. "So what do we do about it?"

"Let's get through this crisis first, and then we can look ahead. But I can honestly tell you it feels so good to have you here next to me. I still love you Kristy." He winced as he shifted the weight of his body to ease the pain.

"Good, because I love you more than ever." Kristy leaned down to kiss him. "Why don't you tell me what the doctors know about this poisoning that Greg did to the two of you?"

"In laymen terms, the poison attacked the cells in our blood and started to kill them off. I was fortunate enough to have caught Greg slipping something into my coffee, which was lucky for the both of us. It made me force myself to vomit to get today's dose of the poison out of my body. I originally thought we both had the flu, but when I saw him put the liquid in my coffee, I knew otherwise. The doctor thinks Angel was getting a heavier dose than me causing her to be in critical condition right now, which makes sense with her being so small. My blood was contaminated, but I still had a good supply of red and white blood cells. Angel was not as lucky. The poison practically killed off her entire blood system. They gave her two blood exchanges, but she needs your stem cells because the poison killed hers off. The doctor said the poison worked similar to a snack's venom, except the poison attacked the blood different than that of a snake bite. It's scary to think he actually did that to us." Kristy's hate for Greg was evident in her tone and her look.

"It's frightening knowing he went to all of that work to try to kill you two. How do you think he found out that Angel wasn't his?" Brad asked, intrigued by the mystery.

"I don't know, but one of these days we'll find out. I wonder how the transplant is going?" Kristy asked as her mind focused on Angel again.

Brad looked at his watch. "It should be over soon."

They stared at each other realizing how much they had missed one another. The silent stares spoke of strong feelings for one another, and then suddenly the smiles replaced the serious look on their faces as they each recognized nothing would stand in the way of their destiny to be together.

The door opened, and the doctor reentered the room. "It went well with your daughter. Now it's a matter of time to let us know if that will do the job. We'll check her blood every half an hour until we see some positive signs. How are you doing Brad?" the doctor asked, feeling confident he had filled them in on the girl's condition.

"Just a little sore, but I feel fine. Can I get up and see my daughter?" Brad asked, anxious to get back to his daughter's side.

"Yes, you both can. She needs you right now. She's a little frightened about what's going on. Come on and I'll take you to her," the kind doctor said.

Brad's parents were anxious to see Angel, so Kristy led them in her room first to see their granddaughter.

Margaret thought the same thing as Brad when she looked down at her granddaughter. Angel did resemble Brianna more than the photograph portrayed. But she was more taken by the resemblance of Brad.

Angel looked up at her visitors and smiled weakly at her new grandparents sensing them to be good people.

Miles watched his wife marveling over their granddaughter. It was such a miracle to suddenly discover that this special girl was Brad's daughter. Miles looked back down at Angel and had no doubt this was his son's daughter. She had several features that were definitely from Brad.

Miles and Margaret reluctantly left Angel's room. They didn't want to be selfish and not allow Brad time with his daughter.

"She's so beautiful Brad," his mother said after she left the room. "Everything will be just fine Brad, just wait and see."

Brad rushed to Angel's side. He couldn't get enough of her.

Kristy could see the gleam in his eyes, and she smiled to herself knowing he would be the best father there was for her little girl. Her thoughts were focused on the future because she had an instinct that Angel would now be healed after receiving her father's stem cells. She knew in her heart that God would not take another daughter away from Brad, knowing she had experienced too many miraculous things concerning Angel.

Tears were running down Brad's face at the thought he could lose his precious girl. He nervously stroked her blond hair whispering he loved her.

Kristy read his mind. "She'll be fine Brad. I know because she has been blessed since birth. On the morning of the day she was born, I suddenly had a warm glow go through my body. It stayed with me through the entire delivery. I didn't even have to take any pain killers to have her. Something was inside me and worked with me until my baby was born. That's why I named her Angel," Kristy explained.

Relief was instant for Brad from hearing Kristy's story. He knew the feeling, and suddenly remembered it had happened to him the day Angel was born. He just interpreted it in a different way. He looked into Kristy's brilliant blue eyes and shook his head to acknowledge he knew what she had meant by what she had just told him. He reached for Kristy's hand and held it tight while he held Angel's hand in his other.

Angel gave her father a slight squeeze that brought chills to Brad. He stared at Angel until it was time to pull blood to check on her progress.

The rest of the night was spent looking over Angel and praying she would be alright.

Brad's parents waited patiently while talking to Carol, and Kristy's parents. They would go in to see Angel periodically for short visits.

Morning came with still no change in Angel. The good news was she had not regressed, but there was no indication that she was getting better.

Brad's parents relieved Brad and Kristy since Angel was sleeping, allowing the two to stretch their legs and get something to eat.

Brad and Kristy were reluctant to leave, but knew they needed a break, plus they wanted Brad's parents to spend some time with their granddaughter. They walked hand in hand with cautious optimism concerning Angel as they approached the cafeteria for some fresh coffee and a sweet roll.

A song started playing on the radio causing Kristy to stop walking. She told Brad to listen to the song.

I let you go not so long ago,
And we went our separate ways.
But now I know how wrong it was,
To let you walk away.
I want you back in every way,
But you have gone your separate way.
So now I'm left to hope and pray,
You will come back to me some day.
We are on our journey to fate,
And all I do is wait for destiny to find its way,
To hold you in my arms again forever.

You touched me once nine months ago,
And now I hold a child you don't know.
It hurts me everyday to see the baby girl,
That you may never know.
So I pray to God to guide the way,

And remove the devil in our way.
The only thing that keeps me going,
Is when you let me know you care.
We are on our journey to fate,
And all I do is wait for destiny to find its way,
To hold you in my arms again forever.

I go to bed most every night,
And dream you are here with me.
You show me love in so many ways,
That you help me find my way.
But when I wake my dream is fake,
So I pray to God to guide my way.
And then one day he answered my prayer,
As you carried our Angel and me away.
We are on our journey to fate,
And all I do is wait for destiny to find its way,
To hold you in my arms again forever.

"That's a beautiful song," Brad said. "It sounds like us."

"It is about us Brad, I wrote the song," she said proudly.

"It's great Kristy. Congratulations." Brad gave Kristy a hug and a kiss.

"Thank you, but I couldn't have done it without you. You're the only thing that kept me going, as well as Angel of course. But it was your strength that got me through this mess, giving me the inspiration to write the song." Kristy stared into Brad's eyes. "I have missed you so much."

"We have time for us now Kristy. Let's just make sure our daughter is fine, and then we can go on," Brad stated as love for her spilled from his eyes.

"And what happens if she dies? Where does that leave us?" she asked as her smile left her.

"Heartbroken, but left with each other to help each other through it. It won't change my feelings for you Kristy," Brad promised.

After a quick snack and some coffee, they walked back to the room slowly, stopping briefly to look outside at the falling rain.

A sudden fierce flash of lightning struck next to the hospital, followed by a long angry thunder that shook the large structure they were standing in.

Brad smiled as he had a feeling that something was about to happen. He grabbed Kristy's hand and rushed her back to Angel's room.

"Still no change," Margaret said when they entered the room.

"It will change soon," Brad said with confidence. "Why don't you and Dad get some coffee and a quick bite? I think we'll have better news after that."

His parents left the room as Brad stroked Angel's hair.

Angel was awake now and she smiled at him affectionately.

Brad then walked to the window and opened the blinds. The rain was starting to fade, and there was a hint of blue skies as the clouds cleared in such a way that it appeared it opened a door to heaven.

"Come here Kristy," Brad said.

"What is it Brad?" she asked curiously.

"It's a sign." He waited for the special painting in the sky. The sun came through the clouds, and suddenly a beautiful rainbow accented the sky. "There it is Kristy, the sign I was looking for. I feel like everything will be all right now with Angel. Trust me."

"After what I've witnessed, I do believe you Brad," Kristy said, racing towards the window. She looked towards the area that Brad's finger was pointing to and saw the colorful rainbow. But this was not an ordinary rainbow, because the colors in this one were bold and unique. She looked at Brad for an explanation.

"On the day that Brianna died, I went home that night to try to sleep and go through some of their things. As I left the next morning, I saw a picture that Brianna had painted with Anne's help. It was a picture of the most colorful rainbow I had ever seen. It was so unique that I saved the picture knowing it meant something. I saw this same rainbow one Sunday morning, and that is what brought me back to life. I felt something unusual then, just as I have felt it several times before, and a few times since," Brad explained.

They both turned around and smiled when they heard the sweet voice of Angel say, "I'm warm."

Kristy and Brad hugged each other so hard that they almost crushed each other's ribs. They rushed over to Angel and saw more life in her face than they had seen since Brad had arrived.

"Why are you happy?" Angel asked the two of them.

"Because we know you're better now," Kristy said with enthusiasm.

The nurse came in to draw blood from Angel and Kristy. "Oh my little one, you've gotten some color back again."

The doctor entered the room shortly after the blood was drawn with the test results. He had a smile on his face as he walked towards Angel. "Good news. Her blood is looking better. There was a significant improvement in it this time. And your blood work is normal," he said, directing his last comment to Kristy. "We'll keep monitoring her blood, but we'll go an hour now before testing it again."

The doctor examined Angel thoroughly and left satisfied that she was on the road to recovery.

Kristy and Brad just looked at each other knowing they witnessed another miracle.

Brad asked Kristy to go inform the others of the good news while he stayed with his daughter. He did not want to leave her side at this time.

Kristy kissed him on the cheek before she left the room, thankful that Angel had a father that truly loved her.

The others were relieved by the good news, and Brad's parents came back in the room to see Angel before they left for a while to get some real rest and a change of clothes.

Brad agreed with them that it would be a good time for them to get some sleep since things were looking good for Angel.

Brad and Kristy thanked Carol for her support and for the hard job she had to perform to bring Brad to Indianapolis. They knew it wasn't Carol's job to tell the Prestons about Angel, but they appreciated her for doing it.

Angel's next two blood tests showed steady improvement, and so did she, as she wanted out of her bed. She was hungry now, so they brought her some breakfast she eagerly ate. Angel kept staring at Brad with a big smile.

He returned her smile, but didn't push himself on her. He wanted a natural progression of her knowing him as dad.

Just after noon, there was a slight commotion outside Angel's door. Brad peeked out to see what was going on and was surprised to see the entire Dodger team in the waiting area. He rushed out to see his friends and let them know he really appreciated them coming to see him and his daughter.

"We didn't know at first what happened to you," Tony said. "We stopped popping the champagne when Coach told us the entire story."

"You guys shouldn't have waited to celebrate your championship on me," Brad stated.

"You're the reason we won Brad. Your great pitching and leadership made everyone of us better. We'll wait until you're around before we celebrate, right guys," the first baseman stated.

"That's right," the team yelled in unison.

"How are things going here?" Coach Elders asked, concerned about the serious matter.

"It's looking good now Coach. I appreciate the way you handled the whole thing by the way," Brad said thankfully. He couldn't imagine too many coaches approaching the problem the way Coach Elders had.

Brian walked up to Brad and gave him a hug of friendship and to let him know he was glad Brad survived last night's killings.

The rest of the team followed suit as each one hugged Brad, touching his heart as they did it.

"When do you think we can plan the celebration?" Coach Elders asked.

"It should only be a few days now. Angel is improving hourly," Brad replied with a pleased smile.

"We'll be waiting for you son and praying for you and your family," the coach replied as he patted Brad on the back.

CHAPTER 47

▼

Four days later, Angel was released from the hospital, allowing her to go home. The doctor praised the efforts of the hospital and staff for her recovery, but he thought there was another part of her quick recovery that was a miracle. He gave orders that Angel was to wear a mask while outside or around strangers for another two weeks, so as not to pick up any germs. He explained to Brad and Kristy that her immune system would return to one hundred percent by then.

Brad had already contacted an attorney to go forward with a change of name motion for Angel. He did not want Somanski on her birth certificate or as her last name any longer.

Kristy was in full agreement with having Preston as Angel's last name and pushing for the name change.

Following Angel's final release from the hospital, the Dodger organization had ordered a helicopter for Brad, Kristy, Angel, and his parents. It would fly them to the airport where a private jet was fueled and ready to fly them to Los Angeles. They would then join the other teammates for a celebration parade through Los Angeles to allow the loyal fan base to see their beloved heroes.

Kristy and Angel, along with Miles and Margaret would have their own private area to watch the parade for Angel's protection.

Angel did not want Brad to leave them when they arrived in LA, but he eased her concern when he promised her he would soon be back.

Brad joined his fellow teammates and was surprised when they popped open the champagne bottles for the championship ritual. They finally whooped and hollered with joy for winning the World Series. Brad truly appreciated his fellow teammates waiting for him to share in this special moment with them, and showed it as tears flowed from his eyes.

Tony stood on a chair and asked for silence. "I want to say that this past season was the best year of my life. I owe it all to this great organization and every one of you in this room. I know he doesn't believe this, but I owe much of our success to Brad." He raised his glass to Brad and the other teammates.

Everyone in the room agreed with Tony and let Brad know it.

Brad took the chair from Tony and stood over everyone in the room. "Don't listen to him," he said as everyone in the room laughed. "No seriously, I'd like to thank the Dodger front office for bringing us all together, and I want to thank each one of you for the hard work it took to get us here. I'd also like to extend my sincere thanks, as well as my family's, for the way this organization stood by me and went the extra mile to help me and my daughter, and my soon to be wife through our crisis. Now I only have one more thing to say, let's do it again next year."

The entire room erupted in applause and a cheer to win the championship again next year.

The celebration was then directed towards the fans and the city of Los Angeles. The complete Dodger organization formed the parade and waved to the faithful Dodger fan base as they went through the downtown area.

That night, Brad and Kristy joined the rest of the team for a wonderful dinner and ball while the happy grandparents stayed with Angel. It was a great night that Kristy relished. She loved being with Brad, and she enjoyed being out in public again to have a good time.

Brad and Kristy danced the night away after the dinner and awards presentation, having the confidence that Brad's parents would take extra special care of Angel.

Brad had been awarded the most valuable player award for the World Series earlier in the evening and modestly accepted the honor, all the while crediting his teammates. He pointed out to the crowd that the most important award here tonight was the World Series Championship trophy.

Brad then went on to say his daughter's recovery from her dance with death was the most important thing that had happened in the last week, and everyone applauded in agreement.

The next morning, Lisa Collins opened the newspaper to a picture of Brad and Kristy from the night before at the celebration dinner and ball. As she sipped her coffee and read the article, she smiled for Brad and his new family. She knew all along that she could never compete with Kristy, especially when she learned that Brad was the father of Kristy's baby. Lisa vowed to take her lessons learned through this episode in her life and apply it to the future. She knew she was a much better person now and a better actress, thanks to Brad.

Brad and Kristy took a short drive with Angel the next morning to see the beautiful sights of Los Angeles. Kristy was impressed with the beauty of the town as well as the great weather.

"Well, do you want to live here?" Brad asked her.

"I don't know if that's a good idea," she replied seriously.

Brad turned to her stunned. "What's wrong?"

"I'm not sure I can put up with a Los Angeles Dodger and a California Angel in the same house," she laughed, knowing that she got him on that one.

"Oh, you're so funny. You could write a song about it," he added, kidding her about it.

Kristy played along with the joke. "That's a good idea."

Brad was in heaven having Kristy back in his life again. She regained her old wit and laughter making her a pleasure to be with.

Angel sat back and watched them while she laughed along. "Funny, mommy and daddy," she said.

Epilogue

Opening day of baseball had arrived once again as Brad climb the hill to toe the rubber. The Dodgers were picked to win the World Series again after dominating the spring training exhibition games. Brad was better this year than last, causing grief to the opposing teams.

Kristy and Angel were sitting with the rest of the wives in their reserved section. Angel was wearing her Dodger hat that she had requested for Christmas. She rarely took it off.

Kristy didn't mind though, because Angel had developed a deep love for her father and she wanted to be like just him. Kristy couldn't think of anyone better for her daughter to base her life on than Brad.

Brad and Kristy had purchased a house in Los Angeles a few days after the big dinner celebrating the World Series victory. Brad made a call to Jim and told him what he wanted, and Jim produced a perfect house for the happy family. They married two weeks later having a small wedding with family, and good friends, as well as the entire Dodger baseball team.

Brad, Kristy, and Angel couldn't have been happier.

Lisa Collins had just won the academy award for best actress for her latest movie. She thanked Brad in her speech for making her a better person and actress. She was dating a great guy who worked in banking, with hopes of marrying him some where down the road. She wasn't going to rush into a marriage though.

Bill Matthews was voted businessman of the year in North Carolina. The invention of the CAMM had led to several other advances in the world of prosthetics. He still wants Brad to take over the business when he retires.

Tony and Brian married their fiancés a month after Brad wedded. Brad was the best man at each wedding. The three of them are still great friends and made a pact before opening day to win it all again this year.

The entire Preston family was pleased with the marriage between Brad and Kristy as they truly loved Kristy and Angel. They were especially pleased the marriage concluded Brad's journey to fate.

978-0-595-40405-
0-595-40405-7

Printed in the United States
67199LVS00004B/89